Love's Like That

Love's Like That

by

Lewis Miller

The Pentland Press Limited
Edinburgh · Cambridge · Durham

First published in 1994 by
The Pentland Press Ltd.
1 Hutton Close
South Church
Bishop Auckland
Durham

ISBN 1 85821 146 8

Typeset by Elite Typesetting Techniques, Southampton.
Printed and bound by Antony Rowe Ltd., Chippenham.

To all young lovers

Chapter 1

The Palais de Dance was moderately full with a crowd of happy go-lucky youths and a sprinkling of the not-so-young, mostly in pairs or small groups with a lesser number of singles. There was nothing to distinguish between them in their attitude except to say, the men stood around in groups propping up the refreshment bar or leaning against the wall. They were visibly eyeing the girls and obviously making ribald comments from the coarse laughter that emanated from them. A small minority that did not appear to be concerned with the opposite sex, at least at that moment in time, were debating the current news of the rise of the moustached man that had become Germany's leader. When the band struck up, the groups would disperse or integrate as the men in confident stance and smile, approached the girl of their choice and asked for a dance. By the time the third or fourth tune had been played, the crowd was at its fullest.

Every bus or tram that paused outside the hall, disgorged more cheerful participants for the dance. At the same time, the curbs outside and all the side-streets around became crammed with the revellers' cars. The dancing season was in full swing again, and despite what the weather was like, be it bitterly cold, raining or just plain dull, the crowds will congregate nightly throughout the autumn and winter season, but more so during the weekends. The majority of pleasure seekers at the Palais found no problem in attracting the opposite sex for the exercise of dancing, but now and then a gentleman was snubbed with either the excuse that 'I'm tired' or 'I'm

1

booked this one' or similar. The man in question would move away, either in bravado attitude or occasionally somewhat downcast and disconsolate. But it was rare for any lad not to find a partner. From an observer viewpoint, it appeared that the lads led the chase; they selected and the lasses accepted. This trend is age-old and probably will never change in pattern or style.

Of the young ladies on the other hand, very few lolled around, as mostly they sat on chairs that needed reupholstering and strengthening, at the numerous tables that were partially littered with lemonade bottles, handbags and ash trays. The tables had seen better days, days before they wore scorch marks of numerous cigarette burns. Some, usually the older girls, showed their presumed experience in a more nonchalant attitude in an extroverted way. Most of them sat holding a cigarette between their finger and thumb in a pose of indifference. It was invariably these that snubbed the young men if they thought that they were too young, without prospect of buying them a drink or known not to possess a car, a major attraction being that car ride home. Other young lasses obviously not so experienced as those, that sat with a presumed blasé air, sat quietly looking under their eyes at all the young men in prospect and hope. Some realised that on an occasion when the floor was already crowded and very few possible partners remained, those that were not too demure and youthful and lacked the courage to approach a potential partner, that a pair of girls would arise and join the throng on the floor. The attendance here as on numerous other seasonal occasions was not merely a discipline in dancing, but invariably from both sexes from the ogling that went on, it was also an exercise in sizing your possible partners that may be better or superior than the one you were with at that point in time. Outside, the weather could be very blustery or even exceedingly cold, but inside the Palais it gradually became progressively warmer as the hall filled to capacity, but the atmosphere was the most paramount one of gaiety and joyfulness.

The hall itself could not be said to be run-down, but it was approaching that stage in its long history of entertaining the youth of the neighbourhood, as well as those that travelled by bus, tram or increasingly, by car. It was a typical hall of the thirties, where shoulders had been rubbed against the walls, the paintwork showed the signs. The bar counter was permanently blotched from various drink spills that remained too long before being wiped off. Strip lights emblazoned the bar area, but the dance floor depended solely on a central rotating globe that reflected a mirage of multicoloured spotlights throughout. At the end of the bar counter, sat three nicely attired young ladies and one youngish man. These were the professional dancers that could and would partner anyone that paid over the six pennies per dance to an attendant that sat nearby.

At the other end of the hall, facing the bar, were the five-piece band. They performed on a raised rostrum with the leader, affectionately known as Tubby Tommy, who stood to the front holding his saxophone. He acknowledged many as they swayed around the floor and looked up towards him.

One pair of young ladies that attended the dance that evening were Anne and her friend Joan. Anne Hopkins, an eighteen-year-old that had not long ago left school and was now employed as a shorthand typist with a small firm of accountants, not too far away in the City. She was of medium build and of fair complexion and modestly dressed. With a little bit more sophistication, she would be considered very pretty, if not beautiful. At her place of employment, she found that as the youngest there, all the male staff, of which there were not too many, were either married or already paired off, and the odd few that were otherwise single and unattached found her too junior or immature to consider as an escort. She had the feeling of isolation; consequently she sought the companionship of the opposite sex outside the work environment. Her companion, Joan Marchant, was a matter of but a few months younger than Anne but still at school, where she hoped to achieve success in her forthcoming duel with her matriculation examination. Although she was of modest ambition, with perhaps more than necessary foreboding and apprehension, she did hope to be successful in the examination and so get to University. Having only been at school, and not having emerged from her chrysalis, she viewed Anne with a slight feeling of awe as one that had already entered the world of work and as a 'woman of the world' that had broken her juvenile shackles away and had entered that great big universe that faced her. Although she was in no way dominated by her companion, she weighed up any advice or

3

comment made by her and considered it with normally more thought than it possibly deserved.

Our pair of friends sat at a table that already had two other occupants – not unknown to either of them, as although they had not attended the same school they knew each other as near neighbours and having met frequently on similar occasions as this weekly Saturday night dance. The taller of this pair of friends that shared the table was Tracey Bristow, a girl of nineteen who carried an air of minor sophistication and looked down upon all and sundry with a patronising air. She appeared to be the leader not only of the pair but of the other two friends that had joined them at the table.

Tracey sat looking at her companion, Wynne Roxbee, who had accompanied her this evening as she usually did on all adventures. Tracey could not understand herself for keeping company with Wynne, who was so extrovert without a trace of sophistication, that Tracey presumed put her own mannerism on a higher plain. But she did see a slightly younger girl of modest dress that appeared really quite attractive in all respects and was very popular with the opposite sex. She also knew that Wynne was not so demanding and invariably threw strictures to the wind in her desire to enjoy herself and please others too. It was always Wynne that kept the party going with her witty conversation and at times bawdy comments. She realised that they did not match up together in outlook yet she would not forsake her and search out a new regular friend. They both filled in the gaps that the other left out. Whereas she would decline an invitation to dance for some hidden unknown reason, Wynne was never known to refuse anyone's request, and, as a consequence, was always in demand and constantly being partnered. She glanced over to where Joan and Anne sat demurely talking in a low, hushed voice to appreciate that that pair was not so ebullient and so did not capture so many partners. She could not see her own shortcomings but readily saw those of her table companions.

Obviously, the four girls comments were of the men then around them. Wynne had most to say both relevant and not so relevant and at times derogatory as well as pleasant remarks, but in all cases there was the unspoken hope of finding a nice suitor. Wynne, our most extrovert, pointed out John who stood almost opposite to them with

4

a remark that he was a lovely dancer but not much good as a lover! To this Joan asked what she meant by that comment, which caused the others to smirkish titters but from Wynne she responded, 'Don't tell me you're *that* innocent.' Then she observed Tom nearby and gave him a wave of the hand, to which he responded in like manner, whilst saying in general terms, 'Now that's a fine chap who treats a girl to a slap-up meal and drives her home in his own car; not like some guys I know that buy you a drink and then think that gives them the right to squeeze it out of you.'

So the evening wore on, each enjoying the hours to varying degrees. By the time it was the last hour of the dance, all our four ever-wishful friends had separated into the company of a male companion, who each hoped and presumed, would lead to further entertainment and perhaps further 'dates'. But by the time the last waltz was played, many of the assembly had already departed the hall so as to enable them to get a late bus or tram back to their home. And as the last note tunefully died away, the crush at the exit matched the crowd at the bus and tram stop on both sides of the road nearest the hall. With an evening chill, those that came unprepared for the autumnal weather felt the cold. But despite the lateness of the hour, the transport service was good, and the merrymakers did not have long to await their ride homewards. Within some ten minutes of the last dance concluding, the street was deserted. No one stood at the bus stop nor were any cars parked nearby. The night drew on inexorably to the next day.

'Hullo Anne, how did you make out with your beau last night?' asked Joan when she came round to see her friend the Sunday evening following the dance, and preparatory to going out again that night.

'My beau was quite nice and you know him I believe,' responded Anne.

'Yes, I have met Jack before but we have never dated though. But do tell me, what did you do when we separated last night?' questioned Joan wondering what she was about to learn.

'Oh, we just went to a café for a hot chocolate and a cig, then we took a turn across the park,' replied Anne in a nonchalant manner, hoping that small amount of information would suffice.

'And I suppose,' retorted Joan with a smirkish smile on her face, 'that he made love to you.'

'Well, not exactly. He tried to but I held him off and that was not easy,' replied Anne in a quiet tone.

'And are you seeing him again?' questioned Joan.

'Yes, I am to meet him again tonight at the station at eight,' came the reply.

'Oh, that's fine,' returned Joan in a hurried voice. 'I'm to meet Angus also at eight, so if you wait a while at the station, we can all meet up together; what you say to that for a foursome?' proposed Joan.

'I'd like to, but he proposes to take me to the cinema tonight,' answered Anne in the same tone.

'OK then, we can all meet up in the foyer of the cinema at a quarter past; how would that be?'

'That will be fine with me if Jack also agrees and does not object – though can't see why he should really,' replied Anne, who secretly hoped he would as she did so wish to be alone with him.

To this Joan added, 'There is safety in numbers you know and together there will be no hanky-panky.'

'Well, I suppose there is something in what you say, so let's get ready, otherwise we will both be late,' commiserated Anne.

And so they skipped down the stairs in a happy frame of mind, Anne announcing to her mother that she was going out with Joan and would not be home too late.

Anne walked with her friend to the crossroads where they parted on the understanding that they were to meet up again very soon. They both individually went their way to their tryst. Joan proceeded towards the meeting place to greet Angus, a tall slim young man of some twenty-two years of age that had the apparent wherewithal of a go-getter who knew what he was after but invariably never attained his objective despite his dogged perseverance. He saw Joan approaching so walked towards her calling to her the mutual salutations of the evening. They greeted each other with a shake of the hand after which she placed her arm under his and turned him towards the cinema saying, 'I have just left Anne and she is meeting Jack at the cinema and we would like to make a foursome if that's in order with you, Angus.'

'Why, that's fine – I would like to see that film it so happens, so let's go. But what about after the show – are we to have company again?' questioned Angus with a look as if to say that he hoped as not.

'Well, we could all go for a snack together and then separate; how would that be?' ventured Joan turning her head towards him as they continued the walk.

'That will be the order of the day then,' responded Angus. So arm in arm they made their way towards the local cinema.

'Hullo Anne,' said Jack as he came forward to greet her as she entered the foyer of the cinema, and with more than a peck on the cheek asked after her welfare.

'I'm fine, but let me tell you that we have Joan and Angus coming any minute to join us. I hope that's OK with you?' questioned Anne looking into his face as she spoke.

'That will be nice but after the film would you not like to have me all by your little self?' suggested Jack beaming a broad smile on his face showing a good set of dentures.

'Yes, but why not join together for a milk shake after and if you would still like to separate, that's fine with me, lover boy,' peeved Anne in a mischievous manner.

So they awaited the arrival of the other two which was not for more than but a few minutes, when all greeted each other; then the two young men walked to the pay box whilst the young ladies moved towards the stairs that led to the circle seats.

Some two and a half hours later, they all arose and made for the exit and observed that the night air was decidedly chilly. So each young man placed his arm around his partner and proceeded along the street to a local late-night restaurant.

The conversation during the meal was mostly of the film but now and then the young men asked each other where and what each proposed after refreshments. It became apparent that both couples desired to be on their own, so after Jack settled the bill on behalf of them all, they all walked to the exit door of the restaurant and, in a nonchalant way, Jack led Anne to the left and bid the other two 'good night.'

'Hope you enjoyed the film and the meal Anne?' asked Jack with his arm still around her.

'Oh yes, thanks. I think the film was very enjoyable and the meal and the restaurant well worth a second visit,' responded Anne in a happy mood.

'So where would you like to walk, unless you have a better suggestion?' questioned Jack as they still meandered along the deserted highway.

'It's getting late, so we must not stop out very much longer, otherwise my pop will be at me for coming in late, so I'll leave it up to you where we wander – but not too far please,' begged Anne.

'In that case lets stop right here in this shop doorway – its all quiet in the street now,' suggested Jack as with a little nudge and a slight career, he manoeuvred her into the nook of the doorway. He then placed his arm around her shoulders and drew her towards himself as he pressed his hot lips against hers. Anne responded very happily and kissed and mouthed each other quite passionately. But gradually one arm that held her to him, slipped so that he fondled her breasts. She made no objection, so again he lowered his hand until he held her from behind and pressed her to him strongly.

She became aware of his manhood very compellingly against her, and although she enjoyed the sensation she began to think apprehensively that she had better call a halt to further movement between them. But whilst she was contemplating her strategy, his lower hand was raising her skirt to expose her panties, and as she struggled to release herself from his tight hold, during which time he was already probing the legs of her panties, by dexterously moving his sensuous fingers onto the inner side of the elastic top against her skin, she realised that she would have to act quickly before she would lose her self-control, as his action was assuredly creating an aura of desire that she knew was very risky.

She placed her arm under his and wedged him away from herself a little, but enough to make him comment, 'Please no, let's.'

She responded very sternly as she could, indicating that no way would she permit this sexual attack upon her without her consent and that would not be given now or ever. Perforce, he had to release his hand from her clothing which gave her the cause to presume that the episode was over – but no, it was not, as he then exposed himself to her and asked her to hold him. She knew her natural desire to oblige but she also knew that it would lead to more attempts on her so she raised her voice and asked him to desist. He remonstrated in a quiet, pleading voice with her that he wanted her and if she refused she should at least help him to relieve himself, and whilst making his begging plea he drew her hand to himself attempting to get her to grip him. His hold upon her wrist was too strong to resist, so she closed her fist as tightly as she could which caused him to plead again for her co-operation. She realised that she was unkind to him but at the same time she also knew that she was wise to refuse his advances. But she considered that she would allow him his own pleasure by moving aside a little and telling him to get on with it and leave her free. He understood that it would be useless to attempt to force the issue any more so he got as close as he could to her until he climaxed, after which he felt more at ease with her, yet a little upset that he had not conquered her the first date out.

After this exercise, he closed up to her and just kissed and fondled to mutual contentment and delight. And from Anne's feelings, she could not deny that she enjoyed the interlude, even though it took all her courage and strength to keep her self-control. After a while she suggested that it must be time that she got home. To this he agreed, but begged another hug that she willingly gave with all the ardour that she had left. Then after adjusting their dress they moved away from the doorway and he escorted her homewards chatting generally until they arrived at her abode. Then at his suggestion they made plans for a further meeting with the proviso, that he would not attempt his advances again against her, to which he reluctantly agreed but begged a good-night kiss that was given with passionate delight, as they hugged and wiggled for the last time that night to their mutual pleasure, then parted.

Anne went indoors and found all was quiet, so she made herself a drink that she took up with her to her room, thinking over the events of the evening and wondering if she was right to refuse him his advances or maybe she was wrong? She had heard so much from others of what can happen that it unnerved her to think that had she succumbed she may have become pregnant. But then the thought, 'What if he had a disease; how was one to tell? It must be thrilling to have sexual relationships but whoa! what a risk it must be.' She fell asleep

9

dreaming of intercourse that she submitted to and rolled around in her bed in sleeping delight until it awoke her to find herself in a sweat bodily and all wet underneath too. She felt cheated having slept through the episode of her dream, so she pondered without realising that her own hand had travelled down her thigh until she felt her fingers all wet inside her. She moved them about which gave her delight until she climaxed; then she understood the element of intercourse that she would have to achieve to enjoy the same feeling. She again fell asleep tossing over the choice of submitting or doing what she had just done, not knowing that it was a common practice among many young girls of her age. And so the night passed and a new day dawned.

The following morning, Anne prepared and dressed for work. The house felt comfortably warm but looking out of the window she saw dark clouds above that forebode of a miserable day ahead weatherwise. She descended to the family room for her breakfast, where her parents asked her in the normal manner of her adventures of the evening before. She indicated that she was escorted to the cinema and then went for a meal with her latest boyfriend without any elaboration. After breakfasting, she bid her parents adieu and left to walk the short distance to the station.

On alighting at the City station, she was carried up the escalator with the throng of other commuters to the concourse and made for the exit. As she approached the exit she observed Angus rolling up his newspaper and hitting the crippled news-vendor with it across his head and then as if nothing unusual or untoward had occurred, walked away. She hailed Angus who turned on hearing his name called and with a gleeful smile turned and approached Anne.

'How nice to meet you again so soon Anne,' he said; then added, 'Hope you enjoyed yourself last night.'

'Yes thanks. I did enjoy myself last night, but tell me, why did you swipe at the cripple fellow – you know he is harmless and cannot defend himself.' Anne responded in a half-pleasant tone that was caused by his action with his newspaper.

'Truthfully, I do not know why I do it except that it has become a habit that I must cure. But how did you make out with Jack last night?' he probed.

'First I agree with you that you should cure your bad habit as the poor chap is harmless. Yes, I enjoyed the evening and thanks to you for helping it along too. And how did you make out with Joan though?' she questioned by way of conversation really.

'Joan is a lovely girl but a bit immature and frigid. But I bet you're not,' posed Angus as he looked at Anne with a wicked twinkle in his eye.

'That my dear Angus remains to be found out if you ever get the chance,' came Anne's quick reply that matched his mood.

'Well, I would like to find out so what about a date one evening this week. Any night except tonight which is my evening-class night,' retorted Angus still with a broad smile.

'But what about my friend Joan – I don't play doubles,' quipped Anne in reply.

'I am seeing her again for the weekend, and presume that you will be along too with Jack. But I'm free during the week, so why not?'

'All right then, but I feel a bit of a cad going behind Joan's back as it were, so where and when?' questioned Anne.

'Firstly, you are not a cad as Joan and I are not on regular terms any more than you are with Jack, so can see no reason why we cannot date up. But if you like we could meet again outside the cinema on Tuesday say at eight. In the meantime you could think up where you would like to go and we will – how does that appeal to you?'

'That's fine, then at eight at the cinema and will give it some thought as to where to go,' responded Anne in a happy mood.

So they parted there and went their respective ways to work.

Chapter 2

Anne entered her office block along with many others who all seemed bent on discussing the weekend adventures more than the thought for the purpose or the reason for entering that building. A great hub of voices sounded, but as they separated onto different floors off the elevator, the sounds became progressively less. She entered the suite of offices in which she was employed and found a number of staff already there. Again the main topic of conversation was the weekend. She replied in monosyllables when spoken to with her mind on both the adventures with Jack and the prospect of a night out with Angus as she made her way to her desk.

Anne's immediate superior was Felicity Fawley, who was in her mid-twenties or so and had been with the firm since leaving school. Anne looked up and observed that Felicity was approaching her. She noted her poise and attractive outfit she wore and how her blonde hair was set in a most becoming manner. Anne often wondered how it was that such a beautiful young woman should still be single, as she felt sure that a girl . . . no, lady she reflected, would be the more fitting appendage to her superior, would and should have no difficulty in attracting wealthy suitors.

'And how are you this morning Anne – you look as if you have lost a penny and found a pound – or is it the other way round – what's troubling you – don't tell me your date did not turn out so good, or what, eh, you know you can always talk to me, so give.'

'Actually I had a nice weekend but this sex business is a bit too much for me to grasp.'

'That's no problem, you have come to the right person who claims to know all the answers. Just pop into my room before you go off to lunch. But in the meantime, here is a short screed for typing then another reconciliation to do, and we would like it completed as soon as possible, Anne.'

With that, Felicity moved away and left Anne with her workload to get through. Anne felt flattered to be given these extra tasks as it gave her scope and hope of advancement.

Approaching lunch time, Anne remembered Felicity's bidding that she should go to her room that was but a few paces from her own room along the corridor. As she entered the corridor, her mind seemed to immediately forget her work and fall into reverie about her weekend and all its passion. She knocked on Felicity's door and entered without awaiting the call to do so. Felicity was on the telephone as she entered, but she was motioned to be seated in the chair that was at the side of the desk. Anne could not but observe that Felicity had her leg resting up on an open drawer of her desk which caused her dress to drape above her knee and semi-expose her elegant negligée. It made her wonder what it was like above there in the dark recesses behind the lace trimming. 'Did she also get the same feelings that I got last night in bed and the feeling that came about from the proximity with Jack? But I am here to confide in her and not the other way round. But what lovely undies and the faint smell of perfume that emanated from her made her very desirable. I wonder how long I will have to be with the firm before I can afford to buy such pretty things.'

The telephone conversation continued for only a few minutes, but long enough for Anne to ponder what to say to her and how much to tell her. But she need not have worried, for as soon as Felicity put the telephone back onto its rest, she opened up the conversation with, 'It looks as if you are beginning to enjoy life with the opposite sex but do not know how to respond and handle the situation – am I right, Anne?'

'Well yes, you are more or less right but how can you tell?'

'You look as if you are puzzled and from what I know of you, it could only be one thing, and that's men. So you can be confident in the fact that we cannot be overheard in this room and anything you tell me will be considered very confidential. But maybe it may be better if I asked you the questions then you can reply – that way you are saved the partial embarrassment of coming out with your story. So let's ask first, have you had full sex yet?'

'Am not sure what you mean by "full sex" but the fellow I was with last night tried to finger me in my private parts and when I pushed him away he asked me to hold his thing which I refused to do, and that's what bothers me – should I have let him touch me and should I have held him, that's what I would like to know?'

'The answer is simple but not easy to do. You did the right thing in getting away from your boyfriend as his fingers would excite you very much, but that is only the prelude to his inserting his "thing" as you call it and that spells trouble if you are not wise and careful. Once he has his fingers in you, you would find it very difficult to refuse or want to refuse him, as you would be too excited with emotion. But if you go out with him again he will expect to be given that privilege, so it is up to you how far you go. To start with, you know that if he does put it in, you take the risk of getting pregnant, so don't; it's not worth it if you are not married. And if he is very adamant and you find it a struggle to control him, it may be better to hold him and help him that way. But remember, if you do hold him and you have your pants down and he ejaculates onto you, it is still possible to get pregnant, so be careful.'

'Then how can one enjoy sex without the risk of getting into trouble, as it seems that whichever way one turns there is a risk factor?'

'Are you free tonight Anne?' was her only reply.

Anne was puzzled. She raised the question and instead of getting an answer she is asked if she is free tonight? She looked across to her superior and noted that she had a warm smile on her face as she sat back in a reclining manner. She deflected her eyes as she responded to the question not knowing if the answer would be what was expected in response to the query.

'Actually I am free tonight but have a date for tomorrow night, why?'

'You have never been to my flat have you, Anne?'

'No.'

14

'Well, I think that it is time that we cured that deficiency, so meet me downstairs after work. But you had better phone home first and let your folks know that you may be home late.'

'Where do you live?'

'Not far, about ten miles from here, but do not worry as I have my own car in the basement, so will see you as agreed, OK?'

Joan returned home by all reckoning much before her friend Anne. She was somewhat annoyed at the way Angus endeavoured to make love to her. She knew that the theme of things was that it was expected but his approach was too much. He invited her in for a coffee as a pretext to his one-room digs on the first floor of a small house in a nearby street containing a row after row of similar dwellings. The room was rather nicer than she expected as the furniture appeared to be of good quality and the drapery equally so. The bed was almost centrally situated and alongside it towards the wall was a small table-type cupboard. Behind the door was a medium-size wardrobe and near to it was a small table with two chairs. In the odd corner of the room was one easy chair, and immediately behind that was a small wash-hand basin. Without any ado, he took off her coat after divesting himself of his, and placed them together across the easy chair. And with a dextrous move sat her on the edge of the bed with him alongside her. No sooner was she so seated that he immediately pressed her back onto the bedcover and simultaneously pulled her skirt up above her knees and made a grab for her pants with one hand whilst with his other hand unbuttoned the fly's of his trousers. Her immediate and quick response was to roll over twice to the other edge of the bed and then stand up and adjust her clothes.

'Sorry, lover boy,' said Joan in as normal a voice as she could muster under the strained circumstance. 'I'm not in the mood for frolics so I had better be going.'

'Oh don't be like that,' was his eager response, 'but I did not think you would be so frigid; so what gives with you to be like that?'

'What sort of girl do you take me for if you think you can get me to bed the first night out with you? If you think I sleep around with any Tom, Dick or Harry you are very much wrong as I don't and won't, so I had better be off.'

'A'right, you win,' replied Angus somewhat taken aback, but prudently realising he was on a losing wicket. 'So come and sit next to me and talk.'

'Only if you promise you will behave and not start interfering with me again.'

'I'll promise, but you will not refuse me a kiss now, will you?' he pleaded with a mock sorrowful face.

For answer Joan walked round to his side of the bed and sat beside him and putting her arms around him, hugged him to herself tightly and they kissed and fondled, which she did not object to. He asked her why she did not object yet refused to 'go all the way'. Her reply was logically that she had no intention of having intercourse with him or any one else as she had not and would not until married. He indicated that he appreciated her stance and said that he would like to go out with her on a regular basis, as he felt now that he could trust her unlike many others that submitted early in their relationship.

And whilst speaking he undid her blouse to which she raised no objections. He exposed one of her breasts after attempting to get both out of its encumbrance of the blouse and took the nipple to his mouth, whilst they both held on to each other. 'Oh dear,' she thought as he progressed in his ardour with her nipple. She was beginning to feel swoony and faint and in need of petting. But she knew that as far as she allowed Angus this liberty, she felt that he would keep his word and not endeavour to seduce her as he had tried earlier. She could not deny that she enjoyed the sensation this fondling created, but after a while she became a little sore and asked him to desist. Immediately she asked him he withdrew his mouth, and holding her breast in his cupped hand asked if she preferred him to suckle her other one or would she like him to try lower down. She jumped up away from him misunderstanding his suggestion on hearing him and responded that she would not allow anyone to touch her in her private parts and she thought they had had enough and that she must now go home. He apologised for the suggestion and said he had no intentions of upsetting her and agreed that it was time to escort her home.

After adjusting their dress, they left the house and proceeded on their way, during which period they made arrangements for a further mutually convenient meeting.

Tracey left the dance hall somewhat early in company of Andrew Gilmour, whom she had met and danced with on previous occasions but had never dated with before. He led her to the local car park where he had parked his M.G. sports car. 'My, my,' thought Tracey when she was in the car into which she was invited to be seated.

'Is this your own bus or whose?' queried Tracey by way of opening conversation.

'Yes, it's all mine and not on HP either,' retorted Andrew with a smirkish smile of satisfaction on his lips.

'OK, then Buster, where to?'

'Well, what would you say to a nightspot?' replied Andrew.

Tracey eyed him somewhat quizzically as she re-appraised him in his smart suit with silk shirt and matching tie. He was an attractive fellow that appeared to be well-endowed with cash but it seemed too good that he was offering her this treat – what price would she have to pay, she pondered before she replied.

'Well, if you think you can spend your dough on a defenceless girl and ply her with drink then try to squeeze it out of her, I'd rather not go but would appreciate a lift home.'

'If you think I'm a cad, you are wrong – I ask for your company because I think we are on the same wavelength and can get on well with each other. But have you been to the Starlight nightspot yet, because if you haven't, you will be missing a treat that I am sure you will appreciate.'

Tracey stared at him pondering how to answer. After a hesitation of but a few moments, she replied, 'OK then, let's try this Starlight for what its worth, but what time do they close as I have no intention of staying to three or four in the morning?'

'It actually finishes about 2 a.m. after a beautiful cabaret, and I could then run you home unless you have the courage to stay out, then you can come to my pad and stay the night.'

'I said I will go with you to this nightspot but thanks also for your offer of a bed – that I decline. And I hope that my going to this joint with you does not mean there are other strings attached.'

'Oh no,' replied Andrew, smiling at her trepidation. 'But any time you are lonely you can always give me a buzz and I would come and pick you up – and there would be no strings to that either.'

So without further ado, he switched on the ignition and with a smooth show of gear work, they moved out of the car park and made their way to the nightclub. Within a matter of minutes they arrived and after carefully parking his car, escorted Tracey into the club. The head waiter greeted Andrew in an affable manner and led them to an advantageously positioned seat from which they would be able to view the cabaret easily. The manner in which they were ushered to the table led Tracey to believe that Andrew was a 'regular' at this nightspot. Although she herself was somewhat attempting to style herself as sophisticated and tried to carry herself in that manner as she thought befits a cultured adult, she could not but have a feeling of admiration with a tinge of jealousy at the apparent smoothness Andrew displayed in his reception and greeting.

She immediately felt and knew that she was going to enjoy herself and as they were led to their table, she took momentary stock of the company that made up the customers that night. She observed to her pleasure that they all without exception were neatly dressed and that no riff-raff appeared to be present. That gave her additional feeling of pleasure. The table they were given was in a good favourable position for viewing both the assembly and the stage that was set for the cabaret. But then it appeared that all the tables had a splendid view as the arena was laid out in graduating steps, each step semicircling round the floor that was purpose-built to hold a number of dining tables comfortably. But she was distracted for a while as she was presented with a copious menu from which to choose. In fact she secretly admitted to herself that she had never seen such a seemingly inexhaustible menu nor could she admit to knowing what some of the items were. Whether she appeared with a brow of consternation or not in her study of the menu, Andrew came to her rescue by suggesting a bill of fare that he desired for himself. She said that on reflection she too would like the same. But her sophistication rose when he asked her for a preference for wine.

'I think that a nice cool bottle of Chablis is called for with what we have ordered,' indicated Tracey without any trepidation or hesitation.

'And I think that would be just the ticket,' responded Andrew and immediately appreciated that his partner was able to choose so wisely.

18

So the meal progressed and after a couple of dances on a small area destined for that recreation in front of the stage, the drum roll sounded for the cabaret.

The whole atmosphere of the venue changed, as everyone returned to their respective table and, turning the chairs to face the stage, poised themselves for a happy and entertaining interlude.

The cabaret lasted about three quarters of an hour and the verdict of both Tracey and Andrew were that it was well-performed even if it was at times near to the bone suggestively. So after another turn on the floor, Tracey suggested that it was time he escorted her home, to which he immediately responded that he would do so. He hailed the waiter and settling the bill with a handsome tip, they rose and departed the venue.

As they passed through the exit to the outside, they felt the cold night air with a touch of dampness around. Solicitously, he suggested that she wrap herself up well as they walked to the car park arm in arm, both in a happy frame of mind. The car was where he had left it and without any bother, the engine purred silently away the moment he switched the ignition on. Asking her for direction, they made their way to where she lived. She asked him not to stop outside her home as she feared it might attract her parents, so he pulled up a few doors away and alighted with her to walk her to the door. In soft voices, as if afraid any louder would attract and awaken sleepers, they discussed the evening and made arrangements for a further meeting. And much to Tracey's wonderment and delight he just gave a nondescript peck on the cheek and bid her 'good night'.

She let herself into the house and without awakening anyone, made for her bed. She lay for quite a time going over in her mind the adventures of the evening, trying to debate what was the most enjoyable part, but found that she could not ascribe any portion as better than another, so rightly concluded that the whole evening was in her own vocabulary 'topping'. The only part she could not make out was why Andrew did not attempt to make love with her despite his promise that he would not. Surely he was not the shy type she ventured, so can it be that he is 'that honest' which she found hard to understand. Every other escort she had been out with always expected as part of the entertainment and pleasures of the evening to be

19

allowed a certain amount of licence. But then she thought, for the wonderful evening she enjoyed, should she have succumbed had Andrew made advances. And then he did invite her to his 'pad' which she knew meant that she would be expected to submit to his desires. So why was he like this, she kept going over in her mind until sleep conquered her.

Felicity walked half a pace ahead of Anne as they made their way to the firm's private underground car park. It gave Anne the opportunity to view her companion surreptitiously as she led the way. It made her wonder how much she earned to be able to set herself up in such a smart and beautiful attire. Although she had no envy in her she did admire quality when she saw it and Felicity assuredly had that. They were about the same height but her senior was dazedly carrying a more polished stance in her whole way she walked. Anne even observed that the hair style at the end of the day was still excellent and the slight waft of perfume was indeed very pleasant. She wondered and not for the first time, how it was that such a beautiful and attractively smart female that oodled such charm should not be having a number of men awaiting her outside the office building.

Felicity had everything Anne had ever admired, poise, clothes, good figure which she enjoyed looking at. Everything but everything was her secret verdict of Felicity and she was being invited back to her home. But before she could expand on her wonderment theory, Felicity was holding open the door of her car for her to take the front seat alongside her. Felicity likewise entered the car and with a nonchalant manner and without further ado set the engine into motion and gearing the car, moved off.

It seemed that they arrived at the point where Felicity stopped the car and alighted in but a few minutes. The air was still mild as they left the car to enter the entrance hall of the large purpose-built block of apartments. Anne observed the marble floor of the entrance hall and the acknowledgement given them by the uniformed hall porter as they made their way to the lift. Within a few moments they arrived at the floor of Felicity's apartment. Again Anne was astonished at the apparent affluence of the flat. They walked through the small entrance hall that housed the telephone on an elegant console table made of exquisite wrought iron painted in multicolours and gold that was situated under a small chandelier. Felicity led into the door to the lounge. This was a most lavishly furnished room of very comfortable looking settees with small coffee tables and lamp standards, radio, record player and other elaborate appurtenances.

Felicity asked Anne if she would like a pre-dinner drink, of which the response was in the affirmative. They both had a light sherry, whilst Felicity asked Anne in continuation if she would like to rid herself of the day's dust and have a shower as she herself normally did before putting her meal into the oven.

'I should love to have a shower but I feel I would be imposing upon you,' she replied, with hopeful thought of the luxury of a delightful shower.

'It is no imposition and you are very welcome any time you come to my home, so let me show you the way,' she said with a broad smile upon her red lips, as she took Anne by the elbow and led her back across the small hall to the bedroom. And whilst Felicity went to a purpose built-in wardrobe to take out a dressing gown, Anne had a moment's opportunity to take in the opulent lushness of the room.

'My,' said Anne. 'You sure have a fine flat and exquisite taste; I almost envy you, but envy is not in my character, so I can only compliment you on your achievements', and adding 'It's worth coming home too.'

'As I've said,' replied Felicity, looking at her guest with a charming smile, 'you are welcome and if we become friends as I feel we may, then this flat is as much yours as it is mine. But how would this gown and cap suit you?' she added as she handed over a Chinese kimono in shining cream silk with coloured birds nesting upon flora of distinctive patterns with the cap to match.

'Felicity,' said Anne reddening in the face. 'You are going to spoil me and I do not know why.'

'That's simple to answer my dear girl – we appear to be on the same wavelength, we work in the same place, and both have equal ambitions, so why the puzzlement? So now let me show you how to operate the shower, then you can undress in here and enjoy the delights of a refreshing hot and softened water for as long as you feel inclined – I'm in no hurry and hope you are not either.'

'In a flat like this I could stay for ever, but I suppose I must go home sooner or later,' she opined with a trace of regret in her voice.

'Well, we will discuss how long you can stay after your shower and after we have eaten – so go along and get your shower.' With that, Felicity turned and walked out of the bedroom and left Anne to her own devices to undress and enjoy an often-felt but never-attained luxury. So methodically, she laid out her clothes on the adjacent bed and then returned to the bathroom and entered the shower cubicle and turned on the hot water and began to soak away the invisible dirt of the city.

After seven or eight minutes she heard Felicity call out to her if all was in order and was she enjoying herself. Anne called back that it was wonderful as she should know.

'In that case you are going to have my company too, so make room for here I come', and as she spoke Felicity opened the shower cubicle glass door, and entered the shower to Anne's somewhat consternation and puzzlement and not to say embarrassment.

'Don't look so alarmed Anne; it is quite alright if I come in as I feel you may appreciate a bit of company as I do. And now we are in together we can get better acquainted and I will wash you down as you do for me too – how does that appeal to you, eh?'

'Well, really I do not know, as I have never shared a shower with anyone before but it's your home so I suppose it must be all right then.'

'I knew you would agree,' responded Felicity with a broad smile on her face, 'so let's have the soap and turn round and I will give you a good going over.' And as she spun Anne round she took the tablet of perfumed soap from the holder and rubbed it across Anne's neck and small of her back and down to her buttocks. She replaced the soap in the holder and begun to systematically massage her, beginning from the top at the neck and working her way down. After a while, she asked Anne to grip the crossbar and lean forward so that her back protruded. Again, as Anne held onto the bar she felt the soothing hands of Felicity gently rubbing her back getting gradually lower and lower until she reached her buttocks.

'Now just move your legs apart like a good girl so that I can finish your back,' said Felicity, and without thinking, Anne did as she was bid. So the hands now reached her thighs gradually rotated them round her sides and also under her legs until Anne realised she was being fingered in her private parts. 'Oh' thought Anne, 'now what shall I do; this feels lovely but shall I tell her to stop?' But before she could make a decision she felt an ecstasy she had never felt before and all she could do was draw her breath in fast gasps as she felt first a small intrusion then little by little the intrusion became stronger as she rightly presumed that Felicity was rotating her finger inside her at the same time as she moved it in and out. So there she stood in the hot shower leaning forward with Felicity warmly abusing her yet she could not call out to her to stop, and before she could make up her mind upon what action to take, she was asked to turn round and face her. She was half-minded to ask to stay as she was as she enjoyed the elicit thrill of abuse; then she considered perhaps she would turn round as she felt sure it would continue from another angle. So without a murmur she turned and faced her new friend, who again picked up the soap and began to wipe it down her again from the neck to her knees. Again Anne simply stood dumbstruck but not unwilling whilst she was massaged all the way down and showered off. And when no soap remained, Felicity continued her gentle rubbing and after a while with both her hands she cupped first one breast then the other and took the nipple into her mouth and drew them in, and as she held the second nipple in her mouth Anne felt a hand lowering to her knees and then gently moving upwards with a slight pressure that compelled her to spread her legs a bit apart.

Again she felt fingers entering her but this time it delighted her still more, and with her hand resting on Felicity's shoulders to keep her balance, she felt that she must throw her arms around her so that both could be closer together as it thrilled her. This she did to the obvious delight of Felicity who increased her action until Anne could not contain herself any longer and climaxed whilst she let out an indistinguishing scream from her throat.

Then she heard her friend say that it was only fair that she should try to give her the same treatment and at the same time released her and handed over the tablet of soap to Anne as she turned round and held the bar. It took Anne a few seconds to reconcile herself to this demand, but in a flash realised that she enjoyed the new experience so why should she not do the same for her new friend. So with a little prompting, Anne proceeded to reciprocate in the same manner as she enjoyed and asked continuously if what she was doing was as wanted, to which the constant reply was that she was doing just fine.

Altogether, the bath adventure lasted but half an hour in which time Anne was initiated into the mysteries of woman and woman. After they wiped each other dry, they emerged from the cubicle to don gowns already laid out in readiness and then proceeded to the kitchen, where Felicity had prepared a very attractive and wholesome meal, which she served in the adjoining dining room. The conversation was somewhat stunted in as much as, most of the talking flowed from Felicity.

'Now you know what it's like but without the risk of a man and all the trouble that that can fetch you. When you are old enough and feel that it's time to marry, then go for a man, but until then you and I can be partners.'

So demurely, Anne answered with her head down still somewhat doubtful and unsure, that she would like to be her friend and now understood why a smart girl like her had no regular male escort.

'Oh don't get me wrong Anne, I do go out with men now and then, but they are such beasts that they think they can take you out and then own you. So I make it a point to stop a guy in his tracks if he gets too fresh. We will not miss the thrill of love if we can get together so what do we need a man for?'

After a pause and Anne not replying Felicity added, 'Are you troubled Anne, because I feel we could love each other as well as a man and be free from all that trouble of pregnancy and VD too, so what do you say, and further, if you would like to stay the night, just telephone your folks and tell them you are staying here and give them this number in case they wanted to check it out.'

After a somewhat one-sided conversation Anne agreed to stay and telephoned her home to indicate that she would not be home, but gave the phone number as advised to.

After a reasonably good meal they jointly washed up, then resorted to the sumptuous lounge. Felicity asked Anne what her likes were in music and ascertained that despite her youth she desired classic to

24

modern jazz. This apparently pleased Felicity, as her face took on a shine of delight and she immediately placed on the record player a Mantovani. Obviously, Felicity was inwardly as well as outwardly delighted to have captured a new lover that liked the same as she did. After general discussion, Anne began to tire which was observed by her new friend. With great concern Felicity said, 'We must stop prattling away as you are tired, so let's get to bed.' So with that, she led her back to the bedroom and without any embarrassment, undressed and jumped into bed naked. She indicated to Anne to do likewise. By this time Anne was half asleep and not her own master so she did as bid and lay down on the uncovered bed alongside the naked body of Felicity.

Anne felt the arms of her friend enfolding her as she lay drowsily and gradually sank into a deep sleep dreaming of the wonders she had enjoyed with her new friend.

Chapter 3

Wynne had accepted a second request to dance from a well-dressed young man of some twenty-two or -three. He appeared to be a man of the world by his manner and attitude. He looked down his Roman nose in both defiance and indignity, when he felt it warranted that attitude to those whom he knew but were still sitting around. From Wynne's point of view he appeared about the best dancer she had experienced and this made her somewhat apprehensive in case she missed a step. To her credit, this did not occur.

During the first dance no conversation ensued between the two, but during this second dance, which perhaps as a slow tempo waltz, gave both breath and time to engage in conversation. After the preliminary introductions in which he enunciated that he was Richard Crosby and was employed as a salesman for a large insurance company, the conversation was of a general nature for a few minutes. Then he asked if she was in the company of the other girls at the table; to which she replied that she was, but raised the query as to why the question. Richard responded with the question that if she was in company, could she leave them to join with him at another table elsewhere in the hall. Wynne being what she was, would not reply direct but began to tease until eventually she agreed to join him, after she took him over to meet the other girls. They then sat in a corner and after a few seconds he asked her what she would like to drink, and then left her for the bar counter to comply with the request.

As only half the session had been danced away, they were able to enjoy each other's company on the floor a few more times that evening. The more Wynne danced with Richard, the more confident she became, so much so that he complimented her on her skill on the floor. As they became more acquainted with each other, they opened up on their own history. Richard indicated that he was twenty-five years of age, to which Wynne evinced that he looked younger. He appeared to enjoy her repartee and was not lost for replies, which were at times as risqué as she was indelicate.

The way they reacted to each other appeared to any interested onlooker that they had been acquainted with each other for a considerable time. This attitude made both very contented and happy, so much so that their mirthful tittering went down well with the throng nearest them. She did not object when he drew her into a tight squeeze to himself nor when he deliberately kissed her at the close of a dance. And when the last dance was announced he asked her if she would care for him to escort her home or perhaps join with him for a late meal. She elected the latter, so before the last dance ended, they left the hall.

He led her along a few streets to where he had parked his Vauxhall which he indicated was a firm's perk. From Wynne's point of view she did not care, so long as he had the means of conveyance. As she gave him the choice to which restaurant to go to, he took her to a reasonable place that was not too overcrowded that time of night. Background gramophone music was still playing and with the general hub-bub of the patrons, it was not easy to hear one another. However, they managed to make a good choice off the ample menu and did not have long to await the meal to arrive.

It was then gone midnight when they stood up to leave the restaurant and Wynne suggested that it was high time she went home. He escorted her back to his car and, asking her for location as to where she resided, he moved the car in that general direction. 'You will not mind if we stop for a few minutes before we get to your home, will you Wynne?' asked Richard in a nonchalant manner.

'And what do you want to stop for?' responded Wynne, knowing full well what his intentions were.

'Well, perhaps a kiss and a cuddle would be a nice way to end a nice evening,' said Richard.

27

'And will a kiss and a cuddle content you or is that a prelude?'

'Now that you ask I will be frank with you. Nothing would please me more, to take more, if you would allow me to!'

'Just stop here and let's kiss and cuddle but not for long as I will get into trouble at home,' suggested Wynne.

To this, Richard brought his car to a halt and switched off. Then without any trace of embarrassment, as if they had known each other a long time, they turned towards each other and embraced passionately for a few minutes, after which his hand began to travel to her hem. She appeared to ignore this movement so he braved it and continued his hands travelling until he felt her pubic hairs. Both were silent during this period of lovemaking. She still held him in embrace whilst he was by then with his fingers inside her, at which she moved in concert with his finger rhythm.

'Undo my buttons, Wynne darling,' he muttered in her ear.

'Sorry my love, if I did that you would want to seduce me, now admit it?'

'Yes, that's true and you would enjoy it too, so please take it out or I will have to, and that would spoil your oozing and you can feel that now can't you?'

'You can do as you like, but you are not going to put it in as I will not let you, and if you try I will kick you where it hurts!' Wynne replied without much emphasis, but extremely happy in the progress so far.

'Then take it out and if you hold it, you will know where it is and can control it; how would that be darling?' he ventured to suggest perhaps more in hope than expectation.

'So long as you do not make a mess on me or break your promise, I will do as you ask; now do you promise?'

'My love,' replied Richard who was so excited in his ardour that he would have promised the moon if he could have availed himself of it, 'I will do everything you ask for but do be as nice as you can as I'm falling in love with you.'

'You are falling in love with sex, not me, lover boy,' riposted Wynne as she moved her hand down to the crotch of his trousers and as carefully as she could, undid the buttons and moved her hand between his leg and pants and drew out in her terminology, his dickey.

'This is not a dickey but a rod, lover boy, but you'd better control it!' she said as she focussed it away from herself.

During all this time he had not relinquished his motion of his hand around her and she felt herself swimming in clamminess as he continued exciting her, and now she was holding him. She peeped at it and realised it would have hurt her had she consented to have full sex. Then she had never had full sex, and although she succumbed to playing very close to submission, she was confident she was able to control herself against attack from Richard or anyone else.

'What do you want me to do with your rod, if that's what you call it?' asked Wynne still holding on to the throbbing length of manhood that was silently asking for relief within her.

'I think even if you let me have you, it would be too late, as it wants to go and I cannot hold it back any more, so get a hanky out of my side pocket and cover it, unless you would like to bite it off?'

'You filthy sod; what do you take me for? Because I allow you this liberty the first time out, you ask me to do something I have never done before and nor will I ever do,' she replied, yet wondering what it would be like to do as importuned – but that would be a deferred pleasure maybe some time in the future, she thought.

'Sorry darling. I did not wish to upset you as you have been so nice to me, so get that hanky quick before I let go, as I feel I cannot hold it back any longer.'

So without further ado, Wynne let go his dickey and went rummaging for the handkerchief, noticing that as soon as she released her hold it appeared to lose its stiffness, but the moment she placed the muslin handkerchief over it and again gripped it, it waved and expanded visibly and throbbed heavily until she became aware that her hand was sticky with that which had oozed through it. And that was not an easy thing to do, to place the hanky over it, as a split second before, he engulfed her with his free hand in a tight grip as if life itself depended on it; so with his one hand holding her pressed to him whilst his other hand still wandered around inside her, she felt his whole body go into a strong throb that shook the very car. Then after a few minutes that seemed like an age, he released her, or at least took his hand away from her and with his free hand wiped himself, then felt in his pocket and withdrew another handkerchief that he gave to Wynne and suggested she wipe up.

After straightening their clothes, he took out a packet of cigarettes and lit one for her and for himself, and putting his arm around her shoulder, they both reclined to recover.

'Wynne dear, I must say thank you for the great girl you are. You were marvellous tonight and I really appreciate it. I cannot say how happy I am with you. I respected your wish and I hope you enjoyed what you had from me. I can promise you I would not do anything to mar our relationship.'

'Well, that's nice to hear you say that, but what relationship are you talking about?' she asked with a broad smile of wonder.

'Wynne, I'm really falling for you and not just because of the sex interlude, believe me. I would like to see you again if you would agree, so how are you fixed for tomorrow night – I could call for you at your home now that I know where you live, so how about that, darling?'

'Nothing would please me more than to see you again Richard, but just promise you will not try to push your luck and try going further than you have tonight, and if so, call for me say at eight tomorrow night,' responded Wynne with open eyes beaming pleasure.

'Darling, I will be there, so now let me drive you to your door where you can give me a good-night kiss, eh?'

So they moved off and drove the hundred yards or so to her door where he left the engine purr whilst he put his arms around her and pulling her to himself, gave her a long lasting kiss to her delight. They then bid each other adieu, she alighting from the car, at which point he sped off to his own home.

Wynne entered the quiet house and went to her upstairs room and closed the door on herself as silently as she could. She felt the need of a bath after the rummaging she had had, but knew that was out of the question at that time of night. So she undressed and went to bed hopefully, to sleep, but that normal body function evaded her for quite some time, as her mind went over the adventures of the evening. She inwardly congratulated herself on the strength of character in withstanding Richard's attempts to seduce her.

She was pleased with her achievements and was equally pleased in the thrill she received and felt that he was also grateful to her in the co-operation she had given him. She was confident that had she declined to co-operate in holding him, he may have become more demanding; then it may not have been such a pleasant interlude. Gradually sleep overcame her and she slept but not without dreaming of her exploits of the evening. She dreamt of making love with Richard whose dickey yet expanded still more as he inserted it in her to her hurt and equal delight, as she screamed with pain and thrilled emotion. She awoke the following morning more wet than she had been the period she was with Richard and wished that he was there right at that moment. Then she knew that she was foolish, for had Richard walked in at that moment, she would not have refused him anything, so it was safer, she surmised, to be in reverie and reserve her thoughts and pleasures until that night.

Felicity drew the sheet over them as she observed her companion, Anne, had drowsed off to sleep. She felt highly contented with her new attachment and staring into the blank white painted ceiling, began planning her strategy as to how to proceed with Anne. It appeared to her that Anne succumbed too easily and that made her somewhat apprehensive. Was Anne overawed by all that Felicity had to show her or was she genuinely happy with her new adventure. She was confident that the joint play they enjoyed in the shower was Anne's first such contact, but she did so wish to cultivate her as she appeared so intense and interesting that she would be sorry to let her go. She did so wish to give her a present in the morning, but feared it may be construed as a bribe. 'Oh, what should I do?' recited Felicity in her contemplation. 'Would Anne make a magic transformation, metamorphose, convert and remodel to her desires?' She looked to her sleeping friend and wondered if she would be willing to join her as they had the night before? She could think of nothing at that moment but then dwelt on the possibility of getting her promoted at work – that would perhaps be more acceptable to Anne opined Felicity in her mind's eye. So gradually she too succumbed to nature's demand and fell asleep with her arm about her new lover who turned towards her as she lay quietly dreaming.

Anne awoke first that morning and found that she was still in bed with Felicity. She could not recall her dreams of the night but knew they were pleasant. It was a mild surprise to find herself with Felicity in bed with half the bedsheet just covering the lower part of their bodies and the top half exposed, as the whole experience of the night before replayed itself before her as on a film. She looked at Felicity sleeping so apparently contentedly innocent and quiet, with her beautifully-shaped bosom gently heaving in rhythm to her breathing. She looked so sweet and really attractive that she wondered again if what had happened one night ago really did happen. One of her arms was still under Felicity and she wondered if she should move it away, as she feared the weight would hurt her arm if left there much longer. So with great care she moved herself slightly away from her sleeping companion so as to relieve the pressure on her arm, but as she did so, Felicity in her sleep, flung her own arm across Anne's chest. After a moment or two, she observed and felt the hand encompass her breast and at the same moment, Felicity's body rolled over towards her, as a leg moved over her and entwined between her own legs. All she could do in that position was to place her own arm around her as she lay on her back. What appeared to be ages but in reality was probably but ten or fifteen minutes, Felicity awoke still in the same position. She raised her head slightly and said, 'Good morning darling; hope you had a good and restful sleep.' To which Anne responded, that she had and thanked her for all that she enjoyed.

'Did you really enjoy your sleep with me. I do hope you did and I see that I have made myself comfortable by holding you – and I hope you approve of it too, darling.' ventured Felicity.

Anne appeared to hesitate in replying to this last gushing question, which made Felicity somewhat afraid that she had overstepped the mark, so surreptitiously she began to remove her hand from off Anne's breast, and at the same time, disentangled herself from their lower extremities. Anne became aware of this move and realised that her reticence in responding had probably give the wrong impression, so opined, 'Oh Felicity, I think I love you as much as you love me, and you can do whatever you like to me; I'm all yours,' and as she spoke, she rolled over on top of her friend and placed her arms around her in a strong embrace. Inwardly she realised that what she had just uttered, was an instinctive response without meditation, so it must be right, so she smiled as she lay over the prone yet supple body of Felicity.

'Oh my darling,' countered Felicity, 'you have made me very happy to hear you say that. I have dreamed all night that you would utter those words, yet feared that you would not – you cannot guess how happy you make me feel as I have loved you sincerely and have for a long time and was not able to show it to you.' And as she spoke, her hands that had encompassed Anne, began to rotate around her body in a sensuous and deliberate manner, that compelled Anne to roll off so as to face her new lover and said, 'What would you like to do to me? Please show me so that I can repay you as you deserve with all my affection.'

'My darling Anne,' answered Felicity as she closed with her friend in a tight embrace, 'we can only do what we can within the limit of time, as we are working girls, remember, but let's repeat what we did last night, and perhaps add a bit here and there; what do you say my sweet?'

'Please lead on as I am all yours – how do you wish me to lie – as we are or in a different position; I cannot wait as am all eager, so please hurry before I expire,' she said, as she feigned exhaustion and with an appealing look, she again hugged Felicity in a strong embrace, raining kisses upon her with her tongue probing into the depths of Felicity's mouth.

After a few moments in that loving grip in which neither could speak, they separated momentarily, but with enough time for Felicity to suggest that Anne should lie on her back with her legs wide apart. Without replying, Anne did as she was bid and simultaneously, Felicity lay over her and with her mouth began to suckle one of Anne's breasts and at the same time inserting two or three fingers into her that had the immediate effect of causing Anne to go into spasms of motions of raising and lowering her body notwithstanding the weight of Felicity upon her. Anne realised that she was enjoying all the thrills, as she could not reach her friend, so muttered in halting breath, that Felicity should move up a bit, so that she could reach her as she was reached. Without reply, the movement of bodies coincided with this wish and that gave Anne the opportunity to respond in like fashion, but only into the lower extremities, but they kissed in an enraptured and aggressive manner.

How long they lay like that thrilling each other was without time factor. They both became exhausted from the heated exercise and more or less separated at the same time to mutual satisfaction. The first to raise her torso was Felicity, who suggested that they had better get up as she comically put it again, that they were after all 'just working girls'. So without further ado, both arose from the bed and resorted to the bathroom.

After a modest breakfast they left the flat to enter Felicity's car and made their way to the office. As they approached the rendezvous, Felicity suggested that she would put Anne down as near as she could before entering the firm's car park, so as not to be seen together. Anne thought that would be a prudent move and so alighted within a block or so of the office. They did not meet again until the afternoon of that first day of their new understanding. The few minutes it took Anne to walk the remaining short distance to the office block from the point where Felicity had put her down, gave Anne the opportunity to review herself, her reaction to Felicity, her attitude towards this new theme of lovemaking with her senior, to whom she had confessed her love. That confession of love that provoked the reply of love from Felicity. Was all this real or was she dream walking?

As Anne reached the corner of the street, a cold blast of wind swept across her face. This awakened her to the realisation and realities of where she was and to what she was then doing. She was on her way to work, and all other considerations of the previous evening and that very morning must be put aside, for day-dreaming was not what she was paid for. As if with a renewed gait, she strode forward over the last remaining paces to the office entrance and made her way to the elevator with the throng of other members of staff, both of her own firm and that of other firms that occupied suites in the building.

Chapter 4

As arranged, Anne met Angus on that Tuesday, at the agreed time of eight in the evening. She observed his approach as she stood in the shelter of the cinema canopy, shielding herself from the slight drizzle. She noted with inward satisfaction that he walked upright and not with the proverbial common slouch that appeared to be the mode of the day, even with the upheld umbrella. His suit was neat with nicely creased trousers. She spotted a matching handkerchief to his tie out of his top pocket that added a sense of propriety to his manner. His hair was well-groomed and not in the manner of today, but only comparatively short cut. Overall, Anne felt that she would not be ashamed to be seen out with Angus, except she still held a sneaking feeling that she was 'stealing' him from her friend Joan.

But then what of her own emotions? Had she not made this date, she felt that now she had a lover even if it was another female as herself, would she be so pleased to be going out with a man. One half of her mind said that she should not, yet the other half said there could be nothing wrong, so long as she reserved herself for Felicity! Then even she would not object. So with a pleasant smile she greeted Angus as he made his salutations. He appeared quite gentlemanly, as he even did not attempt to greet her with the expected kiss, but simply took her arm in his and wheeled her round towards the street, and at a slow pace, walked her along asking her at the same time where she had planned to suggest they go. To this suggestion, Anne proposed a small restaurant she had passed many times but had as yet not tried. So with agreement reached, they walked the short distance and entered the establishment referred to.

Anne enjoyed the evening very much and found that Angus was indeed a very good conversationalist. He kept prattling away asking and telling her many things. He would not expand on his comments about Joan, as he indicated that he had already said more than his custom by indicating she was somewhat 'frigid'. This inwardly pleased Anne to learn that he had a good sense of honour and could thus be trusted, but then she did not have anything to trust him to or for. This did not stifle his interest in Anne's escorts to which Anne gave but vague responses, having taken a leaf out of his book by being reticent on the subjects that concerned herself with others. So they spent a pleasant period of time over an enjoyable meal, following which they agreed to just take a turn around the park, after which he promised her he would escort her home.

It was no longer twilight as they entered the park. The rain that threatened more heavily had faded away instead, but it was decidedly very fresh. The only inhabitants appeared to be other young couples, some walking abroad, others seated on the infrequent benches. These latter occupiers appeared to be oblivious to others around them in their bent of embrace. This created a slight mirth between Anne and her companion Angus. Without being too pointed, they made comments of the possible behaviour of the lovers. But as soon as an empty seat became available, they both instinctively went for it before another couple could occupy it.

As soon as they were seated, he placed his muscular arm around Anne's shoulder and drew her towards himself, and with his free hand turned her so that they faced each other. At that point they embraced unashamedly and with seemingly full passion. Their kiss went beyond the lip to lip, as they both sought the mouth to probe with their tongue. His hand that had turned her towards himself now dropped off her waist, as it travelled to her chest. Without any objection from Anne, he undid the front buttons of her top coat and placed his hand within; then probed her blouse, grasping her breast that he rubbed in a rotating motion. As her arms were around his shoulders, they felt compatibly comfortable in that position but after a short while, he lifted off his arm from her shoulder and taking her hand from off his, he attempted to manoeuvre her hand to himself. She became aware that he had placed her hand over his rod that she felt was very strong and appeared to be somewhat big too. She did not appear to object to holding it whilst it was still encased within his trousers, but the moment he managed to undo his fly and extract it and put her hand over it, she slapped it and with a cry, moved away.

'Angus,' she said in a loud and somewhat angered voice, 'please do not take advantage as I will get up right now and go home on my own.' As she spoke, she moved further apart from him, much to his consternation, anguish and embarrassment.

'Anne dear, I do not wish to upset you, so please forgive me. But I did think as you did not object that you would go that far with me', and as he spoke he retracted and re-buttoned his fly's having momentarily lost his passionate ardour, as now he had to resurrect his standing with Anne. Now in obvious piteous mood, he snuggled up towards Anne and endeavoured to re-establish himself in her congeniality.

'Please understand, Angus,' replied Anne, 'because I allow you a liberty, it must stop at that, as I am no free-for-all girl. I like you, but not that much to permit me to allow you such freedom with me. So if you insist on that I must leave you and walk home.'

'Please Anne, I respect you too much to go beyond your desire. Please forgive me and let's kiss and make up.' As he spoke, he shuffled along the park bench towards her and held out his arms as if to receive her. With a wry and comical face and half a smile, Anne entered into his embrace with him, which appeared to clear the heavy atmosphere that pervaded them a few moments ago.

'Why did you take it out?' asked Anne.

'If it's going to upset you, I would rather not dwell on it.'

'So long as you tell me the truth, I will not object, as I feel you owe me an explanation.'

'I will accept your word that you will not get cross with me then. The reason I took it out was that you got me so heated that had I left it in my pants, I would have released it there and it would have been very uncomfortable as you can imagine. But the moment you pounced on me, I lost it and it went like a damp squib as it is now and you can feel it if you like.' As he said that he held out his hand asking in its way, to take hers, so that he could place it over himself. Her hesitation was but momentary, as she considered that no harm could come of fondling so long as he kept his word to keep it beneath, so she allowed her hand to be taken up and placed as it had been before. She felt the slight throb and as it remained there with Angus's hand over hers, she felt it gradually rise at which point in time he pressed her fingers around it and moved closer towards her and with his free hand embraced her.

'Now what are you going to do – let it go in your pants and be uncomfortable as I can feel it getting to mammoth size?' said Anne with a wicked grin on her face in devilment.

'Well, what else can I do my sweet?' countered Angus.

'You can either let it go off again and let it get little, or you can go behind that tree and let it off, which may please you and help you feel relieved. So just enjoy yourself as you wish,' added Anne, still with a grin in making him cringe with frustration.

'I would love to relieve myself, but would you come with me to the tree and cuddle me there, and I promise, you will not have to touch me but I would feel happier with you there too.'

'So long as you do not attempt to get me to hold you or to look at it and do not make a mess on me, I will. But how can I be of any help in that?' opined Anne, with a secret giggle to herself.

With that, Angus arose and holding on to Anne by his arm around her waist, they moved into the shadow of the large overhanging willow tree, in which position they could not be seen by any passer-by. He leaned her against the trunk of the tree, and still holding her close to himself, managed to undo his fly buttons and take it out. She held onto him with both arms around his neck, as he bid and pressing as close as he could. He went into an ecstasy that made him shiver all over, much as Anne had herself experienced when in the state of climax or orgasm. During this period he held her tighter, if that was possible, raining kisses on her, that appeared to please her as she responded to them, knowing he would not attempt anything against her that night. When his trembling ceased, he released his hold and withdrew a handkerchief from his pocket with which he covered himself and then replaced it and rehooked the fly buttons. He asked her if she was all right and not upset at him.

38

'Why should I be upset with you – you kept your promise and have not made a mess on me, and you are happy now, so what?'

'All I can say is *thank you* for helping me. I know, as you know, I would have loved to give it to you, but you have made it clear to me that is as far as you will go, so I respect you for that. Then I can ask you out again, can't I?'

'At least you are not wet in your pants and have got rid of it, not like me. You got me equally excited and I can't hold it out to dispose of it like you,' retorted Anne with a humorous chuckle.

'Would you like me to wipe it up for you then; I can if you wish as it's no bother,' Angus replied with a broad grin on his face as he made a jocular show of getting out his handkerchief again.

'I bet you would like to wipe it up, but I will suffer it as a reminder of our night out and if I get back soon, it would not attract attention if I slip into a bath when I get home, so let's get going, otherwise you will spoil a very pleasant evening.' With that she moved away slightly and he taking the hint, moved with her to where the car was parked and drove her home. Before letting her out of the car, they made tentative arrangements to meet again and exchanged telephone numbers.

At first, Anne felt it impossible to concentrate on her work, as she was full of thought over her interlude with her senior, Felicity. At least now she knew that she could indulge in lovemaking in the quietude of Felicity's flat without exposure and without risk. But was she right to do this or was it wrong? And that she should be with man and not with woman? Again she could not reconcile herself to making a decision, so contented herself with the thought that she would enjoy what was available and work it out when the time was opportune. The pressure of work that was placed upon her soon gave her reason to forget her mental turmoil, and so concentrate upon her job in hand. So a few days passed without any happenings until near the end of that week, when she was called into Felicity's office for the first time since their meeting at the flat.

She was bid to enter the room but not to close the door. Anne did as she was asked, wondering why now that they were on such presumably intimate terms, she should leave the door ajar. Felicity, in a very soft voice, so as not to be overheard, indicated that she preferred the door left open so there could be no hint or talk of impropriety between them. It was then that Anne understood her companion and the reasons. She took a chair as invited to, and was asked in a normal tone of voice by Felicity how she was progressing with her work and how she liked to be at the firm. From Anne's point of view, it was her first and only job she had ever held and enjoyed working there. To this Felicity said, 'I have been asked to choose a new person to join the audit department, to work with a couple of good lads and have recommended you to the boss.'

'That's marvellous, Felicity,' came the eager reply, in a first blush of pleasure, but on reflection, did not assuredly know exactly what went on in the audit department.

'First, I must ask you not to be so informal whilst here in the office – you must continue to address me as "miss" otherwise two and two may be put together, which would not enhance either of us, now would it Anne?'

'No miss,' responded Anne in a subdued manner with her eyes half averted. 'I agree with you, so please forgive my error. Now about this audit post; do you think I can do it as I do not know the slightest thing about it really?'

'I have already indicated to the boss, Mr Meredith, that you have proven yourself in work outside typing, and I feel that you will fit in very well. Now remember, you will be working with a couple of lads and that means they will be making passes at you, not forgetting the boss, who may take a fancy to you, too, despite being a married man with a family. Together we can resolve all those little problems; what you say Anne?'

'You know you can count on me, but when do we meet again, as I feel I would like to as has been indicated that we made a good team.'

'First I must compliment you on your very formal manner in which you address yourself to a very personal point; keep it up as I have suggested whilst in the office, as we can forget formality elsewhere, can't we Anne?'

Anne nodded her head in acquiescence and smiled covertly and added, 'When do I see the boss and when do we meet?' she added the last request in a softer tone so as to be doubly sure of not being overheard.

'The last question first; in the car part tonight if that's OK with you Anne. Now go directly to Mr Meredith's office.'

'Shall I telephone home first or leave that until I have met the boss?'

'I think it would be wise to pop in to his office right away now, otherwise he will be buzzing me; so off you go and the best of luck.'

With that, Anne left Felicity's room and made her way along the short corridor to Mr Meredith's office.

She had walked past that room on numerous occasions, but had never had the call to enter. So she felt a tinge of apprehension as she quietly tapped on the door whilst reading the legend on the brass name-plate affixed thereto, that announced that, 'Norman Meredith, FCA, Senior Partner' was within. She tapped a second time but then she heard a shout to enter, which she did still feeling shaky.

'Come in, come in. I answered your knock but apparently you could not have heard me, Anne.'

'Yes sir. Miss Felicity said you would like to see me, as you wish to transfer me to another section.'

'Well, before we deal with the proposal of a transfer, I would like to ask you a few questions to make doubly sure that you are as good as I have been told. Now I understand that you have, with little instruction, mastered Bank Reconciliation's. Is that so, my dear?' He asked her with a very pleasant smile upon his countenance.

He was a well-dressed man of some forty years of age, maybe a year more or less, but he appeared as usual, well-groomed with a neat pinstriped suit and college tie and a wisp of a moustache. He appeared to wear a permanent smile on his face, and he had called her 'my dear'. Now was that his regular way of addressing his junior staff or was that special to her, wondered Anne.

'Reconciliation's did not seem to hold any mystery to me sir, as I found it was common sense when it was explained to me,' replied Anne still wondering the implication of his term of endearment.

'Then you will have no problem with auditing,' replied Mr Meredith. 'Now you will start Monday in the Audit department under two very experienced lads; the senior is Ian McDonnell and called Mac for short and under him is Braddely Ford. You probably

41

know them well already.' Anne nodded in acknowledgement to the question. Mr Meredith continued, 'After four weeks, they will report to me and if the indications are as expected, you will get a substantial increase in your pay packet. But between now and then I would like you to pop in to see me as there is a small thing I may wish you to do for me. Is that understood Anne?'

'Oh yes sir,' replied Anne very much puzzled by the last injunction. Feeling that the interview was then over, she arose and was about to leave the room when Mr Meredith said, 'Turn round Anne please.'

She stood for a moment with a slight gape in the mouth not quite understanding the request. He observed her hesitation so added, 'I just asked you to turn round, as I would like to see what you look like. As you may know, in auditing you may be called upon to visit clients in their own offices and work there.'

So with an understanding smile, she turned as if on a catwalk parading herself to the best advantage.

'Now that's just fine; just you respond and smile and you will always win. Yes, you look OK but I feel that your pay increase you will be able to smarten yourself, not to say that you do not appear very attractive, but you know what I mean, don't you Anne?'

'Not really sir, but I like to be happy so I smile naturally and I also enjoy my work and that makes me smile when I have achieved results that are appreciated.'

'Now that is a good topic for us to chat about when you pop into my office as I have suggested, one day next week.'

'Thank you very much sir; I will pop in as you say, but may I go now sir?'

'Off you go and the best of luck to you,' replied her boss.

So without further ado, Anne left the room and returned to her own desk and looked around before wondering when she should start getting her things together, but decided to defer to the last moment.

As arranged, Wynne met Richard but she had trepidation as to going anywhere with him that evening. She was now having second thoughts as to her quick response to his advances. Despite the fact that she enjoyed the interlude, she knew that she was wrong to have permitted those advances so soon in their acquaintanceship. 'No, that's not right,' mused Wynne. 'Even if I have dated him umpteen times I should not have been so foolish to have gone so far with him.' What was she to do that night, repeat the same performance or say strong and clear that the 'shutters were down' and incite his possible wrath?

Richard for his part was looking forward to the tryst with the eagerness of a cock among a battery of hens. He knew that he came very close to being frustrated and felt that luck would be with him that night. If he got no further in his arduous demands than before, he considered that he would still count himself lucky to have met such a fine girl that was also co-operative with him. He had thought perhaps he may even take her to his home even though he had only dated her that once.

'My, you do look nice tonight, Wynne,' said Richard as they met.

'Thanks, and it's nice to see you again, Richard,' replied Wynne. 'And where to tonight, lover boy; do you fancy the movies or just a coffee some place?'

'Yes, why not a movie. There's a good one on at the cinema this week and I believe it's worth a visit. After that we can have that coffee and then, who knows, eh sweetie?' said Richard in a chirpy voice full of innuendo.

So with that they made their way to the cinema, and obtained a rear seat. After taking off their outer coats and laying them across their laps, they sat themselves down and with an arm around each other, they posed themselves to watch the film. After but a few moments he drew her free arm over to himself and placed her hand, palm downwards over himself. He whispered into her ear that she may if she would like to, undo his buttons and put her hand inside for comfort, indicating that the coats were covering them so they would not be seen. She declined and said there is a place and time and that was not there then. He did not answer but as a sort of compensation, placed his arm under hers and held very lightly her breast which he gently squeezed. So they sat and seemingly both enjoyed the film show.

Chapter 5

After the film show, Wynne and Richard left the cinema, but donned their coats on reaching the foyer, as it appeared to have chilled weather-wise somewhat since they entered to see the film. They walked aimlessly arm in arm talking of the film, making both compliments and criticisms. Then realising that they had wandered without purpose, they discussed where to go for a snack and coffee. Thus, they had an aim and proceeded there as agreed.

After that interlude, being a little after eleven, he proposed that they walk to the park as before. She was at first reluctant, reminding him that his behaviour was not of the best. He promised that he would not attempt to go further than before, to which she responded that on that occasion he went too far, but nevertheless, they continued their walk in the park direction. Being perhaps because it was a week night, they found the seats in the park not so popular as at the weekend. He proposed and she consented to take the same seat as before if available. Fortune smiled upon them as the seat was vacant, so they seated themselves thereon. Wynne commented that it was getting somewhat chilly and that she did not feel like staying out late in the cold damp park too long.

'Well, to start with we could cuddle up close and that would keep us fairly warm, now wouldn't it?' proposed Richard as he drew her closer to himself and placed both his arms around her so that they sat side by side but half turned towards each other. After an apparent introductory kiss, he asked her to place her hand below as she had done in the cinema.

'Now do not spoil the evening by starting that all over again,' pleaded Wynne somewhat hurt yet not surprised.

'But darling,' replied Richard, 'you only covered it in the cinema and did not hold it, so I did not get any relief and you would not like to go home thinking of me so frustrated that I would have to do the alternative, now would you?'

'And what is the alternative?'

'Well, you know. I would have to do it myself as I could not go to sleep pent up like this as it would keep me awake all night. So be a darling and hold it.'

'But that won't satisfy you even if I did hold it. You would want me to excite you and I'm not in the mood as it's too cold.'

'Then what we will do is that I'll warm you up first and then you will be in the mood to do for me; how would that be darling?' asked Richard with his mind racing ahead of his emotions, but still very hopeful of his persuasive powers over Wynne. And as he spoke his hand went under her coat and travelled beyond her knee and then negotiated the lower elastic of her pants. Rather than stretch them, he drew his hand over the pants to the top of them, then drew them down slightly but enough for his hand to reach her as he had on that previous occasion. During the period, Wynne sat with her arms around him and did not raise any objection as she immediately felt a flush of warmth come over her as she felt the hand reach her and the fingers entering her in a piston like motion, creating in her an aura of excitement that made her glow all over. After but a few moments without any preconceived plan, she realised that despite her earlier objections, her hand had travelled, as if on its own volition, and had undone his buttons and, as if by charm, was gripping him in a tight fist-like hold that made him shudder and pull her towards himself violently and passionately. They were in an amorous embrace kissing each other around the face and neck as he repeatedly prodded and withdrew his fingers, whilst she gripped him in a pulsating hold, when he pulled away slightly and said, 'Hold it away from you as it is about to explode darling.'

Wynne instinctively understood the request and realised that he would be making a mess over her clothes if she did not focus it away from herself. So just in time she managed to see it release its fluid

45

away from her into the air. The moment this occurred, he seemed to relax his fingers in her and go limp all over and lay back a little and breath a deep sigh. He made no attempt to adjust his clothing but remained in a semi-comatose position whilst she held on wondering what to do next. She realised that he had spent himself with the exertion and excitement, but she had not climaxed, so she said quietly in his ear, 'Lover boy, you have enjoyed yourself but what of me left in the cold holding on to this limp lump. Are you going to give me satisfaction or are you finished?'

He immediately realised that he was behaving in a cavalier way, getting the best out of her without reciprocating, so he quickly got out a handkerchief and gave it to Wynne with the request that she wipe him up. Whilst she did this without any qualm as if it was a normal duty, he wound his finger back again into her and proceeded to please her with the motion as before. As soon as he restarted, she left his shaft that had now become a mere winkle, and threw her leg over him and embraced him strongly in an intense vice-like grip whilst she went into climax that shook both of them with the park bench too.

He realised that he was too quick, for had he held back until now, she was in the position he dreamed of and entry would have been achieved easily. She was astride him jockeying up and down as he fingered her whilst she held on to him in her passion around the neck raining kisses and biting him with ardour.

Gradually, her passion became spent and she released her hold and straightened herself out on the park bench. He too realising that emotion was spent, it was useless to attempt anything more that night. So for a few minutes they both lay back and reclined to recover their equilibrium. Richard was the first to fully recover and took out a packet of cigarettes and proffered them to Wynne who declined but indicated that he may smoke if he wished. He extracted a cigarette and lit it up and after a puff or two offered it to Wynne. She looked at it for a moment, then said that perhaps she would just have one draw, which she hoped would cool her down but also suggested that it was time to make tracks for home.

'Yes, I agree it's time I took you home, Wynne darling, but let me have a quiet smoke first unless you feel you must go this minute.'

'No, no, it's OK for a while, then we can both get our breath back again, can't we lover?' interjected Wynne.

'Well, Wynne, was it satisfactory tonight? You are not cold now are you and *did* you enjoy yourself, admit it darling?'

'Yes, you make a wonderful lover but that shows your experience I suppose, doesn't it now?'

'Truthfully I have not been out with a girl before more than once as I have unfortunately found them lacking in common sense and passion.'

'And you worked up my passion all right, haven't you?'

'Shall we agree that we match each other, as we gave each other good satisfaction without intercourse, which perhaps we will enjoy next time.'

'That's what you think, lover boy,' countered Wynne.

'Well, why not, because I could have done it and you know well I could have when you went into ecstasy.'

'In that case you can get me home and we will not meet again, as I have told you before, and will tell you again, I will not allow anyone to seduce me and what we have done tonight is in truth, further than I thought I would allow, but then I'm possibly falling for you and that's a waste of time I suppose.'

'Darling,' responded Richard with his eyes opened as far as nature would permit as he solidly looked into the face close to him. 'I too have a strong feeling for you, otherwise I would not have dated you. And if you like on our next date, you can come to my home to meet my folks.'

'Do you really mean that, Richard?' echoed Wynne with a look of happy wonderment on her face.

'Of course I do. Have you found me speaking out of my hat yet? I always say what I mean and you have by now realised that, or have you?'

As if new life had been pumped into her, her face lit up and if it was not dark about, it would have been observed by any passer that her face beamed with smiles and glee as a first love had come into her life.

As if by spontaneous motion, she almost leaped at him and threw her arms around him and after but a moment put one hand into his still unbuttoned trousers and gripped him. He was for a moment aghast and taken aback, but welcomed the unexpected exhibition of love that Wynne showered on him. He began to feel higher emotion and began to debate what he should then do. He was sure that she would be easy prey if he so desired to have her, then and there, but reflected that he would assuredly lose her that way, so he compromised and cuddled her with one hand, the other fondling her to apparent delight again.

She asked him to reconfirm that he wanted her as his regular girl with plans that he would wed her. He then saw that she had taken him very much at his word and had even jumped to the conclusion that marriage was in his mind. He reflected and stealthily stole a glance at her and thought that he could do much worse by far, and as things stood at that moment he felt it may be a good thing too. So he answered that it was his intention to show her to his family as his future bride if she would have him. Instead of replying she went into another spasm of showing her love by gripping him still more and raining kisses all over him. Her passion appeared to be endless. He realised too, that his emotions were being aroused by her grip and before long it would have to be released. In forethought he drew out a spare handkerchief and laid it at the side of him and then replaced his hand and fingers within her as before. This action appeared to rekindle her once again into the flame of excitement that threw her into contortions with her legs over him and her free arm pulling him towards her in a strong passionate hold, all the whilst she held on to him as it grew and grew. Richard became aware in his aroused emotion that in the position she had placed herself it was virtually a fraction away from entering her full and strong, and it appeared to him that she was deliberately drawing it towards herself. 'Oh!' he cried silently to himself, 'I can have it for the taking, but should I and then get into trouble and what of the consequences?' He was getting near to the end and a decision had to be made. As if someone guided him, he withdrew his arm that had encircled her and placed it over her hand and, deflected her hand whilst still holding his now bursting thing and not a second too soon, as no sooner had he, he moved her hand with her grip still in place he let fly and ejaculated into the air.

She still did not release him but began to moan that she wanted him and why did he take it away.

'Darling, you would hate me if I took advantage of you whilst you were in that state. Frankly, I have dreamed of having you just as you were, but when it came to it, I had too much respect and love for you to take advantage; so let's wipe up and I'll get you home.'

Still holding on to him she cried that she wanted it and he must give it to her. He then realised that he was still exciting her, so gently he withdrew his hand from under her and at the same time took hold of his handkerchief that he put on the side of the park bench and with great care began to wipe her under her clothes. This seemed to cause her to lose her excitement he was pleased to observe. When he had to some degree wiped her, he gave her the then damp handkerchief and asked her to wipe him up. This she did with seeming reluctance to let him go. And as she completed her task she laid it as in repose back within and buttoned it in and said in a soft voice, 'Good night, my little love – you almost had me, now rest until next time.' And with that, she returned his now very wet and very clammy handkerchief.

In an attempt to change the subject, he told her that she may have become pregnant if she had wiped him up first then wiped herself with the spermed handkerchief. To this she replied, 'Then you would have had to marry me but perhaps a bit sooner. Would that be in your plan?'

'Truthfully, no, it would not, but marry you I think we will as we seem to get on so well together so far. But I think you will agree it is too soon after only dating a couple of times. So let's make a few more dates and then if we are still as happy together, then we can seriously talk about that; what do you say to that?'

She did not reply immediately but went into another spasm with her arms around him smothering him with her wild kisses and in between them, she called him various names of endearment, indicating that she was in love with him.

'If we meet again in a couple of days, you can tell me if you still love me as I feel it may be your frustrated emotion that's talking and not your sane self, so let's get going otherwise your folks will be asking questions.' So with that he stood up and gently pulled her up too. Reluctantly, she complied and followed him to his car and entered the vehicle and with a last turn towards her and with a slight peck on the cheek, he started up the car and drove off towards her home. When he pulled up outside her home, he did not get out but she turned towards him and again throwing an arm around him and placing the other over his lap gave him a strong kiss and bid him 'good night'. She left the car with the reminder that they were to meet in a couple of days time.

Chapter 6

Wynne stood in the doorway and waved Richard off. She stood there but a few moments until the darkness swallowed up the receding car. She stayed yet a while and contemplated the area and wondered what it was like where Richard lived. He did say that he proposed to have her home to meet his family. That gave her a nervous shudder, as it made her feel vulnerable, but of what she was not sure. Then she considered that everyone has to face that ordeal – if it was an ordeal? Then it may be the same for Richard and his family when she arrived to meet them. They may also be on edge wondering if she will like them. But then all meetings of this kind are usually preceded with misgivings that invariably are groundless as both sides intend to be at their best at the first introduction. Standing in the doorway contemplating, she did not realise that the door behind her had opened, until her father spoke to her asking if she intended to stay the night there.

'No, Dad,' replied Wynne, 'I've just had a lift home and wanted to see the car on its way, that's all. But thanks for waiting up', and with that she gave her father a hug and a greeting kiss and entered the house.

After a few casual questions and answers as to how she enjoyed the evening, she said that she was for a shower and bed. Her father bid her 'good night' and promised to put a glass of hot milk by her bedside for her.

In less than half an hour, Wynne had showered and got into bed and drank the milk put there for her. Within minutes of laying her head on the pillow, she was fast asleep. Visions appeared that confused her. She saw herself being married to, presumably, Richard and to his questioning her as to her past sexual behaviour. She frankly admitted that she had played around. He wanted to know in detail so she admitted throwing herself into a position for sex but she had not actually indulged. When she described what she had done, and how she had held a man, he was very angry and called her awful names that upset her. 'Only a tart does those things,' he said and it made her cry and ask for forgiveness. For that he said she would have to do exactly as he demanded and no arguments. She promised to obey his every wish and the first request was to re-enact what she said she had done before. To comply with her promise she immediately moved her hand to him and took it and held it until it grew and grew. She cried and wanted to know what to do with it and was told to place it where his fingers were. She obeyed and began to feel the throb of the organ within her. She was in an extraordinary state of ecstasy and felt his body upon hers and his thrusting rhythm as she clung to him. She followed his motion in his thrust and heaved and sighed in consort with him. Then she felt him expanding to a point where she thought she would burst if it became any larger, when to her satisfaction, she felt his ejaculation at the very moment she herself had an orgasm. She screamed out in simulated passion and the noise of her own shout awoke her.

She was in a sweat all over and very dishevelled as if she had been in a tussle. Then she realised that she was not in a sweat just bodily, but underneath too. Her fingers had apparently been in as they too were wet. She realised that she had been dreaming and fantasising over her adventures of that evening. It was then too late to get out of bed and go to the bathroom as it would awake her parents. So she lay there going over her dream and then going over her actions with Richard.

She did not think that she was sufficiently sophisticated to control herself, and she felt ashamed of her actions. She realised that she succumbed to temptation and had it not been that Richard had spent himself, she would be in a worrying state. Then she began to analyse her innermost thoughts. She had declared her love for Richard. Could she really be in love with him or was it just sexual infatuation?

She had heard of love at first sight but did not really think it could happen. Then she reflected that it was not at first sight as she had dated him twice. Was that a point in her favour? She could not credit that she had physically flung herself at him in her excitement of lovemaking and felt very low and miserable. How could she, who claimed to be sensible and sane, do such a thing? After tossing and turning for a considerable time she came to the conclusion that it was, in truth, not love but sexual intoxication. Now how should she react when Richard called for her? Should she refuse to join him or what? Was she likely to succumb again into that trap of silly infatuation and make a fool of herself as she now felt she had?

She clenched her fist in determination and with a tight lip mumbled to herself that she would prove herself capable of looking after her own destiny and would go out with him again if invited, but would be more careful. So after much inner searching, she fell into a dreamless sleep.

It was a quiet evening when Tracey removed herself from the dinner table and went over to switch on the radio. At the same moment, she heard a telephone call that was answered by her mother. She was called to take the 'phone by her mother who indicated that a gentleman named Andrew was calling. She felt a flush reach her face as she took the hand piece from her parent and announced herself.

'I thought I'd give you a call as a new show is on at the Starlight tonight and may be you would like to join me there?' she heard Andrew say into the mouthpiece. Without covering the mouthpiece, she called her mother and said that she had been invited out and had she any objections; to which she was told to go out and enjoy herself but not get back too late. Tracey told her mother that it was the Starlight nightclub and did not terminate until 2 a.m. but that she would get home as soon as the cabaret was over.

She then spoke into the mouthpiece and said, 'You probably heard all that; if you can get me home as soon as the show is over. I'll be delighted if you came for me in about half an hour so that I can get dressed up.' It was then agreed that he would call for her as suggested and promised to return her home as early as possible.

Tracey won the championship for speed that evening in preparing herself. So rushed was she that she was ahead of time and was awaiting Andrew's call before he arrived. She began to debate with herself whether she should invite him in or perhaps she would do that after they had dated a few more times. Before she could deliberate any more, he arrived. He suggested that she go in and fetch a coat, as it did get somewhat chilly late at night. She was rather surprised at his solicitude in her interest and made a mental note of it. He was dressed in a dinner suit and she posed the question that she felt that her low-necked tinted blue organdie dress may not be suitable for the occasion or with him. To this Andrew responded that her dress was just right and he thought she looked very attractive in it. So having agreed that detail, they made their way to the nightspot. As before, great deference was shown him by the ushers which made Tracey feel important.

Tracey indicated that she had already eaten at home so Andrew suggested that she just have a sweet and coffee unless she felt she could tackle the hors-d'oeuvre, too. On reading the menu, she succumbed to joining him in the appetiser. In between the courses they danced, which gave her an opportunity to look around at the assembly. She observed that most of the men wore dress suits, so she raised the point as to why it was not so apparent on the last occasion.

'As it is a first night, it is a courtesy to do so if you are a regular client,' responded Andrew. This gave her an inner sense of feeling somewhat important to be with a 'client' that is considered a regular. She also noted that the others all appeared to be of the well-to-do bracket and this also gave her the feeling of well-being. She realised that her escort must be better off than those she normally mixed with. This too added to her happy feeling. So they danced the night away and enjoyed the new cabaret, at which time she proposed that he take her home.

Without any hesitation, Andrew called the waiter and settled his bill and then arose to escort her home. He helped her on with her coat that she brought at his instigation and glad of it she was. The early hour of the morning was indeed very chilly and the short walk to the car made her feel quite cold! When they had both seated themselves in the car, he asked if she really wanted to go directly home.

'You heard what I promised when you telephoned me this evening, so I feel that I must ask you to get me home, please.'

'Actually, I asked you that because I thought you may like to see my flat and have a good night drink with me.'

'Is it only to see and drink or perhaps you have other ulterior motives?' quizzed Tracey with her mind racing away as to the possible reason.

'I never take advantage of a girl without her express consent, so you need not worry on that score, Tracey.'

'Would you be upset if I promised to go with you next time but right now, just get me home?'

'As you wish, my dear, but when would you like to see my home?'

'You say, as I am mostly free except at the weekends when we all go to the Palais where we first met. But are you all on your own in that flat of yours?' queried Tracey with a slight feeling of misgiving in going to a man's flat on her own, as she imagined she would be walking into a trap with open eyes and tantamount to consenting to anything that may occur there. As if he read her mind, he revealed that he was on his own in the flat and that she would be quite safe there with him, as he was not an ogre. If she liked to join him any evening from work, he would prepare a meal that she would enjoy.

'You surprise me, Andrew, as you do not look the type that is domesticated too. And as I do not know any other man that can cook, I feel I am up to the challenge and would be happy to try your efforts. So I will nominate the day,' countered Tracey.

'Then what about Friday night. I could call for you at your place of work if you let me know where it is. And if you really feel adventurous you can if you wish stay the weekend.'

'And you said there would be no hanky-panky and now you ask me to stay with you for the whole weekend! What do you think my parents would say if they heard your proposal?' retorted Tracey with a slight smile on her face as if to say, 'Now here goes; he is asking for it', and whatever that meant she knew inwardly.

'Whatever you tell your folks is really up to you, but as far as I am concerned, you are very welcome to stay over. So why not just come for the first time on Friday and take it from there – you can always 'phone your folks if you decide to stay over, can't you?'

'OK then, I am employed at Brown's, 99 Cheapside. I could be downstairs in the foyer at 5.15 p.m. How would that suit you?'

Without immediately answering, Andrew switched on the engine and after moving off he replied that he would be there. So he drove her home and with but a peck on the cheek as before, he alighted and escorted her to the door of her home.

Tracey entered her home somewhat bewildered. Every time she had been on a date, the escort had endeavoured to make love with her despite her protestations. So far she has won all the battles as she could claim that she had never succumbed, however she may have been inclined, tempted or badgered. But here was a very likeable man who appeared to be well off and all he did was to give her a peck on the cheek, yet spend a considerable sum on her in entertainment. Surely it could not be that she put him off as he had invited her to his home. So why was he so restrained. Could he be a homo – he did not appear to be, but what do they look like; she did not know. This feeling of puzzlement made her determined to find out the truth whatever it was about him when she visited his place on the coming Friday. She knew that she would not allow sex, but did enjoy and possibly expected to frolic a while with a male escort. So what was wrong with him if it was not her fault? Or was it her fault? She looked at herself in the cheval mirror and saw a pleasant slim young, reasonably attractive female, whom she imagined any male would be happy to bed! He had admired her cocktail dress so it was not her outfit that could have made him reticent, so what could it be?

The more she pondered the more she felt that going to his home next Friday would resolve the mystery. But that sneaking suspicion that it was just a catch did not dissuade her from her plan.

However she looked at the question, it intrigued her the thought of seeing where he lived.

So she prepared and eventually went to bed, only to have pleasant dreams of what was to come and with some misgivings of not having had that expected hug and its consequences. And the first thing that came to her mind on awakening the following morning, was Andrew.

Chapter 7

Anne was at her desk perhaps a few minutes after her interview with her boss Mr Meredith, when she had a call to go to Felicity Fawley's room. Her mind went blank for a moment when she had that request, as she had completely forgotten her superior and now her sponser for promotion. In a split second, she recalled her adventures with Felicity and that made her wonder if it was likely to be repeated. At that precise moment in time, she was full of promotional prospects and could not think too clearly of her lovemaking with Felicity. But she wanted her in her room, so she thought she had better go and see her. So leaving her desk as it was, she traversed the corridor and tapped on Miss Felicity's door, and was bid to enter.

'Ah, Anne, just the person I wanted to see; just come in, but please to leave the door ajar as I told you before.'

'Yes, miss,' responded Anne with a correct show of deference. She walked across the room and unasked, took a seat and looked up at her superior with a somewhat quizzical expression.

'Anne, you look at me as if you are looking at a ghost or some such apparition or something!' said Felicity in a quiet calm voice.

'I am so sorry miss, but I was in deep thought, for as you know, thanks to you, I have had a successful interview with the boss.'

'Then I am pleased to hear you say *successful*. But if you have any problems in your new capacity, just pop in to see me. But tell me, how did you get on with the boss – did he ask you to visit him again soon or what?'

'Yes – how did you know?' asked Anne looking surprised.

'I have been with this firm long enough to know almost everything that goes on and by whom, but tell me exactly what he said and asked.'

So Anne dutifully disclosed to Felicity all that was said and indicated, including with whom she will be working, and the request to look in to see him in a week's time.

'We will discuss all that at the flat. How are you placed for tonight?' And in a hushed voice continued, 'I must see you tonight, so please do not refuse, as am really desperate for you my love.'

Anne's face went slightly red when she heard this appeal and simultaneously felt an aura of sexual desire come over her. She still felt she was not in a position to refuse. Then why should she refuse – did she not also enjoy the interlude. So in a low voice she whispered that she could hardly wait to get to the flat and presumed that she would meet her at the car pound.

She left the room somewhat in a daze until she had to answer a telephone call. That reminded her to call her home and let her parents know that she may be staying overnight with the chief of her department and briefly indicated that she had been promoted.

That information seemed to suggest to her parents that she was celebrating her good news, so they saw no objection but suggested that she come home first to collect a few fresh clothes for the morrow. That she promised to do.

The evening was very cold and drizzly as Anne left the office block to make her way to the car pound. Just as she was about to enter the portals she had a tap on the shoulder and a voice spoke.

'Hullo, Anne.'

She turned to see Angus that gave rise to confusion in her mind, 'Now why should he be here just at this moment when I have a lovely date with Felicity. Had he been waiting for me or was it by chance that he happened to be at that point at this time?'

'Now what are you doing around here, Angus?' queried Anne looking at him with a stern yet quizzical countenance.

'I did hope to meet you and as you see I have. I wondered if you would like to join me for a meal this evening and perhaps a film or dance,' responded Angus.

'Sorry, Angus. I already have a date for tonight and I do not like it if you spring these surprises on me, nor do I like it for you to be here where I work.'

'Please, Anne, don't give me the brush-off. I did not mean to upset you but have thought of no one else but you since our last meeting. But are you really dated tonight?' queried Angus with a somewhat demure voice and sorrowful look.

'Yes, Angus, I really have a date and before you ask me, it's a girl that I work with and we are off together and not with men either. But why not give me a ring one night and we can make a date. How would that be, eh?'

'So glad to know you are with a girl tonight. I know I have no right to be jealous about you, but I cannot help feeling a tinge, now can I?'

'OK then, give me a buzz and we'll arrange a date, but I must be going now, so be good', and with a slight wave of the hand, she turned and left him.

Angus stood there for a moment to watch Anne disappear into the covered car park. With his hands deep into his pockets and a glum look upon his countenance he moved away.

Anne saw Felicity awaiting her in the car and made towards it with a happy smile upon her face. She had at the moment of seeing Felicity forgotten all about Angus. Her mind seemed to eradicate all thought of him on seeing her with the pleasures that promised and she hastened her step and entered the car. Felicity appeared equally happy, as she was full of beaming smiles, and as Anne boarded the car, she moved her hand over and gave Anne's leg a friendly squeeze. They both looked at one another with eyes that seemed to say that they craved each other. It took a few seconds before the spell was broken and Felicity switched on and moved the car forward out of the car park on to the road and towards her abode. All that was said during the journey was that Felicity asked Anne to place her hand on the upper part of her leg for comfort. This she did and doing so seemed that both derived some satisfaction therefrom.

Just as the car moved forward, Anne remembered her promise that she would first return home to collect a few items of wearing apparel.

She made this request to Felicity who immediately redirected the car in the correct direction on Anne's instruction. Despite the traffic, they reached the house in reasonable quick time. Anne alighted from the car and, with her own key, entered the house.

Within a few minutes, Anne re-emerged from the front door followed by her mother. Whilst her mother remained in the doorway, Anne came over to the car, and invited Felicity into the house as her mother had requested. With a wide smile, Felicity swung herself out of the car and walked across the pavement with Anne towards the open door.

'Mum,' said Anne slightly flushed and decidedly happy, 'this is my senior from work, Felicity, with whom I am staying over tonight; and Felicity, this is my mother, Mrs Hopkins.'

Mrs Hopkins, an attractive woman whom one recognised as Anne's mother so much alike did they appear, proffered her hand and accepted the outstretched hand of Felicity.

'I'm pleased to meet you,' said Mrs Hopkins. 'Would you care to come in for a cup of tea whilst Anne is getting a few things together.'

'That is very nice of you to offer me some tea, but really I did wish to get home as soon as we could, but perhaps another time, eh?' responded Felicity with a very pleasant manner and smile on her face.

'Then do come in for a minute or so whilst Anne is rummaging, please do,' rejoined Mrs Hopkins.

With that, she turned and entered the house leading the way for Felicity to follow. In the meantime, Anne chased up the stairs into her own bedroom, and as quick as she could, collected a few items that she proposed to wear the next day. No sooner did she do this, than she tumbled down the stairs and with a peck on her mother's cheek, she indicated to her friend that they were all set to go. They then both made their adieus with the mother giving the admonition to Anne to have a good time! To this injunction, Anne replied with one word, 'Sure'; so they left the house and re-entered the car. As soon as they were out of sight of the house, Felicity said she thought they would never get away, but she was delighted to have met her mother.

As they arrived at the flat, they both appeared to have developed straight faces. They both walked through the foyer, just nodding to the people there and made for the lift. Within a couple of minutes, they entered the flat and closed the door behind them. Immediately, Felicity caught Anne's shoulder and swung her round towards herself and embraced her very passionately. This was reciprocated with pangs of lustful desire.

After these preliminaries, they entered the lounge and discussed the programme for the evening. Should they eat first or shower first. They decided to forego and eat first, so Felicity introduced Anne to her kitchen, and between them they prepared a very delectable meal. By unspoken agreement, they made no reference to what they both anticipated but spoke primarily of their respective jobs. When the meal was over, and the table cleared and things put away, as if by intuition, they both moved towards the bedroom.

Again, as if by prearranged agreement, yet neither had spoken, they began to undress each other. Each time a section of the body became exposed, a hand would smooth it over. Eventually, both stood looking at each other completely divested of any clothing.

'Come,' said Felicity, as she lightly grabbed Anne by her arm, 'do not let us waste time here when we have such nice hot water awaiting us.' So with that, they both entered the shower cubicle and without ado, each took up a bar of soap and began to massage each other. They made great emphasis when they soaped the breasts and between the legs. This seemed to take ages as if it needed that amount of time to make it come clean!

After both had spent their sexual energies, they both jokingly started to frolic and splash each other playfully, until by consent, they ceased and emerged from the hot shower to help each other to dry off.

Felicity suggested that they go into the lounge and listen to some records in preference to the radio that evening. As the flat was comfortably warm, they could dispense with dressing gowns? By now, Anne had lost her caution and any inhibitions she may have had, and with a great show of forwardness, Anne heartily agreed and proposed that they have a bottle of wine instead of coffee. So like a couple of babes in the woods, one went for the wine whilst the other

61

chose a record and placed it onto the turntable. So they sat and inconspicuously fondled each other between the sips of wine.

It was getting late when they both began to endure muted yawns. So they agreed it was time to go to bed that they did after extinguishing the surplus lights.

The morning light penetrated the heavy brocade curtains. Anne awoke first and found that they were still in an embrace and lightly covered with a sheet. She stealthily withdrew her arm from under Felicity, and moved out of the bed. It was then that she realised that they both had gone to sleep in the nude. Anne felt a slight brazenness attitude to this discovery. She drew the curtains first to let the daylight in, then to the bathroom for a rinse. Sneaking in as quietly as she could, she entered the kitchen and put the kettle on for a cup of morning tea. She poured out two cups and with them returned to the bedroom, and placing them aside, she gently nudged her friend to wakefulness. As Felicity awoke, Anne was faced with the top half of a torso whilst standing over her at the bedside. Without saying a word she stretched out her arm and placed it under Anne and pulled her towards herself. This action toppled Anne onto her friend and caused both to laugh heartily. Anne indicated that she had brought her a cup of morning tea, to which Felicity responded, that she thought what she had grabbed would have been more appetising but would be content with the tea this time.

After a little frolic, they both emerged from the bedroom fully dressed for work and after a quick snack left the flat for the car and road. En route Anne reminded her friend that she had promised to give her a tip or two about Mr Meredith. To this she replied, that she should tell her when the boss asked to meet her for dinner, which would probably be at a good class hotel.

'And am I expected to join him for a meal, Felicity?'

'If you want promotion and a good pay packet it would be wise and prudent to accept the invitation. But as promised, I will give you further advice when the time comes.'

'It sounds mysterious the way you put it but I take your word, and will let you know when the date is to be; that is if he thinks I am any good?'

'Don't worry, my pet, I know the boss better than most, so you can anticipate a request. And if you have already got a date, regardless who it is – break it.'

By now they had reached the point where they considered it prudent for Anne to get out of the car and walk the few remaining yards to the office block. So they went their separate ways and did not meet again socially during that day.

When Anne had arrived at her home that evening, she found that Joan was awaiting her. 'Hullo Joan, hope nothing's wrong that you are here, as I do not think we have a date for tonight, or have we?'

'I had to come in as I've heard that Angus came to see you last night, but you would not go out with him and the fool got himself into trouble with the police!'

'I did not refuse to go out with him, but told him that I would be going out with my senior from work. And you can ask my mother, as she came home with me first. But why and how did he get himself into trouble with the police? What has he done to deserve that?' retorted Anne with a rising mixture of anguish and temper.

'Well, I got a call from the police to say that he had asked for me, so I went down to see him, but it was not me that he wanted, it was you and he did not have your address so asked me to contact you for him. So here I am doing what I have been asked to do.'

'Look Joan, I have been out with him only once, so why should he ask for me? I am not his regular and for that matter I do not think he has a regular girl. You have been out with him more often than I have, so you can visit him.'

'Anne, do not be like that. I do not care that you have been out with him, but he has asked for you. Why he should I don't know, but you will have a shock when you see him.'

'What you mean "shock"? Has something happened to him too?'

'Well, you know that paperman at the station. It appears that when he left you last night, he bought a paper and the guy hit him on the head with his crutch and bust his head, so that an ambulance had to take him to hospital for dressing.'

'But if he got a crash on the head, why should he be in trouble with the police?' ventured Anne with a puzzled expression.

'It seems that Angus swiped the guy with his paper and he resented it, so hit him back with the crutch.'

'Oh, now I know what happened. When we met last, he swiped the guy on the head; may be playfully; and I told him not to, as one day the chap would retaliate and it now seems that he has. Well, serves Angus right!' retorted Anne, with colour rising in her cheeks.

'Then are you going to the police station?' queried Joan with a frown that spoke volumes of her feeling of indignity that her own friend was being escorted by her boyfriend.

'Join me for a quick snack and come with me, eh?'

'If your mother does not mind I will gladly come with you.'

'My mother will not mind, but do ask her with whom I was last night, please.'

A slight perennial drizzle was falling as the two girls walked to the local police office. The sky was heavy with dark clouds and it seemed that the light drizzle would turn to a heavy downpour. It was an old building and smelt musky as they entered the station. Anne made enquiries at the desk and was asked the relationship. She indicated that she was not related but had been asked to call to see him. The station sergeant opened his counter book and turned the pages over until he came to the point, that suggested that she could indeed visit him but only for five minutes. He instructed a young constable to escort her downstairs.

'Anne, I'm so glad you've come. I have been waiting all day for you. And thank you for coming.'

'Well Angus, looks as if you have got yourself into trouble, and I told you it would happen, now didn't I?' she said in a terse tone yet she could not help feeling sorry for the fool!

'Yes, you did, but I could not help myself. I felt so frustrated last night that I do not think I knew what I was doing, truthfully.'

'Now look, Angus,' began Anne with her arms akimbo and stern-faced. 'I do not understand that talk about being frustrated. I have nothing to do with your feelings and, as you know, I went out with one of the girls from work, so there was nothing you could say about that, not that you could even if I went out with the King of Timbuktu. But you do look a sight for sore eyes, yet I think a fandango around your head suits you', and over her sternness, she let out a chuckle.

'Please Anne, do not take the mickey out of me,' replied Angus looking into Anne's face with appeal. 'I deserved the wallop on the head, but I do not think I should be pinched as well. And you know I think a lot about you and have asked if you would like to come home with me to meet my folks, haven't I?'

'You took unfair advantage of me in a weak moment and I would rather you did not refer to it ever again,' Anne retorted still with a stern appearance. 'If you cannot control yourself with or without me, then I think it would be better if we did not meet at all. I am sorry Angus, but that's how I feel and, in any case, I can do nothing for you here, now can I?'

Angus looked at Anne with his mouth agape in consternation.

'Anne please, accept my apology, if I have acted somewhat high-handed. It was not my intention, I can assure you as I do care for you. I am expecting my father to call here to bail me out, and when he does, may I call on you, please?'

'Angus, I do not wish to sound hard, but I have just been promoted, and I dare not get mixed up with anything associated with police, so please leave me out of it for a while and if this episode blows over, you may give me a call.'

'But Anne . . .'

'Sorry, but times up,' said the young constable that entered and ushered Anne out into the foyer of the station and there bid her good evening.

Anne sauntered home with her friend Joan. Neither spoke until they entered the house and sat down. Then Joan opened the conversation with 'And what did he want you for, Anne?'

'He was looking for my sympathy and asked for a date when his father has bailed him out. But I told him I would rather not see him again, as he cannot control himself too well.'

'That was rather hard, wasn't it Anne?' rejoined Joan, her friend.

'Well, if you must know, when we first dated, I told him I did not like to go out with him as he was your beau. But he implied that there was nothing serious between you two, so I thought it was all right. I

65

am very sorry now that I have been out with him and as far as I am concerned, he is all yours to keep and to hold for as long as you like.'

'Well, I suppose it was my own fault for refusing to go out with him. You see, I'm swatting for my Matric, as you know and when he called on me, my mother told him I was studying so he must have caught you on the rebound.'

'That may be but I will say it again, Joan, he is all yours and leave me out of it.'

With that, the conversation drifted to other topics, until it was getting sufficiently late for Joan to suggest that it was time she went home. Joan left after agreeing to meet for the Saturday night visit to the dance hall.

Chapter 8

The few warm days that constitute the British summer had already departed. On this Friday evening, it was drizzling incessantly yet muggy and warm. This left Tracey in a quandary as to whether to don her raincoat or carry it over her arm, as she stood in the doorway of her office block awaiting the arrival of her tryst with Andrew. During the few minutes she stood there, she wondered if she was wise to accept this invitation to see his flat. So far he had behaved in a very gentlemanly attitude of not forcing himself upon her but had treated her with great deference. This disposition of his made her feel very superior, as she found that she could converse with him on a higher level than other boyfriends that she had been out with. Each and every one of those boyfriends had attempted to take sexual advantage of her and she had a task to keep them in order. But not so with Andrew. He had never yet made an approach beyond a courtesy peck on the cheek. Then they had been in public places except for the car ride home! Could it be possible that he would maintain this stance even in his own flat; that was worrying her.

Further thought on the subject was terminated, as Andrew hailed her as he approached the office block on foot.

'Hullo there,' he called as he approached with an outstretched arm. They shook hands politely as Tracey responded to his enquiry by indicating that she was well as could be seen. Without replying, Andrew placed his arm under hers and gently turned her towards the street so that they could reach his parked car. This was reached in minutes. They entered the car and Andrew started up the engine and, with a gentle purr, moved off. It was at this point that he was asked exactly where they were heading, as she had mislaid his visiting card, thus did not know his address. He gave her his address as a street well-known in Hampstead. Within some twenty minutes or so, they arrived at a smart block of apartments into which Andrew drove his MG car and parked it in the underground area assigned in a place obviously marked with his car number!

'You even have your own personal car space here. You have told me you own the car, but what of the flat; is that yours too?' queried Tracey with her eyes wide open in wonderment, that such a young man should be in a position to possess such opulence.

'As I've told you, the car is my own and the flat too, so now let me take you up to it and you can see it for yourself.' With that he held her arm and led her to the elevator that they entered and drove upwards to the level of his choice. Still holding her arm, he led her along the heavily carpeted corridor to his apartment door, where-upon he opened the door with an affectatious and flourishing bow, ushering her in.

They entered a small but neat hallway off which led various doors. Before entering any of them, he asked her for her raincoat so that he might hang it within the clothes' cupboard situated in that hall-way. Taking her arm again, he led her through the door leading to a beautifully set-out lounge. It was a squarish large-dimensional room with two windows overlooking the street far below, each window most elegantly draped in attractive brocade that overlaid the flimsy net curtain. The furniture was of classic design rather than what she anticipated. She looked taken aback at the apparent luxuriance of the room. Andrew observed her look of astonishment, so asked her opinion as to what she thought of the room. She stuttered that it was actually nicer than she had really anticipated. He countered that observation by suggesting that they now look at the bedroom, as he proposed to show the dining room area last as that was where they had to sit for the meal that he would prepare.

'There he goes,' she thought, as he led her to the bedroom. 'This is where he begins his monkey business, so Tracey, beware! You must now be on your guard, as this is where the exercise of attack upon you is likely to begin.'

Much to her amazement and relief, as well as loss of understanding, he preceded her into the bedroom, again with a theatrical flourish. Again she was dumbstruck at the apparent sumptuousness of the room. Having stood there for at least a couple of minutes without uttering a word, he moved her towards the door, and as he opened, the light came on in the room that she realised was the bathroom, complete with shower and corner bath. But in the recess she noted, that where the toilet was situated, was also a bidet. 'Now what would a man want with one of them?' she mused, as she ventured at long last to open her mouth and ask.

'I did not design the flat but bought it as it stood and the bidet was already *in situ*. If you would like to use it, you are at liberty, as I have never used it myself yet,' he replied with a comical look in his expression.

'Thanks for the offer,' she opined. 'I too have never used a bidet and do not think that I will start with yours.'

'And what is your view of what you have seen here, Tracey?'

'You really take my breath away, as it is much nicer than I dreamed it would be. But you must be in a very good situation to be able to afford this obvious luxury.'

'That is true to a certain extent. I have had a few wealthy members of my immediate family that have left me money and coupled with that, I have a good post that pays handsomely.'

'Perhaps over dinner you can fill me in about all that. I am sure that it would interest me,' responded Tracey.

'Well, if you are interested in my history, that is no problem. I am more interested in you. So we can exchange stories about each other over our meal. For that matter, there is now but the kitchen to see, where I have prepared our meal. So let's go and see what there is to see.' So with that, he led her back towards the kitchen that adjoined the dining area.

Tracey did not think she could be surprised any more. But she was mistaken. Although the kitchen may have been considered smaller than average in size, it contained all the modern electrical contrivances she could think of. It was a neatly planned kitchen in attractive oak fitments. On the side was a number of packages which Andrew indicated was to be their meal eventually.

'So now that you have seen my apartment, let me sit you down in the lounge whilst I prepare the promised meal for you. Now you can either listen to some of my records or I can switch on the radio for you. Which would you prefer?' asked Andrew in a very conciliatory manner. Then as an afterthought, 'Or would you like to glance at my evening paper?'

'I think some music would be appropriate, then you too can enjoy it whilst I glance through your paper,' answered Tracey as she wondered what he was about to prepare for them to eat.

'And what sort of music do you like to hear, modern, jazz or classical?'

'Oh please, if you have any classical dance music I should love to hear it,' replied Tracey hoping that he would have just what she liked to listen to. She should by now have realised that he seemed to possess everything so why should she be surprised that he offered a choice of bands of quality dance music. She chose one of Victor Sylvester's classic recordings. He placed the long-playing record onto the deck, and suggested that she sit down and made herself comfortable, whilst he withdrew to the kitchen.

Without a word echoing from the kitchen, and the pleasant music playing very softly and reclining on a very comfortable settee, Tracey began to doze off. She did not hear Andrew enter the dining area until she was awakened by a cork popping. She opened her eyes and looked towards the table that was just visible between the arched opening betwix the lounge and dining area. She observed that the table was laden and by appearance, it was all ready. But where was Andrew? Then from behind, a pair of hands gently passed over her cheeks until it rounded her chin, and with a slight pull, her neck was turned upwards. There was Andrew looking down at her with his head within inches away from her. She gave a pleasant smile as she saw him standing over her from behind. As she became aware, he bent forward and gave her a passionate kiss full on the lips. And in a most uncharacteristic manner, her arms arose to encompass his neck from above her and with equal passion pulled him towards herself, and kissed him in return.

'Now that is what I call a very nice prelude to dinner,' said Andrew as they disengaged themselves. Then going round to the front of her, assisted her to get up off the settee and leading her by the elbow, escorted her to a chair that he pulled out for her at the table. Once she was seated, he took the chair opposite her and began pouring out a white wine which he handed to her and raising his glass, proposed, 'Bon appetit'. The dinner was remarkable in as much as, it was as good a meal as she herself could possibly have produced. They began with a half of an avocado pear with a topping of some pleasant fruit that she was too embarrassed to ask what it was. This was followed by a very nice cutlet of lamb beautifully seasoned with herbs and trimmed with more than required of sauté potatoes and diced carrots and minced corguettes. This was succeeded by a choice of various ice-creams and fresh fruit. Throughout the dinner, he plied her with wine.

After they concluded the meal, he suggested that they sit on the settee and have a brandy. This she declined, but saw no objection to him having one. So they sat quietly listening to the recorded music, whilst he sipped his brandy. When he had placed the empty glass down on the side table, he suggested that she knock off her shoes to make herself more comfortable. Without thinking, she did as he suggested at which point he placed his arm around her shoulder and pulled her towards himself.

'And this is the point where I have to pay for the dinner,' said Tracey with a quizzical smile on her face, as she prepared to do battle for her honour, knowing that she could not resist too much, after all the drink she had consumed.

'My dear Tracey, I was of the opinion that I have demonstrated that I am a gentleman and never take a liberty,' countered Andrew looking with a mock hurt mask on his face. 'If you are willing to indulge with me, nothing would be more pleasing to me and am sure to you too. So it is up to you how far we go tonight.'

'Then put your arm around me and cuddle me,' replied Tracey somewhat mollified.

With that invitation, Andrew did as he was bid. But he let his hand fondle her breasts, to which she showed no disagreement. With unobtrusive motion, he undid her blouse front and then asked if she would object to him taking them out. As he was already fondling them, she considered that to have them exposed for his pleasure he would not attempt more than that, so she consented. By carefully pulling off her blouse over the back of her shoulders he was able to expose both of her breasts together. As he cupped them in his hand he said they were very nice and firm and beautifully shaped. With that he pulled one up and took the nipple between his lips and sucked it to the obvious delight of himself and Tracey too. She lay back resting her head on the back of the settee in a semi-state of swoon, and wondered what was next on the menu of desire. He appeared to enjoy the thrill of first taking one then the other breast within his lips and suckling them copiously. And all she did was to lie back with her arms around his neck enjoying the interlude.

'Do you mind Tracey if I feel you below whilst I kiss you here,' he indicated with one hand upon her breast whilst the other moved to her nether regions.

This is something that no one would believe if I told anyone. Who would believe me, that a man asked if he can do this or the other! Most men, if not all, to my knowledge go the whole hog and hope that no objections are raised. Then I like it and at least he does ask, so I suppose that he would ask if he wanted more than just to hold me!

'So long as you do not hurt me, you can touch me there,' she replied.

'Now how can I hurt you. My nails are nicely filed and you know I have too much regard for you to hurt you. But just say the word and I will stop,' whispered Andrew in her ear as he deftly put one hand under her skirt and pulled down her pants until they dangled at her feet. He suggested that she wiggle her legs to rid herself of the encumbrance which she willingly did, even if thoughtlessly. Then subtly lifting her skirt, he exposed to himself her private parts that she could not see because, the roll of the skirt obliterated her view. Retaining one hand still on her breast he began to soothe her with the other hand. After a while, he inserted his fingers to her pleasure upon which she began to squirm and twist in excitement of desire.

All the while he had his two hands in occupation upon her person, he remained fully clothed. This gave her many thoughts as she began to wonder when he would ask for further liberty and what were she to reply. Whilst she wondered what the next move would be he pulled her legs apart, so that he could play with her more easily. She did not object to this, as it gave her further strong feelings of desire.

Then he whispered that it may be more comfortable on the bed. He asked in such a begging tone that foolishly she consented. And much to her amazement and surprise, he lifted her bodily as if she weighed but an ounce, and carried her reclining in his two strong arms into the bedroom. He could not release her there as she clung to him in the walk to the bedroom, so he gently bent down and placed her on top of the bedcover and released himself. So there she lay, with her blouse fallen apart with her two beautifully-shaped breasts fully exposed standing up like sentinels, and her skirt around her middle exposing her lower parts. He deftly undid her skirt at the side hooks and with a slight tug, pulled then down over her naked legs and removed the skirt. So there she lay partially naked and more than partially exposed.

'It is not fair, Andrew, that you should do this to me and you stand there fully clothed, now is it?' whispered Tracey in an askant manner looking for sympathy, yet foolishly.

'I agree it is unfair of me, so I will remedy the defect pronto,' exclaimed Andrew as he unbuttoned his trousers and let them drop with his pants to the floor and simultaneously divested himself of his shirt too. He stood there with even less clothes than Tracey, as she lay slightly propped up on a pillow he had placed for her. She looked at him in both amazement and semi-shock to see a man for the first time in her life almost naked.

As if struck by something comical, she burst into ribald laughter in which she could hardly contain herself. 'Whoa!' she exclaimed. 'Where do you hide that big thing that's sticking out like a ramrod?'

'That my dear is for your pleasure whenever you want it, but how do you like it? But what the hell are you in such stitches over? Please let me join in the joke so that I too may laugh.'

'You look like a policeman on point duty with that thing sticking out controlling the traffic; that's what makes me laugh. It looks like an awful weapon to me, and am sure that it would hurt anyone that tried it, now wouldn't it?' she replied.

Before he answered, his face lit up in a smirkish smile that seemed to say that he understood her mood. He replaced his hand over her nether region whilst he took her hand and placed it over him and, as she made contact with it, he moved her fingers over it in a gentle rubbing motion. She became aware that as she progressed in this action over it, it became stiffer still and throbbed.

'Why is it throbbing, Andy?' questioned Tracey.

'That's because you are getting it on heat and if you keep that up, it will fire all its got and from the position it's in it will catch you in the eye,' he answered in a laughing tone.

Before she could reply, he left the standing position, and mounted the bed, and kneeling, he straddled her as she lay beneath him. And still before she could respond, he asked her if the new position they were in was better.

It was then at that moment that she realised that she was in a very vulnerable situation. Here she lay in a semi-nude state with him over her with even less on, with his thing fully extended towards her. All he had to do was to fall upon her and insert his thing, and hey presto! she would be in trouble. Her face turned somewhat with an anxious and troubled look that he observed as she pondered.

'What's worrying you darling?' he asked in a comforting manner.

'Please don't do it. I am afraid that you will force yourself and get me into trouble. I will do anything but please, please, don't do it to me,' pleaded Tracey with tremor in her voice.

'Darling, you know very well that I respect you and have already told you that I would not do anything against your will. As you so nicely say, you will do anything instead; let us recite the options, shall we. As you know, I can put it in which you have asked me not to. In any case, I would not insert it without a French letter. You know what that is I presume?' he queried. She shook her head in a negative way, so he continued, 'They are also called "sheaths" and you may have heard of them.' To this query, she again shook her head but in the affirmative way. Again he continued, 'That's number one option. Number two is awkward. You have the most lovely pair of breasts but they are too small to close the gap, as I will show you.'

As he spoke, he placed both his hands over both her breasts and tried to draw them together. He then placed his thing between them and said, 'You see my dear, they are really a lovely pair, but not yet big enough to close over me, but in the position that I am in, it is almost touching your chin. So option three is for you to put your tongue out and reach in as I move it between them and catch it and then if you are brave enough, grab it between your teeth and draw it in.'

'Oh please, no!' cried Tracey. 'What will happen if it touches my mouth. I understand that it releases something and I do not want it all over me or in my mouth.'

'Darling, please trust me. I have told you I will not do anything that may upset you. But first may I suggest that you hold it, and if you wish, you may examine it so that you may understand the anatomy of man.' With that, he took her hand again and placed it on to him and tightened her grip on it.

'Now don't just hold it like a lemon,' asked Andrew. He continued, 'I have suggested that you take advantage and examine it for as long as you like, and in the meanwhile, I will hold it back especially for you. Then when you have seen enough and want to finish playing, then I will let it go; how's that my darling Tracey?'

So with that invitation, she moved her hand over it and raised and lowered it to examine it fully. She felt under it until she reached beneath his leg.

'What are those two things hanging here?' she asked holding them in her cupped hand.

'That my dear, are correctly known as the testicles but are commonly called "balls". That is really the motor of the sexual parts of a man. Inside it, it manufactures the sperm that comes out at the tip. You can see that if you hold the knob and press it back and expose the little hole through which it squirts. That's it,' he said as she did as suggested.

'If these are your balls, what is the thing called then?' questioned Tracey as she smoothed her fingers over it.

'My darling, the whole thing is the male organ and that's called a "penis". It's also called various colloquial names such as cock, prick or even rod. You may call it what you like. Now would you like to taste it and draw it in a bit – just a little way, to begin with and if you like it, then take it all in.'

75

'Really, Andy, do you expect me to draw that length in my mouth. It's impossible! And if I did I would surely choke. But if I do, will you keep still and not push it in too much and please stop if I ask and on no account let your motor make any sperm and empty it out in me.'

'Darling, I can promise you I will not hurt you and will also promise you I will not let it shoot inside you. And whilst you are sucking it, I will put my fingers inside you so that you can enjoy the thrill that you deserve.'

So with that, he moved higher up towards her head and with one hand steadied himself whilst he positioned himself so that she was able to take in his thing between her teeth, as she barely opened her mouth wide enough for it to enter. By the time he had managed to get his free hand down towards her, and probe her with his fingers, she gradually relaxed her tension of her lips and opened her mouth fully and took the whole of it in. Little by little, she began to enjoy the sensation and appeared to relish the sucking motion with seeming delight. While they were in that position, he expressed himself in many amorous words interlaced with many love words that she had never heard before. As she lay there with her mouth full, she held onto it so that it should not penetrate too far into her mouth. She looked up to him in an askant manner as if to say, 'How is that; am I doing it all right?' And as if he heard her unspoken words he said, 'You are doing marvellously, darling. Now wipe your tongue around it as you suck and you will enjoy it still more – that's it – that's lovely. How are you feeling with my fingers there? Really wet, I can tell you, and that means that you are getting heated very much. Do not be afraid to let me go if you get a climax and want to scream; it is natural that you may, so just you enjoy the experience. Now stop sucking me a minute my love, otherwise it will be all over with me and you will get a mouth full, so just hold it gently in your hand and when you see it get a bit smaller, you can take it in again – got that? But stop now, please, otherwise it will go off – stop now.' he called and as he did so, tried to withdraw it from her now tight lips. Just as he succeeded in getting it released, she grabbed him around the waist with one hand and with the other grabbed again for his still large and sopping wet thing and pulled him on top of herself and let out

76

screams of delight as she wriggled and squirmed and flung her legs about in climax. So for a few never ending minutes, she lay gasping with hot bated breath whilst he whispered sweet words of encouragement.

'Do you feel like taking it back again, my love?' Andrew asked as she lay spent.

'Please forgive me Andy, I'm really whacked and cannot move an inch,' she murmured.

'Then I presume you enjoyed it. You will also note that I kept my word. There is now only one item left – I too would like to get a climax, so if you do not feel like taking it again in your mouth, I will lie on you, but do not fear, I will not poke it in as I have already promised I would not. I will cover it with whatever I can reach.' And as he spoke, he reached for and caught hold of his own shirt that lay nearest to him on the floor. With that as a cover, he ejaculated.

They lay nestled together for quite a while until she evinced that it was time she left for home. He agreed and together they walked unashamedly towards the bathroom. With a little prompting from Andrew, they washed each other down and dried themselves off satisfactorily. They then returned to the bedroom where Andrew extracted a clean shirt out of a drawer. Then they donned their outer clothes and, with a few quiet gentle words between them, they sauntered to the door and made their way to the underground car park. On the journey home they made arrangements to meet again the following Friday as that evening.

Tracey entered her home and as it was somewhat rather late, she found it in quietness. She made as little noise as possible and went up to her room. Within a few minutes, she had undressed and got into bed. She did not toss or turn as she expected too, but almost immediately fell into a deep sleep. Although she could not remember having had a dream, she found the following morning, that she must have flung herself around the bed by the state it was in. She speculated that perhaps in her subconscious she had re-enacted the time she was with Andrew! She reflected that she had gone further than she had planned, yet it was all the time with her consent. So how was it that they indulged as far as they did? They had committed to meet again the coming Friday. Would that be a repeat of the previous night or would they be expected to progress from that state of play to real and full sex? She did not appear to worry just at that time but reflected that she would have to make strong determinations for the next meeting. Her further thoughts on the subject were interrupted by a call from below that it was time she made an appearance for breakfast. So without further ado, she called back that she was about to get up, which she did that Saturday morning.

Chapter 9

One has never discovered why, during a working week, the weather can be average but as soon as it is a weekend, when a spot of sunshine would be appreciated, the weather deteriorates. So it was on this particular Saturday evening. The wind was very blustery and gave the appearance of rain to come. The clouds lay heavy in the sky and one wondered if they could get to their journeys' end before the heavens opened up. So each and every individual had to make the choice as to whether to don a light raincoat or some other form of possible protection against the elements.

At the cloakroom of the Palais there was a larger than usual shuffle of coats and umbrellas being deposited. In the adjoining vestibule, friends met each other whom they had not seen since the last Saturday evening dance. Here it was that Anne and her companion Joan met up again with Tracey and Wynne. They arrived unescorted but did not remain unattached for long at the table they settled on. Jack appeared on the scene first and was followed within a few minutes by Angus. Both lads joined the ladies at their table and joined in general conversation, which appeared to be a regular enquiry of how they fared during the past week, and casual comments of the actions taking place in Germany under the new leader, Hitler. Richard came in very much later, accompanied by Roger who was introduced to the assembly.

Before the arrival of the last pair, Joan asked in a quiet voice in Angus's ear, what had transpired since they last met. This reference was an obvious illusion to his apprehension by the police. As Angus sat between both Anne and Joan, the others did not hear all that was said; thus did not understand the reply given by Angus, that he was released on bail to attend Court in a few weeks time. No more was said on that subject at the table but Anne with whom he danced, raised the point more outwardly.

'And how are you going to plead when you are in front of the Magistrate?' queried Anne as she glided smoothly across the floor. 'Are you going to say that you were frustrated in love and as a consequence lost your temper?'

'No; all I can plead is that I was at fault and apologise and pay up,' answered Angus who had been advised that to fetch up outside matters would not only prolong the hearing and add to the costs, but also possibly raise poor publicity for him too. He continued, 'But the truth is, that it was a feeling of frustration that caused me to be so foolish, particularly after you told me to desist. But, perhaps tonight, I will not get the feeling of frustration with you Anne,' added Angus as he looked down towards Anne with an appealing glare.

'Whether you get frustrated or not is not my problem, Angus, but I am not having you to escort me home tonight or any other night. In courtesy to you and in respect of our mutual friends, I have not raised the matter at the table, as I know the exposure may embarrass you. So do not press your luck with me, please, for if you do, it may spoil both our evenings.'

'Anne, please believe me, I am truly sorry for what I did and more than sorry for not obeying you when you told me to leave the cripple alone. Please, can we not start all over again and I promise you will never have reason to complain of me,' pleaded Angus in a tremulous voice, as he looked down towards her whilst gliding across the floor.

'Angus, let me make myself clear to you. I only accepted this dance with you so that we can discuss this question privately and not at the table. After this dance, please do not ask me to dance with you again as I will refuse. I will acknowledge you, but go out with you I will decline. I made the mistake of going out with you when you had palled up with Joan. Perhaps Joan will go out with you but I will not. I hope I have made that clear and understood,' she said as she looked up towards him with a stern face.

'I feel very ashamed, Anne, but I hope you will not slight me if we meet. And thank you for your consideration and only hope that I can somehow prove to you that I wish for your company. I will do as you ask me and speak with Joan.'

'Yes, please do, and I hope she asks you, "Where did you get those big brown eyes and that tiny mind from?"' retorted Anne in an unfriendly manner. So they finished the dance and returned to their table both looking at odds with each other. Only Joan mentioned the fact to Angus as to why he looked so terse. Angus replied that he would appreciate a dance with her so that they could converse.

Joan and Angus arose from the table as the band struck up again. As soon as they had traversed the floor about halfway round, Angus confided to Joan that her friend Anne had told him categorically that she would not associate with him again. He hoped that her feelings were not on the same wave!

'Angus, I have a problem. I am very loyal to Anne as she is to me, but I also like you so I feel that I may have to side with Anne and say adieu. I do not wish to have friction with Anne.'

'Please Joan, do not desert me too. That would be too much. If you do not wish to upset Anne, which I can understand, can I suggest that, if she is escorted home tonight, then I can see you home, but nothing will be said; so what do you say, my dear?' added Angus with a pitying look that seemed to melt the imaginary butter in Joan's mouth.

'Well, let us play it a while and see how the evening progresses. Perhaps if Anne enjoys herself she will forget all about you and will not notice us together. So do not monopolise me all evening but spread yourself around. Then it will not be so obvious that you are hanging onto me,' advised Joan in reply.

'You know Joan, I think you have a good brain and feel that you have solved the problem and so easily. But you will not get too upset if I ask another girl to dance with me, I hope. You will not refuse to join me for a coffee during the interval, now will you?' asked Angus in a slightly better frame of mind.

'It seems that all is agreed between us so let's return to the table now please, Angus.'

So as the band had concluded the number, they made their way back to the table among their friends.

81

Richard had asked and was accepted for the dance with Wynne. They spoke a lot of their last meeting and he said that he really appreciated her company. This was his prelude to asking for assurance that he would be given the privilege of seeing her home. Wynne queried having a meal first to which Richard implied that he had taken that into account and, if she had any particular restaurant she would like, then they would try it out that evening. It was therefore agreed between them where they would go. So they danced, with Richard holding her if anything, somewhat closer than was normal but, as Wynne raised no objections, he enjoyed the feel of closeness.

In the meanwhile, Roger having been introduced all round asked Tracey if she would care to dance with him. As they happened to be the remaining couple at the table and, as no others approached her, she considered it prudent to accept. So they arose from the table and joined the throng on the dance floor. She observed that Roger was possibly the tallest of the men at the table yet possibly looked the youngest. May be that was because he spoke so much and spontaneously joined in every conversation with banter and facetiousness. She did notice that he was well-dressed and smelled pleasantly of aftershave which she considered nice in a man, so long as it was not applied to hide body odours.

'Do you come here often?' asked Roger by way of opening up the conversation with the oldest cliché in the book.

'Well, yes I do, and generally with the same crowd at the table. But I have not seen you here before; so where do you usually go on a Saturday night?' questioned Tracey.

'This is not the first time I have been here, but as I know Richard and walked into him a couple of days ago, he asked me if I would like to join him as he has good company. That I must agree with. As to myself, I like to vary my points of pleasure. I find that more stimulating that patronising the same place week after week. But then it's a free country and each of us has our own choice as it should be,' replied Roger with a gay insouciant manner. At this point the floor cleared of dancers who all returned to their respective tables and awaited the next number being struck up.

So the foursome with their partners enjoyed the evening. They occasionally exchanged partners for variety but invariably returned to the chosen one of the evening. During the halfway break, the four men joined together to collect the drinks for the ladies, who remained at the table conversing among themselves.

Tracey was the first to speak whilst the menfolk had left the table for refreshments. She opened up the conversation with, 'Well, it looks like we are all fixed up with an escort tonight, or am I wrong?'

'Richard has not actually asked me but I shall presume that he intends to get me home,' responded Wynne. 'And I suppose you, Anne, will be off with Jack again and Joan with Angus. That leaves you Tracey! Has Roger asked to see you home or are you anticipating him to ask?' queried Wynne.

'Oh, he will be seeing me home tonight all right. He has asked and I have accepted as I can see no reason otherwise,' retorted Tracey.

Both Roger and Richard came back to the table preceded by Angus and Jack with two trays of refreshments. After much confusion the drinks were distributed amid some chaffing and general jollification. The noise level in the hall was now greater than when the band played. Whilst they sat drinking and conversing, each took the opportunity to view their partner surreptitiously so as not to appear too pointed in their perscrutation.

Each of the men found only beauty, as they were much too young and possibly too inexperienced in the worldly way to recognise blemishes. They looked for overall acceptable appearance and smartness of attire. But the main point of the search was for a sexually willing partner, that any blemish they may have observed would have been overlooked in the excitement of achievement. As they sat at the table you would detect that each one at different moments had to put his hand in his pocket, or place his hand beneath the table on his lap. You would also have observed, that none of them drew anything out of his pocket. So why did they go to the pocket or place their hand on the lap? A man would know, and he would tell you that the reason was, that the man in question was at that moment in time on the point of excitement, excitement created by his own anticipatory thought or may be, just wishful hope of how he wished to sexually indulge with the chosen partner. So it became necessary to place his hand in a position, that could shift his rod that had risen, due to his thoughts to an awkward length and was uncomfortable in the angle it

83

then lay! Such it is for the young men as they view the lady of their choice, not so much for beauty but for attainment and the very thought of that raised their expectation of a sexual high!

And how did the ladies view the menfolk? Did they *too* look for erotic excitement from their partner? The answer was both yes and no! They all desired to indulge yet they all knew it was unwise to do so, so all hoped that no attempt would be made on them, for if it were it would have to be fought off. Each one of the four young ladies knew how far they would permit the man with them to advance and each one also knew that if unchecked the men would go too far. They would all agree that it is the one thing that makes the world go round. What was a happy medium? Was there such a thing as that? Is there a kiss to be counted or is that of too little a consequence to be considered an approach to sex? Then there are kisses and there are kisses. One is the respectful closeness on the lip or cheek whereas the other is a tongue probe that excites and possibly leads to other things! So where does one draw the line? Allow the probe type of kiss and then have a tussle or fight to control not only your partner but your own emotions!

So the evening drew to a close as the band struck up the last waltz. All our four pair of friends mutually agreed to separate some time during the last dance. Thus, couple by couple danced a few steps then disappeared into the cloakroom to reclaim their belongings. In the vestibule of the hall, the crowd accumulated where the young lovers awaited each other at the exit from the cloakroom. There they greeted each other and invariably, arm in arm, they left the precinct of the building on their way homewards. Some made their way to the underground station whilst others amassed at the bus and tram stop. But by coincidence, all our four couples went their way to wherever their escort left his car.

Angus asked Joan if they should go to the restaurant as agreed. He raised this point fearing that she may have changed her mind, as he espied Anne giving them a quizzical look as they arose to have the last dance preparatory to leaving together. His luck held! Joan agreed that they should proceed as planned. This they did and after the meal, Joan proposed that he take her home. So together they walked the few paces to where his car was parked and entering it, he started the engine up and drove it a short distance, then stopped in a quiet spot.

'What have you stopped here for Angus?' questioned Joan.

'Would it be too much to ask if we kissed a while, as I would like to, Joan?' replied our gallant. Without waiting for the reply, he drew her towards himself by placing an arm around her shoulder until they were cheek to cheek. Joan did not reply and did not object to the move but appeared to consent to it. So Angus feeling brave, hugged her and kissed her, and allowed his hand to travel to her blouse, which he was able to unfasten easily and place his hand within. Still Joan did not remonstrate against him, which emboldened him still further to not merely fondling her but to attempt to withdraw her breast from its encumbrance behind the blouse. He managed to get it partially exposed, so he withdrew his lips from her lips, and arched himself to enable him to reach her semi-exposed breast with his mouth. He began in a most ardent manner to kiss and suckle the nipple and rotate his tongue around it, which made Joan feel swoony. She did not seem to mind this attack upon her but appeared to lie back and accept it in a nonchalant way that still further emboldened him.

So there he was, with one arm around her shoulders and the other hand onto her breast that he drew towards his mouth. 'Oh, how lovely,' he thought to himself. 'So unlike the last occasion they were together when Joan behaved in a sterner manner, but she now appears so much softer.' Thus with this premise he could be forgiven in presuming that Joan was a complete consenting party as he dropped his arm from her shoulder and moved it to the hem of her skirt. With great adroitness, he moved his hand from the hem upwards to reach her laced underpants, and with equal deftness reached the top of them and gently rolled them down as far as he could. The moment he placed his hand upon her where he should not, he heard a shout emanating from Joan to desist immediately. Without replying, he obeyed the command and withdrew his offending hand.

'May I hold you there if I cover it up then, please Joan?' pleaded Angus in a quavering voice.

'You are beginning to take too many liberties again with me, Angus. You spoil yourself. Kindly pull my pants up as they should be, and if you behave, then you may place your hand there for a very short while,' replied Joan wondering why she allowed this, when she knew it would only arouse him still more as well as excite herself, which she also knew may make her lose full control.

Wisely, Angus did as he was bid and drew up her pants, and with the flat of his hand, placed it over her and gently rubbed and gyrated his palm. At the same time he returned his attack upon her breast, which he again placed in between his teeth and suckled and drew it in. So for an indeterminable period, she lay back whilst he lay arched over her. She had her two arms placed around his neck pressing tightly against herself, whilst he held her nipple between his teeth. She began to fantasise and imagine she was lying upon a flowered bed with the smell of floral perfume around, whilst her knight in shining armour made love to her. Her body began to make involuntary motions as if in the act of lovemaking. The more she moved, so the more were her desires stimulated. Fortunately for Joan, Angus feared that any further advance would see the end of their friendship, so he did not make any. Had he done so, Joan would have been very receptive just at that moment, as she was experiencing a great desire for more involvement in lovemaking. So there he was with his manhood at full stretch, but afraid to touch it, as he was not able to control it, whilst she lay there in desperate need, yet afraid to countermand her injunction that he should not attempt anything against her. So time passed when, as if by mutual consent, they ceased probing each other and desisted whilst both remained very frustrated.

They spoke quietly together, each appreciating the other's allowance or liberty. Angus was the most profuse in his remark and thanks to Joan, for what was permitted. Joan acknowledged his acceptance of her wishes and on inward reflection was very glad he abided by them. So outwardly they were pleased with each other, yet inwardly, they desired still more. Time not yet caught standing still, they moved off in the direction of her home. During the ride, they laid plans to meet again during the week.

With some slight hesitation and perhaps a little reluctance too, Tracey accepted the offer of a meal with Roger. She somehow felt she had to reserve her loyalty to Andrew. But then he was not on the scene, and here was a very nice young man offering her a meal and a ride home. So why should she feel obligated to anyone? If Andrew wanted to reserve her to himself, he would have to declare his intentions, then she would assuredly be beholden to that obligation. Until then, she felt that she could go with whomever she wished! So having satisfied her own conscience she felt contented towards Roger, whom she perceived was a likeable fellow. He appeared to be quite liberal when it came to tipping, so she felt that he was accustomed to escorting ladies and treating them handsomely.

After the meal, he proposed a walk in the park which Tracey declined, as it was getting too cold. So they sat in the car in a quiet street, just chatting away until Roger openly and without any blush, asked her if she would care to indulge in sex with him.

'Well, I must say, you have some courage to come out with that suggestion, Roger. How do you expect me to reply, "Come and get me"!'

'If you feel like saying "come and get me" and meant it, then that's fine, and we would get on with it, but why the hesitation? I will still go through the foreplay so that you get built up to the point of desire. I know the drill and presume you do too,' retorted Roger, looking angelically towards her, whilst at the same time putting one arm around her and drawing her towards himself, and with the other hand he raised her skirt as high as he could, which was not too high, as she was seated on her skirt and that held it more or less in place.

'Sorry, lover boy, but I am not in the mood for frolicking tonight. Now put my skirt down, if you please,' emitted Tracey with only half reluctance.

Instead of lowering her skirt as he was bid, he began to explore the area that he had exposed and found his hand wandering under her, until it reached a hot and fleshy part that excited both of them. Instead of telling him as she should have done, to stop, as already requested, she demurred and lay her head back and accepted the advance. After a few minutes of attention, during which period she was becoming very heated sexually, he ignored her earlier request and tugged at her pants. Although she did not remonstrate against him, neither did she assist him, by raising her bottom to ease the pants off. She held her place and he achieved some small measure of success in getting them partially pulled off. He fondled her there until she was exceedingly and uncomfortably wet, and still did not give the signal to stop. He took advantage of the situation as any man may have done, and dexterously unbuttoned his flies to expose himself to her. With the one hand occupied fingering her and his other hand now free, he pulled her hand over towards himself and placed what he had unbuttoned into her hand! She began thinking of Andrew as soon as she touched his flesh and that brought her to her senses. She immediately withdrew her hand and endeavoured to straighten herself in the car as best she could. As she drew her hand away, she pushed his arm from under her, which caused him to postulate and ask why the sudden change.

'You are getting too fresh and I don't like it nor permit it, so please be a good fellow, and pull my skirt down straight,' countered Tracey in a semi-terse voice.

In response, he removed his hand from under her clothing and in a kneeling position, placed his own hand on his rod outwardly in front of her, and without any embarrassment, and cried, 'Look at it; it is crying out for you and you know it needs you, so please be a pal and help it along, as you too need it as we both know, don't we?' remonstrated Roger.

So there he knelt in front of her holding it under her in full view. She blushingly took a peep at it and saw it as a shining throbbing pinkish weapon that was asking for help and only she could help it. She wanted to say, 'give it to me strong' but she could not get the words to her lips! 'Oh Andrew, where are you? It is you that I need and not Roger! So tell me what to do as I can see I will soon lose control and then you will not love me any more.' Then just as he raised it closer to her so that she could not fail to see its full potential, she became inspired by sensibility of purpose, and with one sweep of her hand, pushed him backwards and so released herself from the position she was in.

'Tracey, Tracey, what are you doing? You want me I know and it is ready for you, to give you the thrill of your life. Please do not stop something good for both of us,' implored Roger who had regained his posture and was still holding on to his tool, which by now had by appearance, shrivelled somewhat.

'Enough is enough, lover boy,' countered Tracey. 'I allowed you too far and now you ask me to go further. You ask too much too soon, so please do not lose control and please stop, as it is really time I got home.'

Roger looked downcast as he looked first at Tracey then at his hand, which now covered the whole of what was earlier a shining example of manhood and now hardly visible. He realised that for the time being, he had lost the battle of the sexes and with a lot of misgivings, reluctantly accepted his defeat, but thought of future assaults with Tracey, who may be by then more co-operative. So in a resigning manner, he replaced his shrunken orb and fastened his trousers and simultaneously assisted her to straighten herself too. With one long spontaneous kiss and hug, they separated and regained the sitting posture for the drive onwards.

Most of the evening, Richard danced with Wynne. She excelled herself in an extrovert way in making a joke of everything that was said or done in flippancy. Even as they danced across the floor, she was making comments on all and sundry. From his point of view, he enjoyed her quips of repartee and tried to match them. Then he was not such a past master as she was. Any observer would have been correct in commenting that there was a girl in the throes of love – or very near to it! Her whole attitude enthralled Richard. He really felt that he loved her, even though they had only dated each other a few times, despite the statement that he did love her. Conceivably she was right when she suggested that he did not really love her, but the sexual interlude, perhaps it was that too. If it was only that, then now he began to feel a deep passion for her that he had not felt earlier. Was this love then? All he wanted was for the night of dancing to end, so that he could have her on her own and then test if his passion was merely sexual infatuation or was a real deep-down feeling.

They left that last waltz in the middle of the tune and resorted to the cloakroom, to recover their outer garments before the rush of patrons. They did not bid the others at their table the customary 'good-night', but no one was surprised that they had gone off – it was presumed by all that they would be off together. So arm in arm they made their way to the car park. By the time they reached the car, a decision had been agreed that they just have coffee and a cake, then ride to some place quiet. This they did and with some manoeuvring, he placed his car in an alley not overlooked and where they would be undisturbed!

No sooner had he parked, than they went into a hug that seemed as part of the switching off the engine. Without hesitation they hugged and kissed and automatically each began to explore the other. He was the more adventurous, as he was by now probing his fingers within her, but she had not unbuttoned him; she just poised her hand over him and gently rubbed away until she felt beneath her hand a mound thickening up!

'Darling, take it out, otherwise you will lose the thrill of it,' implored Richard.

'Only if you solemnly promise not to try and put it in me, then I will happily take it out for you,' responded Wynne in an excited manner.

'Darling, I will do anything you ask, but get it out before I burst a blood vessel or something. I don't think its been so big as that before; it just shows what you do to me, my love!' replied Richard with his face getting redder and redder all the while, and inwardly hoping that he could restrain himself long enough for both of them to enjoy the titillations. Before he had said that, her hand was already unfastening his buttons and dexterously she wove her fingers around it and withdrew it in its full glory in full view of them both.

'My, you sure do have a weapon on show tonight. Can you hold it back to stop it going off or are you about to let it go?' she commented with a gleeful and giggling expression, whilst with her thumb and forefinger she passed them over it from the top to the bottom – or at least, as far as she could in view of the fact that his trousers prevented her from fingering him very low. She continued, 'You sure do have a whopper tonight, Richard. Is that specially for me? But can you get it all out as your pants are in the way?' she added.

'Nothing would please me more than to oblige,' he replied with a great feeling of excitement as he delved into his crotch to clear the way for full exposure. All the while, she held on to it with her thumb and forefinger, that ran up and down the length of it. And at the top she pressed a little harder to cause the aperture to open which gave her a chuckle as she asked, 'Is that where it comes out from as well as the water works?' As she spoke, her fingers continued to travel downwards until it had passed the length and continued under him.

'Yes, that's where it all comes from. If you get your hand up a wee bit, you will feel the other end, the balls, and hold them very gently as they hurt very easily if you squeeze them harshly. Yes, that's right, you have them. How do they feel to you?' asked Richard in a one of strong desire. 'Oh how lovely it would be to be like this for hours on end, Richard old boy, you have got yourself a girl in a million, so behave and play the game correctly and you will enjoy yourself for a long time to come!' So he mused as she appeared to take a delight in studying his anatomy by first pulling one way, then pulling it the other way, all the while her fingers continued to travel up and down the length of the heated and reddened shaft.

'Let me have something to cover it with, quickly, Richard please,' she implored him aware that before many more seconds it would explode!

With that request, and in the knowledge that he may yet be too late to cover himself, he managed to extract from his pocket a clean folded handkerchief which he gave her, and not too soon.

With apparent skill learned from the previous episodes, she placed the square still folded over the shining knob, just in time as she felt it expand, as it burst through. She retained her hold and gently squeezed it as it throbbed itself to its climax.

'Now you have enjoyed that I'm sure, so you can now put it away,' Wynne whispered in his ear as she moved back a little out of range.

'But what of you? You haven't climaxed yet, and I feel you too should enjoy that at least,' replied Richard somewhat taken aback at the sudden withdrawal.

'When you have buttoned up you can give me a cuddle and you can hold me there until I have come, and that will be all tonight.' And as she spoke, she replaced it within and buttoned it up for him. Then without any misgiving, she clung to him and drew his hand down to her so that he could continue to fumble!

'Oh, that is lovely. Keep it going for a minute more and it will be good. I can feel it coming all over and your hand swimming. Oh . . . hold me tight, please. I am coming – I am coming! Hold me tight . . .

. . . tighter . . . hold me tight . . . oh!' she kept repeating until she was spent!

After adjusting their clothes, and making preliminary proposals for meeting again very soon, they moved off to the location of Wynne's home. He let her alight with a good-night kiss, and drove off with a happy song in his mind. He whistled along until he reached his home. Parking his car and entering his home, took him but a few minutes. The house was as expected at that hour, quiet, so equally quiet, he mounted the stairs to his room. After his nightly toiletries, he flung himself into his bed to sleep happily.

But sleep did not reach him for some time. He was reliving his experience and trying to decide if it was love or mere infatuation that he suffered. Would he be so keen on her if she was not such a willing partner? As she was so apparently willing, was she also willing with others as she has been with him this night? 'Then should I look at her past history when I myself have run around with numerous dames? So, OK, I have enjoyed the interlude with her but I have not seduced her, and does that mean she has never been seduced – in that case, she is for me! Oh yes, I will try to go the whole hog with her and what then? Do I jilt her then after I have had her or keep her – that is a knotty problem and I should be able to resolve that question at perhaps the next meeting.' So he debated with himself, staring up at the ceiling until sleep conquered him.

Jack felt an obligation to escort Anne home but he also felt an unwillingness and reluctance. He was still mindful of her attitude towards his advances. Oh yes, she was a fine partner at the dance and an equally fine companion. She was gay and pleasant, and one could enjoy an evening with her. When it came to lovemaking, she was a failure! Then he reflected – he had only escorted her that once. Perhaps this time she may grow towards him and be more responsive. The best thing would be, if he was charming to her and may be she would be a bit braver this time, as she may have felt nervous before. So he mused as they walked out of the hall towards the car park.

They held on to one another by arm and arm. Anne appeared to Jack to be very bubbly and enthusiastic over the pleasures of the evening and thought it boded well for the night. So as they entered the car he asked where she would like to go? She proposed only a light snack, as she did not feel like a full meal, so they drove to a known establishment for the purpose. They sat chatting away there over their snack, as if they had the whole night in which to eat. It was Jack who suggested it was time they moved if they wanted to have a hug! This made Anne laugh with a very broad grin and, with her consent, they returned to the car.

He drove slowly along until he found the spot he had decided upon as a quiet place where few if any people passed that late hour of the night. He came to a halt there, and leaning over towards her, drew her towards himself in a gentle hug. Anne responded happily and placed her arms around his neck and accepted the kisses and reciprocated with apparent pleasure. They sought each other's mouth and followed that by travelling hands. Even Anne allowed her hand to move from his neck down his back and draw him towards herself within the limit of being in a car. He whispered in her ear, that if she felt uncomfortable in the front of the car, they could roll over the backrest of the seat, but with his help she achieved her object and got to the back; yet not before all her clothes had risen above her waistline in vaulting the seat. He slipped over without any problem and immediately took advantage of the situation, and placed his hand above her knee. She did not appear to mind, so he moved his hand upwards to where her pants showed. Still she made no objection as he pulled them down a bit so that he could place his hand over her hairy part. The while he was progressing thus far, she was holding him around the waist and pulling him towards herself in a passionate hug. With his free hand he managed to get his fly unbuttoned and attempted to get it out. The moment she became aware that he had partially exposed himself, she let go of him and said in a slightly cross tone, 'Now Jack, you know I will not allow liberties, so put that away like a good boy.'

'Anne, my love, I am not taking liberties. I am just placing it for you to hold and then you could control it and make sure it does not reach you. So please take it and play with it whilst I play with you,' he pleaded with a cajoling tone and innocent smile.

'No, I do not wish to hold it, so please put it away.'

'Please Anne, you will not know what you miss if you do not hold me. Do please try just this once, and see for yourself if you do not enjoy holding me,' pleaded Jack in an earnest begging voice, that Anne found hard to resist.

'Then if you pull my clothes down, I will hold you,' responded Anne.

'You will miss out if you do that as you cannot climax if I pull them down. And it is hardly fair for me to get excited without you also getting excited, so let us play with each other, and I promise I will go no further,' again pleaded Jack with greater earnestness.

'I will hold you to your word Jack – no monkey business, and I will go along with you. But the moment you take advantage, I will raise my knee where it will hurt you good and proper. Is that clear and understood?' said Anne with a chuckle in her voice as she laid down the law to him.

'Message received clear and understood, Captain,' replied Jack in a very jocular frame as he felt he had won the battle of the sex!

So they fondled each other. He placed his fingers within her that made her think of Felicity, and how her fingers did the same yet she could not decide which felt the better, Jack or Felicity? The while he was doing this, she was gripping him. He whispered again in her ear, not to just hold it but rub it up and down. He placed his hand over hers and moved her hand up and down in demonstration and then let her proceed on her own which followed as instructed. So they both enjoyed each other's company to reasonable fulfilment.

So Monday morning dawned like any other day, but this Monday was somewhat different to Anne. Today she was to commence in her new assignment and work with the two lads in the audit department. She felt a slight element of apprehension, not of the work involved but for working in close proximity to a couple of lads. Although she referred to them as 'lads' they were older than herself. She was confident that she would be able to keep her head up with them whatever happened.

'Good morning, Brad,' said Anne in a pleasant manner and continued, 'Hope you had a pleasant weekend.'

94

'And good morning to you Anne. Yes, I had a very pleasant weekend and I hope we get on well together so that the week will be equally pleasant,' replied Braddley Ford as he looked upon his new workmate with mixed feelings.

'Where's Ian this morning, late or something?'

'No, I am not late,' answered Ian as he entered the office just at that moment. 'I've just seen the boss and he has asked that we complete our assignments in hand and fetch it to him all together. Then he will give us new instructions. I am also to show Anne the first ropes, so when you are ready, Anne, come on over to my desk and fetch your chair with you!'

Anne did as she was bid and transferred her chair alongside Ian's so that he could instruct her in her new programme. For the next hour or so, they had their heads down over the pages and sheets of paper, that comprised the workload that Ian had to demonstrate to Anne. On more than one occasion, Anne spotted a point that Ian had not observed. The first time he was pleased at her attention to detail, but the second time he felt discomforted by her astuteness.

At noontime, Ian suggested that Anne go off for lunch. This she did. During her absence, he spoke with his colleague Brad of Anne's perceptiveness.

'You will have to watch out for your own job, Ian, if she is as good as you say, ol' boy,' speculated Brad after analysing the problem. But Braddley knew that Ian's job was secure as they were both articled to the firm. It may be embarrassing to have a learner spot items that had escaped them.

'And she does not appear to me that she would be unwilling for night work either!' prompted Ian as he considered if Anne would make a willing escort for him on an evening's entertainment.

'Well, why not try chatting her up whilst you have your heads together?' suggested Brad who had thought of doing just that himself. Ian had the opportunity, whereas he did not at that point in time.

'I suppose I can broach the subject some time and go from there,' replied Ian with misgivings in his mind. He added, 'I think I will pop out for lunch now as it is half past.' With that, he donned his jacket and left Brad on his own in the room.

'Well, how's that for luck! With you all the morning and when we should be lunching, who should I sit down with but you, Anne.'

'Very nice indeed. Perhaps we can talk of other things here than work I hope, Ian,' replied Anne who had almost consumed her meal and had contemplated leaving the café for a stroll to do some window-shopping.

'Now that's a good idea. I heartily approve of the sentiment that we should not engage in shop talk during our lunch break. So let me ask, what do you enjoy doing in your off-duty periods; do you like cinema, dancing or what?' queried Ian in his best possible manner.

'I enjoy both the cinema and dancing. I also enjoy good restaurants. How do you spend your free time then?' replied Anne, and as she spoke, she took general stock of him. He appeared to be perhaps twenty-one or -two. He was reasonably dressed with a clean shirt but tie loosened at the neck. He had a nonchalant manner that appealed to her. She noted that he was studying her as she was studying him. Although he had been with the firm longer than she had, this was, in truth, the first time they chatted together for any length of time.

'Then we have something in common I am happy to say. So would you like to try either a dance or cinema with me tonight, Anne?' asked Ian in his best and most charming manner he could put forward.

'Thank you for the invite, but must get my beauty sleep in tonight, as have been burning the midnight oil over the weekend. So thanks again.'

'Do you mind then if I ask you again another day, say during the week?' queried Ian looking up at her in an appealing way, yet felt a trifle annoyed that a slip of a girl like Anne should refuse him!

'That's very charming of you but if you would leave out this week, as I am really booked out almost every night,' answered Anne with a smile.

'Lucky you. You must be very popular with the boys then, hey?' suggested Ian in a new look of wonder at this raw slip of a girl in front of him that found errors that he did not and was too busy to date with him – or was it another way of telling him to get lost? She must have her head screwed on all right and yet in the past, he paid her scant heed but now reviewed his consideration of her as a smart cookie and was worth bothering about. Oh yes, the boss must have observed she was worth the promotion – so how come he did not, who possibly saw more of her than the boss?

'Had a good lunch, Anne?' asked Braddley as Anne walked back into the office from lunch.

'Yes thanks I did have a good lunch and also had good company. Ian sat with me when he came in for his. Are you not going out yet yourself though?' queried Anne.

'I must not go out until Ian is back, as we must always have one of us available at all times,' said Braddley in a condescending tone to Anne to emphasise his superiority.

'That will be OK with me then,' responded Anne feeling hurt by the tone of his utterance. 'You can pop off now and I will look after the shop – I am quite capable you know!' added Anne in pique.

'You know, I think I will, just to see what would happen?' said Braddley with a gleeful twinkle in his eye. Anne caught that glimpse, so she thought to herself that she would show them that she was no fool and could cope unaided.

So the first week vanished and the habit of leaving Anne alone was firmly established. But on the second Monday that Anne was alone, her proposal was put to the test much sooner than she expected. She became aware that someone had walked into the room quietly as she bent over the journal, as she was going over the figures. She turned her head and observed Mr Meredith looking at her from behind!

'Oh, hullo sir. Is there anything I can get for you?' asked Anne in a pleasing and happy tone of voice that appealed to her boss.

'Not really, but I came in to see young Ian, about the work he is doing. Where is he?' asked Mr Meredith.

'He is not back from lunch and is not due until about ten minutes. But I have the journals that Ian is working on, and if you wish to know anything about them, I may be able to give you the answers to your queries, sir,' said Anne somewhat bravely.

Mr Meredith smiled to himself as he looked at her and thought, 'Here she is with just over a week's experience at the job and is offering to tell me what I want to know. At least she is showing willing, so why not try her out and see what she does know.' With that decision made, he started firing question after question, and to his utter amazement, she replied in a nonchalant manner as an old hand would have done. He was indeed nonplussed and left her and went into Felicity's room.

'Licy, that girl Anne you proposed to me as a keen and capable brain,' began Mr Meredith with a straight face.

'Why, whatever is the matter Norm, nothing wrong I hope as I do feel she has a lot of potential. Perhaps the lads have upset her and she has fluffed it,' echoed Felicity with a tremulous and nervous voice.

'No no, you have it all wrong! She is fantastic. She has only been in that office one week and a day, and she has virtually taken over. I asked her umpteen questions and without hesitation, she knew the answer to every one that I made. Now that's better than the lads at any time and they have been on the job for three months. I compliment you Licy on your observation. I must keep an eye on her, eh?' replied Mr Meredith in a most delightful manner of pleasure, as if he had just found a gold-mine.

'Norm, you will keep your hands off her if I know what's good for you. She is a good girl and if you want to cultivate her for promotion, you will have to play it very carefully. I know what's underneath that brain and I can tell you it is explosive, so lay off,' said Felicity with a strong feeling of fear that her boss was thinking not merely of the work, but of a bedmate, and made her very jealous.

'Don't worry, my pet, you are the only one I want. But let me have her personnel card out. If she has the educational standard, what you say that we article her?' replied Mr Meredith who hoped notwithstanding the admonition he had just received from Felicity, that Anne was both of the standard for articles and not so 'explosive' as suggested.

He took the card handed to him and with a sly wink left the office to return to his own room. As soon as he left, Felicity rang through to Anne's room and asked to speak with her. Anne lifted the receiver and heard Felicity ask for her to come to her room right away.

'You asked for me Miss Felicity?' posed Anne as she entered that chamber.

'Yes I did, to have a word with you. I understand the boss has been in to see you and you impressed him dutifully. Now what was it he wanted and where were the lads at that time that he should be asking you the questions?' queried Felicity.

Anne gave a complete statement without missing out any detail in reply and looked at her superior with a worried look.

'I hope I haven't done anything wrong as I only answered what he asked of me,' murmured Anne still slightly worried.

'Quite the reverse Anne. You have flabbergasted him with your brilliance and I am very pleased for you. Keep it up and you will be going places I can tell you. But do not forget my injunction – if he asks you out, you had better not decline as I feel he may yet,' added Felicity trying to look supportively helpful yet worrying herself of potential competition. 'Now you know the latest, I think it would be wise if we made a regular date. How would Thursday be for you, Anne?' asked Felicity with a look of appeal in her eye.

'I am glad you asked me that as I had hoped you would. I feel that Wednesday may be better as it is a halfway break of the week and Thursday is already close to the weekend,' replied Anne looking at her companion wishing that it was that day right now. She felt every time she was in her company that she desired her.

'Sorry Anne, it will have to be Thursday as I am otherwise engaged Wednesday's. I will tell you about that next time we meet. But right now I have a lot of work and so have you. So off you go and see you as agreed, eh?' countered Felicity with authority in her tone that brooked no answer.

Chapter 10

So Anne left and returned to her own room and noticed that both Ian and Braddley gave her quizzical looks that made her feel very uncomfortable. She got on with her own work and became aware that they were ignoring her. She wondered why this was. Could it be because she had refused to date with Ian? Surely they could not be so infantile as that. No, it could not be that as before she joined them that day, they virtually did not notice her. There must be some other reason, so why not ask?

'What is the matter with you two. You both look as if you have seen a ghost or something. Or is my hair out of place and you do not like it?' queried Anne looking askant at them both.

'Your hair is fine as far as I am concerned Anne,' replied Ian. 'But we understand the boss has been in to see you whilst we happened to be out. Is that so?' retorted Ian.

'Surely the boss is entitled to come in here if he wants to. After all, he *is* the boss isn't he?' responded Anne.

'Of course he may come in here, but we understand that clever Dick has been answering all the questions and put us in the shade. That was not nice of you, now was it?' retorted Ian in a bit of a contrary voice.

'If you ask me a question, I answer it. If the boss comes in and asks questions, I answer. So what is wrong with that, tell me please?' queried Anne looking at them both with a quizzical look.

'It's not that you answer as you say, but you answered to embarrass us, that's what. How come you are so cocky to answer audit questions after just over a week in here, that is what we would like to know? We are convinced that you have had experience before you came into this room in that field, now haven't you Anne?' queried Ian still looking quizzically at her.

'Actually, I find your attitude very puerile to say the least. I have not had any experience in auditing before and find this work very juvenile. I reckon a kid can do this work easily. But if you do not like me in here and would rather I asked to be transferred to another section, I will oblige with pleasure. But one thing you can be sure of, that I will not work with sour pusses,' she sallied.

'Please Anne,' answered Braddley, 'we think that we would all make a good team together, but we did feel put out by your obvious knowledge that you must have spouted to the boss. Perhaps we can learn from you instead of the other way round, eh Anne?' added Braddley.

'Well, if that's how you both feel, we can call a truce and get on with the work that pays us, shall we boys?' responded Anne in a better mood than hitherto.

So by mutual consent, the peace was declared and they proceeded with the work in hand.

Anne had just finished her evening meal and was in the throes of assisting clearing the table when the bell rang. Mrs Hopkins went to the door and upon opening it, welcomed Joan and asked her in. Without ceremony, Joan went into the kitchen and there found her friend, Anne, just about to immerse her arm into the soap suds in the sink to wash up. She turned on the entry of Joan and after a surprised exclamation of her call, asked Joan to wipe as she washed, so that she could be done the quicker. Joan, poor thing, had just had to do that chore at her own home and did not relish having to do it again, but with prudence, assisted nevertheless. Anne spoke first after that commencement.

'I did not expect you tonight, so I suppose something has happened and you wish to tell me,' sponsored Anne without looking in her direction but concentrating on clearing the washing up.

'Yes, you are right as usual, Anne,' Joan responded in an almost inaudible voice. 'I took the day off to attend court to hear the trial of

Angus and that poor cripple. If you would like to join me for a coffee round the corner rather than stop in, I am dieing to tell you what happened,' reported Joan still in a subdued manner.

'OK, that's no problem. I should in fact like to get out for a breath of fresh air after being in the office all day. So let's finish these few plates and go,' replied Anne in a pleasant tone and pleased for the company.

So after finishing the chore in hand, and letting her parents know that she was taking a stroll with her friend, she left the house.

The two friends walked a short distance to a familiar coffee house where they had resorted to on many occasions. After taking their seats and ordering, Joan began, 'As you know, Angus was summoned for common assault by the police and causing actual bodily harm and causing an affray. The cripple whose name, apparently, was Tom Banks was also summoned for exactly the same thing! As you may know, I have never been in a court before so everything was new to me. Banks was called to the witness stand and the usher asked him to swear on the Bible, but he remained dumb and refused to answer any questions. The magistrate that sat in the middle, presumably the senior of the three there, spoke to him but he still did not reply. The magistrate then asked who was defending him. A barrister in a wig got up and said that he was counsel for the defendant, Mr Banks, and that he could get no word out of him either. The magistrate then asked the arresting policeman that was in court if he knew anything about the man. The policeman answered that when first arrested after the affray, he was indeed very voluble, but since he has been in the court buildings, no one has been successful in getting a word from him, either about the case or the reason for his silence. The magistrate again spoke to him and again he failed to elicit an answer.

'The lady magistrate called to him and asked if he would like to approach the bench and explain something that may be troubling him. But he still did not answer! The magistrate was now red in the face and called on him to reply to questions, for if not, he would be committed for contempt of court and would be imprisoned. He would then have to remain in prison until he purged his contempt and could then come before the court again and apologise. After all that

102

he still refused to reply. So the magistrate got very angry with him and hit his desk with his gavel and referred to him as an obdurate, obstinate and stubborn individual who had no respect for law and order and ordered the constable to take him down to the cells.

"'It took you less than ten minutes to lose your temper and I have had to bottle up my temper for more than ten years," shouted out Banks as he stood up and waved his crutch at the magistrate.

"'Ah, I see now," responded the magistrate as he leaned back in his leather armchair with the court crest on it. "You are a bit of a philosophist, are you Mr Banks? What you imply is that you have held your peace against a lot of provocation until you could not take it any more. Is that it?" questioned the magistrate now with a smile on his face as if to say, "I understand you my man." By this time the constable had reached the defendant and was gripping his arm to effect his removal as directed.

"'Constable," called the magistrate as he saw that the defendant was about to be removed from the court as he instructed earlier, "You may leave him now that he has explained his reasoning, thank you, constable."

"'Yes sir, I have indeed had a lot to put up with and I doubt that even you sir, with respect, would have tolerated the hitting, slapping and insults I have had to endure from my so-called clients that purchase the papers from me. They think that because I am a cripple I have no feelings and that I can be called all sorts of names and be smacked in jest. That still hurts, sir," he answered back as he looked towards the magistrate with an appealing yet firm look.

'The magistrate then called upon the barrister to say what he had to say and that was very little, except to retail the chap's life history and to add that that was his first offence.

'The policeman was then called and he corroborated that indeed the defendant, Banks, who was not known in court but was well-known as the local news-vendor.

'The magistrate then asked Banks a few questions, then turned to his two colleagues and conferred. He then spoke to Banks and told him to stand down until after he had dealt with Angus.

'Angus was then called and this time all questions that were asked were replied to. Angus showed himself in a very sorrowful light with regret shining out of his face. Anyone could see that he was truly sorry for the trouble he had caused. Again the policeman admitted that he was not known and that he had a hitherto clean record. Angus was asked if he had anything to say and he offered his apologies to both the court and to Banks.

'The magistrate then called Banks back to the witness stand and said the bench had arrived at their decision. He fined Banks five pounds but Angus as the *provocateur*, he fined twenty pounds and ten pounds costs. I met Angus after he left the court having paid up and had a coffee with him and he asked me to call on you to tell you, as he seems to have a very soft spot for you, Anne.'

'Whether he has a soft spot or not, is not my concern Joan. I have told him I do not wish to go out with him, and that is how it will remain. You appear to have a crush on him, so why should I interfere in your pitch, Joan. It would not be nice of me. But if we meet, I will be as pleasant as can be and will not refer to this sordid scrape he has managed to get off. I hope that meets with your approval, Joan?' questioned Anne with an askant look on her face.

'You are right, Anne. I do like the guy even though he was a fool to do what he did. But I believe that he has learned his lesson and feel that he will be a credit hereafter – don't you think so Anne?' appealed Joan.

'I hope so for your sake, Joan. But please tell him to try and avoid me, even through you, as I too may lose my temper,' added Anne without any heat.

Then after a few other topics of conversation, they left each other to go their own way home.

Anne had told her mother that she had been invited to Felicity each Thursday to stay the night. Her mother only asked if she was expected to return the invitation? When Anne said that the point had not emerged, but would raise the question and let her know. Anne indicated that as she had a rather large single bed the two could be comfortable if Felicity came to stay with her at her home. Her mother agreed and the conversation there ended. Anne met Felicity in the car pound and entered the car as soon as she saw Felicity get in. With but a nod and look, they moved off onto the main road and made their way to the flat.

After a very pleasant meal, Felicity turned up the central heating then proposed a shower. She said that after the shower, they could listen in comfort to some music uncluttered by clothes. Anne's face lit up at the thought of sitting in the lounge in *in puris naturalibus* with Felicity. Anne so admired her figure that she could sit and look at her all day long. So it transpired that Felicity thought that Anne's figure was also worth studying and enjoyed looking at her too. So without further ado, they both disrobed each other as had become their custom and entered the shower to freely indulge in play that had become the norm between them.

After wiping each other down, they entered the lounge with an arm around each other and sat themselves down upon the settee. With the music turned low they sat and mused until it was time to retire to bed.

'Do you wish to go to sleep, Anne darling?' asked Felicity when they jointly entered the bed and pulled the coverlet over themselves.

'I am not really tired so if you would like to play with me and anything else, I may appreciate it very much. Then perhaps we can both enjoy a good night's sleep after, eh Felicity?' replied Anne looking at her bedmate with ardour.

'Now first I must ask you when you are here to call me Licy. I too am not ready for sleep. So how about a bit of *soixante-neuf* as an interlude to enjoyable sleep?'

'That's French isn't it Licy, but what does it mean?' queried Anne realising that for the first time she had called her friend by the abbreviated name of Licy.

'It's so nice to hear you call me Licy. Thanks, my love, but remember, only when we are together here. Yes, that's French and means "sixty-nine". Now if you wrote that number down and turned it up one way or the other, it would always be the same. Is that right, my love?' asked Felicity.

'Ye . . . es . . . so it would be,' said Anne in a hesitating and newly understanding manner, 'but what does that mean as far as we are concerned tonight?' posed Anne.

'It is easier to explain practically than to go into reams of explanation. So you, Anne, reverse yourself and put your head where your feet should be. In other words you will by lying the opposite way to normal. Got that – so do it,' instructed Felicity with a great deal of humour in her voice.

Without understanding, Anne did as she was bid and as soon as she was in the presumably correct position, Felicity rolled over on top of her, and placed her two hands under her. As she did she instructed Anne to do exactly as she was doing. And as she was nudging Anne's legs apart, Anne did the same to Felicity. Then Anne felt Felicity tonguing her awhile around then suddenly inserting her tongue into her and rotating it within. Anne hesitated for a moment then realised that Felicity was raising and lowering her body over her in an invitation to do likewise. So in a flush of excitement, Anne put her tongue out and searched out between Felicity's legs and commenced a rotating motion with her tongue as she felt being exercised on her, and at the same time put her hands around Felicity's buttocks. After a few minutes, she felt that Felicity was rolling her over so that she appeared on top instead of being underneath. So they probed each other to contentment. Anne found her new experience quite exciting and wondered how Felicity got to know all these ways of exciting a person! She pondered and then realised that in the reverse position, she would then be the teacher!

How many times they each had an orgasm could not be counted. But they went into spasms so frequently that they lost count. But one thing can be indicated – they exhausted themselves so much that they fell asleep in the position of lovemaking and did not realise that they lay uncovered until well into the night. In the morning, when they awoke, they could not remember who covered who or who was the wrong way round in the bed.

'And how did you enjoy your new experience, Anne darling?' posed Felicity as a form of morning greeting.

'Oh lovely, Licy. You sure know the ways and positions. Where did you get to know them or mayn't I ask?' queried Anne with a healthy morning flush on her face.

'We will not have any secrets between us if we wish to remain true to each other. So anything that is asked must be answered. Now how I got to know the arts of female lovemaking is simple. There are books about it and there are shops that sell certain items to encourage it, too. I have sent for a special treat for us by mail order and hope it

106

is here next week,' answered Felicity with a happy glow on her countenance.

'I will not ask what it is, but shall look forward to the treat with real eagerness, my love,' said Anne sweetly.

Thereafter, they both arose and after their ablutions and breakfast, they left for work.

Inexorably the summer receded as the autumn moved forward. Light coats are now giving way to heavier coats. Umbrellas are now carried daily instead of occasionally. Boilers are lit, fires nurtured, extra blankets are put on the bed. So the days pass to weeks and they pass to months. We now light up earlier as the days draw to a close earlier by minutes each day.

It is now over a month since Anne began to work with the two lads in audit. Her progress has been very rapid, so much so that the lads now look to her for help and advice instead of the other way round. And with unspoken approval, she is presumed to be in charge. Anne had an interview with her boss about a week after commencing there and that day she was requested to present herself again. She accepted the request in a very mature and nonchalant fashion. Her last meeting with the boss gave her the idea that he was eyeing her with perhaps a lecherous, lustful look. This gave her the confidence that she could achieve her point, whatever it was, easily. She did not think that it went beyond the look but perhaps she saw into his attitude more than was there. Well, she would be in to see him very soon and then she would know if he was going to make a pass at her or if it was mere conjecture on her part. She hoped that it was an error in her presumption yet she hoped that it was the other way round, just to prove to herself that she had noted right and that she could look after herself.

'Come in, Anne. Please be seated as we have a lot to discuss,' said Mr Meredith as Anne entered his room. It was a very large room with bookcases lining the walls between the windows that overlooked the small rear green below. His desk was equally large yet did not appear to contain so many files as on the other desks in the firm. She also noted for the first time a cabinet which she later discovered contained the drinks that he offered clients. The ceiling lighting was subdued but there was ample lighting on the desk.

'Now,' continued Mr Meredith, as he sat comfortably in his leather-upholstered swivel and tilt chair, with his elbows resting on the desk as he leaned forward, 'I am pleased to hear that you have made excellent strides in your work and as I understand, you have taken charge. This pleases me greatly as it makes what I wish to say so much the easier.' He paused for a few moments looking at her as he did on the last occasion she came into his office. He continued, 'I have a few points to make to you, but which I place first should not imply that is the most important. In fact I shall start with the least important. I would like you to take one of the lads at your choice to do an audit at one of our clients. I have especially chosen you as I think you have the ability and what is more important, the pleasantness, calmness and charisma to pacify the client. He is an ogre and feel sure that you will handle him excellently. Are you willing to try this assignment?' he said looking at her with a hard stare as if to say, 'I dare you refuse.' For answer, Anne just nodded but did not speak.

'Good, I'm glad about that. Your friend Felicity will give you full instructions where to go and you give her your chit for expenses on your return. Now, an important point I wish you to consider. I have checked your file and see that you have matriculated yet no subjects apply to our work here. That's surprising, seeing you have shown that you can do the work. However, I have obtained the necessary forms for you to be articled here as a future accountant. It means that you would be tied to this firm for the period of articles and sit your examination as from here. You will also be given leave of absence to go to college for extra tuition. This will be paid for. Further, your next monthly pay packet will contain as promised, a handsome increase. Now, every time I have the occasion to speak with you, you give spontaneous replies. Can you now, Anne?' he concluded as he looked at her with a most pleasant smile as his hand twiddled with his pen on the desk.

'Well sir, you have overwhelmed me with your generosity. Let me first thank you collectively for the bounty. Thank you indeed for the pay rise – that I will enjoy. I will do my best to justify your confidence. But how can I possibly thank you enough for accepting me as an articled clerk to this firm?' responded Anne with a hallowed aura around her with cheeks glowing pink blush as she reflected the future that was before her.

'That is delightful to hear, Anne. I knew you would see that advantage of accepting and am sure you will justify the confidence I am placing in you. Now if you would like to thank me practically, turn round and go to that cabinet,' he said as he pointed to the closed cabinet that stood between the door and bookcases.

'That's right. Open it and pour me out a small whisky and yourself a drink as you wish. That will cement our arrangement, eh?'

As he requested, Anne opened the unlocked cabinet, although it held a key in its lock, spotted the whisky among the many bottles there available, poured out a small tumbler full and placed it at Mr Meredith's hand. Returning to the cabinet she sought out a light sherry and poured out a very small measure for herself. She did not wish to overdo herself on such an occasion and spoil his obvious confidence in her.

'This is to your good health and success, Anne,' said her boss as he raised his glass towards her.

'And this is to you, sir, in appreciation and thanks for the honour you have bestowed upon me and for the pleasure of working in this company that I enjoy. I hope I will never let you down or that you never have reason to wish you did not offer me the bounty that you have, sir, and if there is anything that I can do for you, you can be sure I will do everything in my power to give satisfaction,' she replied with a full heart.

'Now that is very nice – you will do everything in your power to give satisfaction. Yes, there is one thing I would like very much and hope that it comes in the category, "in your power". Pop in before you go home on Thursday night for a drink with me, would you Anne?' and he looked at her with an appealing eye.

'I would love to join you for a drink but can we make it Wednesday, as I have a date on the Thursday,' answered Anne wondering what she has let herself in for in accepting this invitation. But then could she very well refuse after all that she was to get from the boss, also having in mind the words of advice from Felicity that she should forego any other date to accept one from the boss?

'Oh dear, and I have an appointment on that evening, so it will have to be Tuesday, that is this evening. Can we agree on that, Anne?' he said with a pleasant smile that said a lot yet implied nothing.

'Very well then, I will pop in later, and as I have a lot of work on my desk to clear up, will defer my call for instructions from Felicity until tomorrow morning. Would that be satisfactory, sir?' she asked in as normal a voice as she could muster.

'Sure, that will be fine with me. And one other thing. We are presumably going to be friends, so do not call me "sir", call me Norman if you would, please, but of course not in front of anyone else,' he replied with a smile across his clean-shaven chin.

'Yes sir, – I mean Norman,' returned Anne hesitatingly. And with perhaps a too bewitching smile, left the office and returned to her own desk.

What had she let herself in for, mused Anne as she sat at her desk just looking at the pile in front of her without any concentration. She did not know too much about the boss but presumed him to be married. As she had to get instructions from Felicity, she would consult with her, and then she remembered, that she was to have told her something or other about the boss. Then Felicity had been with the firm for a number of years so probably knew about the boss's pedigree and all that she should know. One thing she was sure of, was that if she was to gain advantage that the new status would give her, she would have to play ball and co-operate with the boss. But how old could he be? Possibly in the upper forties. No more she was sure. Then Felicity would be able to tell her. Then he wished her to return for a drink again that evening! What if he started asking for intimacy or that? What with her attachment with Jack and her firmer attachment with Felicity, she did not want any more commitments. Then if he asked and she refused, then her prospects might be over and possibly, dismissal too. She took a deep sigh and thought that she should get on with some work and let those other problems sort themselves out at the proper time.

Chapter 11

Neither of Anne's two colleagues gave it a thought that she remained behind after they had both left the office. They had by now accepted the fact that she was now the senior in the audit department. It was her duty to supervise and share out the workload. In consequence, it meant that she stayed a while after the others had departed to see how to share out the work for the morrow. But Anne had an ulterior motive this evening for staying behind. She had promised her boss that she would pop in for a drink with him. She declined to do this during working hours as it assuredly gave the wrong impression to the other members of staff. So she found something to do purposely with the object of waiting until all the staff had left! When she felt that the firm's premises were devoid of staff, she tidied up her desk, and then traversed the short corridor to Mr Meredith's room.

Why she did it, she still could not say. But without knocking, she opened the door and entered. On later reflection, she realised that it was a move implying great intimacy, a state that she was endeavouring to avoid. But when the door was fully opened, she stopped in her tracks by what she saw. There was her boss kissing *her* Licy and she was responding. She must have stood in the doorway a few seconds before they realised that she was there.

'Do come on in, Anne. Licy was delighted when I told her of your prospects that she could not contain herself as you saw. Now that is what I call a fine friend! I congratulate you, Anne, on cultivating her. Licy is staying to join us in a drink with you. Now isn't

111

it nice, eh?' said Mr Meredith with a broad grin on his reddening face.

Anne looked at both in turn and saw that Licy had a heightened cheek colour and so did her boss. Now, was this little speech a charade, a get out or was it genuine? Somehow she felt that he was very quick on defence and got out of a situation very cleverly and well! She determined to tackle Licy when they got together. As they were all to drink together, she would assuredly be leaving with her. Then she would ask direct if there was anything in what she witnessed.

'Nothing pleases me more than to see happy people around me and what is a kiss among friends anyway?' replied Anne in a quiet tone and hopefully not showing any malice.

'That's very true, Anne. What is a kiss among friends, so now you come and kiss me too and show that we are all friends here tonight. Then we will have a drink to cement our friendship,' responded Mr Meredith with his arm outstretched to receive her and a grin across his face as if to say, 'I got out of that one, didn't I?'

Anne now realised that she was on the spot. Should she decline to go forward and kiss her boss and be considered a spoilsport or should she be brazen and kiss him as if it was a common custom. The same demon that made her open the door without knocking now pushed her forward, and with a great show of levity, threw her arms over his shoulders and kissed him full on the mouth. She delayed breaking apart on her kiss as she became aware of his manhood throbbing against her. It felt nice and enticing but she quickly thought that she had better break, otherwise she would be open to an inquest from Licy later on.

As they separated, he said to Anne that she should pour out the drinks, so without further ado, she resorted to the drinks cabinet and opened it. She first poured out a large whisky for her boss, although she was not instructed to do so but took it upon herself, and as she already knew Licy's taste, poured her out a sherry as she did for herself. Then for the first time, Licy spoke as she raised her glass and proposed the toast of the evening.

'Here's to your success, Anne, in this firm. I think you merit the reward as I know that you deserve it, having watched your progress.

But do not let all this go to your head and spoil things.' And with that, they all raised their glasses and drank of their contents.

'I feel that I should respond, but in truth I do not know what to say. Perhaps I should apologise for barging in in the first place, and in the second, I can assure you that I will not do anything to spoil my opportunity here. I appreciate my good fortune and will make the most of it as best I can. I will endeavour not to fail, and should I, it will not be for the lack of trying,' voiced Anne with a blush on her face as for the first time she had made an impromptu speech, even though there were only the three of them present.

Mr Meredith seemed to be emboldened as he put down his now empty glass and drew both ladies together, and with an arm over each of their shoulders, said he felt very happy to have two such brainy and beautiful girls with him. He dropped his arm and placed it around their waists and turned them both towards himself and first kissed one then the other, both in a passionate manner that was perhaps more than expected from a boss but not from a lover.

He did appear to be very familiar with both of them, not differentiating with Licy who had after all been with the firm a long time. It made Anne wonder if this was normal attitude of bosses or was her boss somewhat different to others? It made her wonder too, about Licy. She seemed to accept the attitude as natural and was she expected to accept this procedure every time she met up with her boss? She would have a lot to ask Licy when they got out.

'Anne, fill them up again, will you my dear?' called her boss.

Without hesitation she did as she was bid, although she did not desire a second drink herself but thought she should do so. She handed them out and with one large swallow he gulped his whisky in one. Both Licy and Anne still held their drinks when he first approached Licy, and taking her drink from her and placing it on the desk, grabbed her in a strong embrace and hugged her tightly to himself. He did this with one hand around her middle but the other hand Anne observed travelled down to her bottom that he pressed towards himself. To Anne's amazement, Licy did not fight him off but instead put her arm around him and encouraged him. He was now rubbing himself against her very violently and suddenly stopped and turned to Anne. Again he took her glass and placed it on the desk

113

and as he did with Licy, so he did to her by placing one arm around her middle and the other around her bottom. She immediately became aware that he had an enormous erection and it would explode any second. She knew that he would stain his trousers. That did not disturb her but should it penetrate onto her skirt she would not be at all pleased.

'Mr Meredith, please control yourself and let me go,' remonstrated Anne very softly in his ear, and then with a strong push to separate themselves, and they parted.

'So sorry, Anne. Please forgive me but it was the drink doing what you witnessed,' uttered her boss with a downcast look of frustration coupled with mild embarrassment. 'But please do finish your drinks then we can go home,' he added with a mellow and sorrowful tone.

For the first time that evening, Anne called her boss, Norman, by replying to his request to finish their drinks.

'That's all right, Norman. You were tempted perhaps. Or perhaps we were too provocative, eh Licy! But please remember Norman, it does not matter what you do in the bedroom as long as you don't do it in the office,' quoted Anne with a heightening colour to her cheeks.

'Well, well, you are a good sport too, Anne. Very nice of you to say that, was she not Licy, my dear?' and as he spoke, he wandered over to Licy, placed his arm into hers, drew her to the desk and handed her her drink, then released her.

After a few more banters, they all left the office together. They all walked up to the car pound. The boss had a special port on the ground floor so left the two ladies to take the lift after first bidding them both a good night.

They both sat in the car in stony silence. Felicity started the engine and without a word moved the car forward and out of the parking lot. They had only traversed perhaps a hundred yards when Anne asked her friend to stop at the café where they normally resorted to for lunch. Again without any response she drove the car and was able to park outside the café. Felicity stopped the engine and turned to Anne and asked, 'Well, what now Anne?'

'I think we have a lot to discuss, so let's go in for a cuppa or something,' she replied in a stern matter-of-fact voice.

As she spoke and left the car, she walked across the pavement and entered the café without turning to see if her friend was following or not. Felicity knew she had ruffled her friend Anne, and was at her wits' end to know how to pacify her. She did not wish to lose her friendship but how was she to explain the compromising position she was found in by Anne. At least that is what she would want to know or was there something else that was troubling her? Whatever it was she was determined to eat humble pie if needs be, rather than lose someone she had begun not only to admire for her brilliance but with whom she felt very much in love. So without further ado, she too left the car and followed Anne into the café and seated herself opposite her at a corner table. Fortunately, very few customers were in at that time of evening, so they could converse quietly with little risk of being overheard. Without asking, Anne ordered two coffees and sat awaiting their arrival.

Despite her being a few years older than Anne and more world-wide experienced, Felicity felt almost in tears as she looked at her friend's drawn face that spoke of aggravation. And who caused this attitude in her but her own stupidity and foolishness of not holding her boss in check when she knew that Anne was due any moment. Of course she did not for one moment think that she would enter the room without first announcing her arrival by knocking on the door. Had she first have knocked as expected, she would have had sufficient time to hide their compromising situation they were found in. But now she awaited Anne's outburst with great trepidation and fear, coupled with the dread of the outcome.

'Now Licy, I think you have a lot of explaining to do. Is Norman your sugar daddy, or something like that? I feel I have a right to know, especially as you told me to tell you that should he ask me to meet him, I should seek your advice. Now that spells to me that you have a strong liaison with him and I wish to learn all there is to learn and from you who claims to be my friend,' she opened up the question period with a strong determined voice that brooked no argument. And she said 'friend' and not 'lover'.

Felicity wanted to begin her explanation by calling her 'my darling' as she was wont to, but feared this introduction would create a ripple in Anne's attitude towards her so she began on a more sober note.

'Please believe me, Anne, I have no intention of upsetting you. As you very well know my feelings for you are the most paramount consideration in me. But to show my confidence in you, I will not beat about the bush but tell you straight out that there is something between Norman and me. And I observe that you, too, call him Norman, so I presume that you, too, have struck up a connection with him and you have not told me about that either. So perhaps we both have a confession to make? But let me go back a bit in history so that you may understand the reasoning of how things developed. I had a soft spot for you so invited you, and you know the results of our mutual meetings. They are happy ones and am sure you will agree. But I did not realise your brilliance in your work and when I realised this, I took it upon myself to more or less sponsor you to Norman. The fact that he listens to me is to our advantage because you have seen the result of my conversation with him on your behalf. I know everything that he has promised because we discussed this programme together and I can assure you I struck out for you very strongly. No, I do not ask for thanks or medals, but did what I did because of our great friendship that we have and hope that wherever our conversation leads us, nothing will prevent us continuing as hitherto.

'Now what you really want to know is how far have we gone. Well, Anne, I can say in confidence that we have had an affair for quite some time, even to this day. The flat is in my name but paid for by him. So if we ever parted I would have the flat but have to pay the outgoings as he has contracted to pay the mortgage. He comes to me every Wednesday night. That's why I see you on another night as I could not very well ask you at the same time. I tolerate him. In truth, since I have found you I hate it when he calls and I long for you. But it is jam on my bread so I put up with it. Now this evening was the first time he made an exhibition of us in front of anyone else. Normally, he is very careful that our liaison should not be known outside and, as far as I know, you are the only one aware of the truth. I do not have to ask you to keep it to yourself as I know you have discretion that can be relied upon.' She paused just then to catch her breath after such a long chronicle. Most of the time she held her eyes downwards but occasionally looked up to gaze into Anne's face to catch a glimpse of the reaction that may be portrayed therein. But

116

Anne's face was stony and stern and unbending. She had already told her most, including that she had an affair going on, so what else should she tell her to get Anne to melt a little towards her? So she continued, 'I asked you to let me know if he asks you out or anything like that. That was to be my day of resolve to tell you what I am telling you now. So you see, Anne, I was not intent on hiding anything from you or keeping it a secret. Because if he wants you too, then we have to talk about it very earnestly. Are you going to squeeze a flat out of him too, or are we to share him together at the same time or on different occasions. Then we have to work together, Anne, so you see we have to have a long chat to make up our minds on a joint policy.' As she concluded she looked up again towards Anne and noted that possibly a slight softening seemed to have occurred.

For a while Felicity held her now cold cup of coffee whilst Anne looked at her friend with her mind in a turmoil. This was a revelation yet she was not *too* surprised to learn the truth. This now confirmed her suspicions of Licy's apparent wealth. But it was getting late, so she must come to a decision if possible and quickly, as the proprietor of the café was looking at them as the last customers there.

'Licy, it is very difficult to know how to respond to your story. I have no hesitation in accepting that you have given me the truth. I did have a suspicion that a man was behind you, for you had apparent wealth that appeared to be beyond a private secretary's standard. But you have sold yourself and you now question me if I will do the same for monetary gain. That is a subject that I would rather not have to face, but it has emerged its ugly face so we must consider the erotema. And as it is Tuesday and tomorrow night you entertain Norman, that will not give us an opportunity to discuss the question then. But I presume that you will have a session with Norman and you will probably give your opinion. Are you going to propose that we all get into bed together, because if you do, you can count me out! Are you going to propose that we entertain him on separate nights whilst the other one is out of the way by arrangement. Or are you going to encourage him to buy me a flat too, or perhaps ask him to leave me alone so that you can keep your apple pie to yourself. Frankly, I cannot make up my mind on such a subject, so would like to know after tomorrow night how you are going to auction me off?

We will meet as usual on Thursday night unless you have cooled off and would rather drop our friendship altogether. Now, if you do not mind, please drive me home as my folks will be wondering what has happened to me for being so late without telling them in advance. Just one thing I can add, I will look in to see you tomorrow morning for instructions about that audit I have to go to.' With that she got up and went to the café counter and paid for the coffees, and then walked to the door. Licy was already by the door that she held open for Anne and both walked across the pavement to the car which they then entered.

Felicity turned towards Anne and with a deal of trepidation, took her hand into her own and looking into her face, asked if she could return to the pleasantness that prevailed between them before Norman came on the scene betwixt them. For a few moments that seemed like ages to Felicity, they held hands whilst Anne returned the look as her mind began coining phrases to say in reply to the appeal.

'Darling,' she began. Immediately Licy's face lit up on hearing that term of endearment. 'You know my feelings for you and despite what has happened tonight, I cannot find it in myself to lose you over a man. Nothing would please me more than to continue as we have begun. But I have a great problem of how to add this new item to our agenda. I shall listen with great interest as to how you recommend what I shall do with Norman. We are both involved, but as far as we should be concerned, we are together, and if the worst came to the worst, we could both leave and get a job elsewhere? I am sure that is a point you can put forward,' added Anne with a better expression on her face now that the air between them had more or less cleared. As she concluded, she took Licy's other hand into her own and looked into her face and asked if she still loved her.

'Anne, my love, how can you doubt me! Of course I love you and want you very much. But please kiss me so that we can part as we should.'

'The saying is '*Tis better to have loved and lost than never to have loved at all.* But in our case, we have found our love again!' With that, they kissed each other as passionately as they could within the confines of the car, and still in a public thoroughfare, then drove off towards Anne's home.

'You are rather late tonight, Anne dear. Hope there is nothing wrong, as you look flushed', so Mrs Hopkins spoke to her daughter as she observed her entering the family home.

'Well, Mum. I have a lot to tell you. Perhaps the flush is because I have had a couple of sherries. I saw my boss this morning, and he told me that I have been accepted as an articled clerk to the firm. That means that after a couple of years and a bit of swatting plus an exam or two, I will become a chartered accountant? He also told me that in my next pay cheque I should expect a goodly increase. How much, I do not know and did not feel I should at that moment question. All this came about because Felicity spoke up for me to the boss. It was on her recommendation that I have been promoted. Tonight I was invited to his office with Felicity, to celebrate with a drink. So I am sure you will be pleased to learn the reason for my being late tonight, Mum.'

'Yes, I saw her car as you drove up and wondered what it was all about. But I am really delighted to hear your wonderful news. I hope that you get what you are after. I wish you every success and good fortune, Anne my dear,' said her mother as she beamed with delight at her daughter's good fortune in her post. She then knew why she looked so flushed, too.

'Thanks Mum, I was sure you would be glad for me. I do not know exactly what I have to do, but I believe I will be getting time off to go to college to study on certain days. And another thing I must tell you. I have now to go to visit clients of the firm to do their audit at their place and take an assistant with me. Me take an assistant who was one herself only a couple of weeks ago! Of course I will be coming home as usual as I do not think I will be called upon to go to out-of-town clients. But one can never tell. So you see, Mum, in a short while, my whole life has taken a turn for the better.' So she spelled out her good fortune to her mother, who sat looking at her with due pride and pleasure.

Anne awoke much earlier than usual. She could not sleep. She had tossed and turned all night going over the problem that had beset her in the last day. She knew that she would be seeing Licy that morning for a few minutes for instructions as to which client she had to go to.

119

She was equally sure that she too had a sleepless night puzzling over the same problem!

She went over in her mind the alternatives she had illustrated to Licy for her consideration and recommendation. Surely she would not propose that they meet with Norman together on the same night! And what if she did! Was she expected to fall in line and accept the proposal? Just imagine, the two of them after a shower together coming out all nice and hot and pink, without a stitch, to be greeted by Norman in his birthday suit too! Then she had never seen a man completely unclothed. And how would he react. With whom would he react first? Would they both, in full view of each other at that time. That would mean we would be sharing the bed all three together!

She dwelt on this hypothetical proposition for a while, conjuring up the picture of the three of them running around the room with nothing on! Who would be teasing who, that was the question? Her mind did not for one moment suggest any shyness. Did that mean she was a brazen hussy? No! It just meant that she had grown up and was more sophisticated! After all, a body is part of nature's wonders, so why should we be awkward about it?

Would she feel different if Norman touched her as Licy did? Then he would not want to use his fingers in her but his weapon? She already had some experience what that felt like with Licy, who recently purchased by mail order an item that was inserted into both of them to simulate proper sex! They smeared Vaseline on it before inserting it. Would she have to do that to his thingumabob, too? But then with the instrument they used jointly, nothing could happen. But if he put it in, there was a double risk; one, that she may become pregnant, that she did not desire to be and two, she may contract that dreaded venereal disease. So what was she to do if he demanded to insert it in her? She would have to think that one out very carefully.

What if he wanted Licy whilst she was there too? How would she feel watching them together? Somehow she could not feel jealous of her friend and even thought that it might be better if he did go with her at least first. As they had already indulged, at least that is the presumption, she could learn from the action play in front of her.

Perhaps he would want to please both and ask them to decide who would be first?

All this kept her awake and still she came to no solution of how to react to what was really imminent. Then she could be prudish and refuse all advances. Would that be wise? She felt that if Licy earned a beautiful apartment out of Norman, she too should have one! She must pay the price and that was sex in some form or another!

Her mediation was called to a halt, when she heard her mother calling her for breakfast. She hurried her shower and donning her bathrobe resorted to the breakfast room for her morning meal. With haste, she dressed in a somewhat severe costume, made up, and left so as not to be late on this occasion of importance. She did not even become aware of the morning chill as she strode along to the station for her ride to work.

As became her new custom, Anne entered Licy's room without knocking and found her already at her desk.

'Ah, nice to see you Anne, so early this morning. I hope you have had a better night than I had? I found it extremely difficult to get much sleep last night. Too much on my mind I suppose – and you can guess what that was about, I am sure,' said Licy with a broad smile on her face that glowed with a happy tinge of blush redness. Anne was sure that it was not make-up but nature's remedy reflecting itself in her happiness.

'I do not have to emphasise that I too found it impossible to sleep. I went through all sorts of possibilities and could not agree with myself on any one of them. So I hope you can help me resolve the problem tomorrow morning Licy, but right now I wish to have the information of where I have to go on this assignment,' concluded Anne.

'Of course, of course, that's your first outside job. You have to see a firm called Blackstone of Hammersmith. They are a firm of engineers. They employ about a couple of hundred people. We've been doing their accounts for them over a long time and twice a year we have to do an audit on the job. The boss of the firm is a Mr Charles Harrington. I must warn you about him. He is not easy to get on with! Perhaps I should not have told you this but I have. He is rude

121

and shouts at you for the slightest provocation. That is, he finds provocation to encourage him to shout. He is a good client financially, but the worse one to deal with! So the best of luck with him. I have full instructions written down for you. Take a taxi there. By the way, who are you taking on the job with you?' concluded Licy looking at her friend perhaps with envy that she was getting out, yet she did not relish her working for a man like Harrington.

'I have not yet decided which of the lads yet. Thought perhaps I would ask them and take the one that may have been there before,' proposed Anne as she returned the look that Licy gave her. With that she took the typed instructions given her and left the office after a gentle wink, perhaps indicating happy thoughts.

'Now you two, who has been to Blackstones on audit?' queried Anne as she entered her room with both Ian and Brad being present. They both looked at her for a moment before Brad replied.

'I do not think Ian has been there but I have and would rather not go again. That Harrington is a tough one to work for. It does not matter what you do, he will find fault. It always takes us three days there and it's hard work so I suggest that Ian can go this time, Anne', and as he finished, he put his head down as if to continue his work.

'Now first of all, I must insist that in future you refrain from addressing me by my forename. You may call me "miss" if you prefer or "Miss Hopkins". And in the presence of anyone else, it must always be "Miss Hopkins". Now is that clearly understood you two?' said Anne in a commanding tone yet not in a dictorial manner.

'As you wish,' retorted Brad with a shrug of his shoulders.

'Now that is understood, Brad, kindly pack up what you are doing as you are coming with me. I prefer to have someone with me that has been there before. So please jump to it as we have a job to do,' replied Anne and as she concluded she turned towards her own desk to sift what she wished to take with her.

After tidying up her desk and assuring that Brad was ready to depart, she ordered Ian to call a cab so that one should be awaiting them by the time they arrived in the entrance hall.

'We are from Meredith's the Accountants, miss,' said Anne at the reception desk.

'Oh yes, you are expected. Mr Harrington requested you to call at his office first. I will show you where it is, if you would please follow me,' replied the attractive young receptionist that left her desk to lead them along various corridors and up in the lift to the top floor.

This floor, Anne observed, was nicely carpeted. Pictures adorned the walls. An air of opulence pervaded the atmosphere, as they walked in file after the receptionist until they reached the door upon which the legend indicated that there within was a Mr Harrington, the Chairman of the Company. The receptionist tapped on the door and awaited the call to enter. On receiving the call, she opened the door and announced that the auditors were there to see him. He called out to ask them to enter, upon which Anne led the way, followed by Brad. They were invited to sit, which they did, and awaited further words from Mr Harrington.

'I understand that you Miss Hopkins are in charge, so you, young man, can leave the room whilst I go through a few items with Miss here,' opened up Mr Harrington, who looked as they expected, an ogre in a suit that looked Saville Row and possibly was so. Brad got up to leave, but Anne interjected.

'Mr Harrington, please let me make one thing clear so that we do not have any misunderstanding.' Then, turning her head towards Brad, motioned him to be seated. With doubt and reluctance, he did as he was bid. 'Braddley here is my assistant and only I can give him any instructions. It is my wish that he remain here to hear your general instructions so that it does not waste my time to relate to him what you have imparted to me. I hope I have made myself clear, sir. Now is there anything in particular you wish me to know before we commence our work?' she concluded looking at him with fire in her eye that made him go red in the face as if he had burst a blood vessel.

'Well, well, we have ourselves a straight Jane no nonsense little bitch, have we?' retaliated Mr Harrington when he could muster the words together eyeing her with malice.

'I am not concerned sir, with petty names. I have come here to execute a job of work and that is what we shall do regardless of your opinion of me. May I therefore ask where we are to work; I hope it is compatible for us wherever it is?' she added as it to add fuel to the already blazing fire that swelled up in him, as they stared at each other.

123

Instead of answering her, he called on his intercom for someone to pop in.

Within a few minutes, a young lad knocked and being invited in, entered. He was instructed to take his visitors through to the account department to Mr Jones' office. With that, both Anne and Brad arose to their feet and were about to leave, but Anne interposed. 'Thank you, sir for seeing us. If you wish to see me again upon any matter relating to the audit, I shall be happy to oblige.' With that, she followed Brad who was already at the door.

They followed the young lad to the office of Mr Jones whom they presumed to be the accountant to the firm. On arriving there, the young lad tapped on the door. They heard the call to enter, so Anne told the lad that that was all and entered the room. It was a medium-sized room that appeared to be a hive of industry by the books and papers that littered the large desks. Mr Jones stood up and came forward to welcome them as they entered. He was a slight man inclined to stoop, probably from the years of bending over his desk in pursuit of his occupation. He was probably in his fifties and with mouse-coloured hair and a wisp of a moustache he appeared to have a permanent grin tattooed on his face.

'Ah, you are the lass that's commissioned to do the audit. If you would care to come into the adjoining room to mine, the papers and vouchers are all there. If you need anything extra, all you have to do is ask.' As he spoke he opened the door to the room that intercommunicated with his. Both Anne and Brad entered the room and found it reasonably large with two desks with little on them. The pile of books and papers for them was on a small table-like desk alongside. Mr Jones indicated that coffee or tea could be had when the tea lady came round which was due in a short while. He would see that she came in to them. With that, he left them and closed the door between them.

'Anne, Anne, oh, I beg your pardon, I mean miss, I do not know what possessed you that way you struck into the boss! He was flaming red and livid, and I thought he was going to raise hell the way you responded to him. Did you do it to aggravate him or what?' queried Brad as they found that they were alone at last.

'Brad, please understand, we have a job to do here and that job is going to get done or my name is not Hopkins. So now let us not waste time and look through this pile,' and with that they both walked over to the side-table and rummaged and sorted out what was wanted just then. Braddley never got his reply to the question he raised then or ever!

Towards the end of the second day, Anne realised that the work could be completed. She decided to let Mr Jones know that they would be departing and not returning after that evening. On imparting this information to Mr Jones, they were told that the boss, Mr Harrington, desired to see Anne alone before they left. Brad looked quizzically at Anne who said that she would see him alone, as the work was completed, and that he was to await her return.

Anne took the lift and walked along the corridor to Mr Harrington's room. She found the door open, so she looked in and called out that she had called as requested.

'Ah, do come in Miss Hopkins. Do sit down, I would like to ask you one or two questions that I feel sure that you can answer. Now in the past, the audit has always taken three days and you say you have completed the work in only two? Are you sure then the work is in fact completed?' and as he spoke he scrutinised her with a commanding look, as an officer may to a corporal, yet with a pleasant smile on his face, which perhaps was the first time he had worn such an expression in front of a slip of a girl as Anne.

'Sir, as far as I am concerned the work is complete. If it is not, I will find out in a very short while when I get back. Now is there anything else you wish to know, sir?'

'Yes there is. You are the first one that has stood up to me and not only that, you appear to know your job, too. So I have a proposition for you. Whatever your salary you enjoy, I will add another thou' to it and come and work here. You will enjoy it, I can promise you that,' he said with, if possible, an angelic smile that would have made her laugh had he not been a client of the firm.

'Thank you indeed for the offer but I must decline as I am very happy in my present post. I am however very sorry if I disturbed you yesterday. It was not my intention to be officious but if I have a job to do, I do it and that's all, sir,' replied Anne looking as pleasant as she could in response to an offer that she never ever expected.

'I will not take "No" for an answer, but ask you to dwell on it for a few days and then call me, but to show you that there is no ill feeling, would you care to join me for a drink?' Instead of awaiting her reply, he rang a bell at the side of his desk upon which the same young lad that showed them to Mr Jones' room, came in.

'Ah, Joseph, would you kindly pour me out a drink and give Miss Hopkins one too', and turning back to Anne, asked her what she would like.

'Now that is very nice of you, sir; I will have a very small sherry, if you please.'

With that, Joseph gave each a drink and then left the room, closing the door as he went.

'Here's to you Miss Hopkins in the hope that you do eventually join me in this firm. And do please call. Here is my direct phone number which I would ask you to use but not divulge. I look to hearing from you very soon, and I hope it will be in the affirmative, too,' he said as he looked at her with as pleasant a smile as he could muster. After a few more questions and answers, he raised no more objections to her departure.

Chapter 12

'Mr Meredith, please,' asked Mr Harrington when his call was connected.

'Mr Meredith's line is engaged, sir. Will you hold?' asked the telephonist in a tired voice having answered umpteen calls that day. 'Ah, it's free now, sir. Who shall I say is calling, sir?' volunteered the same tired voice.

'Tell him it's Mr Harrington,' came the reply in a curt tone.

'You are through now, sir,' said the voice as she connected the two men, bosses of their own empires yet dependent on each other.

'Hullo, Charley; you are going to rouse me for sending a girl over to you I suppose; is that your call?' queried Mr Meredith in a resigned tone as of experience from the past.

'Well now, that's where you are wrong, old boy. I thought I'd give you a call to see if we can make a deal. I want that Hopkins girl on my payroll as I think she is just the one I am looking for. You would not miss her as you have ample staff I'm sure, so how about a proposition, Norman?' sponsored Mr Harrington in the most appealing tone he could muster.

'She's too young for you and also not sufficiently experienced, so I feel you would be getting the worst of the bargain, Charley,' came the immediate reply from Meredith who wondered what had transpired to get that old fox to ask for 'his' Anne.

'Norman, old chap, it is no concern of yours if she is too young or inexperienced. If I want her, I want her. I have offered her a thou' over your pay and she has refused. So have a word with her, you old

127

codger, will you?' retorted Mr Harrington in an inveigling tone that he hoped would not brook any refusal.

'Of course she will refuse your offer. She is articled to the firm and who would be so foolish to give that up. But I am delighted to hear you ask for her. I presume you are pleased with her,' responded Mr Meredith with laughter in his inflection.

'Now don't give me that bull, you old so and so. I suppose you have bedded her, too,' countered Mr Harrington.

'As a matter of fact, she is a very charming girl but straight and no nonsense too. So she should be of no use to you. You need a heifer to keep up with you, so pick another. By the way, how is she doing?' rejoined Anne's boss with a titter of delight to get one over his client.

'Oh hell, she is finished in two days flat. I've never had it done in less than three days and sometimes it has stretched to four. Shall I tell you something, Norman: she stood up to me and made me keep my place. Now that's guts that I admire, so let me have her, please,' begged Mr Harrington to his friend's pleasure and amusement.

'Charley, you have asked her and she has refused. You have asked me and I endorse her action, so what can I do and say to appease you? I bet if you doubled her offer of a grand, she would still refuse you, so leave her alone,' ventured Norman with a chuckle in his throat.

'Go to hell, you old dog,' bellowed Harrington as he hung up.

'Licy, come into my office right away, if you please,' said her boss into the intercom.

'Sorry sir, but I will be two minutes as I have someone with me right now. Will that be all right, sir?' responded Felicity in her casual cultured voice.

'OK then, as soon as you can,' came the reply and a click of disconnection.

'Oh dear,' thought Licy, 'I wonder what he wants now? We had a very long talk last night at my flat and came to no conclusion as to how or where Anne will fit in. We kept going round and round the same point to no end. Tonight I am to meet up with Anne. Probably I will find her at the car or perhaps she will call. She has not yet done so but must I hold on for her. I had better go and see what Norman wants.' So with that decision made, she left her desk and walked to his room and entered without knocking.

'Licy, you will be surprised to learn and hear that I've had a call from Charley Harrington about our Anne,' mooted her boss with a crafty twinkle in his eye.

'Oh dear, I hope he has not bawled her out or upset her, now has he?' queried Felicity with a worried look on her countenance, yet mindful of his expression of 'our Anne'.

'You do not have to look so worried, my dear. She has put him in his place and not only that, he phoned me to ask me to release her and has already spoken to her with an offer of a thousand a year more than I pay her and she has refused. Now how's that for a girl, eh Licy?' chortled her boss with glee that could not be depressed.

'Wha. . .t!' expostulated Felicity with astonishment showing in her face, 'offered her a grand and ticked him off into the bargain and he still, wants her. Well, I'll be damned! What did you tell him then?' asked Felicity now in a dumbstruck voice that she could not comprehend.

'I told him I endorsed her action and that he cannot have her. And on top of that, she has completed the assignment in two days; now that's something too, eh girl?' he added still without control of his suppressed laughter.

'Well, Norman, I told you she was good, but even I underestimated her full potential. You have a prize bird here so you had better give some very strong thought to our discussion of last night. Be careful, otherwise you will lose a unique beauty with brains,' she added with a look of startlement and yet great pleasure.

As she concluded her statement, he lifted the intercom 'phone and asked if Anne was back yet. He was told that she had arrived but a couple of minutes ago and was at that precise moment unpacking her holdall. The recipient of the call then had the request to ask Anne to come to his office immediately. At that point he hung up.

'You wished to see me, Norman?' asked Anne as she entered the room and noted that Licy was there, too.

'Yes Anne, we do. We have heard from Harrington that he made you an offer of a thousand and you declined. Both of us are staggered yet delighted to learn of your loyalty and we are also delighted to

129

learn that you put ol' Charley Harrington in his place. Now what exactly did you do or say that he should call me and tell me that you got one over him?' queried Norman with a smile that went from cheek to cheek.

Within a split second Anne's demon assaulted her again and made her turn towards the drinks cabinet and pour out three tumblers without saying a word. With a broad smile, she handed the drinks round taking a seat unasked, she then explained what had occurred.

'You are marvellous, my girl. Come and kiss me as you delight me more and more each time I see you.' With that he stood up and held out his arms to receive her.

Without any hesitation she approached his side of his large desk and threw one arm around his neck and with the other hand pressed it against his crotch. He did not wish to release her from the amorous hug he was enjoying but Anne did not hold on more than a moment but long enough to whet his sexual appetite.

As became their custom, Anne and Felicity walked together to the car park and took the lift to Felicity's car. They walked arm in arm despite Felicity witnessing what Anne had done to their boss. She made no comment as she feared that an adverse mention may upset her and the result would be only that she would lose her darling Anne. So they entered the car and away they went to the flat.

The talk en route was of Anne's exposure of what had transpired at Harrington's. Speculations were made as to what would have been expected of her had she accepted the offer and post? It was presumed by both that apart from office duty, a demand for sexual involvement would be part of the deal, although no mention was made at the outset. They hypothesised all manner of opinion as to what sort of flat would have gone with the job and what demands he would have made upon her. So they arrived at the flat, both in a very frank and happy frame of mind.

The meal over, they sat quietly with very low background music playing. Felicity gave a full synopsis of her conversation with Norman the previous evening. It was taken for granted that whatever was agreed between the two, Anne would accept without demur or protest! Although Felicity had not yet told Anne and neither had

Anne asked exactly what had happened between her and her boss, from Anne's point of concept, she presumed that Licy accepted full sex in exchange for the perks and privileges she enjoyed from the firm.

'Well, to be truthful,' commenced Anne, 'I am not ready for a liaison with him or anyone else. I am happy with you as it is, and feel that I do not want any more! So if you can hold him off for a while, it would be appreciated, Licy darling,' she added looking up at her with a wistful look.

'Quite frankly, Anne dear, I think he would be afraid of upsetting you to press his claim too strongly. If you will take a tip from me, don't let your hands stray on him to provoke his ardour, otherwise it may be difficult to keep him in check,' replied Licy wondering if she herself had not overstepped the mark by the allusion of what she witnessed in Norman's office only a few hours ago.

'Thank you, Licy, for that tip. Quite truthfully, I do not know what possessed me to touch him as I did. I should not have done, but you know how it is at times we all do things that we should not and know that we should not,' answered Anne without any embarrassment.

The conversation then continued until Anne proposed that it was time for fun, games and bed! So they retired to enjoy each other's company.

Andrew in compassion had already telephoned Tracey to explain the reason why he had not been able to meet her at the dance. Again, he reconfirmed his promise to meet up the coming Friday. It was not then a very pleasant evening. It had been showering on and off all day. As the evening drew in, it became progressively colder. So by the time Andrew arrived to pick Tracey up, it was far from walking-out weather. The best place was indoors and as he had promised to take her to his flat, that was under the circumstances acceptable.

Although it was the normal rush hour of home-going traffic, Andrew made the journey to Hampstead within half an hour. Tracey only had a vague idea of the location and was pleased to get a running commentary from Andrew, as they passed through the City towards the suburbs.

'Well, how did you enjoy that repast?' asked Andrew as they left the dining table to return to the settee in the lounge.

'I came without thought of what I may get but now that I have had it, I must say that it was a very enjoyable meal and you are to be congratulated for your efforts. It is appreciated,' she answered as she did feel very happy after the good meal.

'And what would you like to do now, my dear. Would you like a romp in the bed or are you going to play hard to get?' he asked in an emboldened smile that meant business.

'So you have given me a drink and now you wish to squeeze it out of me; is that it Andy?' she retorted without any rancour.

'I will only squeeze it out if you want it out. But I do like to ask as I feel fun should be enjoyed and not forced. To start with, come a little closer to me here on the settee and let's have a cuddle just to warm up,' he replied again with no hesitation or embarrassment, and as he spoke and without waiting for Tracey to move over towards him, he shuffled towards her, and when they were side by side, he placed one arm around her shoulder and with the other hand laid it across her lap.

'Perhaps this will be almost as good as the bed, but if you feel like changing your mind and trying the bed, just say and we will do so,' ventured Andrew as he closed up still more and turning her towards himself, engaged her in a very passionate kiss to which she reciprocated with equal ardour.

After a few minutes, they separated to refill their lungs. When they had done so, he asked her if she would care to make love with him. She replied that she had never made love with anyone yet and did not intend to commence then. If he insisted, she added, she would don her coat and leave.

'Then we will just play, how would that be, eh, as we did before?' he replied and at the same time allowed his hand that lay on her lap to roam under her skirt until he found his hand smoothing her among her pubic downy hairs. She did not stop him as she felt excited as the hand gently rubbed her there. She still did not object when he first slipped one finger then another into her. She became aware that she was oozing a lot and he accepted it as normal – at least he did not comment on it. She then found the position they had adopted in such close proximity to be somewhat uncomfortable, so she let his arm around her neck slip off as she laid her head back to the rear of the settee. So there she sat with her head leaning on the back of the settee and her legs slightly apart as he had manoeuvred them, with both her arms lying by her side.

With his free hand, he gripped her hand nearest to him and gently drew it towards himself. She did not object as she did not know its purpose but realised as soon as she felt pulsating flesh. She had not seen nor realised that he had taken out his phallus, until she felt it. It was rock hard! He drew her hand to close over it and she had to think quickly her attitude to this movement. She enjoyed her sensation with him so why not a little of give and take! Then would it be a little give and take or just take and from the position, proceed to further advances. Should she speak to him and demand a stop; that would upset both of them, or just say, no further, and hope for the best! She plucked up the courage and said, 'Andy my love, no further or I will leave, promise.'

'Tracey my dear, you should know me by now, I never take liberties. If you are happy to continue as we are, that's OK with me. It still would be more comfortable on the bed; again that you need not be worried – so shall we adjourn to the bed?'

Tracey let go of him and flung both her arms around his neck and kissed him and in a soft whisper in his ear said that she would trust him. With that and much to her amazement, he lifted her bodily and carried her to the bedroom and laid her down very gently. As she lay on her back he pulled her pants off without any objection. Then before mounting the bed itself, he divested himself of his trousers and underpants and then stood in front of her in exhibition.

'Now you promised, Andy. You will not do it again, please promise again,' whimpered Tracey now feeling as a spider in a web.

'You will trust me I know because I have given my word. I will not seduce you unless you ask me to. But we can enjoy a good bit of play until you say enough. Now is that in order?' he returned in passion.

'Yes Andy,' she murmured without being too confident that she did right.

He then lay alongside her and again took her hand and placed it around his weapon that was again as hard as rock. As soon as her hand was to his satisfaction he replaced his into her that made her murmur and breath very heavily with soft moans of delight. She just lay there holding on to him whilst he manipulated his fingers within her with one hand, whilst the other was around her shoulders so that they could lie very close with lips seeking each other.

'Would you like to do something for me, Tracey darling?' whispered Andrew into her ear as they lay together.

'You promised, so what do you want me to do now, Andy?' questioned Tracey not at all happy to get this request.

'What you have in your hand, would you take it and bite it for me as you did before – remember?' ventured Andrew in hope that she would.

'What do you mean bite it? Put it in my mouth; is that what you want me to do?' questioned Tracey with misgivings.

'Do try it, I'm sure you will enjoy it again, so shall we try?' posed Andrew more in hope than expectancy. So as to encourage her to do his bidding and biting by subterfuge and tactical movement, he straddled her with his knees to her side whilst she lay on her back. As he reached that position he wiggled towards her head so that it was not more than inches away from her face. All she had to do was to pull him towards herself and take it in. To his misgiving yet not surprise, she seeing the position they were now in, decided to remove herself. To do this, she simply rolled over to one side that toppled him off the bed. This created a howl of laughter from Tracey when she realised that he lay on the floor instead of the bed in the semi-nude state.

To ensure that she would be co-operative as far as he could get her, he joined in with the laughter. As he did, he rose up and lay alongside her again. With new caution, he again took her hand and moved it towards his tool. The moment she gripped it, she tugged at it and then let it go. This made him scream and jump away from her. She knew that she had annoyed him but she was now in that mood.

'Oh dear, you asked for that Andy, now didn't you?' chuckled Tracey with a broad grin and devil in her eye.

'I did not think you had that streak in you, Tracey, so what's up with you? I am being as nice as I can with you. I have not put it where you asked me not to, so why not a bit of co-operation with me? Now will you have a bite or do you just want to hold it tight for me?' he remonstrated.

'I've had enough of this messing about. So let me go, please?' retorted Tracey in a mock-pleading voice. As she spoke she endeavoured to get up from the prone position.

Andrew realising that he had probably lost the battle made another attempt. He rolled over to prevent her getting off the bed and so lay over her and said, 'Darling, I have not meant to do anything you would not accept, as you well know. So I agree to stop, but please before we do, just hold it nicely for me for a couple of minutes so that I can shoot; then I will be pleased to stop,' he said in an encouraging soothing tone of voice.

'What am I to do?' thought Tracey as she lay there with his body over hers in very close proximity, 'so close, that should he decide to go back on his word and seduce me, I could not prevent it. Should I try to escape somehow and risk his wrath or should I hold him as he asks. I have already been holding him for quite some time so what would it matter if I held him again and let him have his fun. Yes, I think for harmony sake I will grab it and hold it for him so that he can get his climax, but how does he get that if he has not already reached it as I have?' So with a pleasant smile, she half turned towards him and reached for it and took it again in her hand. He immediately responded with a very happy smile and said, 'Now that's lovely my dear, just rub your hand over it and it will grow. You can look at it see for yourself and I will reach for a towel in the drawer of the bedside table.'

'What do you want with a towel, Andy?' queried Tracey as she did as he bid and observed that it had become again very hard and had begun to throb.

'It will be prudent to cover it with a towel,' he replied as he leaned over to extract a small face cloth out of the drawer of the bedside table. 'Any second now it will explode and you will see come out of the knob strong fluid that can shoot across the bed. That is what I wish you to catch in the cloth. Otherwise we will make too much of a mess. But tell me, you knew that, didn't you?' he said in partial puzzlement.

'Actually, I did not know until you explained the last time. How should I have known if you are the first guy I have held? But as you have told me this much, tell me what is this fluid for and why?' challenged Tracey.

'Well, I see I will have to educate you my love,' he said in a pleasing tone to realise that he was the first and that he had a virgin. 'What comes out is what can produce in you a baby if I put it in you and let it go in there. Do you now understand?' he added looking at her.

'Truthfully, I must plead ignorance. I knew if you put it in I risk a pregnancy but I did not know about the shooting bit!' answered Tracey in a perplexed, uncertain tone.

'I will hold it back if you would like so that I can give you a lesson in the anatomy of man and sex, should I?' asked Andrew in a very consoling voice. She wondered exactly what he meant by holding it back but feigned to ask; she just agreed as that is what it appeared would please him at that moment.

He realised that he was with a novice, and that pleased him tremendously. He could not remember having brought a girl back with him that did not know what it was all about. It gave him a feeling of desire with her that he had never felt before. To have a virgin is a rarity and he was going to hold on to her whatever happened. She was also a beautiful creature, slender, nice figure, well-groomed, in fact he would not feel ashamed to be seen with her anywhere. So he will play his cards correctly and keep her against competition. He, of course, presumed there was competition.

'Just sit up on the bed, my dear,' proposed Andrew as he assisted her in getting to a sitting position.

'That's fine, just spread your legs apart. That's right. Now I can stand in front of you and you can examine it now so that you understand what it is all about. So now put one hand underneath it, . . . that's good, and the other one on my shoulder to steady yourself – your under hand, that's good, as I've said and hold it gently – fine,' he added in a disjointed way as he got her to co-operate.

She sat looking at it and observed that it was not so stiff as before. She also now and not for the first time, felt under him, and realised that he had something hanging there. He saw that she had a frown on her face that showed puzzlement as she held him underneath and as she drew it forward so that she could see exactly what it was she was holding in her cupped hand.

'That in your left hand my dear are the "goolies". Some people call them other names but I call them "goolies". The whole thing is the scrotum and they develop the sperm that is ejected when it gets excited as it nearly did a few minutes ago. Now that you have moved your hand to cover it, what you now hold in the other hand is the "penis" or as I call it the "rod". It is only at its fullest strength when it is roused as I said it was a few minutes ago. Now it is halfway there. So before I get it to explode I will let you examine it and ask any question that occurs to you. Take advantage and please do not be too timid to ask. It is for your own good that you should know these things.' So there he stood over or alongside her with her left arm at full stretch under him and resting on her arm it lay at full length and with her right hand she was gently passing over it as it reposed on the arm. He was in a very happy frame of mind as never had he the experience as now portrayed. He thought that she must be so innocent that she had succumbed to doing what he bid and he enjoyed it to the full as it appeared that she did too.

'This seems a mightily long rod and you are supposed to put it into a woman? It must hurt, I'm sure. How can it go in at this size?' puzzled Tracey as she continued to gaze at it as it lay along her arm.

'Ah, that is easy to explain. Nature has its own way. A woman may be tight where it has to go, but nature allows it to enter and with natural lubrication that the woman gives off as soon as it enters, the same as you feel when my fingers are in you, it smoothes itself right in. Of course when it is the first time or second time that you enjoy the experience, then it may appear to be tight. But the tightness may even hurt a little but that creates the thrill and invariably you would call out or even shout for more and more. Would you like to try it a little bit, darling?' he added hoping that she would respond in the affirmative.

'Don't you dare to put it in. You did say that this would be an exercise of instruction for me, so keep your word and please do not test me again,' she pouted back at him to his discomfort and loss of hope.

'All right then, you do not have to put it in but please have a bite of it. It has almost reached it and it wants to go off, so would you do that and help me get my satisfaction, darling?' Again he hoped that despite her earlier refusal she might this time.

137

'I think I've had enough,' and as she uttered those words she let go her both hands and withdrew them and gave him a slight push in the chest, so that she could get up on her feet.

'Oh hell, you are not going to walk off and let me dangle with it at full length when it only needs you to give it a very slight rub and it will flow over and finish; so please be a darling and hold it for just a minute more,' he begged as he held it out in front of her pleading for her hand.

'No, I'm not going to take it again. I have held it for you for a long time so be satisfied. And if you want to do something to finish it off, then please do. Don't mind me I'll just watch; how would that be eh?' she teased.

'Oh, you are being wicked now. But hold me around the waist while I rub it to finish as I cannot leave it now,' he croaked in a pleading voice as he pulled her arm and placed it around his middle whilst he held the face cloth in the one hand and with the other held his rod and rubbed it. Within seconds he placed the cloth over it and turned towards Tracey and hugged her with a strong passionate squeeze.

'Is that it then?' posed Tracey watching him as he now wiped it when he had stopped trembling.

'Yes, that's it, but only half bake. Next time you will try it inside and then it will be a full bake and then we will both enjoy it, shall we my love?' he added in a cajoling tone.

'Thanks for the buggy ride but I don't think there will a next time. I think it is time I went home, so do you mind letting me go so that I can dress myself, please,' she said in a nonchalant manner as if tired of the exercise that they had indulged in.

Andrew knew he was beat, so with as much bravado as he could muster, put on a cheerful countenance and assisted her in dressing. then he did the same for himself and after a small banter of words, he offered and she accepted a lift to her home.

Tracey reached her home rather later than anticipated. Nevertheless, she reached her room without awakening any of the household. She had a shower and after drying herself, went downstairs for a glass of milk that she carried up to her room. She got into bed and sitting up took her milk and sipping it went into a vision that she had just gone through.

Was she her sophisticated self or had she changed? Why had she succumbed to what she did. Did she regret what had transpired? Should she have gone to his apartment on her own? These and many more questions ran through her mind and she felt flummoxed and did not know the answers to her own questions. Should she discuss her experience with her friend Wynne who may know some answers but would she know all? If she knew the answers did that mean she was woman-wise, too? She could not deny that she enjoyed his probing inside her; it made her feel excited. Whatever the answer that appeared in her mind she raised the question of that, too. So no solution came to her in finality. The only solution that came to her was sleep that overcame her at last.

Chapter 13

'Hullo everybody, hullo! Please do come in and enjoy your
selves. Nice to see Anne and you too Wynne. Where's
Tracey?'

Thus Joan welcomed her guests to celebrate her acceptance to
University.

'She should be along very soon, I believe. But congratulations,
Joan. We all wish you luck and great success in your new venture. It
looks as if you are going to be overcrowded here tonight, eh Joan?'
replied Wynne in a happy frame of mind looking over everybody to
see if there was anyone that she did not know.

'My parents have given me the run of the house and have gone out
so we can enjoy ourselves to the full and I hope that everyone does
just that,' responded Joan looking at all yet specifically at Wynne who
raised the question.

'Can I help in anything then, Joan?' asked Wynne.

'Sure you can, if Richard will let your arm go. Help everyone to a
drink if you would please, so that I can stay here for a while longer to
greet the others yet to come. And when the record has finished, turn
it over, or please replace it; there are a number of good records by the
gramo,' acquiesced Joan as she turned towards the door to greet yet
more company.

'Ah, Anne, so glad you have come. It would not be a party without
you. I presume this is Felicity that you have told me about. Welcome
aboard Felicity! I do hope you enjoy yourself here tonight,' added
Joan in a happy manner.

140

'Thank you for inviting me Joan. Anne has told me quite a bit about you – no – all good things so do not be alarmed. I wish you the best of luck in your University and hope you make the final grade, too. Looks like you are going to have a full house here tonight though, eh?' posed Felicity as she saw that the company was as she anticipated, full of fun and happy and light-hearted lads and lasses.

'Come on in,' said Joan as she then turned back to Felicity to thank her for her kind words of encouragement.

'Do come on in and help yourself,' Joan added to more comers as they piled into the house.

Fortunately, the house stood in its own grounds as a detached two-storey home of modern design. Although it was feasible that no one was on the upper floor, all the lights on that floor were fully on. This added to the brilliance of the house, too. Outside, little room remained for the latecomers' cars. They had to park on the kerbside for quite a distance from the house. Inside, the main rooms were opened up as one large hall by swinging back the folding doors. With prudence, Joan's parents had the foresight to have a lot of the furniture removed temporarily to the double garage so as to make more space for the throng, that by now had assembled.

It was difficult to hear one speak for the noise that emanated both from the loudspeaker playing a rhythmic record and the hubbub of the friends there. They all seemed to enjoy each other's company. Some sat together eating the prepared sandwiches or slices of cake with various drinks on offer. Others sat on the hallway steps telling jokes, or at least that is what it appeared to be by the raucous laughter that came from that area. Others seemed to find their enjoyment in being in close proximity to each other. Yet others roamed the upper floor of the house to find a nook so that a couple might get together.

'Hullo, Anne; you look lovely tonight,' said Angus as he espied Anne talking to Andrew and Tracey.

'Thank you for the compliment, Angus. You look happy yourself tonight, too, if I may say,' quipped Anne in reply hoping that he did not join their company as she still felt a slight animosity towards him.

'Would you care to join me for a drink, Anne?' asked Angus in a hopeful and askant tone and look.

'Just for a couple of minutes, then I must return. Will that be in order with you Angus?' answered Anne who looked charmingly at him yet hid her annoyance at the same time. With that, Angus took her elbow and led her to the table laden with a variety of liquid refreshments. He asked what she preferred and was told that orange juice would be fine. He poured her out one and gave her the drink requested. He himself availed of a small whisky. When both held their drinks he asked, 'I do hope that we can be friends again Anne?'

'I accepted the drink with you, Angus, so as to avoid embarrassing you in front of the others. I have already made it clear that I do not seek your company and please try and keep away. If you persist, then I will have to publicly say why I do not relish your company,' responded Anne in a terse manner that gave no room for mediation or argument.

'You do me an injustice, Anne. I have learned my lesson and paid the penalty. Had I have paid attention to your injunction, I would not be imploring you now, would I? So please let me plead with you to give me a second chance as I do really love you, Anne. With all the girls here tonight, I do not care for any; it's you I desire if you will but try again. I promise you will never have reason to be upset with me,' pleaded Angus who felt almost if he was on his knees to his Madonna.

'I appreciate what you say but you are attached to our host, Joan. If she gives you up and she tells me this, then I may reconsider. At the moment I do not feel like starting again as you make too many demands on one. So please let us be on friendly terms from a slight distance and let me go back to my other friends,' she replied with a slight smile on her lips that made him yell inside in frustration.

'I will put up with your conditions so long as I know that in the end you will be with me,' sighed Angus with a look of a torn-hearted man.

Instead of engaging in further conversation she put her half-emptied glass down and walked back to her friends that still stood on the same spot.

'Where's Felicity?' asked Anne when she returned to her companions.

Tracey was now with Richard and Wynne who replied to the question.

'Thought you may have seen her with Andrew as they went over to get a drink,' she said in a nonchalant manner as if to say, 'It is nothing to do with me or you.'

'Oh, I thought that Andy was with you, Tracey,' said Anne turning towards her as she spoke.

'Yes, we came together but we are both free agents. Can see nothing wrong in him going for a drink with a pal, now is there?' questioned Tracey with a mildly belligerent tone.

'No, Tracey; that's what I call true friendship and a good example of democracy,' answered Anne in a quiet voice without trace of the surprise she felt.

'Do you really want a drink or would you like to explore the house upstairs?' asked Andrew as he led Felicity towards the drink table.

'Well, perhaps we can take a peep upstairs then have the drink after. I must say this is a nice house; what do you say?' asked Felicity of Andrew as they walked towards the table.

In a gentlemanly manner, Andrew took Felicity's arm and walked her upstairs. He opened the first door on the hall landing and there to their amusement they both observed that another couple was in the room in a somewhat compromising position.

Both of them giggled and speculated on the outcome of what they saw. They approached the next door that again was closed. Andrew turned the knob and with a bit of discretion this time, put his head round into the room to see if that too was occupied. Felicity pushed close to him so that she too could take a peep into the room. There on a very large bed lay two couples in a disarray in their clothing. One could only hazard a guess what they were up to, but as quietly as they opened the door so they closed it. Both of them gave another giggle and a smirk. They approached the third door and without surprise found this again occupied by a couple enjoying the bliss of lovemaking. The next door they opened was the bathroom. Even here was a couple in a hug! So they approached the next door as Andrew said, 'It looks as if we should have made a reservation for a bed here tonight. What do you think Felicity?'

'Perhaps Joan could have given out half-hour vouchers so that everyone can have a turn that wants a turn. That would be a splendid idea. But why should you bother? We are not here for that purpose,' she added knowing full well that before long she too would be in clutches of passion that she longed for. After all, he was a handsome man and seemed to be well-heeled, too. That was always an attraction to her. Seeing the others gave her an inward urge that even surprised her.

'Let us find accommodation first then we will try the room for size,' he replied as he tried the next door in turn. To their pleasure they found the small room unoccupied. It was a maid's type of room: neat, clean and sparse, with but a single bed, small wardrobe and dressing table to match. Without hesitation, he drew her to the bed and set her down. As she sat down there looking up at him, he divested himself of his jacket and without any embarrassment, unbuttoned his fly, then sat alongside her.

'Would you like to take it out for a while whilst I undo your blouse?' ventured Andrew as he set about unbuttoning her blouse.

She did not remonstrate about his approach to her blouse but asked, 'You are very confident that I would like to hold you. What makes you think that I wish to? Then that would only be a prelude to sex, now wouldn't it, Andy?'

'Sex will be welcome but has to be at your asking. So let us act as adults and take hold of it for me, please,' he added as he took her hand and drew it towards himself and inveigled her fingers in the area of his crotch. She did not hesitate but probed her hand within and withdrew his manhood. During this episode, he had already extracted both her breasts and was merrily sucking away at them to her delight.

Whilst he suckled her breasts, he permitted his hand to wander to the hem of her dress. Without opposition, he walked his fingers upwards until he reached an area both of tightness and heat. He relaxed her breasts so that he could speak.

'Felicity, please do not be awkward but open up for me,' he pleaded with her without looking in her direction as he bent forward immediately to start the cycle of sucking again.

By spontaneous movement she moved her knee so that he could reach her private parts more readily, which he did. First one finger entered then a second later; it felt to her that most of his hand was probing her. By the motion he created and the moisture that came swimming there, she felt an aura of bliss. After a few minutes of this, he asked her if she was going to ask him for sex.

'Please understand, Andy, that hole you are after is my holy hole and you nor anyone else is going to enter, so be content with what you have received,' she continued, 'and I think it is time we closed the shop and returned to the party, otherwise we will be getting questions asked.' And as she spoke, she withdrew her hand from holding him, and with that free hand pulled at his arm that was under her dress and extracted it, so that she was free from his attention. She then with a little struggle got off the bed and stood up. Then, as if by spontaneous motion, he too arose from the sitting position, but took her in his arms and hugged her saying, 'Felicity, I must say you are marvellous but just do one thing for me before we go down, will you?' he said in her ear as he held her close to himself.

'What would that be, Andy?' queried Felicity, yet she suspected what his request would be.

'Take hold of it again to relieve me; then I will happily come down with you,' he said in a semi-pleading voice.

'Sorry, but I'm finished for the day. You can take it out and finish it. I do not mind, and I will go down the whilst you are at it!' she said in a humorous tone with a stifled laugh.

'Please don't be so wicked. It is better if you hold it then I will enjoy the shoot all the better,' he again pleaded and as he did so took it out himself and at the same time extracted a handkerchief out of his back pocket. Having accomplished this, he then took one of her hands that held no resistance, and placed the fingers around it and at the same time moved her hand over it in a soothing backward and forward motion.

She felt the increase in size as she manipulated it until she felt it throbbing. Then he almost strangled her with the terrific hug he gave her, as he rained slobbering kisses upon her. After a few minutes both he and his rod subsided at which point he relaxed and let her go.

'Felicity, you are a brick and a good sport. Thanks for everything. We will have to get together one day as I have truly enjoyed your frank company,' he said with a smile across his face that spoke volumes.

'That's fine, but let us get down and get that drink. We had better be truthful and say that we have been looking over the house, hence the time we have taken, eh?' she said as she made the first move towards the door.

'Hullo, Licy; where have you been? I have been looking for you and lost you?' said Anne as she observed Felicity walking towards her holding a drink in her hand.

'I went for a drink with Andrew but the table was so impossible to reach from the crowd that we took the opportunity to wander over the house and have a look-see,' lied Licy with a blush that Anne noticed.

'Then is that your second or third drink, Licy?' questioned Anne as she looked at her friend with a question in her eye.

'What makes you say that? This is my first, of course?' responded Licy wondering why she had been asked that question as she did not realise that the colour of her cheeks prompted the challenge.

'Because you look flushed as if you have either had a lot to drink or been in a clinch with Andrew; so which is it Licy?' asked Anne in a quiet yet stern tone. Anne noted that as soon as she had said that, that Licy's face went deeper red that gave rise to Anne's further specula- tion.

'Hullo, you two. I have searched all over for you, Anne!' said Jack as he came and stood in front of the two friends.

'We have been talking here for the last few minutes, haven't we, Anne?' replied Felicity thankful of the timely escape.

'Then I do hope you do not mind if I take Anne for a drink?' asked Jack as he took her arm and moved away from Felicity.

Anne's face was still a little clouded and said to Jack that he had come at the wrong moment as she was expecting an answer from Licy as to where she had been for the last half-hour.

'I think I can answer that for you. I saw her going upstairs with Andrew a while ago. Would you like to wander up there also?' asked Jack. Without awaiting her reply, he led her by the elbow towards and up the stairs.

As they reached the upper hallway, a couple not known to either of them came out of one of the rooms in a hilarious mood of laughter.

'Must be something very funny in there, so let's have a look,' said Jack in mock innocence yet he knew instinctively what the couple had been up to. With that he moved with her to the door which had been left ajar and they both entered.

'Well, it's just a bedroom so what made them laugh so much. Can you tell me that Jack?' asked Anne also in feigned innocence.

'Would you like to come out laughing too? Then let's move to the bed and try it for size,' responded Jack as he led her towards the bed then sitting down he pulled her down besides himself, too.

She did not observe that he had, in sitting down, undone his flies, for as he turned towards her to hug her at the same time he moved her hand downwards until she became aware that she was touching flesh. She remembered the previous occasion when they were in very close proximity and he got her to hold him to his satisfaction. Then she remembered that her Licy had been missing for a long time and now she knew she had been up here with Andrew and probably doing as she was, too. So if Licy can, then she can play, too! So much to Jack's pleasure and surprise, she held it as he had asked without any injunctions.

'Ah, there you are, Licy. I understand that you had been upstairs with Andy in a bedroom. Is that true?' queried Anne as she spoke to her friend after she had returned downstairs. She had not been very long herself upstairs as Jack in his apprehension of fear that she would terminate any lovemaking, had reached his climax much too soon even for both of them. He knew in his mind that if he could see her homewards after the party that he would be able to repeat the performance again, but in a more leisurely fashion, so that both would get full satisfaction.

Felicity blushed a very strong carmine colour that spoke for her. She was asked a question and she could either turn her back on her and walk away and thus lose a beautiful lover that was constant with her and long lasting, or admit the truth.

'Anne, I feel guilty. Please forgive me but I have been in the bedroom with Andy and he attempted to seduce me but I refused to permit it. I am so sorry; do say you forgive me my dear?' pleaded Felicity as she looked at her friend with sorrowful eyes.

'Then if he attempted that he must have had it out. So what exactly happened – the truth please?' demanded Anne in a very stern authoritarian voice.

147

'He probed me with his fingers and I held it for him,' answered Felicity almost in a whisper. She turned to look at Anne and was very upset to see that the look in her face was unrelenting.

'Licy, please understand, I am already sharing you with Norman who came before me, so I must accept that. Now if you want me too, it must be alone and not shared with any Tom, Dick or Harry. I will overlook this discretion if you give me your word, as I am very jealous for you and as you know I love you too much to share,' she answered in a hushed tone with both sternness and pleading.

'Darling, I will do anything for you, as you know. So please forgive my transgression. But jealousy?'

'Jealousy is no more than feeling alone among smiling enemies! Yes, I accept your word that we are for us alone. And to show our feelings, please join me to find a quiet corner, if possible, so that we can kiss and make up; come my love,' answered Anne in full earnestness of desire as she half pulled Licy along with her.

It was not easy with the crowd, but they managed after a while to give each other the kiss that seemed to heal the breach between them.

Chapter 14

'Sir John Cuthbertson, sir,' announced the junior, as he showed that gentleman into Mr Meredith's room.

'Oh, do come on in, John,' responded Mr Meredith as he stood up to greet his friend and client. He added that he should be seated as he walked over to his drinks cabinet and asked his visitor what he would enjoy?

'Just a small scotch, Norman, please. How are you these days? Do not see much of you at the Club nowadays,' came the reply.

Mr Meredith walked over to his visitor with the drink in his hand which he placed with care on the desk in front of him then replied, 'Sorry, not had time to visit the Club of late as we have been so pressed with work. Am otherwise quite fit and by the look of you, you are too, eh, John?'

'Yes Norm, I keep myself pretty fit with a round of golf every other day. Do try to come to the Club for a chat, as it is not proper to visit a professional man and take up his time with non-business talk, now is it ol' boy?' said his visitor.

'Your sentiments are really appreciated. I also wish many of my other friends and clients would act that way. Then I would have time to visit the Club more often. Now why are you concerned with change of personnel that I will be sending to you to do your audit, John?' questioned Mr Meredith as he looked at his visitor, wishing that he too could take the time off as frequently as for a round or two of golf.

'Well, though I may still be young, I like to keep the same people around me and watch them grow old! But you have indicated that the senior that you would be sending is a young girl. Now that is whom I should like to see! I feel somewhat apprehensive that you should propose a girl, but had I not known you, I would reject her out of hand. But obviously you must have confidence in her capabilities, otherwise you would not be sending her out on these assignments. So have her brought in so that I can see for myself what and who she is,' instructed Sir John.

'First let me tell you that she is an exceptional worker. She is both speedy and accurate. She is also very loyal to this firm. She has offers of posts everywhere I send her, but she automatically declines! And she only takes instructions from me, and takes no orders from anyone else! You will find her a good disciplinarian too. Now what else would you like to know?' asked Mr Meredith with a hidden smile.

'Just send her in. You have painted a beautiful picture so shall expect an ugly ducklin',' replied Sir John, who wore a smile that said surprises were not new to him.

'Anne, would you please come in right away as I wish to introduce you to a client that you are to attend,' summoned Mr Meredith into the mouthpiece of the intercom. He heard her affirmative response and hung up and sat back to await her arrival.

She was a little put out by this request as she was in the midst of a trying job that needed all her concentration. But she had never yet refused a request from the boss when he called for her. After all, he was the boss! So Anne gave instructions to her assistants not to touch or tamper with her papers and left the office to walk to Mr Meredith's.

Anne tapped on the door and in her custom, entered without awaiting a call to do so. She saw a man of perhaps nearing forty sitting facing her boss, but who turned to watch her enter. He had a full head of wavy hair, a clean-shaven face that shone with a broad smile. A very nice pinstriped suit adorned him that spelled Saville Row. She also observed that his smile broadened still more as she entered. He rose from his seat and held the back of the chair inviting her to the seat.

Anne advanced another pace and asked her boss what it was that he desired and stood looking towards him ignoring Sir John who still stood there holding the chair for her.

'Ah, Anne, I would like to introduce you to Sir John Cuthbertson whom you are to attend for audit next week,' and turning towards Sir John he added, 'This is Miss Anne Hopkins, Sir John, whom I discussed with you earlier.'

With that, Anne stepped forward and, with her right hand outstretched to take Sir John's hand, said, 'Pleased to meet you, sir.'

'Do sit down, Miss Hopkins. May I call you Anne too?' he posed as he stared at her with interest.

'Thank you, sir,' she replied as she took the offered chair, after looking towards her boss and getting his nod; then sat down and continued, 'Yes, you may address me as Anne, but only in here, if you please', and looking again at her boss, asked if there was anything special that he wanted.

'No, I do not need you but thought it prudent to call you in so that you may meet Sir John. Perhaps he may wish to ask you a question or two?' so turning towards his visitor he gave him a quizzical look.

'Well, I am very pleased to have the opportunity to meet you here, as I fear I may have doubted you if you had arrived at my place and said you had come to attend our books. You look much younger than I expected and I also expected an ugly ducklin' and you are far from that!' he said as his mirthful eyes bore into her.

'I am sorry if I have disappointed you, sir. But I hope my work will compensate you for that misconception, and if you would like to know anything else, please feel free to ask,' she added wondering why he sat glued to her with his eyes.

Without taking his eyes off her he said, 'It is my delight to have met you, Anne. I look forward to your visit soon. You may leave us now,' he added then turned towards her boss.

Anne remained in her chair and turned towards Mr Meredith and asked if he needed her for anything else. He indicated that there was nothing else to detain her, so she rose and bid the visitor 'goodbye, sir' and left.

'Did you observe that, Sir John? She did not leave when you asked her to but asked me first! That is what I told you. She only takes orders from me,' he said with a grin of super satisfaction on his face.

'Well, I must say she's a beaut. I did not expect such a girl in an office. She should be modelling or something. You are a lucky guy to have such a lovely female around the place. Now I can believe you when you say other clients have offered to take her on. Frankly, I would make the same offer if it was any good, but obviously, you are wise to hold on to something so attractive and as good as you say she is. But can she really do the work, that's what I would like to be assured?' asked Sir John.

'Sir John, she is a jewel and not only enhances the place but can do the work of two of my lads here. So far I have only had praise for her ability wherever she has been sent. You will find her excellent in her work and a very strict disciplinarian, as I have already said; there is no monkey business with her either. She is straight, so be warned,' he added thinking of his own opportunities that were yet to come.

'Then what, my dear friend, would bend her straightness; I could do with someone like her around all day. I would not need to go either to the Club or bother with golf!' he emphasised as he pondered on having that luscious creature on his knee. He could not concentrate on the reply he heard as he pondered yet more on the lovely attractive slim well-balanced female that had just left the room. What would he not give for a night with her – he was already planning a strategy for the time she called on his establishment. He came out of his reverie with apologies to his friend for not paying attention to what he was saying, but his mind was absorbed by that lovely creature. He asked if he had had any hanky-panky with her.

'Sir John, if you would like a slap in the face, just try it and see. I told you she was straight and there's no nonsense with her either. As far as I am concerned, I would not risk losing her to try playing the fool with her, so be warned!' he lied as he knew that she would be a willing partner with him. At least he anticipated that after his conversation with Felicity which he determined would be concluded very soon, as he too wanted an affair with Anne desperately himself. And why should he not? Everyone else wanted to.

'Thanks for the tip. It reminds me of the old saying, *Brigands demand your money or your life; women require both*, and I suspect that your Anne would be just like that too.

'Twill be a lucky guy that gets her I think,' he posed as he began to look glum at the thought of someone else capturing such a prize and not him.

'Hullo, Licy darling. Come and kiss me,' said Norman Meredith as he entered her flat with his own key. He came with a small bouquet of flowers and a box of chocolates that he put on the side-table as he walked towards her. She walked into his open arms and was happy to observe that he was with a full smiling face. She knew that he had come to discuss Anne apart from his anticipated love scene with her.

'Thank you, Norman, for the gifts. They are appreciated. You look happy tonight and I hope you go home like that, too. But you look as if you are dieing to tell me something, so out with it whilst I pour you a drink,' she said as she led him to be seated on the cushioned settee.

'Well, you know I am always happy to be with you, Licy. You do try to make me happy and that is appreciated. And I hope we can come to some sort of arrangement about Anne. But before we discuss that, I must tell you that I had Sir John Cuthbertson in and introduced him to Anne who is to attend his firm for audit. He was stunned with her manner and beauty. I think she could capture him for the asking, so be warned. We may yet be both the losers!' he speculated but still with a happy smile. He held out his hand to take the proffered drink that Licy offered him as she sat down alongside him.

'Let me tell you, Norman, she is taking over. I fear that whatever we may agree she may not. She has emerged from her cloister, or is it oyster, and is assuming the role of the senior even with me! So do you still wish to discuss how we share you knowing what we do? But tell me more about Sir John,' she added.

'As I've said, he was stunned with her. To crown it, I warned him that she only takes instructions from me and what do you know – when he offered her a chair she asked me first, then when he told her she might leave, she again asked me first before she left. He was lost for words and then began to think aloud that he would like to have her. She seems to capture them all so I think there is something in what you say. We will have to be careful how we play the game otherwise we will be the worse off in the end. So please, Licy, let me ask her myself, and go from there. We can spend the whole evening discussing and planning and then she can throw them overboard just like that,' he said with a click of his thumb and forefinger. 'So let me try my hand with her. If I succeed you will know and then we can plan what we shall do,' he added as he looked into her eyes with a pleading and desiring smile.

'Norman, please be careful. I am afraid that we may put her off. As you know, I have taught her a lot as she was truly innocent when she first came here. Don't go getting her pregnant as that will be more than I can take!' she spoke with a glint of dread in her voice as well as near jealousy that was a new thought with her.

'Darling, you know I'm infertile, so there is no chance that she could become pregnant. But from what you have told me she will not allow anyone near to her there or has she changed her views on that since we last discussed it?' he asked with strong thoughts of the near future when he would test his prowess with Anne.

'You have always maintained your infertility, but how can you tell after all these years? You know full well that things can and do change, not always for the worse either I am happy to say,' evoked Felicity feeling the pangs of jealousy after all at the thought that Anne may yet have an affair with her lover.

'You have not agreed with me yet. Do I get your OK to try her direct, or do you wish to talk about it first?' posed Norman looking at her with a large question mark across his forehead.

'Oh well, there is no harm in you trying the direct approach. I suppose I had better warn her that is what we agreed should she ask. What if Sir John also tries his luck with her, too? What then? I am sure she will tell me if that happens,' added Felicity with her mind running riot at the thought that this conjured up.

'Good! That's agreed then. So now let us get to bed.' And with that he arose from the settee and taking her by the arm led her to the bedroom.

'Do you know, Licy, I feel more at home here in this flat then in my own home. I really enjoy my stay here. I hope that you feel the same too, or am I trying to you?' asked Anne when they had arrived at Felicity's flat that evening.

'Darling Anne. How can you think that I do not wish you here? I look forward to our night together all the week. The day does not come soon enough for me! You are here now, so please kiss me then we can eat.' And with that, they hugged each other and allowed their hands to roam a little.

'Now tell me what has been decided between you and Norman? Am I to be concubine or something. How do you feel sharing him with me, that is if I share him, and by the way, I have a message to visit him tomorrow before home time. Do you know about that Licy?' asked Anne as they each held a glass of sherry in their hand.

'You ask too many questions all at once. I will try and answer, but if I miss one out, then remind me. The reason that he wishes to see you may be, and I said may be, that he is going to ask you for your responses. He is keen on having you as the saying goes. It is entirely up to you if you let him have anything. As far as he knows, we just play but as women and not as man and woman. Now does that answer all your questions, Anne darling?' answered Felicity.

'Have I got to do anything to keep my job or is that up to me? I am not too keen of having an affair with him, so what shall I do, Licy dear?' questioned Anne as she looked into her face to see if that gave her a clue of the action she should take.

'My love, as far as your job is concerned, I think I can say that you are safe as safe can be. I think he would stop immediately if you told him you would be leaving him. He is very keen but also prudent. I will not interfere, Anne. If you would like him to play with you or go further, that is up to you. So if you are thinking of getting anything out of him like a flat, I do not think you would have a problem. He would give you anything you asked; that's the hold you have over him. But be careful whatever you do. Do not spoil a good thing,' returned Felicity.

'Do you really mean what you say. That sounds as he must be in love with me if he would do anything I asked! Surely he's not in love now is he?' pondered Anne with a look of doubt in her expression.

'Whether he is in love with you or not, I cannot say, but he will do anything for you and that's certain. He has had to fight off a few of our clients that have asked for you and you are aware of that, I know. Why not just have a petting session and let him touch you. That may please him,' proposed Felicity wondering just what to advise.

'I would like a flat, but I feel that is a bit too soon, as I do not wish to leave home just yet. I have given my mother a surprise when I gave her her monthly moneys. I gave her exactly double the usual and she thought that I had made a mistake, but I told her that my increase in pay will stand for that. Now if I had a flat too, I would not be able to afford to give my mother that much, now would I?' posed Anne.

'Do not worry about money, my love. You just tell him how much you want and I warrant you will get it and, possibly, more too. It will not come in your pay packet, but he will let you have anything you ask. Just you say that you saw a lovely dress in the store and could not afford it, and I guarantee he will pull out his wallet,' advised Felicity as Anne looked up towards her in wonderment of what she had just uttered.

'But how will you feel if I start playing around with him though?' queried Anne.

'I will feel exactly as you feel right now knowing that Norman and I have an affair going. I am not happy that I will be sharing you, but then I had him before you came on the scene. And if I could throw him over and just have you, that would make me very happy as I know it would you too,' pouted Felicity.

'I do not know what to do, Licy. I do not really want a liaison with him, but also feel that I owe him so much. Who else would have given me the opportunity that he has. Perhaps, when I have inveigled a flat out of him with a further raise in pay, then I will play around with him. But just now I will do what I can to avoid a compromise. Do you think that would be prudent, Licy my sweet?' posed Anne as she looked up to her friend.

'As I have told you, he will do anything you ask. If you tell him to lay off, he will. If you play with him, you make the rules. Do not be alarmed about your job. It is secure and if you ever left, a number of our clients will be fighting to get you onto their payroll. Now that's enough talk about Norm; let's get to bed, darling,' answered Felicity as she rose up and helped Anne to do so and they both walked to the bedroom and closed the door after them.

'Do you know, Wynne, this has been the longest couple of days that I can remember?' said Richard with a very happy smile on his face as he came forward to meet and greet her again. He looked into her eyes, the bluest he had ever seen. Her face was a picture to behold.

156

With a slight and gentle touch of colour to the cheeks she looked ravishing and more than ever desirable. Her close-fitting costume accentuated her natural slim figure to its best advantage. He felt enraptured over her and wanted to grab her in the open public view and hug her forever.

'Strange that you should say that, Richard,' replied Wynne as she looked demurely towards him. 'I too have been counting the hours. Why do you think that we are both that keen to get together?' she added as she realised that he appeared to be wearing a new suit or at least it had that appearance. It suited him so smartly as well as the accessories, too.

'It may be because we are made for each other, my dear Wynne,' replied Richard to the question as he raised the same question in his own mind. 'Yes, that's right. I have been thinking long and hard about her and perhaps my desire to be in her company and that I found the waiting time a trial must mean that I want her. Do I want her just for lovemaking or do I want her for more – that is a question my mind will have to spell out and very soon.'

'Well then, let's make the most of it. So where are you taking me tonight, Richard?' questioned Wynne as she looked into his face and only saw what she wanted to – love blossoming!

'I have been invited to fetch you to Andrew's flat. Tracey will be there too, so shall we?' he proposed as he took her by the arm and led her to his car.

'Come on in, you two,' said Andrew as he opened the door to his two friends. He shook Richard by the hand but with Wynne, he put his arm around her and gave her a gentle kiss on the lips which she reciprocated. Richard walked into the lounge where he observed Tracey getting up off the settee as he came towards her. They acknowledged each other and kissed lightly as he had observed Andrew had done.

'Now this is very nice and cosy to have you all here. So what would you like to drink for a start?' he queried as he walked towards the drink cabinet. Both Wynne and Richard gave their request that he supplied. Tracey did not make a request – he knew exactly what she would appreciate and which he poured out for her.

157

'Let's leave the girls alone for a while, Richard – you come in with me to the kitchen and give me a hand', and with that he rose up and looking towards Richard moved towards the kitchen door. He entered the kitchen followed by his companion.

'You look a blaze of colour, ol' boy,' said Andrew, when they had reached the portals of the kitchen. 'Are you in love?' he added.

'Frankly, I do not know but feel very much so. But does it show that much, really?' quipped Richard somewhat taken aback to learn that his heart was visible to all to see.

'Do you wish to test it then?' posed Andrew with a broad smile on his face. 'Because that's easy. I will call Tracey in to help, and as she comes in, I will walk out and leave her to you. Then you will have Tracey on your own whilst I will have your lady-love Wynne to myself, too. You play as long as you like and I will do the same. We will then know if our feelings are good or indifferent. Shall we try?' he asked with still more devilment in his manner.

'I do not really like the idea. What if Tracey allows me to do things; how would you feel? How do you think I may feel if Wynne allows you to mess about with her in here!' answered Richard in query and doubt.

'Well, let us try and see,' suggested Andrew, then added as an afterthought. 'If we both get snubbed we will know our true love to be. But if one or both responds to our play, then we will learn from that, too. So shall we call Tracey in then?' asked Andrew.

'All right then, call her and I will tell her that we have decided to swap! That will be OK with you, I hope?' posed Richard who felt some apprehension of the scheme ahead. He did not object to trying his luck with Tracey but did not relish the thought of Andrew interfering with 'his' Wynne.

Andrew called Tracey who came into the kitchen, and as she entered he walked out towards Wynne on the settee.

'Can I sit beside you, Wynne?' asked Andrew in an innocent manner.

'Well, it's your home, so how can I object?' answered Wynne somewhat puzzled. So without further ado, he sat down and without invitation, put his arm around her shoulders and drew her towards himself. As he did so, he turned her head to face him and placed his lips onto hers. He drew her into a strong hug and although she kissed in return, it was not given freely but more by compulsion.

'Now, what are you up to Andrew?' asked Wynne who eventually managed to untangle herself from his embrace.

'We have decided to change partners for the night. I hope we can be happy together, Wynne,' posed Andrew as he looked into her face and at the same time feeling a sudden desire attack him, that made his statement more true than he bargained for. Without realising it, he allowed his hand to wander towards her skirt which he tried to lift.

She did not appear to object to his hand touching her, but as soon as his fingers touched her skin above the stocking line, she gave him a violent push that made him lose his balance and he found himself on the floor beside her.

'Now why did you do that, Wynne?' he asked in a hurt tone.

'Because I permitted you to kiss me and hold me it does not give you the right to poke me about. The fact that this is your flat gives you a little privilege, but it does not give you rights over your guests, so please behave, Andrew,' answered Wynne somewhat concerned at the happening.

'What do you think is happening in the kitchen, my sweet. He has by now probably had his fun all the way, I bet!' he exclaimed with a glint in his eye more of wishful thinking than of expecting it to be true. As he finished speaking he again put his arm around her and once again drew her towards himself, and again indulged in a kissing session.

'Now what shall I do and what shall I believe?' thought Wynne as she allowed the second attack on her to proceed. 'How can Richard do this to me? I thought that he was in love with me? And what is he doing with Tracey in there? Is he really having it off with her? But I am in love with him, so what shall I do? And whilst she was in thought, she did not appear to be alive to what was going on around her. Without her realising it, Andrew had his fingers where she had told him not to. Her mind was so taken up in troubled thought, that she forgot herself. She just lay there as if asleep without any feelings as to what was transpiring. Suddenly, she became awake and alive to what was going on by Andrew's probing. As soon as she realised that she had submitted without her basic knowledge or acquiescence, she jumped and pushed simultaneously and freed herself from further

159

attack. She stood up and straightened her dress and told Andrew that she found his behaviour reprehensible and did not believe that Richard was doing what he suggested.

'I am sorry, my dear,' answered Andrew as he recognised that the plan as far as he was concerned had failed. 'Why not go into the kitchen and see for yourself?' he added with a questioning look.

Without answering him, Wynne moved over to the kitchen door and with a slight hesitation, flung it open. She felt a temper arise in her of the conduct of the evening so far, and was expecting the worse as she peered into the kitchen. She nearly fell over in her burst of laughter that she emitted. There was Richard and Tracey enjoying a coffee sitting opposite each other at the small table.

'Well I never!' Wynne exclaimed as she walked into the kitchen. She too sat down and poured herself a coffee from the pot, and turning to Tracey and Richard, asked them if they were party to the subterfuge.

'I did not know of the plan until I came in here,' replied Tracey, who continued, 'Your lover here just gave me a cuddle and a kiss and said it was not being honest and could not do anything even though he admitted he would have liked to, had he been with me before going out with you; so you can have him back Wynny.'

'I'll say again, well I never. We have been waiting for you two to come out of the kitchen whilst we have been sitting in the lounge, wondering on what you two have been up to. All we have done is talk and talk some more,' lied Wynne with a straight face.

'That's right, all we did is talk. She would not even allow me to cuddle her!' echoed Andrew who embellished the lie.

The evening passed off pleasantly with much laughter over the plan that did not come to fruition. They speculated various possibilities of what may have happened and of what could have happened. The only conclusion they arrived at, was that all four of them were lucky in their partners. So the time arrived for Wynne to be escorted home by Richard. They made their adieus and left together leaving Tracey to follow at her will.

'Anne, do please come in' requested Mr Meredith over the intercom. He had determined to discuss the prospects of an alliance with Anne as it was some time since he promoted her, and despite his discussion with Felicity, nothing had so far been achieved. Anne entered his room without a courtesy knock.

'You wished to see me, Norman?' she asked as she walked towards him with a pleasant smile. She did not stop at the chair in front of the desk but as her habit had become of late, she walked behind the desk and bent forward and gave her boss a peck on the cheek.

'Now that was nice,' he responded and at the same moment grabbed her hand, so that she stood over him. As she straightened up, he too stood up but still holding her hand. He put her hand over his crotch and held her still tighter there.

'Do you remember that you did this to me on the first occasion, and that was about three months ago, and since then you have not been near enough. So please, Anne, when can we get together?' asked her boss in a pleading tone yet with a slight sternness.

'My dear Norm, you know that you have piled a lot of work onto me and I have not let you down, now have I?' retorted Anne as she released herself and walked to the other side of the desk and sat down. She looked up at her boss with a pleasant smile that made him all the more eager.

'Anne, I am fully aware of the load that you have capably carried. I am more than delighted in your progress. But that is always during working hours of the day. So what do you say that you join me this evening for a meal?' he replied with as sweet a smile that he could muster.

'Next time I look for a job, I will check that the boss of the firm is a misogynist. Would that be a proper question to ask Norm?' she added with a broad smile that he felt infectious. For he smiled at the thought that an applicant came into him and asked that impertinent question.

'Anne, my dear, you know for certain that I for one am not a hater of women. And I can vouch that if I did have that fault it would not include you,' he answered with a gleeful expression and continued, 'but if you have not said that you would join me, so can I accept that you will?' and he looked across at her with a declaration of desire.

'I am not going to lie that I have a date for tonight so I will happily. But where to, please?'

'Now that's very pleasant to hear. I will meet you in the car park and I will take you to the Eastbury Hotel where they present their food in the most delightful way. Moreover, you will find that you will not better the service anywhere in London. Although when you get used to eating there, I will arrange an account for you. How would that be, my dear?' he said as he looked into her eyes with his passion becoming alive. How could he contain himself, that was the thought that was running through his mind as he watched her with undiminished relish!

'That's agreed then. It does mean that I will not be able to get home to change and I do not feel like going to the Eastbury in my working clothes. So can I meet you there at say an hour, or perhaps I should make it two hours, after leaving the office, Norm. Is there anything else as I have a lot to do before I can leave for dinner, Norm?' she replied.

'Just one thing, Anne, my dear. You invariably kiss me when you come into this room. Would you not like to do the same as you left the room and at the same time pat me you know where?' he replied as he looked at her in hope that she would agree. And much to his pleasure and not quite surprise, Anne arose from her seat and went over to her boss and as she bent forwards to kiss him she placed her palm again over him.

'So glad you made it and that you are here now,' said Mr Meredith as he approached Anne as she entered the foyer of the hotel. He noted that she was well-wrapped up, for the weather was decidedly chilly. He continued, 'I've only been here a couple of minutes, but it seems longer waiting for you. So do come on through and let's get your coat over to the cloakroom, then we can go through to the restaurant. A welcome kiss first, eh?' and as he spoke he placed both his arms over her shoulders and gently drew her towards himself and kissed her full on the lips. Anne reciprocated happily, then disengaged themselves and then both walked toward the cloakroom.

'How did you enjoy that feast, my dear. Could you have had better anywhere else, eh?' chirped Mr Meredith as they sat opposite each other after the waiter had cleared their table.

162

'Norm, you are right in what you promised. It was a fine meal in all ways. In fact I'd call it a feast. Ah, here's our waiter again.'

'Your coffee has been laid out as per your request, sir, if you would care to go up now,' said the waiter as he looked towards the boss.

'Thanks, Tony,' he replied and then turned towards Anne and said, 'Our coffee has been prepared and laid out upstairs, so let us go up, my dear.' And as he said that, he arose from his chair and went round to assist Anne from her chair, and holding on to her arm, led her to the elevator. Without question, Anne followed and entered the lift and made their exit on the fifth floor. Still holding on to her arm and chatting away aimlessly, he walked her along the corridor to the door number five and with the key that he produced, entered the room. She noted that it was a suite and not just a bedroom as she first suspected it would be. A table had been laid by the window with beautiful china, coffee on a simmerer, various pastries and chocolate mints and champagne at the side in an ice bucket.

'Well, my dear, what do you think of this layout especially for you, eh?' asked Mr Meredith as he surveyed the table which reached his satisfaction.

'I think it really fine and I am really dry enough to enjoy a nice coffee and mint, so shall I pour out, Norm?' she asked and without waiting for his reply, began to pour out the coffees.

'Yes, by all means, please pour out whilst I take off my jacket. I would suggest that you loosen up as it is very warm in here.'

As he said that, he divested himself of his jacket and then removed his tie and loosened his shirt buttons. Then turning towards Anne, he began to undo her blouse buttons and attempted to remove the garment.

'Norm, you have not locked the door, so please do that first,' added Anne as she herself removed her blouse knowing that would be what he would ask her to do in any case. When he turned round towards her, having inserted the key into the door, he saw her standing in front of him in her skirt and bra. He invited her to sit, and handing her a coffee and offering her a mint, they just sat and sipped and engaged in general conversation. After a glass or two of champagne and still more coffee, he asked her to take his trousers off and then take her skirt off too. Without any hesitation, she got off her chair and approached him and undid the buttons and belt buckle of his trousers and yanked them off, and then asked him to take off her skirt in retaliation. This he did with gusto and surprise, as he had anticipated a struggle of wills!

'Let's go into the other room, my love,' suggested Norman as he took her arm and led her willingly towards the bedroom. He closed the door after them and approached the bed, and together they sat down on it.

'Norm, let me make one thing clear before we start. I will happily play with you, but the moment you try to put it in, I will leave you where you are. Can we agree on that?' she pouted as she pulled at his underpants to remove them.

'Whatever you say. I will let you be the boss here; how would that please you?' he suggested as he took her pants off too, then put his arm around her to undo her bra that came off without any difficulty.

So there they sat for a long moment looking at each other, she looking at his rod becoming extended as he ogled her shapely breasts and small fluff of pubic hairs. He could not contain himself any longer so he pushed her gently backwards onto the bed and lay alongside her, and began to move his hand all over her. He took his mouth away from her ear where he whispered for her to play with him and moved it down and took her nipple into his mouth and began to rotate it with his tongue to her delight. In reply, she grabbed at him and held it in such a tight grip that made him ask her to ease off a bit.

'Darling,' said Mr Meredith in an ecstasy of emotion, 'if you will not let me place it in you, then you will not object to me putting it between your beautiful breasts.' And as he spoke he moved up on her, so that her head was now in line with his belly button. He then lay his length between the two breasts and asked her to close them up as tight as she could onto him. This she did and found that with his motion that went up then down it almost reached her mouth at times. She was at that moment very tempted to take it and suck it dry, but she refrained and allowed him to exercise himself. With foresight, though uncertain, he had prepared a towel in readiness at the pillow that he soon found the need of. His excitement on ejaculation seemed to know no bounds, as he went into raptures that surprised Anne. She was indeed very pleased that he did show his emotions, as

164

that emphasised that she had given satisfaction. Then suddenly, without warning, as he presumably had finished, he swung round so that he now had his head at her feet and as she lay with her legs slightly apart, he put his head between them and with his tongue entered her. It was not very many minutes before Anne went into raptures of thrilling delight at the emotional effect of the probing below. As she reached an orgasm, she placed her two legs around his neck and drew him towards herself. She had to exercise extreme care to avoid his rod that was around her face all the time he was probing her below. Although he was spent, she knew by now that she could if she so desired, arouse his passion again. She pondered on to whether to or not? 'To take it in would' she thought, 'be too soon in their arrangement,' so she moved her head slightly aside to avoid its temptation. After all, they had stripped on the first occasion together, what else could he expect? 'I feel sure he will enjoy my efforts to please him.' Then a thought occurred to her of her Licy. Should she tell her and possibly upset her or perhaps she would discuss that with Norman first. In the meanwhile Norman was giving her a lot of satisfaction, too. She opined that she enjoyed his tongue probe for some intangible reason more than that of Licy's. She reflected that with Licy, both did the same at the same time, whereas now it was just her getting all the fun!

'My darling, Anne,' said Norman as they both rose from the bed to straighten themselves up, 'you were marvellous tonight and I cannot thank you enough. You have captured me at work and now you have captured me in bed. I am so happy with you that I will give you anything that you want – so if there is – you just ask and it will be yours,' he added as he looked at her beautiful figure standing in front of him in the motion of bending down to recover her clothes that had slipped off the bed. Her firm breasts gave him the desire to take them again into his mouth, and her slender slim shapely body gave him the beginning of an erection again. She became aware as she looked towards him, that he was getting heated again, so thinking quickly, she announced, 'Now Norm, be a good fellow and get dressed. If I have satisfied you this evening, I am delighted, but do not spoil it, so put it away before it explodes. As to giving me anything, I can tell you straightaway, that I need an awful lot of things, so we had better leave that subject out, and discuss it at a later date, eh?' she added as she recovered her clothes and began to dress as he just sat and looked at her dolefully, with his eyes so wide open that she wondered if they would pop out if she stood any longer in front of him. Yet he still did not answer but continued to sit transfixed in front of her.

'Now Norm, I asked you to get dressed and not to sit in a daze with your thing getting all big again. I am sure that you have had enough for one night or are you asking for more, because if you do, you will spoil it for the future. So now put these on,' she said as she handed him his pants which he took from her without taking his eyes off her.

'Darling,' he uttered, as he grabbed her around the waist, pulling her towards himself, 'you have turned me into a love-sick zombie and I cannot get enough of you. So please come a little closer so that I can smother you with kisses before you finish dressing, please Anne,' he added looking at her with appealing eyes and his arm drawing her ever closer to him as he sat on the edge of the bed and as she stood in front of him.

'Oh all right if you must, but you will only be working yourself up again,' she responded with a twinkle of humour in her voice thinking that she has without setting out to, that she has truly conquered him and now he will be her slave!

She ruffled his hair as she stood in front of him whilst he was smothering her with kisses all over her, even to pulling her pants down once again.

'Now that must be enough, Norm. You remind me of a saying I saw somewhere, *An optimist sees the doughnut, but the pessimist sees the hole*, but in your case, it is the other way round,' she added after getting somewhat drenched with the kisses that began to turn into bites all over her anatomy. 'You must stop now, otherwise I will get upset.'

The moment she uttered those last words, he paused and looked into her eyes with his that were semi-glazed from heated excitement. 'Darling, I want you again and I must have you now, please Anne, do not let me go. Help me again and I will give you anything you want, please, please,' he begged as he held onto her, looking into her eyes that cried for more.

166

'Why not take hold of it yourself and let it go again. I will not mind. Here is the small hand towel that you can use if you wish. I will be right behind you and I will put my arms around you too. Now come on, stand up and get it over with, please Norm,' she insisted, as she assisted him to a standing position and then turning him from herself, she placed her arms around his middle. Within seconds, it was over, when he turned round towards her and gave a strong compassionate hug and rained kisses on her again. After a few moments, she released herself from his hold, and again picking up his pants, she handed them to him with a stern face and 'ordered' him to dress.

Without a further murmur or word, but with his head down, he began to dress. After he had covered himself but before he completed his attire, he circled towards Anne who had by now completed her array, and speaking in a soft low voice said, 'Anne darling, I'll say again, you have been marvellous. I know I have already said that, but I must say it again as it is true. It is also true that anything you want you can have, so please say what you desire.'

Anne looked at him for a moment without speaking, then passing his shirt to him and helping him to get his arm through it, answered, 'Thanks, Norm, for the offer. As I've already said, that I need a lot of things, so I feel that we can talk about that another time. But right now, it is time you got me home, otherwise I will be getting questions about where I've been tonight.'

She assisted him in buttoning his shirt whilst he replied, 'Do not be afraid to ask, anything and it's yours.'

'The most important item we should talk about is what we are to tell Licy. If you wish to upset her, and tell her what actually happened here or shall we say that I helped you but we did not disrobe. You can say that I allowed you to touch me, but only lightly. What do you say; will you go along with that or have you any other suggestion?'

'Darling, you are a clever girl. Yes I think we can safely say what you propose. Well, I'm ready now, so let's have a quick rinse then we can go,' he added as he picked up his jacket and placed it near at hand for donning it.

On the ride to her home, she indicated that they were to discuss his offer of gifts when she had determined what she would like. On

167

reaching her home, she went straight up to her room and with a quick shower, resorted to bed, but sleep eluded her.

'Now here I am and I thought that I was the master, and as soon as he is with me I crumble. Now what is the matter with me that I submit so easily. He will now expect to enjoy me every time. How can I say "No" to him. If we continue like this, before long he will succeed in getting his way and I will be helpless. Oh, what shall I do!' Thus were the thoughts that spun around Anne's mind as she tossed and turned in her bed as she went over the adventures of the evening. 'Now I suppose, I will get an inquest from Licy. Will she believe me even if Norman says the same as I do? I am sure he will not let me down, but did Licy give him the same pleasures in the past and what pleasures does he get from her now? Why should he want me, too? Will he want me only now or will he want us both? And what shall I ask him for – a car, a flat, or perhaps another raise in salary? Oh dear, my mind is in a turmoil to know which way to turn.' But her mind went into oblivion as sleep conquered her.

Chapter 15

'Come!' shouted Mr Meredith without lifting his head, in response to the knock on his door. In the last hour he had managed about five minutes worth of work due to the constant interruptions. He was not at all happy in having a further distraction from his labours. But on seeing that it was a client, his manner changed to greet the newcomer. 'Why, it's Charley Harrington. Now what fetched you to this neck of the woods? If it's your balance sheet, it is right in front of me here,' he expounded as he looked at his client with a puzzled frown.

'As I happen to be nearby, I thought it would be a good opportunity to pop in and with your permission, I would like to ask your Anne to tea. As it is near home time, I feel sure you will not mind, eh Norman ol' boy?' said his visitor with a delightful smile that showed his teeth to the best advantage!

'Now that is nice of you to think of inviting one of my staff to tea, but you are unlucky, she's on a job right now,' gloated Mr Meredith as he looked at his client whose face dropped as he heard that she was not available.

'Am sorry to hear that. At least it means that she is still with you and has not forsaken you for another client. But could you give her a ring and see if she would like to join me?' he enjoined with a slight plea in his voice.

'This is quite irregular, you know. Forgive me if I say you look like a love-sick juvenile. And without exception, every client we send her to wishes to take her over. It makes me wonder what she would fetch if we still had the old slave market. I can just imagine you among others all bidding your braces away to get her. *Ho, ho* it makes me laugh at the very thought of it!' he chuckled and grinned at him.

'Never mind the rhetoric. Just do as I ask like a good pal and call her. Or let me have the number and I will call her,' he added with a somewhat sterner look at his colleague.

Without answering, Meredith took hold of his personal directory and flicked the pages to ascertain the telephone number and as he did, he said whilst memorising the number, 'You know I cannot give you the number, that's absolutely out of the question.'

He dialled the required number and asked the telephonist for Miss Hopkins, who had come to do the firm's books. That was sufficient identification and within a short space of a few seconds, he was answered by Anne.

'Ah, Anne,' called Mr Meredith as he heard her response to the call. 'I have Mr Charles Harrington with me and he would like a word with you. It is in order for you to speak with him, Anne,' posed her boss. Without waiting for a reply, he handed the handpiece to his visitor.

'Anne, is that you?' asked Mr Harrington. Getting the affirmative reply, added with a brighter tone, 'I just popped in here in the hope that you too would be available, but your boss indicated that you are on a job. Now I came in to ask you if you would care to join me for tea, but as you are not here right now, can I alter the suggestion and ask you to join me for dinner instead. Just tell me where you would like me to pick you up and what time and I'll be there.'

'It is very nice of you to ask me out, but I must say that it is not the custom for staff to accept invitations from clients. That upsets the proper balance, you must know. It is also unfair that you should be with my boss when you ask me. So you had better ask my boss if he is of the opinion that mixing business with pleasure is permitted. Perhaps you will ask him to pass a word to me for guidance,' she added with a beam of pleasure at the thought of a pleasant evening to come, even with the so-called 'ogre' as Harrington!

'I've heard Charley ask you Anne, and as far as I'm concerned it's at your discretion,' came the voice of her boss who then cupped his hand over the mouthpiece and whispered into it, 'and behave please.'

'I promise, Norm, so do not worry,' replied Anne with a chuckle in her voice at what the thought conjured up.

'Ah, is that you again Mr Harrington? Good. Then I will be at the Eastbury Hotel at eight. That will give me time to get home to change into my glad rags. Will that be all right with you?' questioned Anne knowing full well that if she asked him to meet her on the moon he would say yes even to that.

His reply was as expected and she then terminated the call.

Joan answered the doorbell knowing that it should be Angus, and she was right.

'Hullo Angus, please come in for a moment whilst I get my coat,' said Joan as she held open the door for him to enter. As he walked in she closed the door but opened the door to the lounge for him to enter and await her, which he did.

'Do sit down for a mo'; can I offer you a drink and here's the evening paper whilst I get it,' so said Joan as she busied herself. She left the room after handing the drink to Angus. He took a sip, then opened out the paper and saw the heavily printed headlines of the rise of Hitler in Germany to the general discomfort of the British as a whole.

After a few minutes that seemed to him to be an interminable time, Joan returned to announce that she was then ready to leave. He looked at her in appreciation as before him, was a very attractive girl now blossoming into womanhood who was beautifully attired, but above all else, she wore a happy expression.

'I'm ready, Angus, if you are or would you like to sit and read the paper?' she jested with him.

Angus jumped up and neatly refolded the paper and returned it to where she had taken it from, then replied, 'Joan my dear, you look really beautiful tonight! I feel proud to be with you and as you ask, yes, I'm ready for fun.' With that he took her arm and escorted her to his car that was kerbside to the house.

They had parked the car and were walking to the venue he had proposed. Their conversation was of jollification but nothing specific, when Angus paused in his walk and held Joan's arm and stopped in his tracks. Before he could get the words out of his mouth, he pointed with his hand to the entrance of a hotel.

'Why, I'm sure that's Anne!' ventured Joan who also spotted her as Angus had pointed. 'Let's go in and see if we can catch her.' With that they hurried to the entrance and they both entered just in time to see Anne enter the portals beyond the foyer.

'Well, shall we go in or shall we not?' queried Joan somewhat surprised to see her friend walk in so nonchalantly, as if she was a regular client at that expensive habitat.

'I can see nothing wrong in looking inside, now is there?' quipped Angus as he walked forward and held the door slightly ajar and took a look inside.

'There she is!' cried Angus to Joan as she joined him at the open door. They saw Anne shaking hands with a tall gentleman in dinner suit and black tie. They also noted that Anne too was dressed in evening wear and looked ravishingly beautiful.

Joan moved backwards and closed the door and said to Angus, 'It's nothing to do with us, Angus. It may be her uncle or someone like that, but truthfully, I have not heard her mention a rich uncle before.'

'Would you like to go in there and have a meal, Joan?' ventured Angus in a quiet voice, hoping she would say 'no' as he knew that he could not afford the possible cost that they would charge.

'I should love to, but not tonight, as you had indicated another place for our treat. So let's go and we can enjoy the speculation of who the guy is,' was her reply that relieved him of financial worries.

'It's too cold to sit in the park so let's just stay in the car and have a chat, shall we?' suggested Joan after they were seated in it, having just left the restaurant.

'Sure we can sit in it but I will not stop here but move along a bit to a quieter spot, if that's all right with you my love?' proposed Angus in a hopeful mood. Without awaiting a reply, he put the car into gear and moved away to a deserted cul-de-sac.

'Well, we have not exhausted all the possibilities as to who that man may be,' asserted Joan as Angus stopped the car.

'We have gone through all the nice possibilities, but what of the others? May be she works in her spare time for an expensive dating agency,' Angus put forward.

'I doubt it, yet I wonder sometimes at the new clothes she has. Just look at what she had on tonight? That must have cost a packet if a penny I'm sure; what do you say Angus?' she countered.

'Everything is a possibility. If she is on the game, I wonder how much she charges?' he replied as he looked up at the roof of the car whilst his mind raced in wishful thought as to how much he would pay to have a night with Anne.

'Oh don't be so awful to suggest that she's a tart. I know that she is doing exceptionally well in her firm and that she got a very handsome raise recently so that may account for the togs. No, I do not think we have hit the right answer yet, so I will ask her when next we meet. I am sure she will tell me.'

'Well, whatever it is, I am sure we both wish her well,' acknowledged Angus with his own thoughts still on Anne, but he must pull out of his reverie, as he knew that at least for the immediate moment, Anne was elsewhere and he had Joan sitting alongside him. With that, he turned towards Joan and put his arm around her shoulder and drew her towards himself. They went into rapturous kissing and mouthing which Joan entered into happily, but Angus still had Anne in his mind and imagined that he held her and was lasciviously indulging with her to his heart's content. He even failed in his customary habit of having his hand travel over Joan in search of her body as his mind was so occupied with Anne as he was in a complete state of hallucination and really imagined that he held Anne and not Joan. His imagination told him that he was free with Anne and she allowed him to enter her.

'Hey, stop it!' Joan called out as she pushed Angus away from herself. 'What's the matter with you? You nearly bit my tongue off. Have you got that excited already?' Joan queried as she looked at her companion who sat with a dazed look in his eyes.

Angus then realised that he had ejaculated in his pants as he truly thought that he was holding Anne and not Joan. He felt uncomfortably wet but could do nothing about it unless he told her.

'My love, you got me so excited,' lied Angus as the only excuse he could think of that would equal the situation. 'I've blown my top off so would you like to take it out and wipe it for me as it is far from comfortable right now?' he pleaded with her as he unbuttoned his fly and extracted the subject.

173

'I'm thrilled to know that I got you excited but please wipe it up yourself, as you know how to best,' she exclaimed with a giggle at the thought that he excited himself so much in her company. Little did she know that she was not the subject of his kerfuffle. Perhaps it was as well that she was ignorant of the fact, but she did anticipate that he would have endeavoured to try his hand at wandering around her secreted parts. Although she was pleased that he had not, yet she felt at a loss. However, whilst contemplating the occurrence, he realised that his satisfaction was a false one, so in an endeavour to rectify the situation, even to Joan's satisfaction, he turned to her and again embraced her.

This time he knew it was Joan that he was with and not Anne, so he encouraged his hand to wander to her hem. She did not appear to object so he moved his hand upward behind her skirt to reach the elastic of her pants. Still she held onto him and did not murmur an objection. So with delicate touch, he made his hand travel over her pants to engage the top part and as gently as he could, he pulled them down as far as they would come down. Although they were not right down, it was enough for him to just reach her fluffy pussy! He stroked the hairs softly and eventually managed to get a finger nearer to the orifice that he sought. He massaged it and felt his finger getting gooey as Joan began to move in a wiggling motion. Her movements enabled him to insert his fingers still higher which appeared to please her as she stopped her sideward wiggle and began to make a motion backwards and forwards that accelerated the travel of his fingers to coincide. Her embrace became very strong as she held onto him.

He responded with delight and for the first time he lost his memory as he began to appreciate his adventure with Joan. He was just able to get his free arm down to his trousers and unbutton which he had but a few moments ago buttoned up, and then again endeavoured to take it out. He synchronised his action as she moved to and from him to get it out as she pulled away. He succeeded after one or two attempts and then found that her pants were a little too high to get any action. By dextrous movement he was able to pull them down, so that entry could possibly be achieved. But not without hindrance, as they were seated side by side, so he endeavoured to roll over and lie over her.

She still did not seem to mind but he realised that to engage entry he would not be able to even in that awkward position. Somehow he managed to get his hands under her legs and swing them onto the car bench seat. She swung her body as her legs resided on the seat and now her head rested on the edge of the arm seat. Then throwing her skirt upwards and at the same time lying over her, he endeavoured to insert it in her.

'What are you doing Angus . . . you know that I will not allow you to do that, so stop it!' shouted Joan as she realised that as his fingers had left her for a bare second, after they had switched round their seating, and the moment after she felt not a finger returning but something hard and much bigger. Instantly she knew that he was attempting to seduce her. She pulled away and took her arms off his shoulders as she did so. She looked up and saw his weapon that hung out like a semaphore in front of him! It was a fleshy pinkish red throbbing rod that silently asked for entry.

'Darling,' remonstrated Angus somewhat hurt that he had failed once again to achieve his goal, 'You were asking for it so I really thought that you would not only appreciate it, but also relish it and ask for more. Just look at it, it is almost at full stretch and asking for release, so at least be a sweety pie, and if you will not put it where it belongs, at least take it and do exactly as you would like with it; I cannot be fairer than that now can I?'

'I think we both have had enough, so put it away like a good boy. You will spoil it for another time,' she replied as she endeavoured to move from the position she was in, that was still on her back.

'How can I put it away when it is crying for you, my cherrie?' retorted Angus in a hopeful tone.

'Angus, let me get up, there's a good fellow. I am sure that you have enjoyed yourself tonight. You have already had one go, so don't be greedy and ask for more,' pouted Joan as she endeavoured to straighten herself up from the awkward position she found herself in.

'Please,' begged Angus, who now realised that yet again another opportunity was not fulfilled. 'Take it and get it to go off again, please; then I will happily get up.'

By this time she managed to get herself into a sitting position with Angus thrown off her and half-standing up, as the car would not

175

allow him to stand upright. So there he stood bent over her with his tool hanging out in front of her.

'Oh, do put it away and let me get up,' cried Joan as she gave him a slight nudge that made him sit down alongside her.

Instead of doing as bid, he turned towards her and he made a grab for her and went into a hug once again, but this time in a frenzy that got her wondering. In his ardour he pulled her half off the seat towards him and began to paw her again with renewed vigour. She realised that he would be getting heated again and possibly she would be getting wet all over her skirt, as he had not put it away. She immediately endeavoured to release herself from his grip, sufficiently to be out of range. It was neither easy to move bodily nor to get her face away from his passion and lustful keenness, but with her hand and arm, she moved it upwards towards his face and thus broke his grip.

'Now why did you do that, I nearly got it off again and now you stopped it!' cried Angus still in a frenzy but no longer in passion. He let her go and fell back onto the seat in an exhausted mood. When Joan leaned over him and gently opened his fly and let the now half-sized shrimp flop within, he made no protest but looked at her and wondered what made her do that.

'The waiter appears to know you Anne?' questioned Mr Harrington as he looked at her and preened at the pleasure it gave him to have such an attractive well-dressed lass in front of him.

'I should have thought that may have been obvious to you. I have been here a number of times,' she equivocated and continued, 'and as I enjoy both the service and the food, I suggested that we come here. I knew the standard we would get, and I am sure that you too have found the food excellent.' She beamed up at him as he threw back a broad smile at her.

'Anne, my dear, I cannot fault your choice any more than I can fault the company I am happy to be with. I compliment your taste. In fact I can continue to compliment you as it appears that I should not be surprised at anything you do!' he riposted as he retained his eyes upon her with a feeling of craving for what appeared to be unattainable just then.

176

After a lull for a matter of but a few moments he continued, 'Now would you like to try a nightclub before I take you home, my dear?'

'Thank you very much, Charley, but I think it is late enough for a midweek outing. Perhaps another time, eh?' she replied as she looked up at him and wondered what he would next propose.

'Then come to my pad for a nightcap before I get you home. I am not far from here, so what do you say my dear?' he posed as he continued to gaze into her eyes.

'Thank you for the offer but in sincerity I must decline. It is one thing to accept a client's offer of a dinner, but it is quite another to accept his overtures to go to his apartment. I can get a taxi from here if you like, as I think it is time I got myself home and to bed,' came her rebuttal as she stood up, as a clear indication that the adventure was over.

He knew that any further proposals would meet with a negative response. This did not surprise him, as he had become aware of her strong determined character. So in prudence, he beckoned the waiter for the bill, gave it a casual glance when it was presented him, then left a number of notes on the table and walked after Anne, who now stood by the entrance to the dining hall.

'Well, Anne, I must thank you for affording me such a pleasant evening. As you decline to see my pad, can we make arrangements for a further meeting?' he asked as he ushered her towards his car that the hall porter brought round to the front for them.

'Thank you indeed, Charley. It is indeed nice to have had the pleasure of a dinner with you but feel that to meet again would spoil our relationship. So, as it is so near to Christmas, that you leave it to the New Year,' she replied and hoped that he would not further argue the point.

'That does not make me at all happy, as I did hope to see you again before the festive season and then perhaps you may accept my invitation to going to the West Indies for Christmas with me,' he posed the bait.

'Now on the first blush, I am not at all happy at your proposal, as I do not go off with men just like that. And on the second, that would obligate me to do what would be expected of me, and that is a no go for a start. So thank you very much and now please get me home,'

Anne chirped back in a somewhat stern voice that brooked no quarrel.

So realising that he was on a losing wicket, he switched on the ignition, and put the car into 'drive' and moved off. He asked for the address and moved in that general direction until he reached the area, then sought her instruction to her home.

They reached her home with very little being spoken beyond directional pointers. When he pulled up outside her house and she was about to leave, he asked her to kiss him good night. She turned and without hesitation, she leaned over towards him and kissed him full on the lips and then bid him 'good night' and with a renewal of thanks for a pleasant evening, walked across the pavement and let herself into her home.

'Thank goodness, it's our night together,' said Felicity to Anne as they entered the apartment.

'Yes, the days do seem to stretch. But let's forget work and enjoy ourselves, shall we?' replied Anne in a happy frame of mind.

They entered the lift and made their exit at the appropriate floor and both walked the few paces arm in arm in the deserted corridor to the flat door. They entered, switched on the lights and divested themselves of their outdoor garments, then made for the drinks cupboard. One got out a couple of glasses whilst the other uncorked the sherry bottle and poured out two measures. They both took a small sip and then walked over to the settee; they placed their drinks on the side-table then sat down. They immediately turned to one another and went into a passionate hug with one hand around the neck while the other hand travelled around the body in a sensuous manner as had become their custom. In a matter of a few minutes, they regained their composure and taking their drinks with them, they resorted to the kitchen to prepare the evening meal.

'How did you get on with Norman the other night, Anne darling?' questioned Felicity.

'Oh, he's all right,' Anne replied with a humorous chuckle. 'I think he is a bit nervous of me and I intend to keep it like that. Then he is afraid to make too many demands of me. I allowed him to just touch me but no further. He did ask me to hold him, but I refused

178

and encouraged him to help himself. As I told him, it did not bother me if he wanted to get a load off,' lied Anne finishing in a serious tone that gave Felicity the impression that she heard the truth.

'Darling,' mooted Felicity in a soft voice, 'up to the night that you went out with Norman, I was not for one moment jealous. But since then, I cannot get it out of my mind, so although I love you, I am also jealous of you. Tell me what to do my love, as I must know, as I will not lose you whatever happens,' pleaded Felicity as she looked into Anne's eyes that appeared moist with tears.

'Look, you do not have to be jealous of me, my dear. I did not propose going out with Norm. You knew before I did. But are you in love with him?' queried Anne as she looked back at her friend and lover.

'Well, I don't know. I know I look forward to having him here, and I like him, but how can I tell if I love him? He gives me anything that I ask for and he has never been cross with me, either here or at the office, so tell me?' she posed.

'It sounds like you have some strong feelings for him that amounts to love. Yet when you first mentioned your attachment to him, you indicated that you tolerated him for your job's sake, but now it seems that you have grown fond of him. You know his habits and he is recently divorced, so why don't you hang your hat up and have him. Unless he has someone else on the hook, you should get him to propose and settle the question in your favour. Now why don't you?' suggested Anne.

'Anne darling, I do not know if he would want me. After all, I have been his plaything for a number of years and that is one thing, but to offer marriage is quite another. In any case, how could I propose it; it is not my place, is it?' queried Felicity in a low, sorrowful voice.

'The answer to that question is that if he does not ask, you must suggest it. He has had the best out of you for a long time, so is accustomed to you, so why not?' Anne recommended as she looked at Felicity and wondered if she should tell her the truth of what really happened between herself and Norman. She reflected that if she did, she would lose both Felicity and possibly Norman, too.

'I really think you can get away with it Anne, but I do not think that I have either the power or the charisma to. So we will have to think of an alternative plan. You are the brains in the firm, so get your thinking cap on, my dear, and tell me what to do,' implored Felicity in full earnestness.

'Well, there is one plan that will work, but if I tell you, will you promise me that you will do exactly as I advise?' answered Anne as she looked into the eyes of Felicity and wondered if she had sufficient power over her to command her will and action!

Felicity paused a while before replying and looked back at Anne, and wondered what she had concocted in that fertile brain of hers! She knew that if Anne proposed a scheme, it would work. But in this case, it was herself that was at the end of the ride.

'You know very well that I have absolute confidence in you, and anything that you propose, I know in advance would be in my interest, so I can give you my assurance that whatever you recommend I will do if it achieves the aim,' answered Felicity, still wondering what it was that Anne had in mind for her to capture her boss as a husband.

'Well, let us sit here and I will give you in brief the plan; then tell you what you have to do,' proposed Anne as she sat on the settee alongside her friend.

Anne had been speaking non-stop for at least a quarter of an hour, whilst Felicity just gazed into her eyes spellbound and speechless! Even when Anne asked if she had any questions, Felicity still sat dumb and in thought.

'Anne darling,' uttered Felicity at last as she found her faculties, 'do you think that I could get away with that? What is the likelihood of Norm ever finding out the ruse we played on him?'

'Why should he ever know if we are the only ones that know. I for one will never let you down and you are not a fool to confess, now are you?' sallied Anne.

'I feel a bit nervous so you will have to give me a push now and then. How will we be able to meet if I do eventually marry Norm? That is another point that I would like you to clear, as I will not miss you for any man!' asked Felicity still in open doubt of the plan proposed to her.

'That will be a small problem, so do not worry, my love. I would not like to lose you any more than you would, so be assured that I will plan accordingly. So now let's get to bed,' yawned Anne as she rose from the settee and walked to the bedroom door.

Chapter 16

Since the meeting of Wynne and Richard at Andrew's apartment in company of Tracey, the foursome had met on a few more occasions. But Andrew had planned to have just Tracey as his guest this night. He could not break what had become a regular feature and habit, so he proposed an extra evening out alone. From Tracey's consideration she could see no reason against accepting a tryst with Andrew alone. After all, she knew his flat well now and it held no mystery any more. When they met as a foursome, as if by preconceived arrangement, after the meal, she always adjourned with him to the bedroom, whilst Wynne and Richard held the settee. Whatever happened between the other pair was conjecture, as she had never discussed it. As to what occurred between her and Andrew would also be conjecture for the other two. She could declare that Andrew exercised a lot of restraint when he had guests there.

She still remembered the first time she went to the flat. He had then given her an anatomical lesson of his manhood. Since that time, they accepted the motions as customary between them. He did not make advances beyond certain limits, so she gave in return the satisfaction he craved. She still refused to bite it as he had in the past asked her to do. Now would he ask again that they were at the flat alone without their friends? Was she wise to accept the challenge? Could he control it to prevent her mouth getting filled up with all that ejaculation stuff? Could she conceive if she took it in that way as he said she could if it was inserted in the other place? Somehow, she wished to try the experiment yet with maybe wisdom, she thought it better to reserve that pleasure to perhaps another time, if at all.

Then as they are now to be alone and did not have to exercise caution, would he again make demands that so far she has refused? She had dreamed of this on numerous occasions and longed to put thought to the test of reality. She hoped that she would have sufficient sense and courage to hold off the demand, as she knew the risk inherent if she did succumb. So far, he had never used his manly strength against her will, but could that always be relied upon? She remembered the occasion when she rolled him off her to his discomfiture.

It was a rather fresh evening and the flat emphasised this. Tracey commented on the coldness as they entered, so without ado, Andrew immediately raised the temperature of the radiators by advancing the heat control. She retained her topcoat for a while, whilst Andrew prepared the evening meal. She was becoming accustomed to leaving the meal preparation to him. So she just mooched around the room hugging herself against the cold until he came in with a tray well-loaded.

'Gee, you've still got your coat on and I am sweating,' were the first words Andrew uttered as he entered the lounge.

'Well, it's cold here so what do you expect?' retorted Tracey.

'Oh, come on now, it's warmed up very nicely now, so take your coat off, then we can sit down and enjoy this meal,' returned Andrew as he walked on into the room and put the tray down on the table and began to set the various plates out into a two place-setting.

'All right then,' answered Tracey as she divested herself of her coat, which she nonchalantly threw over the arm of the settee, then followed him to the table and sat down opposite Andrew, looking at the very tempting meal he had prepared and produced.

'Just leave the things on the table and we will see to them after,' proposed Andrew as they rose from the table after their meal had concluded.

'No,' answered Tracey emphatically. 'I hate to see an untidy table, so let's shift them quickly', and immediately took as many dishes as she could carry to the kitchen sink.

'I thought you couldn't wait for your snogging session,' quipped Andrew with a broad smile as he assisted in clearing the table.

As soon as the table was cleared, they automatically walked arm in arm to the bedroom.

They had already reached the stage where she consented to his action. Now he attempted to get himself in a more compromising position as she feared and she became aware of his tactics. She rolled away and freed herself entirely from him saying, 'Andrew, you know I will not allow you to put that in, so why do you keep nudging into that position?'

'Darling, you get me so excited that I forget myself. In any case, is it not time that we indulged a bit more freely?' he replied as he manoeuvred himself into a more promising position for his endeavours.

'You know damn well I will not allow you, so stop harping on that. You are annoying me so I think we will stop right now, as I think I will go home,' added Tracey with a slight show of temper rising in her, which in truth was really just a defence mechanism at work.

'Darling, you know I would not do anything to upset you. Don't you think that after all this time that you could try it just this once. I promise you will enjoy it much more than what we do, so be a pal and say *yes*,' offered Andrew more in hope than expectancy.

'I have said NO, and if I say it again, it will make the thousandth time; so stop and let me get up as I *do* wish to go home.' argued Tracey as she endeavoured to raise herself off the soft bed.

'Oh, all right then. Now don't go yet and I will not press you again,' capitulated Andrew as he knew that he had lost the struggle once again. So he remained in his overbearing position over her that prevented her getting up!

'But I still wish to go home, so please move your carcass away,' she threw back at him, still with a show of rising temper.

Andrew now realised that he had overstepped the mark, and to regain compatibility, he moved away so that she could get off the bed. As she rose, so did he, and as they stood side by side he took her in his arms and rained kisses on her. She appeared to have lost momentum of wanting to depart as she accepted the hugging. But prudence dictated to him not to recommence his assault on her but to smooth her ruffled self into more compliance, which he did excellently.

'Well, now that's over, I will get dolled up and go home,' she said as they separated from their clutch.

Andrew looked at her in amazement as he was of the assumption, that she would have reconciled herself in the last few minutes. His surprise showed in his face as he replied to her, 'But I have let you get up and you still wish to go home? What's wrong now, please tell me?'

'I'm getting bored with this routine exercise. We go over the same messing about each time I come here. You keep pestering me to go the whole way with you and I would like to, but my prudence dictates that I must not. So I am bored and want to go home,' she retorted in a very grave voice that put him on edge as to know the best way to reconcile her to a more friendly attitude.

'But Tracey darling, you know that I really love you, so can see nothing wrong in doing what I propose,' came his considered reply that seemed hardly a reply at all.

'Love,' sniggered Tracey back at him, 'you do not really know the meaning of the word. What you mean is that you are in love with sex, but not with me! So I will repeat, and please for the last time, I am reserving myself for my future husband and now get me home,' she added with but a half smile on her face, which was more a sneer than smile!

'Tracey, that's where you are wrong. The very fact that you have refused me indicates that you are the girl that I would be willing to live with for the rest of my life! I am quite serious now, and am asking you to marry me; so what have you to say? I hope you say "yes",' avowed Andrew as he stood looking at her with an appealing glance.

'Are you proposing to me, Andrew?' blustered Tracey in a surprise with her eyes wide open to their maximum in disbelief.

'Of course I am, you beautiful, gorgeous creature,' he declared, as he again took her into his arms and renewed his hug which was reciprocated. 'But you haven't said "yes" to me, so let me hear you say the word, please,' he pleaded in mock emphasis.

'Andrew, my dear, nothing would make me happier than to marry you. But let me make one thing abundantly clear, so that you do not quarrel with me. That is that I will still refuse your advances until we are married. Perhaps you would like to revoke your offer now?' asked Tracey with a look that said more than words could have done.

185

'My sweet, that encourages me to repeat my question. Will you marry me?' he enunciated as he continued to look into her eyes for confirmation, and as he held her at arm's length from himself, with his two arms outstretched on her shoulders.

Instead of responding to the proposal, she flung her arms around his shoulders and whispered into his ears a feint '*yes*' that gave him the satisfaction he sought.

'Then we can have an engagement party here in this flat any day you choose and then we can fix the big day. This weekend you will come up country to meet my folks. You will find them very nice, even if I say so,' he added with obvious joy in his inflection. 'Don't look so worried; they are as I've said, very nice and am sure they will love you,' he added as he saw that her face had turned slightly white as he suggested meeting his family.

'Yes, I know the thought of meeting them does frighten me a bit. But I suppose that is something we all have to face sooner or later. But you can prime me on them before we meet them,' she entreated him in a trembling voice.

'No need to feel alarmed, my darling,' responded Andrew. 'I will get you home now and, on the way, I will tell you about them. And if your parents are still awake, you may announce the engagement. How does that sound to you, eh?' added Andrew with a broad grin.

So without further ado, they both donned their outdoor coats, and left the flat for the car journey to Tracey's home.

'I say Wynny, have you heard that Andrew has proposed to Tracey and that they are now engaged?' asked Richard as they met that evening after their daily toils.

'Oh, how nice for her; I am delighted, but who told you?' questioned Wynne 'Oh yes, that's very nice,' thought Wynne who now looked askant at her beau Richard and wondered when he would also propose, as she felt at that moment in time, her feelings within her swelling to its height of love and desire.

'I saw Andrew at lunch time in the restaurant and he told me,' replied Richard warming up to the theme, too.

'Then is our date at the flat still on as usual?' queried Wynne.

'Of course it is. I do not think he will propose a swap again, though I do hope that he's not got to marry her or something like that, do you?' posed Richard as he looked at her with wishful eyes.

'I'd stake my last penny on her that he has not had it off with her. So if he has offered to marry her, it's because he trusts her and loves her,' she threw back at him hoping that he would take the bait with her emphasis on the words 'trust' and 'love'.

'It's all very well for him, he can afford to wed. I cannot in my present state even if I wished to. If I did it would be you that I'd ask and you know that also,' he answered with a solemn tone.

'Would you really ask me, Richard?' she challenged.

'Yes I would, and I think you are aware of my feelings. Although I have a good post and a commensurate salary, it is not sufficient for the standard that I would like to maintain when we wed. Marriage is not all bed and breakfast you know. So if you have patience, I do not know for how long, I will ask you to marry me. What would you say if I asked you, Wynne?' he questioned.

'If you will pardon the pun and if's money that is the problem, I will tell you that "*Money doesn't talk any more, it goes without saying*", but it's no good me saying "yes" now and then in umpteen year's time we are no nearer. So let us forget that subject for a while and come and celebrate with our friends in their joy,' proposed Wynne in full earnestness but with a heavy heart at her own dim prospects.

'Ah, I'm glad you have come in. But my kiss first, as I have some special work for you,' said Mr Meredith to Anne as she entered his room.

'And I have some special information for you, Norm,' answered Anne as she sat down opposite him after her salutary kiss. She was about to continue, but he began before she had time to utter the opening word.

'I will be taking you to Sir John Cuthbertson. I will spend an hour or so with you over his problems, then I will leave you there to complete the work. After coffee, if you can make it?' suggested her boss.

'That is only a small problem that we can see to soon. But first I must tell you that Licy will not be in today. I had a call from her yesterday, Sunday, and have been with her all night up to now. She is far from well! And before you ask, I will tell you. She has had a bout of morning sickness rather badly. You know what that spells, Norm?' she implied as she looked into his face for the reaction.

'Morning sickness, what do you mean, morning sickness?' he repeated looking back at her with his mouth half open in puzzled wonderment.

'You know very well what I mean, Norm. After five or six weeks pregnancy, a woman gets "morning sickness". In her case it's rather bad and had called in a doctor who came yesterday afternoon and told her she should rest awhile,' she retorted.

'But it cannot be me. I am infertile and she knows that too. So who is it, Anne?' he flustered.

'There is only one man that has been having it with her and that's Norman, and you know it. As to infertility, you also know that it can sometimes happen even if you have been like that for a long time. So the question is, what do you propose to do?' she pouted at him with a stern no-nonsense tone.

'Oh heck, it cannot be me. What should I do? Shall I ask her to have an abortion or what, Anne? Please tell me what to do – you seem to be the new adviser to us both, so now advise,' he muttered in partial distress and anguish.

'An abortion is completely out of the question as she has objections and on the current legal position. You have been having an affair with her for a very long time, and have had the best of her for that time, so you must now, I think, pay the price! You cannot tell me that you have no feelings for her, as you obviously have a lot of affection for her. And as you are free, I think it would make you both very happy to tie the knot and get married. But you must do that quick for the sake of the infant,' she detailed as she continued to look at him.

'Oh dear, oh dear,' he muttered with his head in his hands as she walked round to his side of the desk and put an arm around his shoulders. He looked up at her in dejection and said, 'If it comes to marrying, it is you Anne that I would want. Not to say that I do not love Licy too. So what do I do Anne? Please tell me,' he stuttered in desperation as he looked up at her in appeal.

'If you are thinking about us two, whatever action you take, that will continue; you can depend and rely on me to achieve and connive to it. So do not think our arrangement will be affected. I am sure we can continue as we have begun. You must become a two-woman man but one of them now has a prior claim on you, and you must satisfy that claim. But I repeat, our plans will continue as long as you desire, as I know you have a bit of love for me as I have for you,' she remonstrated to him still with a soothing arm on his shoulder.

'I have told you both that I love you both, and yet it is true. I want you both. Are you sure that you will still desire me if I married Licy?' he replied with a pitying appeal.

'Norm, my dear, you mean a lot to me and even Licy will not object to our continuation as now. After all, we all have agreed to the arrangement and cannot see why you getting married now should really be the reason to change things. If it would make you feel better, then we can if you wish, tell Licy that we will no longer meet. I can take over her flat, but in my name of course; and Licy can move into your house. Then as she will be housebound, it would not be too difficult to arrange for you to pop in now and then to me, now would it, Norm?' she proposed as he tried to fathom her face for hidden meaning that he had failed to find.

He appeared to brighten up at the mention of their continuation of meeting and said, 'My little dove, do you really mean that you would let me come to see you even if I get married again? That makes the whole situation look very different. Yes,' he added with emphasis, 'I will give her a ring and tell her that I will marry her and that she can come to my house at any time. Will that be the right way round, do you think?'

'First, pick up the telephone and call her and tell her that I have told you her problem, but please do not tell her that I proposed that you marry her. It would be much nicer if that suggestion came from you – she would love you all the more I think. In fact, you can say that I simply told you and am not in the room with you but you thought it over and have decided to wed her. As to transferring the flat over to me, that can be done after, at any time. But you must get to the registry today,' she propounded for him.

'You know, Anne my dear, I feel now quite elated. The thought that I was going to lose you was what upset me. Yes, please dial Licy and hand me the phone and I will break the good news to her,' he announced with a bright smile on his face.

As requested, Anne dialled the required number and as soon as it began to ring, she passed the instrument over to Norman. He held it for a short while and then obviously received a reply, as he said into the mouthpiece, 'Licy, I have had Anne in here with me this morning, and she tells me that you are in a spot of bother. I am awfully sorry that it's happened but feel that it's for the best, as I wish to marry you, and as soon as we hang up, I am popping into the registry to fix a date. How do you feel about that, my sweet?'

He held on to the handset for at least a very long minute and apparently received no reply, so with a slightly raised voice, called into it and asked if she was still there.

'Yeeeees,' came the whimpered reply, 'I am still here. I heard you say you wanted to marry me. Do you really mean that, Norm, because I would not like you to offer to marry me because you got me into trouble.'

'Licy my dear, I do not know why I have not asked you before. You know that I love you and it has taken this news to awaken me to reality. I have to pop out this morning, but I will be with you, say about midday, and will discuss details with you. So if you have any plans, then we can agree them. One thing that I will suggest, that you may care to dwell on, is that I will transfer the flat to Anne and you can come and live with me in my house – which is getting too big for me on my own. So all I want you to say now is that big YES that you will marry me and we can then discuss the trimmings later. So now let's be hearing you, my love,' he quipped with glee.

'Norm my love, you have made me the happiest woman and you know I have always loved you. I'll say YES to you a thousand times. I will look forward to seeing you as you say. So cheerio my love till then.' And with that she hung up and lay back on her bed with a sneaky smile on her face.

As Felicity lay back in reverie, she wondered what exactly had Anne told Norman. At least the plan so far was working and Anne was getting the flat now for herself. That would indirectly be saving

him a lot of money. It would not now be necessary for him to buy
her a flat and so maintain two. Now she had to be sensible and act as
Anne has advised her to. 'Gee,' she thought, 'that Anne sure has her
head on her shoulder's all right. How did we manage before she came
on the scene. She must have twisted her little finger around Norman
to get him to propose. I would have loved to have listened to how
she conquered him. That would be very revealing.'

'The taxi is waiting downstairs, Norm,' said Anne as she poked her
head into his room. He was already standing at his desk and, grabbing
his briefcase, made for the door, then accompanied her to the elevator.

They entered the taxi and he gave the driver the necessary instructions.

'You are a great girl, Anne,' said her boss as he took her hand and
held it in his own, as he looked into her face.

'And I think you are a great guy. I also think that you have done the
right think and am sure that you will be very happy. You can count on
me if there is any problem, as I will always be with you, as you well
know,' added Anne as she leaned over to kiss him on the cheek.

Any further conversation was not possible as the taxi had arrived at
its destination; so paying off the driver, they both entered the building of the 'Sir John Cuthbertson Enterprise'.

Within a matter of minutes they were both seated before that
gentleman. Sir John offered them a drink, but both declined and
opted for coffee. He ordered this and within a short space of time, the
tray with coffee pot and three cups plus biscuits were placed on the
desk. Without asking, Anne took the pot and poured out the coffee,
presuming to know exactly how both men liked it. They both
acknowledged her gesture and continued the general conversation
until Anne interrupted them and asked the purpose of the visit.

'Anne, my dear,' commenced Sir John, 'you must learn to relax a
bit. I am interested in what your boss has to tell me, particularly, that
he is getting married again. I am surprised that it is not you, but that
makes it better for me, as I have been thinking of doing the same, and
if I do, it would be to you. How would you reply to that, Anne?'
quipped Sir John gaping at her with a beaming smile.

'Sir John, please can we get on with the work that I am to do. I have a heavy load back at the office and have no time for inane talk,' answered Anne somewhat taken aback by the suggestion and more than a trifle annoyed at being the butt of his questionable humour.

'Oh well, as you wish. If you would both go into the accountant's office, the books and vouchers are all ready for your scrutiny. When you have completed the assignment Anne, please pop in and see me before you leave,' Sir John added as he rose from his desk and walked to the door to hold it open for his two visitors.

As Mr Meredith and Anne walked the corridor to the accountant's office and at a point where he considered they were out of earshot, he caught her arm and halted her and said, 'Anne my dear, why did you respond to Sir John as you did? I have never known him to waste words but, I agree that his semi-proposal could knock a girl sideways.'

Anne hesitated for a moment whilst she looked into his face to check the depth of the question before replying.

'The reason that I said what I did, is because I am of the firm opinion he was playing silly buggers! I am not paid to mess about but to do a job of work which I enjoy. So say no more Norm, please. I will look in to see him before I leave as he has asked, and I suppose you will too, eh?' replied Anne as she detached her arm and walked on towards the office assigned to them.

'I think that you are probably right, but I will take the liberty of asking what it was all about. I do not think he should come out with statements like that. Ah, we are here, so let's go in and see what's to be done,' concluded Mr Meredith as they entered the room.

They found a Mr Smith awaiting their arrival. He ushered them to a large double desk laden with account books and folios. He took up the position between the two and began to explain the requirements. Mr Meredith on seeing the purpose of their visit said to Anne, 'I do not think I need to stop, Anne. This is within your capacity to see to. So if you haven't any questions before I disappear, I will leave it to you,' he concluded and awaited for any possible reply.

'It all appears straightforward Mr Meredith, but if I hit a snag, I will buzz you,' she replied as she in turn looked at her boss. In acknowledgement, he thanked her and with a brief word to Mr Smith, he left the room.

'Is he leaving you to do all the work, miss?' posed Mr Smith with a big question mark across his face when her boss had left.

'My name is Miss Hopkins, Mr Smith. As you know, I was here a while ago to do the audit, so see no reason why I should not be able to do a simple task that is before me. Or is there something that I have not observed?' she questioned.

'Ah, so you are the young girl that was here whilst I was away. I was told that you came and did the work in less time than usual, and I had to check it over. I am happy to acknowledge that I found the work dead on,' he quipped and looked at her in a sort of amazement and mild awe.

'And who may I ask asked you to check my work, Mr Smith?' queried Anne as she posed with a slight upturn of her nose as if to say, 'How dare you?'

'Why, Sir John, of course. But don't get het up with me over that. I am only doing a job and confidentially, one does not question Sir John. If he asks for something, he gets it and no messing about,' he replied still with a look of awe.

Anne looked at him and realised that even if Sir John asked him the impossible, he would try to do it to please. Poor chap, he was not that old, but obviously wanted to keep his post with the firm, so accepted any injunction imposed on him.

'As far as I am concerned, you may check my work as often as you like. I can guarantee that you will find it satisfactory. If Sir John wishes to create extra work, for you, that's his privilege.'

With that, Anne sat herself down and proceeded to do her job.

'Ah, Sir John, I have left Anne to do the work. It is not necessary for me to stay as she is capable on her own without my help,' said Mr Meredith as he again entered Sir John's room.

'I thought she would be helping you and not the other way round. Are you really confident that she can do what is required without assistance?' queried Sir John.

'Sir John, you do not know what a jewel that girl is. Not only is she beautiful and elegant, but knows her job too. I should add that there is no monkey business with her either, so be warned!' added Mr Meredith with a broad smile as if to say, 'I dare you to try your hand on my girl.'

'Now that intrigues me, Norman. You have given me a reference without prompting and I could not have asked for a better one. When I proposed to her before, it was only partly in jest to test her reaction, which pleased me. But I have seriously begun to think in terms of a proper proposal. How do you think she will react, Norman old boy?' he asked, as he gave a smug smile and leaned back in his heavily upholstered swivel and tilt chair.

'Wwwwhat do you mean, Sir John?' stammered Mr Meredith as he perceived that his client was in earnest.

'Exactly as I have said. I think that she would be just the person that could look after my household in a fit and proper manner and be a credit to me with my guests. She seems to have her wits about her and speaks with a nice calm voice. In fact I could quite happily sit and listen to her all day with that charming tone of hers. So what do you say Norman?' asked his client.

'Look, you have only met her a few times and I do not suppose you have even been out with her, so why this keenness to marry − I presume that's what you mean now, is it, Sir John?' cross-examined Mr Meredith in disbelief, as he felt at a loss to know what to say to this revelation.

'It is quite true we have not been out together but you have already indicated to me that she has been sought after by most of your clients. And damn it man, I have no impediments, so why should I not contemplate such a step. Can you see any reason against that idea? Please air your views. I will take it literary and not be offended, so speak up man,' demanded Sir John in a cavalier and judicial tone and manner.

'I really thought you were ragging her before when you made that proposal. But the only thing against you is that you are at least twenty years her senior. Then maybe she likes older men, that I cannot gainsay,' he lied as he continued to gaze at his client, wondering if he was not after all pulling his leg in jest with a sham proposal!

'Norman, the more you talk to me the more I am determined that it would be a wonderful plan to wed Anne. You cannot tell me anything against her, and from what I have observed there does not appear to be anything against her, so I will ask her out for a meal or so and take it from there. So if there is nothing else you can add, I will only ask that you do not mention anything we have said in this room and bid you good day.' As he finished, he stood up to shake his friend's hand and usher him out by the door.

'Hullo, Licy, how do you feel?' asked Norman as he entered her flat with his own key and noted that she was reclining on the settee.

'Feel a bit woozy, but with you here it may help me get rid of that feeling,' she replied as she looked up at him as he came towards her. She observed that he appeared flushed and excited. This pleased her innermost self as she presumed that he was truly pleased at the prospects of marrying her, and was doing it with love and not for having been coerced.

He took the few paces to the settee and kneeling down alongside her, he put both his arms around her neck and drew her towards himself and hugged and kissed her, and whispered that he loved her. She attempted to raise herself, but he put a restraining hand on her as he rose to his feet.

'Now you just take it easy, my love. I have ordered a nice meal to be brought up for us both, which should be here in a few minutes. Then you can get up when I have laid the table. But tell me, when did you discover that you were pregnant?' he asked as he busied himself with the preparation of the table.

'I was overdue a couple of weeks and I have never missed a period, so I went to the clinic for a check-up, and they confirmed it. And when the doctor called again, he confirmed it too. You are not angry with me, are you Norm?' she questioned.

'No, my dear. I think it's time I settled down again. It is miserable at night on your own. And we have had a very good relationship and understand each other well enough to make a good go of it. So why not? This has made me realise that it is for the best, but I must say I am surprised that I can still father a child after all I have been told. So as soon as we have had our meal, I shall be off to the Town Hall to book the date. Now how about that my dear?' chirped Norman as he sat down again awaiting the restaurateur.

'Darling, you know I have always loved you, and this will surely seal it. Now as you will be with me every night, there is no need for you to look elsewhere, is there?' she questioned as she peered at him with a beaming smile especially for his benefit.

'My dear, if you mean Anne, there are two things I have to say on that topic. Firstly, I have told you before, and you can ask her, nothing happened between us. Oh yes, I have been keen on her, but things have changed now, have they not my dear?'

'And what is the second thing that you have to impart to me, Norm?' probed Felicity as she heard the confession, and as Anne had already told her the same, she was inclined to believe it.

'Ah yes, I almost forgot. But first I must have your promise of secrecy, as I have given my word I will not divulge my knowledge to any one. Have I your promise, my dear?' asked Norman as Felicity gave her acquiescence as he looked at her with a quizzical expression.

'You could have knocked me down with the proverbial feather. I had left Anne at Sir John's place and then had a chat with him. Now you would never guess what he has in mind! No, I will not ask you to guess what he said, as I know you would never in a million years!'

'Oh come on then, do not keep me in suspense but out with it. You have got me all excited, so please be quick and tell me what Sir John said,' butted in Felicity.

Norman looked at her, and taking both her hands into his own, and with a big grin on his face, as he enjoyed the suspense he had created, he added, 'He only spoke of wanting to marry Anne! Now how's that for a surprise, but please don't tell her as it will take the wind out of his sails.'

Felicity just dropped her jaw and was for a while absolutely speechless. She just looked at him with her mouth gaping wide open. After a few elongated minutes, she was able to muster sufficient words together to say, 'You must be joking Norman', but still looking at him agape. Norman made a peculiar chuckle and with a grin, he replied that he was not joking but really very serious.

'Then he must be joking or else he's crackers!' hypothesised Felicity and again she was both transfixed and speechless.

'Don't look like that. He asked her in front of me and she took it to be ragging and ignored the question. Then when I looked in to see him before I left, but without Anne, he questioned me without me realising what he was getting at. Then he blithely announces he was in mind to take her on and has charged me to secrecy. Of course, you know that if it does come off, she will be Lady Cuthbertson, not just plain Mrs.'

'Sorry Norm, I still cannot believe it. I admit that she has sprung up among us with our own asking, and if I may say, with our encouragement too. She has certainly earned her place with us, but to marry a titled fellow takes some beating. Do you really think he was in earnest or could it not be that he was pulling your leg or something like that?'

'Darling, I came away quite convinced that he meant every word of it. All we can do is to sit back and watch it happen. That's if her Ladyship Anne agrees? How do you think she will respond to the offer, my love?' asked Norman as he continued to look at her amazement with more than a little delight that he had brought her a thought to keep her mind occupied.

'Well, I really don't know! I suppose it's a good bid as he is reputed to be very wealthy, but he has a very strong personality and does not brook corrections or answers back. He appears to me to be the type that commands the senior position even in marriage and I wonder how she would accept that. I really don't know Norm, but I must add that it is just as easy to marry a rich man as a poor one, eh?' enunciated Felicity, with a little chuckle.

'Then let us keep our secret and say nothing, but sit back and watch developments. Ah, that must be the lunch that I ordered at last. Just stay there and I will open the door.' And as he spoke, he walked over to the door and opened it to receive the twin-packed lunches as ordered.

Chapter 17

'Nice to see you again, Angus,' said Anne in a straight tone as they met, and she continued, 'and what are you doing around these parts?'

'Actually, I was for calling on Joan and asking her to see you to invite you both to my farewell party and wanted her to come and ask you. But as I have seen you myself now, will you come this Sunday, Anne?'

'And what is it in aid of then?' posed Anne still in an unconvinced manner.

'I am being sent to the States for a period to get to grips with their methods, so that I can be of greater use when I get back here. So I do hope you will come. But we can walk on to Joan's together if you like and we can both ask her too, shall we?' he asked as he peered into her eyes and thought he detected a glimmer of approval of himself.

'Well,' paused Anne as in deep thought, 'I do not think I will go with you to Joan, as she may not believe us that we just met. You may tell her that we have met and if she goes to your party, then I too may join her. Will that be in order, Angus?' she queried.

'That would be lovely, Anne. I do hope that you do come as you know my feelings for you. But would you care for a quick coffee before we separate as I would like to ask you something else, eh?' he asked as he paused in their walk as he stood contemplating for her reply.

'So long as it is just a quick coffee, we can pop in over there,' she replied as she indicated a small tea bar within view.

They entered the tearoom and took a seat. As the waiter appeared to walk towards them, Angus indicated in a voice loud enough for him to hear, that they desired a couple of coffees.

'Anne, it is that I am still in love with you and would like to ask you very seriously if you would be engaged to me, and then we could marry on my return from America. I should be getting a handsome raise in salary on my return and will be able to afford to wed. Please say yes and we could make the party a dual affair, for my going off and for our engagement,' he asked as he peered into her face hoping against hope that she would be inclined towards him.

Anne did not respond directly but without looking up, took another sip of her coffee, then placing the cup back onto the saucer, eyed him, then spoke, 'Angus, you know I had very nice feelings for you when we first met, but you shattered them over that spot of bother you got into. I still like you, but cannot say that I love you. In any case, I am not marrying for at least a year or so, as I have my finals to do first. But Joan is in love with you, so why not ask her?' proposed Anne as she thought that she liked him more than she cared to admit.

'I also like Joan, but it is you that I love, Anne. I have a very good job and am well-liked, otherwise they would not send me on this course, so you can be sure that I could keep you in the style that you would appreciate. Please think it over, and let me phone you, perhaps tomorrow or if you would permit me to, I will call for you at your home,' suggested Angus again more in hope than expectancy.

'All I can say, Angus, is that the last time we spoke, I told you in no uncertain terms that I did not wish to see you again, and here we are talking together as if I had not given you that injunction. Well, I cannot be angry with you forever, and if you are going away, the least I can do is to let bygones be bygones. But you may call on me tomorrow night and tell me if the party is on. I must go now so let's leave it like that, shall we?' As she finished, she stood up to leave. Angus also arose from his seat and they both walked out together and bid each other cheerio.

'Is Joan in, please?' asked Angus as he stood at the open door of her house and asked presumably, her mother.

'Yes, she is in, but who shall I say wishes to see her?' asked her mother in a pleasant voice and with a smile of welcome on her countenance.

'Just tell her it's Angus; she will know who I am,' he ventured.

'Then come in and wait in here,' she replied as she showed him into a large pleasant furnished room to the front of the house.

Before he was able to take stock of the room, the door opened and in walked Joan in a dazzling white frilled blouse and flared skirt, looking like a stage star.

'Hullo Angus, this is a surprise. To what I owe the pleasure of your call?' she asked in a flippant mood.

'I came to ask you to my "farewell" party next Sunday, as I am off to America for my firm for a while, so that's the reason for my visit. I do hope you can come and anyone else that you would like me to invite, I will,' he suggested as he continued to gaze at her with the thought of Anne's suggestion still lingering in his mind.

'Um, er,' she hesitated, 'I think I can make it, but what of Anne; have you considered asking her, too,' proposed Joan.

'Actually, I met her by chance yesterday and she said that if you would go, then she would too. So that will be nice then, won't it?' posed Angus happy in getting the confirmation, but still with his eyes glued on her.

'Then if you met Anne, did you ask her if it was her at that posh hotel we were passing a while ago?' queried Joan.

'Oh dear, it completely slipped my mind. I have been asked to call her tonight to let her know if you would be going, so can mention it then or should I leave it till we are together?'

'I think it may be better if you left it alone until we are all together. I still cannot get over it how high she is flying,' insinuated Joan but without malice.

'OK then,' he replied as he stood up to leave.

'Why, where are you going. Surely you will stop for a cup of tea before you go, or am I to see you again tonight?' she posed in the hope of an evening's entertainment.

'Well, I did say that I was to call on Anne tonight, but if you would like to come with me, that would be fine. But if not, would you like me to call for you after, perhaps for a coffee some place then?'

recommended Angus who did not know which way to turn between the two.

'That will be fine. You go off and be back say in about an hour. Do you think you can make it by then?' Joan put forward having her doubts that he could get back that soon.

'I'll do my best so had better be off then,' returned Angus in a fluster to be off, so much in a hurry that he failed to offer Joan a kiss on account, that he realised on getting into his car.

'Good evening, may I see Anne, please?' asked Angus as the door opened to his knock by Mrs Hopkins, Anne's mother.

'Then you must be Angus. I have been told to expect you. Please do come on in. She will be down soon I hope. She has brought work home and she does not like to be disturbed until she has completed her task,' she said as she showed him into their lounge.

He followed her into a neat small lounge and suggested that he be seated, then offered him either a beverage or a sherry. He declined and said he would await Anne first, then he may have a cup of tea.

'Anne tells me you are going to America for your firm. They must think a lot of you if they are sending you I suppose?' questioned Mrs Hopkins by way of conversation.

'I have been with my firm since leaving college and am, I believe, considered to be in the running for high promotion some day in the not-too-distant future. I look forward to seeing the States and hope to learn a lot from them. That is really the object of my going there,' Angus advanced in the hope that may be Anne's mother may like him and that may assist his endeavours with Anne.

'How very nice. And I suppose some day you will make a girl very happy with your prospects for the future,' schemed Mrs Hopkins.

'Then you do not know that I have already made a proposal of marriage and have been turned down,' he answered in a pathetic tone.

'My, my, who would have thought that! A nice young man like you to be snubbed. Never mind, there must be other fish to catch, so do not despair,' declared Mrs Hopkins not knowing that it was her own daughter that had turned him down.

They sat looking vacantly for a while as both appeared to be lost for words. Angus reflected that at least her mother appeared to like

him. He was not surprised that she did not know that he had proposed to Anne. When she came into the room, should he mention it
in front of her, or would she react against him for the exposure of
stating the truth? 'Oh dear,' he reflected, 'life is not that simple
however much you plan it to be!'

Mrs Hopkins was surreptitiously looking at Angus and wondered
why he had been rejected. She knew very little of him but it was
apparent that he was on the way up in the world and would make a
good husband to a sensible girl. She reflected inwardly, that he would
also make a very nice son-in-law. He was well-mannered, polite and
apparently well-endowed by external appearances. Must have been a
hussy that turned him down. That's girls of today, so unlike in her
day, she mused.

'Ah, I can hear Anne's door closing. That's her coming down
now,' said her mother as she rose to open the door to her daughter.

'Your friend Angus is waiting for you, Anne dear,' said her mother
as she entered the room.

'Oh, hullo Angus. Hope I have not kept you too long, but I always
insist on finishing my work before I can see anyone. My apologies if I
have been too long.' Then turning to her mother added, 'And why
have you not offered and given him a drink, Mother?'

'Anne dear, he has been asked and declined. Now that you are
here, perhaps he would like a drink with you, eh Angus?' she posed.

'I really cannot stop that long as I have a further appointment, so
thank you all the same, perhaps another time may be,' he replied
wondering if he could now make it in time to get back to Joan in the
promised period of an hour.

'Then I will leave you two together, but before I go I must say that
I commiserate with your Angus for being turned down as he will no
doubt tell you,' said Anne's mother as she rose to leave the room to
the young couple.

For a few moments they sat opposite each other without saying a
word. Anne was partially puzzled to know what exactly he had told
her mother about being 'turned down'. At last she felt her faculties
returning to her, so she asked him what he had told her mother. He
reiterated the conversation, much to Anne's anguish and dismay that
her mother should even know that he had been rejected, even if she

202

did not realise that it was her own daughter that did so. She knew that sooner or later her mother would ask her, and she did not wish to lie to her mother, yet she did not wish to confess that it was she who had rejected the suitor. For the moment, she reflected that she would be prudent to change the topic, so she asked about Joan.

'I am very happy to say that Joan is coming to the party and you promised that if she would, you would too. Is that still on?'

'I always keep my promises, Angus, so you need not ask again,' pouted Anne somewhat still ruffled.

'And can I also announce that the party is both a farewell and engagement party, Anne, my dear?' pleaded Angus as he looked at her in hope, that she dashed with a stern look that spoke for her without her need to say a positive no.

'At least, Anne, please be my escort at my party,' again implored Angus with almost a tear in his eye.

'That is definitely out of the question. It is known by all that you have been escorting Joan, and if I should be at your party with you and Joan is there too, that would be asking for a lot of discontent, so be satisfied that I will come to your party. Now you had better be off to your other date,' added Anne as she rose from her seat as a prelude to showing him out.

'Then let me take you out tomorrow night as a last venture, please,' he asked in supplication.

She stood looking at him and could not decide whether she should be critical of his attitude or commiserate for his presumed sufferings. She could not hate him as she thought she could, but then she was not in love with him, yet she could not disguise the fact that she did like him an awful lot. Then on an impulse, she walked over to where he sat, and offered her hands to him in the pose of assisting him to get off the seat. He took both her hands as offered and rose from the seat and as he did so, she embraced him in a strong hug that he happily reciprocated with untold relish. She allowed him to fondle her as he desired without a murmur of restraint. Even when he took her hand and moved it down towards himself, she did not raise any objection. He had begun to wonder how far she would permit him to go. Would she allow him to take it out, and would she hold it for him or would it be as before, she would jump away from the touch.

'Angus, if you want to get it off, do it quick as my mother is only in the other room,' she whispered in his ear, knowing that he was in a high state of excitement being in such close proximity to her.

As he spoke to her in reply, he took it out and pulled her hand over it to hold and said to her, 'Darling, you make me love you all the more, yet you are so loving to me and so nice.' Then suddenly he cried, 'Quick, cover it, as it is coming,' as he put a handkerchief over to avoid making a mess on the carpet. She assisted him in wiping it and even put it back for him and buttoned him up, then said, 'Angus, that's your farewell present. I never thought that I would ever do what I have done just now, but I have, so please never tell on me. And to make up for it I will see you tomorrow night; you need not pick me up, as I know the way,' she added.

'I'll be there, my love. I do not know how to say thank you for what you have just done. You can rest assured I will keep it to myself.' So with that he gave her an extra long embrace. Then she took the proffered slip of paper with an address thereon, and moved to the door.

'I was expecting you at least a half-hour ago. What kept you, so long at Anne's?' questioned Joan as she let Angus in at the door.

'So sorry, my dear, but I had to wait a hell of a long time for Anne. I saw her mother, and sat with her until Anne came down. Apparently she does not come down until she has finished her work that she has brought home. So that's the reason for the delay. Am I thus exonerated Joan?' posed Angus with a full smile on his face.

'Yes, of course you are, but I did begin to wonder if you had gone off with her or something, that's all,' hinted Joan with a wry look.

'Well, I'm here now, so how about popping out for a coffee or a walk around or whatever?' he proposed.

'I fancy a ride round the park, so let's go.' And as she spoke, she put on a heavy coat that had lain draped over a chair and walked to the door looking at Angus in a 'come on then' stance.

They drove around at first aimlessly, until Angus stopped the vehicle in the same spot they had parked not so long ago.

'It's too cold to sit in the park, so let's have a kiss and cuddle in the car, shall we?' he said as he pulled Joan towards himself.

Without a murmur, Joan embraced him and retaliated his smother of kisses. She did not even murmur when he took her hand and she found that she held a throbbing length of his manhood. Still she did not murmur when he started to tug at her pants to get them lower, so that he had access to her below. He observed that she even wiggled a bit to assist him in his fight with her lower garment. When he did eventually get his fingers within her, she appeared to go straight into ecstasy and frenzy.

This was a new Joan to him, and he began to wonder why she was so co-operative now as against before when she was so frigid. Perhaps she had begun to love him sufficiently to trust him and was willing to offer herself to him! 'But caution old boy,' thought Angus 'Do not go and spoil it, so take it slow?'

'Would you like to lie on the back seat, my love?' whispered Angus to Joan.

Without responding, she half rose and looked over the back seat and muttered, 'Why not'. They helped each other climb over instead of simply leaving the car at the front and re-entering at the rear. Of course to have done so, would have entailed redressing and that meant time, which to both appeared they had none to spare. So they clambered over and she reclined in the position he placed her quite willingly, and much to his pleasurable surprise and wonderment.

'Darling,' breathed Joan, 'I love you Angus and you can do as you like, but please please don't put it in, as I am still afraid!'

'Darling,' he reiterated in his overwhelmingness of his almost complete success. 'You know I wouldn't do anything to upset you, so we will play until you say stop. To be sure that it does not go in you, you will hold it all the time and play with it, eh, my love?' proposed Angus as he placed it in her hand, as he lay almost over her within the confines of the car.

'Well, maybe I should think more of Joan as Anne suggested. She is a nice girl, very charming and pleasant and appears to genuinely love me enough to allow this exercise with me. She does not appear to be so dogmatic or so hard as Anne. Perhaps I should reconsider my proposal. Then again I have dated with Anne. Oh hell! That will upset my contemplation's again. I will now be too confused to know which of the two I really desire and love! Perhaps I will confess to

Joan and get her opinion! Oh dear, No! That will not do, as she will want to know about our adventures, and if I told her that this very night, before we met, I was in a clinch with Anne, and she did what she did, it would I am sure compel her to throw me out.

'Then can I talk to Anne and explain our predicament. Would I have to tell her of my success with Joan? Would that be loyal to Joan if I did? No! I cannot be disloyal and tell anyone of what Joan and I do together. I have to think this one out on my own. After all, I am supposed to be a man of responsibilities, so think man, think and decide.'

All the while he was dreaming, whilst wide awake to what was occurring, he realised that Joan was setting the pace between them now. She was clamouring for his probing with her constant motion and simultaneously was pulling at him, until he felt that it would bleed if held that tight any longer, or it would burst in full flood. He re-asserted himself in his ardour and that appeared to give her instant satisfaction. Then she flung her legs upwards and screamed out and pulled him closer towards herself and began to bite his neck and face. At the same moment he found that he could not contain himself any longer, and could not get anything out to stop the expected mess, which did occur and spread all over the floor of the car.

They both lay exhausted whilst she still holding onto his now shrunken example of manliness, yet his hand still pondered with a finger or two stirring her within. Then without releasing each other, he managed to get on his knees over her, and looking down at her, spoke in a quiet voice.

'My dear, how was that? I am sure you enjoyed the experience and had a nice orgasm. At least you bit me hard enough to emphasise it.'

'Angus my darling, you were marvellous. I must have had what you called an orgasm as I've never had before. And look what you have done on the floor!' she added with a giggle.

'You have the evidence in your own hand. So if you would like to do a bit more, you can wipe it for me and I will wipe you in return. Then instead of biting my neck and face, you can bite that for me. What about that, my dear?' proposed Angus full of expectancy.

'Angus, my darling, I would love to do that, but let us leave a little for the next time, shall we?' We have after all, explored further than before and after all, we are only lovers and not even going out on a regular basis, are we now?' propounded Joan as she looked up to his face that was above her, and smiled as sweetly as she could. She hoped that her reference would perhaps goad him to reveal his true feelings he had for her.

'My sweet, we are going out regular and you know it. You are the only one I am out with these days. So tell me just what is on your mind and then we can talk about it like adults, eh?' he replied.

'You know very well that I love you, otherwise I would not have permitted you to have done what you have to me. But you have never said that you love me, now have you? I do not mean sexual love but personal love, enough to want to marry and all that,' she added wondering how he would respond to an almost reverse proposal.

'My darling Joan, I do love you very sincerely, but as to marriage, I will answer that to you on Sunday at my party. So now let's be straightening up,' he implied. That appeared to pacify her sufficiently for her to co-operate with his suggestion.

'I know all about that, mother. I know what Angus has told you of being refused, but I must go to my room as I have a lot of analysing to do, so please do not disturb me for any reason. I hope you will not bother me with any calls or whatever, please,' requested Anne as she rose to leave the room after hearing her mother retailing Angus' story of humiliation.

'Very well then. If you get any calls I will tell them that you cannot be disturbed to your orders! Will that please you, Anne?' chirped her mother rather put out by Anne's constant removal to work in her room.

Anne withdrew to her room and threw one leg onto the seat of an adjacent chair, but left the other dangling onto the floor. She leaned back and with a sigh, said aloud as if she had company, 'Anne, what the hell is the matter with you? Let us analyse your behaviour latterly and see where you have gotten to. You are acting as a slut and that will not do?' she uttered then went into a muse subconsciously.

'Now why did I behave with Angus as I did this evening. Can I be in love with him? – no – I cannot be! So why then did I masturbate

207

him? Yes, that's what I did and I thought I was sophisticated and blasé, but it seems that I am an immature kid! First of all I accept his overtures and allow him to poke me about, then I snub him. I then permit myself to a reconciliation and what do I do? I masturbate him right here in my own home! And to add insult to injury, I have agreed to date with him tomorrow night. Then it is not unreasonable for him to expect a repeat performance of this afternoon. So what is wrong with my make up that I act like that? What must I do to be with more poise and culture?

'Now, my boss, Norman. If anyone has a right over me, it is him! After all, he has given me such a wonderful opportunity of advancement. And what do I do the first time I get into a clinch with him, but touch him up? Now that is not ladylike! Then when he gets me to an hotel bedroom, we both strip as if we are old timers at the game! Then I go and promise him that even when he does marry Felicity, we will still have our little affair. Am I playing fast and loose?

'Then there is the episode with Jack. Now he is a very nice guy, but why did I hold him and permit him freedom of my body for him to probe at will? Goodness me, it is no ending my going from pillar to post with Tom, Dick and Harry? With Jack I had more than one affair, too. So what is the matter with me?

'But my familiarising with Licy makes me a lezzy? Was I that innocent that I fell into her trap just like that? Is there no end to my degradation? And Licy's bargaining with Norman about my giving myself to him. What have I let myself into? Am I a fit person to know. And my mother downstairs thinks her daughter the heights of high and I feel the lowest of low!

'What would happen to my reputation should any of these persons that I have had affairs with talk? I cannot for one moment think anyone of them would talk, but one never really knows. Where would I be able to put my face, if it ever came out? How would Norman react if he knew his precious Anne was a double player and a cheap thriller? If he sacked me, I would not even get a reference and there goes my chances of taking my finals soon? I can go on all night levelling these criticisms, but they lead me nowhere. So what I must do is, from now on, without fail, to behave in a cultured and refined a manner as I can possibly muster as a cultivated adult. Keep my head up and perhaps a little snooty. Refuse to get into compromising situations. No more bedroom scenes or elsewhere for fingering about and definitely no more holding a man's tool!'

Anne felt considerably relieved when she had formulated a decision for her future. How long she had spent in her room she could only guess, but now feeling a lot happier with her plans ahead, she ignored her task that had compelled her to adjourn to her room, and descended the stairs with a happy smile.

'So glad to see you, Anne, and am glad you are right on time. I was getting apprehensive about the police floating about. Now where would you like to go for the evening, Anne?' gallantly asked Angus as he met her as agreed the day before.

'Tell me, which standard do you ascribe to, the upper class or the otherwise class?' returned Anne now wearing her new severe look.

'Anyone and anywhere you like! I am in the funds, so you say and we will go,' merrily replies Angus full of himself and full of expectations too.

'Then do you know the Eastbury Hotel. They have a most delicious table and that is where I would recommend; that's if you can stake it though?' posed Anne.

'Anne, my dear, it will be my pleasure. I know just where it is and we will be there in a matter of minutes. Can one park at the rear, Anne?' asked Angus as he twisted and turned the car from street to street with obvious confidence and knowledge of his whereabouts on the West side of London.

'No, you cannot park it, but leave it outside and give the hall porter the key. They look after it and fetch it back when we are ready to leave. Ah! We are here already; that's quick!' answered Anne as she made a move to get out of the car. Angus switched off and followed her to the entrance of the hotel.

Anne spoke to the porter and told Angus to pass him his keys, then led the way to the beautifully decorated dining hall, where quite a number of diners sat, despite the earliness of the hour.

They stood for but a moment in the entrance, when a waiter approached and said, 'Miss Hopkins. Nice to see you again. Just the two of you or are there more to follow?'

'Just the two of us tonight, Harry. Can we have my usual table please, if it is not already taken?'

'It is free. Must have guessed you would be here tonight,' he replied and led the way much to Angus' surprise at the acknowledgement and deference she was receiving.

They seated themselves when they were handed an enormous-sized menu to choose from. Whilst they sat studying the menu, the wine waiter approached and said affably, 'Good evening Miss Hopkins and you too, sir. You could have sat in the lounge whilst your meal was being prepared, but you know that, so can I take your order?' he asked as he presented a copious wine list to Angus.

'Angus, what would you care to drink? The waiter knows what I will have, don't you?' she asked as she looked up at him.

The waiter affirmed the information and took Angus' order.

'They seem to know you pretty well here, Anne. How come?' queried Angus when they were free from the waiters' attention.

'I have to fetch clients here for meals and I have a firm's account here, so I am well known; that is all. Being known gives us the best service that you could wish for, you will see,' added Anne looking pleasantly happy in a neat two-piece costume that seemed to him much too good to have used for work. Then she appeared to be on a high-level income, so could obviously afford to.

'You must be high up in your firm for that perk?' questioned Angus now looking at her in a new light of awe.

'I would not say high up, but I'm considered capable enough to run a department and attend to clients direct. You met me tonight at a client's firm where I shall be for a few more days in charge of the whole of their accounts,' she replied in a nonchalant manner.

'By your dress you must be in the top bracket salary-wise I should speculate, Anne,' challenged Angus now growing more and more alert to whom he had been playing with and to whom he had proposed.

'Yes, I do get a commensurate pay-packet which gives me all the comfort I desire. And in a couple of weeks, I shall be in my own flat, too. Pity you are off so soon, as I am sure you would have liked my new apartment and you will miss my opening party soon after I take possession of it,' ribbed Anne with a trifling gloat in her voice that did not escape him.

He seemed to shrivel inwards and felt at a loss as to how to recuperate her manner of affection that she showed him but yesterday. He realised that she was in the upper pay range and could possibly be topping him. How could he approach a woman like that when she was a higher earner? His pondering made him somewhat quiet and sullen to which Anne spoke sharply to him, indicating that he should be happy, as she has agreed to join him for that last date before his departure to the United States.

'So sorry, Anne, but you have put me in the shade and I do not know how to snap out,' whimpered Angus looking at her sorrowfully.

'You had better snap out of it, Angus my boy, as I am too well-known here to put up with sulks. So snap out of it and be a man!' she remonstrated with him. His immediate reaction was to smile in a half-hearted way and say that he was sorry for his untoward feelings and that it was over.

'Ah, it is just as well, as the first course is coming. Now enjoy yourself and try to be happy. I will not bite you!' she threw at him.

'I wish you would bite me any time you like, Anne my dear,' he dared, looking at her with appealing eyes.

'Angus, let me get one thing straight with you. What has happened in the past is the past, and will never reoccur. And if you desire my friendship, you will respond as becomes a friend and not a lover. Do I make myself clear, Angus?' quipped Anne with a slight hostility in her voice.

'Anne my dear, whatever you say will not stop me loving you. But I value you too much to lose you as my betrothed and friend. So I have no alternative but to accept your dictates. You can forgive me and I promise you will not have reason to be upset with me again, Anne dear.'

They silently ate their meal listening to the background music with but a comment now and then. The atmosphere seemed to have soured since his apology, but when the table had been cleared for coffee, he mentioned that he had seen her entering the hotel with a gentleman in dress-wear whilst out with Joan.

'That is possible. That would be a client and I usually make my entrance here about eightish, so that by then some of the tables are

211

removed making space for dancing. Why did you not hail me if you saw me?' questioned Anne as she looked at him anew.

'We did not like to disturb you, as you appeared to us to be engrossed, so we did not,' answered Angus wondering now if he should have mentioned that fact at all.

'Angus, you will recall that at the time I told you not to approach me, I called you over to the side to tell you. I would never embarrass anyone by ticking them off in front of someone else. By the same token, if you ever approach me when I am in company, I will respond politely. So you do not have to walk past me and hide if you see me out with someone else. In any case, I am not ashamed to be seen with whomever I am with, not even you,' countered Anne without any belligerency.

'Thank you for telling me, Anne. As we are finished, would you like to stay on now that we are here and have a dance or two or would you prefer me to give you a lift home now?' uttered Angus quietly hoping that they would stay behind, yet he would be glad for the evening to come to an end.

'I should like to go now but only if I see a smile on your face. It grieves me to see you on your last days here on a farewell dinner in such a poor mood. Remember, laugh and the world laughs with you, but snore and you sleep alone! So what do you say?' replied Anne looking at his face as he put a forced smile on it.

'I tell you what, Anne. Let's just have one dance to get us both in a better frame of mind and then we can go; how about that, eh?' he said looking decidedly happier.

'OK then,' came the reply as she rose from the table and sauntered to the edge of the dance area.

As they danced around the floor he brightened up and thanked her for her companionship and understanding. He noted that she made no comment on the fact that he held her tightly and felt himself getting heated as she was obviously aware too. They did the one dance as agreed, then returned to the table to settle the bill; then he took her arm and they walked out to the bids of good-night from a few of the staff.

Joan and Angus stood side by side in the church hall to receive the guests invited to his farewell party. His father was fiddling with the new fangled tape deck endeavouring to get it to function better than it appeared to be able to. He eventually achieved a modicum of success and set the tape going to a modern rock tune.

His mother was checking over the laden table laid with a great variety of food. First, she changed the place of one tray then replaced it with another. Eventually, she put them back as they were originally. Somehow, she could not get it just right as she thought it should be, until her husband came over to her and complimented her on the way she had set the table. That gave her the satisfaction to preen at the goodies and walk off with her husband.

Meanwhile, a gathering of lads and lasses had accumulated. They appeared to be lost as they mooched around the hall, first sauntering over to one then to another.

'Ah, Anne, so glad you have come,' said Joan as she greeted her friend.

'Well, I did say I'd come and here I am. How are you Angus?' she said as she turned towards him. He acknowledged her arrival then gave her a peck on the cheek, as if old friends. Anne raised no objection that gave him momentary pleasure.

'Be a darling, Anne. Could you get the folk into dancing or something. They seem lost without a leader,' asked Angus of Anne.

'No problem,' she replied, then walked over to the tape deck and changed the tape to a modern dance. As it struck up, she called out, 'Everyone on the floor, please.' And like lemmings, they all turned lifelessly to see who called out, then spontaneously, took a partner and danced.

'Thanks Anne, you're marvellous. Don't know what we could have done without you,' echoed Angus, who left his 'post' to thank her immediately when he saw the success of her call to dance. 'Now would you care to stay with me for a few minutes to relieve Joan?' he added. Anne consented and joined him at the door to greet the arrivals whilst Joan left her station to mingle a while.

'I have not mentioned that we had a meal together the other night, Anne, to Joan, as I do not know how she would take it. Do you think I should tell her or not? For that matter, if I do tell her, I will then tell her that I told you that we saw you at that hotel,' challenged Angus.

'I see nothing wrong in having a meal with a friend. But if you are afraid to tell her, if you think it will disturb her and your chances of wedding her, then I will forget that we met. Is this the real reason for asking me, because you have decided that you want her after all?'

'To be truthful, I have not slept at all last night pondering over the question, and all you have told me . . . Welcome, come on in, the cloaks are over there . . . I thank you, Anne, most sincerely for all you have said and really believe that although I do love you, I realise that marriage . . . Hullo, yes Joan is . . . ummm . . . yes, she's over there . . . sorry for the interruptions, Anne, now where were we, . . . ah yes, as I was saying, a marriage between us would be like a ship in a gale, tossing, turning and rarely smooth. Joan has hinted very strongly, that she would like to marry me, so I have decided to ask her tonight and announce it here. I ask you Anne as a trusted friend, am I wise?

'Hullo Bill. Come on in Mary, yes – she is here. I can see her just over there,' expressed Angus to new arrivals as they came in. A few more friends and relatives came in together followed by a lull. He turned back to Anne and asked for her advice and opinion.

'I endorse your proposal Angus. You could not get a finer girl than Joan. Now as far as we are concerned, we are old friends, but have never had anything going between us, as we have always been, perhaps you may say, a bit prudish, now haven't we Angus? You have never even lifted my skirt and I definitely have never touched you, now have I?' announced Anne peering at him with a glint of devilment in her eye.

It took Angus but a second to realise that Anne had given him a clean ticket. She had in a couple of words, wiped out all that had transpired between them, so that he could approach Joan with a clear conscience that he would not be betrayed.

'Darling, I have already said tonight that you are marvellous and now I say it doubly. You always have the right answer and thank you. That means I have not asked you about seeing you at the hotel. Mustn't say any more, Joan is coming back, but thanks again.'

'Glad you're back, Joan. Was about to ask Anne about seeing her the other night at that hotel. Perhaps, as you are here, you will ask her, eh?' suggested Angus.

'Will in a minute, but have had a nice long chat with your folks. They are nice and chummy, aren't they? They wanted to know if I was your number one girl, and I told them to ask you. What should I have said, Angus darling?' quipped Joan with an appealing gleam at him.

Before answering her, he turned to Anne and asked her if she could look after the door for just a few minutes, as he had an important statement to make to Joan, as he surreptitiously gave her a broad wink. Anne understood the object of his request and waved him off with her arm in a gratuitous manner.

'Come with me Joan, please. I wish to ask you a question,' said Angus as he led her by the elbow towards a corner he had pointed out. She followed wondering why in the middle of a party he should want to have a private chat with her. She remonstrated, but he just mumbled, 'Come on please.' When they reached the corner, she turned and asked him what it was that was on his mind.

'On my mind is you, my love. I have been trying to pluck up courage to ask you to marry me and I am taking the bull by the horns and doing so now. Joan, my sweet, will you marry me?' and placing his two arms on her shoulders, he looked into her face as it lit up and coloured slightly.

On hearing his proposal of marriage, she flung her arms around his neck and hugged him and whispered in his ear, 'Yes, yes, my love, I will marry you because I love you Angus.'

'Then let us go over to my parents and tell them, shall we?' suggested Angus as they disengaged themselves.

'My parents are not here to tell, so I think I should tell Anne first. Then we could speak to your folks, shall we?' replied Joan glowing all over.

'Darling, I propose and intend to be the boss, but this time I will let you have your way. We will let Anne know first, then my parents, then we can make a public announcement later.'

Holding hands, the newly betrothed couple barged through the growing crowd to the door where Anne still stood.

In an excited manner, Joan announced to Anne that Angus had proposed to her. Anne took Joan into a hug and kissed her, and congratulated her. Anne then turned to Angus and said generally, 'May I kiss the groom to congratulate him too?'

'Of course you can, Anne,' and with that permission, she accepted his hug and kiss, which this time was of the modest and courteous kind.

'Now Anne, with Joan's permission,' began Angus first looking in the direction of Anne then turning towards Joan, 'it would be our pleasure if you would make a short speech or announcement of the object of this party, that of my going to America, then please add mention of our engagement, would you, please?'

'Oh yes, please Anne, will you?' begged Joan in conformity with Angus.

'I will providing you speak with your folks first, Angus. You must not shock them however pleased they may be. Now it appears that possibly all your invited guests are here, so I will accompany you both to your parents Angus, so that you can make a parental announcement – so lead on you two,' jested Anne as she pointed towards the crowd, and then together they searched out his parents.

'Mum, Dad, I have something very special to tell you,' proclaimed Angus as he came up to his parents, sitting quietly in a corner, each with a drink in their hands. Both parents looked up and cast their eyes upon the threesome, but did not speak, as they awaited the further comment by their son. 'I have proposed to Joan and am happy to say that she has accepted me. Can I have your blessings and congratulations?' added Angus as he pressed Joan forward to be in front of him as if on exhibition.

'Why, I'm delighted my dear,' responded his mother as she stood up and held out her hand to welcome and kiss her future daughter-in-law.

In a somewhat slower tempo, his father also arose from his seat and imitated his wife's gesture and enveloped the bride to be to his bosom in a parental welcome.

'Also,' began Angus again, 'I have asked Anne here to make the announcement this evening. I hope you do not object,' he added as he peered at his folks still in a very happy frame of mind.

'By all means. She is the friend of both of you, so we think it very proper,' replied his father.

'Oh dear,' thought Anne. 'Me again!' She began to dwell on what she should proclaim and from where. The stage was not accessible. She thought. Then she decided. She requested all of them, Joan, Angus and his parents, to stand near the tape recorder. Then placing a chair in front of it, and asking the parents to stand on one side and the betrothed couple on the other side, she asked Angus to stop the tape. As he did so, she mounted the chair. As the sound of music died away, the crowd turned towards them and sensed that an announcement was about to be uttered, so they stood and watched and waited. With her hands raised indicating a command for silence, Anne asked the assembly for a few moments hush! Within seconds, it was possible to hear that proverbial pin drop!

'My dear friends, it gives me great pleasure, first to be asked to speak to you this evening, and still greater pleasure in the announcement that I have been asked to make. But first things first. As we all know, the reason why we are here, is to celebrate Angus' tour of duty in the United States of America. This in itself speaks volumes for the esteem his firm has of him. It means, in basic, that he is considered worthy of spending a lot of money on, because they are aware that he is worth every nickel of it and will repay them in his value to the firm. I am sure that you concur with me when I say on all our behalf, that we wish him bon voyage and success in his future in his chosen career. (Hear hear – good old Angus etc. was shouted out by a number of the guests). Now an important extra piece of information that I must retail to you tonight – if not the most important. This evening in this very hall, Angus here (as she pointed to him) has asked Joan here, to be his betrothed (again she pointed to his betrothed) and I am happy to proclaim that she has agreed. As you all may already know, they have known each other for quite some time and have been keeping company for the same period. To me it is not surprising as I saw love shining in their eyes long ago. I am also happy to tell you, that both his parents that are standing right here (she pointed to them) have accepted our Joan with great affection and am sure that her parents will accept Angus. As Bernard Shaw once said, "You know, marriage is popular because it combines the maximum of temptation with the maximum of opportunity." (A gust of raucous laughter.) Now a further point – I hope I am not boring you, please forgive me if I am, but must also announce that Joan has been accepted by Oxbridge University and will be away much of the time her betrothed Angus will be away. But it is hoped that they will meet again during vacation time. So will you all take a glass and please raise the roof with your Hip Hip . . .' (Hooray came the response, not just once but the traditional three times.)

Before Anne had time to dismount from the chair she had been standing on, the crowd gathered around the couple to personally congratulate them by shaking of the hand, and from those more intimate, by showering them with kisses. For the next ten minutes or so, the medley stood around the couple until one by one they dispersed and the music was again restarted. All the young men now clamoured to partner the bride to be, and Joan found herself the most popular girl of the evening.

The very next day, Monday, Anne was back at her task on behalf of her firm at Sir John Cuthbertson's establishment. As she entered her room allocated her, Mr Smith told her that the chief wanted to see her in his room as soon as she came in. Without ado, she wended her way through the corridors to his room and politely knocked. On receiving the invitation to enter, she did so. They exchanged greetings as she was asked to take a seat.

'Anne, I like your loyalty and approve, and I know you have been offered many posts as evidence of your quality. Now I do not offer you a post here, even though I would gladly have you here, but have something else in mind that I will tell you of later. But right now, I would like you to join me tonight for a meal at the Ritz. Will you come with me?' he entreated as he peered into her face that did not appear to respond!

'Well, Sir John. I have not finished my task so feel that I should not. But if you insist, then I must insist on asking you to join me rather than the other way round,' retorted Anne still without a glimmer of apparent interest on her face.

'Well, I never expected a young lady to offer to take me out for a dinner before. That sure is a novelty,' expostulated Sir John with a broadening smile.

'That is quite all right, Sir John. I am authorised by my firm to take clients out and as you are a valued client, I am asking you to be my guest? An additional reason why I ask, is that I am proposing to ask a couple of friends out tonight who have become engaged last night, and he is off to the States on behalf of his firm. So I will be killing the

218

two proverbial birds with one stone, sir,' replied Anne with now a look of keen interest.

'You are allowed to take clients out at your own discretion, Anne!' challenged Sir John as he again looked at her in wonder and disbelief with great emphasis on his words.

'Just say yes, sir, then telephone Mr Meredith to confirm. I will meet you at the Eastbury Hotel at eight in the foyer. Black tie, of course. All agreed sir?' she asked as she observed that his face coloured slightly, no doubt by the unexpected turn of events and reversal of invitations.

'Well,' spluttered Sir John, 'it looks that you have cornered me and left me without an answer. I did really desire to have your company alone, but in the circumstances, I will meet you as you suggest on the promise that you will join me, say on Wednesday, for a meal out and perhaps theatre. Can we agree on that or are you going to manoeuvre out of that?' he ventured to make that mild pun whilst he wore a big grin.

'Urr . . . I think I am free on that night, so I accept. Perhaps you will give me the itinerary later, eh, Sir John?' questioned Anne now looking a bit more pleasant and reasonable. 'I hope you will not mind my calling my friends to confirm too,' she added as an afterthought.

Thereafter, small talk ensued of little consequence until the assistant brought in Sir John's morning coffee. She was requested to fetch another cup for Anne, who consented to remain and enjoy the break, even if rather early in the morning. This gave Anne reason to question why he had a kind of breakfast here in the office and why he did not have it at home. It was then she learned that he was a bachelor, and his housekeeper did not arrive until after he had left for work, thus his routine.

'I'd like to speak with Mr Angus Finch, please,' asked Anne into the mouthpiece of the telephone. She was requested to hold on.

'Mr Finch here; can I help you?' came the reply in Anne's ear.

'Ah, Angus, Anne here. Got home all right last night?'

'Oh, Anne, yes sure, but what makes you phone me here?'

'Because I would like you and Joan to be my guests at the Eastbury Hotel at eight tonight. That will be my engagement present to you

219

both. And I must tell you, I will be having a client with me too, but you will not mind that I'm sure. So what you say, my ex-lover?' chirped Anne to his consternation.

'I'd love to come but will it not be open to question if I am recognised there,' came the answer in a strong doubtful tone.

'You have always trusted me, Angus, so do check with Joan and get her to join you. Meet you in the foyer unless I hear to the contrary, in black tie.' And with that she hung up.

Chapter 18

She had already agreed with Angus to meet him at the Eastbury Hotel that evening at eight in company with Joan. It was not until after lunch that he called back to confirm. This delayed Anne in calling her boss Mr Meredith to indicate that she had Sir John for a meal that night and that the other guests were on her account. Her boss insisted that she should charge the whole in appreciation of her efforts. With a little persuasion, Anne agreed to do so. What with the number of calls she had to instigate, which also included a call to her mother to say that she should not prepare a meal for her that night, her day did not last long enough to get much work completed. She viewed her day's output with apprehension, but determined that the morrow would compensate, as she would refuse all interference.

As the appointment was not until eight, she was able to stay a while longer, which gave her some satisfaction in her output of work. She also missed the home-going traffic, as she had to return home, where she had to change into her evening wear. Nevertheless, she proposed to be the first at the hotel, as she did not wish to keep Sir John waiting. She therefore arrived about ten minutes to time, so she entered the bar and ordered a light sherry whilst she sat and waited.

Joan, in the company of Angus, entered the bar and spotted Anne sitting there talking to another client of the hotel. They both walked towards her calling out their greetings. Anne acknowledged them and offered them a drink, too. As she was about to order, Sir John walked in and approached Anne with a hand outstretched in greeting.

'Ah, Sir John, just in time for an aperitif. But before I order that, let me introduce you to the engaged couple that I mentioned this morning. This is my friend Joan and her fiancé Angus. Joan, Angus, this is Sir John Cuthbertson. Now that you are all acquainted, let me order you that drink Sir John. What will it be, whiskey, sherry or what?'

They had all shaken hands and exchanged smiles of greeting. Our betrothed couple were a bit nonplussed to be in the company of a titled gent. Sir John sensed this, and kept up the chatter to draw them in so as to get them at their ease to act natural and not stunted.

'Would you and your guests Miss Hopkins, like to choose from the menu and I will call you when the table is ready?' asked a waiter from Anne, as he handed out a menu to each of them.

'Yes, why not. If you would care to make your choice and let Harry know, he will see to it, won't you, Harry? By the way, Harry, my regular table, please,' added Anne as she raised her head to look towards Harry, then looked down at the enormous menu both in content and size.

They all eventually gave their orders and the waiter withdrew. In the meantime, they sat facing each other around a circular table in the bar. Sir John was asking and getting answers from Angus, as to his planned trip to the United States for a few day's time. The two ladies just sat back listening until the waiter returned and intimated that their table was ready.

'You all go in; I must make a call first before I sit down. Hope you will excuse me Anne?' asked Sir John.

'By all means. We will not commence until you return, as a few minutes more or less will not matter, we are sure.' With that, she led the way to her favourite table.

'Say, Anne, you did not indicate that it was a titled guy joining us, did you?' questioned Joan.

'Why, does it really matter. You will find him a nice fellow and as you have already witnessed, he has taken to you both, so say no more, here he comes,' concluded Anne as she rose to greet her guest.

'Hope all is well, Sir John?' asked Anne as he drew closer to the table.

'Yes, thank you. I had to contact an acquaintance that would not be available during normal working hours, hence my late call. I hope

222

I have not upset your table plans however, Anne,' he added with a disarming smile.

'Not at all, as you can see the plates are not all filled. So you are in time to enjoy a good meal. And I can assure you that the food here is good.'

It was nearly midnight and they still occupied their table enjoying an occasional dance and a drink in between. In the dancing, they exchanged partners to mutual pleasure. Anne was in high spirits that Sir John appeared to dance very well and lightly, too. She found him an admirable guest with a fund of topics to keep the conversation at a constant pitch.

'I do think that it is time we thought about getting off home. I have work tomorrow, and if I am late, that ogre I am with will slaughter me!' chirped Anne in a humorous tone.

'I am sure that if the ogre does slaughter you, it would be a nice tasty bit of lamb well worth the bite!' interceded Sir John in retaliatory mirth that the others appreciated and understood.

'Then let's go. You two also ready or do you wish to remain a while longer?' Anne asked looking first at Joan then at Angus.

'Oh no, we two are also ready,' they replied and arose from the table to walk to the cloakroom to regain their topcoats.

Anne went on ahead to sign the chit and ask the head waiter to fetch Sir John's car to the entrance. Angus, who was directly behind Anne, asked the same from the waiter before he disappeared. So all in company, they entered the entrance porch and awaited the arrival of the cars. Anne kissed both her friends good night and Sir John asked in mock timidity if he too may kiss the bride. To a chorus of 'yes' from the three, he gave Joan a sweet peck and a nightly greeting. By now, Sir John's car arrived, so he took Anne by the elbow and walked her to the car, which for the first time she realised that it was a Rolls Royce. He opened the front passenger door and insisted that she enter, as he proposed to escort her home. Without any reluctance, she took her seat alongside and before she realised, they were gliding away. He asked and she replied as to her address.

As it was that late, traffic was light. And although it was very cold, it was dry. They arrived at Anne's home in a reasonably short space of time. He switched off the engine and seemed reluctant to let her get out and enter her home. He plied her with questions. When she heard the neighbouring clock strike the half hour after midnight (or was it one o'clock), she suggested that it was time that she left otherwise she feared she would oversleep and that ogre would really be cross with her.

'My dear Anne, I have really enjoyed myself so much that I am reluctant to let you go. I know I must and as an ogre I demand my price! Will you kiss me good night in the good old-fashioned style?' he put forward in a sang-froid manner.

'I do not know how to kiss in the old-fashioned manner, so you will have to content yourself with all I have to offer in the only way I know. So kindly raise the armrests, then it will be my, and I hope, your pleasure to kiss good night.' retorted Anne in a humorous tone.

Sir John did as he was bid and doing so realised that once again, Anne was telling him what to do. It seemed so incongruous in both their characters, yet it seemed so natural.

As soon as he had raised up the armrest that was between them, he slid closer towards Anne across the leather upholstery, and within the confines of the car, held out his arms to receive Anne. Without hesitation, Anne also slid closer and entered his embrace. She endeavoured to kiss him on the cheek but he turned her so that they kissed on the mouth. He held her somewhat tightly and that made her realise that he was possibly getting excited and that would not do.

'Come now, Sir John, enough is enough!' she cried as she tried to disengage herself from his hold.

'On one condition will I release you. Please, when in company with me, kindly drop the "Sir" as I would like to get to know you better. At least we have broken the ice this evening, for which I am grateful and now look forward to our engagement on our own. Now ask me again.'

'You're the boss John, so kindly release me,' answered Anne in compliance to his request.

'I wonder if I would always be the boss with Anne,' mused Sir John to himself as he pressed another kiss on her lips then let his arm drop away from her.

With but a few more words she left the car. He awaited until he saw the door of the house close after her that he re-engaged the car engine, put it in automatic gear and moved off.

'Darling, wasn't it a lovely evening?' posed Angus to Joan as he pulled up his car a street away from her home.

'I think she is a very lucky girl to have a job that allows her to take clients to that hotel. I agree with you that both the food and dancing was glorious. And did you notice how they all appeared to know Anne and more or less, fawned over her? She sure has a way with her to get the best out of everything and I admire her for that. Also she is a really true and good friend. I have never known her to fail me yet whatever I asked of her. Have you had that experience?' queried Joan.

'Well,' hesitated Angus, not really knowing how to answer, in case he gave himself away in a small detail that would lead to a larger exposition. 'I really cannot think of anything but am inclined to agree with you that she is a topping sport,' ventured Angus as a way round that question.

'I could name a few items that you know of. When you asked her at a moment's notice to make the announcement on our engagement, she did so very nicely. I truly believe it was her that engineered us together, despite the fact that she has a soft spot for you. No, do not look at me like that, I know she likes you. Do you think she would have invited us to that expensive night out if she did not have a high regard and feeling for you?' asked Joan in a thoughtful intonation.

'Joan, I am sure you are right. She does speak a lot about you and very much in your favour. She is the best of friends that you could possibly find. I suppose you must be right that she likes me, but perhaps it's because of you. However, do not let the night disappear altogether without a cuddle, my love,' he replied as he snuggled closer to Joan and placed one arm around her shoulders and the other across her lap.

Joan accepted the overture of the arms placed as they were and moved closer too. She turned her face towards Angus and engaged with him in a kissing bout, whilst he moved his hand to the knee of her long gown.

'Darling, pull it up. It's too long for me to reach,' he implored.

Without releasing themselves, she tugged at her ball gown until it was above her knees, then placed her hand around his neck. Before he took advantage of the raised dress, he unbuttoned himself and pulled her hand over himself. With a slight hesitancy, she gripped him as he motioned without words, then attacked her hem. Without any objection, he was able to get his hand onto her pubic hairs that invited him to smooth them both upwards and downwards, then rotating his palm around her there. He felt that it was oozing even before he penetrated his fingers within her. As he moved in and out with his fingers, she sighed very heavily and at the same time, squeezed her grip in time to her heavy exhalation. All the while, they were mouth to mouth breathing and sighing in heavy gasps. He was able to get a hand to his pocket to extract a handkerchief, which he held in case he would need it, which he knew that he would in a very short space of time.

'Darling, would you like me to put it in?' posed Angus who now thought that Joan may even say yes to him after the pleasures of the last couple of days and particularly that evening.

'Please don't press me. I would like to but am afraid, so please don't,' she replied in a partially frightened manner as she felt that if he insisted, she would now have to submit. To make it more difficult for him to achieve this action, she moved slightly away.

He realised that her movement was instigated by fear, so did not press the issue again, but closed up as before and then suggested, 'Then if you would not like me to put it in, will you bite it for me? I am sure you will enjoy that too.' As he spoke, on the assumption that she would, he moved back a bit so that she could reach him all the more readily.

'No, no. Please, Angus. Don't ask me to do those things. I do not like to!' whimpered Joan in a very apprehensive manner.

'Darling, we are engaged so it is all right. Look at it; it is asking for you.' As he uttered those words, he put his hand onto her chest, and pushed her gently away so as to expose himself to her. So there they sat almost side by side, within the confines of the small car; he with his hand almost invisible, hidden beneath the long skirt with his fingers still probing her, and there she was holding onto his erect throbbing rod of human flesh that he first proposed to place where his fingers now resided, and now he was asking for her to take it within her mouth in place of his tongue. She did not wish to do either, but how to overcome the situation and yet make her beau happy, in what she had given and allowed him.

226

'My love,' she answered, as she moved back again so as to make it difficult to enact the proposed biting, 'you know I will do anything to make you happy, but you should also consider to make me happy, too. You know my feelings about sex before marriage, so please, my love, do not press me as it grieves me that I cannot give you what you ask. Now look what I have in my hand. Surely you cannot expect me to put that in my mouth without injury to me; it is so big and long!' she implored.

'Then at least, if you will not put in all in your mouth, at least the knob alone then. Then you can suck in as much as you feel able to, and in that way we can both enjoy the thrill. What you say, my love?' pleaded Angus now in more hope than before.

Inspiration came to her rescue as she grabbed for the handkerchief that reposed beside her, and at the same time, she squeezed and pulled at his rod, so that it expanded and throbbed, and just as he completed his sentence, he ejaculated into the prepared handkerchief that she held over it.

'You are now expecting me to mouth it now that you have done that?' asked Joan in a quiet voice in private victory.

'Darling, you got me on too soon. If you had just held it, then it would have lasted another minute or so in your mouth. But you have pulled it and got it off too soon. Never mind, next time, eh darling? But wipe it up for me, there's a dear,' he begged as she was about to let go.

She responded in his call to clean him up, and after that she replaced it within his trousers and buttoned them up. She wished she could only wipe herself too, as she felt far from comfortable in the gooey mess there.

They made their plans to meet again prior to his departure, at which point she asked him to drive around the corner to her home and allow her to alight there.

Wynne and Tracey still accompanied Richard to Andrew's flat on their weekly entertainment. Of late, the major topic of conversation was the impending marriage between Tracey and Andrew. Richard began to feel uncomfortable at the constant gibes at his lack of enthusiasm of proposing to Wynne. He had times without number,

227

stated his case that he would happily offer to wed, but felt that he was not in a financial position that he would like to maintain. If he married now, his standard would of necessity be very reduced, and that would only create unhappiness between them.

'Love flies out of the window if there is no money in the kitty,' argued Richard. Then added, 'You know the quip, *Money doesn't talk any more, it goes without saying.*'

'But you pool your joint resources and that should give you the start you need,' haggled Andrew without any strength, as he knew, that he too would not have offered marriage if he could not maintain a wife without dropping his own standard.

'Wynne darling, would you be happy to marry me and live in a little semi in some back street? Then if we had a kid, we would not be able to live even in that low substandard and would have to stay home, as we would not be able to afford the luxury of friends at home, or visit. Now truthfully, could you tolerate that for more than a week before you would be screaming to go back to your job and home!' hypothesised Richard with a glum face, very weary of the constant attacks.

'My love, I would not be having a "kid", as you put it. I would screw it off to make sure that would not happen. I for one, vote that we do not raise this topic, as it is up to me more than Richard to say the word, is it not?' she challenged.

'I agree with Wynne, and now that the inquest is over, may we retire to our respective love quarters. This time, with Andrew's permission, I claim the bedroom. What you say, Andrew?' chimed Richard now more alert as the tiring discussion was over.

'Just this once only, because you have put up with a lot of ragging,' answered Andrew as he arose and at the same time both Wynne and Richard did so too, but they went towards the bedroom, which they entered and closed the door after them.

As the door closed, Richard turned the key in the lock and on being asked why he did that, he retorted that he did not feel like being caught in a compromising position. To that Wynne said there would be no compromising position to worry them. But he led her to the bed and pressed her down to be seated thereon. He bent forward and removed his shoes, then bent again and pulled Wynne's shoes off.

He stood in front of her and then without any embarrassment, unfastened the buttons of his trousers and took out his already throbbing tool and asked Wynne to take it from him.

'Now don't go too far, Richard,' she replied to his request as she took it in one hand and held it somewhat nervously.

'No, no, hold it like this,' he remonstrated as he demonstrated how he liked her to place her whole hand around it and gently rub it up and down. Dutifully, she complied to his request and observed that it enlarged still more.

'What are you going to do when it blows its top, Richard?' questioned Wynne, who knew that before very long it would spill and make a mess if not careful.

'Then move over and I will get closer to you and hold you, and at the same time get a hanky out ready for you to catch it. Will that be OK, my love?' asked Richard as he assisted her in moving to a more suitable position, so that he could lie alongside her and reach under her clothes.

Wynne did not reply but accepted the move, as she felt in the need of some stimulation too. She relished feeling him play with her, despite the fact that she told him to the contrary.

He asked her to relax it now so as to cool off, as he did not feel that he wanted to get it over so soon. In any case, he said, she was entitled to some feelings too and that would give him the opportunity to give her some happy satisfaction, too. So he played with her until she began to feel sore beneath her, so she asked him to finish. He posed the question then, if she would like to rub him to get relief or would she like to take it between her teeth, which she declined. Feeling sore as she did, she did not take long to get him to ejaculate and then she kindly wiped it and with care. After it had subsided, she replaced it, by which time he had left her alone.

'Hope they have the coffee on,' ventured Wynne after they had tidied up. As she spoke, she went to the door and knocked, which was the agreed signal that all was clear within. In a second or two, the door was opened by Andrew who called them out for coffee before leaving the flat for their respective homes.

Sir John Cuthbertson sat engrossed reading a lengthy document that morning after his excursion with Anne at the Eastbury Hotel. He was interrupted by the ringing of the telephone. He took the handpiece to his ear but still kept his eyes on the report. He spoke into the mouthpiece and instructed the caller to ask the visitor to wait a while.

He began reading the document again the second time, but this time it raised some mirth into his manner. Having devoured the contents again, he engaged the intercom and asked that the visitor be brought in.

'Mr Gary Peck, sir,' announced the assistant as she ushered that gentleman in to Sir John's room.

'Do be seated Mr Peck. And is that your real name, Mr Peck?' queried Sir John as he looked at his visitor who appeared quite composed. He had a very short crop of mouse-coloured hair but a ruddy complexion as an indication that he was an outdoor man. The suit he wore was a nondescript make, but the most important feature, that was apparent to Sir John, was his searching eyes.

'No sir, it is my adopted and abbreviated name. I was brought here as an infant from Poland and if I used the name I was born with, it would take me a day to assist you in the correct pronunciation. But I see that you have my manuscript on your desk. I hope you found it good reading, sir,' replied Mr Peck.

Sir John gave him a quizzical look for a second or two, then said, 'I compliment you on your detail. You have been very thorough in your research. I like your comments too, particularly the one in which you say that I am an *entrepreneur extraordinaire*. But tell me, how did you come by so much information about me in such a short time?' asked Sir John.

'It is my job as a journalist to sift for information until I get what I want. But is it all true, sir, that I have recorded?' asked Mr Peck in a light vein, feeling confident that the report he had submitted was a satisfactory one.

'Shall we say that any error is an acceptable error. Now you have asked me for any private commission that I may have and you would let me have a report on this basis. Is that so?' asked Sir John as he continued his quizzical gaze at his visitor.

'I'd be happy to execute another commission for you, sir. I will also add for your information, that when I do a private enquiry, it is never used for any other purpose, as it belongs entirely to the one that pays me.'

'In other words, you do not keep a copy of the report that you would submit,' Sir John demanded to know.

'I always have a carbon copy in case an extension to the enquiry is sought. But if no further information is required, then I release the copy too, on payment of account. I hope that answers your question, sir,' replied the journalist who looked towards Sir John again as a potential client.

'In that case, here is a slip with the name of the person I wish you to make full enquiry about. Also, there are a few names of persons that know the individual in question. I have given addresses where I know them, but feel sure with your methods you will soon find all the acquaintances and check them out, too. It is, of course, clearly understood that my name is not divulged as your client in this enquiry. Is that so?' asked Sir John. Then added as an afterthought, 'The last-named on the list is due to depart in a day or so out of the country, so would suggest that you see him before his departure. Now is there anything else you need from me before I ask you to leave and get on with your work and leave me to mine?'

'No sir,' he answered as he rose from his seat and with a pleasant handshake left the room.

Gerry Peck left Sir John Cuthbertson's office rather pleased, yet puzzled. He was pleased that he had obtained a further commission of enquiry which looked very interesting. He found these in-between jobs more stimulating than routine newspaper journalistic scouting. That implied a rush to get the story then type up for the editor. But a private commission meant an in-depth research that goaded him until he achieved his goal.

But whichever way he looked at the question of this enquiry he could not see the purpose that was behind it. If it was for the instigation of a fidelity insurance, it would be done by the insurance company and not an outside enquiry agent? Then, was she an employee of Sir John? That was not stated. If she was, or is an employee, did he obtain the courtesy references from the previous employer. Perhaps the references obtained gave rise to this extra enquiry. In that case, a job depended on it? Or did it, that was a question he could not see and perhaps he would have to check back with Sir John.

231

Gerry Peck duly contacted Sir John who reprimanded him for asking questions. He was told that the enquiry was to proceed regardless as to whether she was an employee or not. He was to ascertain a complete picture of her character both in a social and commercial sphere. Mr Peck reconciled himself that he was getting paid for a job of work, and that was all that was required to get the best out of him.

Gerry Peck had already found out from the locals what Angus looked like, so he took up a position near the exit of the firm to waylay him as he left his office. The weather held to a mild temperature, so his vigil was not uncomfortable. He did not have to wait long.

'Excuse me, but I believe you must be Mr Finch?' asked Gerry Peck as he accosted Angus as he left his place of employment.

'And who wishes to know?' questioned Angus without any rancour.

'Here is my card. I am Gerry Peck, journalist, but would like to ask you, if you can spare the time, to have a drink with me, as I am commissioned to make an enquiry which I think you can help me on. Shall we pop into that pub opposite?' he ended, pointing to a familiar place of retreat for Angus.

Angus was rather bemused, and presumed that it was in connection with his planned journey to America. He replied to the invitation with an outward sigh of delight.

They entered the bar and Angus replied to the question of what he fancied and Gerry called the barmaid for the two drinks. With the two in hand, he motioned to an empty side-table. Both moved towards the indicated table and sat down. After a small sip, Gerry opened the conversation.

'I am aware that you are due to leave shortly for the States, but that is not the purpose of my enquiry. I am commissioned to make a commercial and social report on a Miss Anne Hopkins whom I understand you know. Now before you ask the question, I am not at liberty to indicate who my client is. Now I also understand that you cannot give me much on her ability, etc., of her work, as you have not worked with her but you can tell me something about her from a social background. So take your time and tell me all you know.'

Angus was at first nonplussed to get this enquiry and wondered who would want to know. 'Oh yes, ask about her work, but her social life too. That was a bit much and then I am involved.'

'Well, what exactly do you wish to know Gerry – you do not mind me calling you Gerry, I hope?' queried Angus looking into his eyes to try to dissect them.

'Not at all, Angus. I understand that you have known her for sometime and have been out with her socially. Is she quiet or extrovert or what? How is she at a dance, at the table in a restaurant and how is she in bed?'

'I will answer the last point first. In bed is a myth. I have never managed to get beyond a kiss on the cheek, but that is not to say I haven't tried and would still love to have her there even though you may know I am now engaged to marry her friend,' he lied with a glib tongue.

'So you find her a straight Jane, no nonsense girl, eh? You must have used the wrong techniques, but the other points now?' he asked.

'As you say, I do not know about her work except that she must be highly thought of, as she takes clients to the Eastbury Hotel for dinners and just signs the chit. On a social plane, she is a beautiful dancer, a champion pal to share an evening with as she keeps the party happy and squashes any quarrels on the spot with marvellous astuteness. You cannot get cross with her as she always has an answer for you. As far as I am concerned, she will always be a friend to me and I would do anything she asked. That is the regard I have for her. Now what else would you like to know?' questioned Angus.

'Thank you for the information. You can let me have the names and addresses of her other friends, so that I can get a complete picture, if you would please. Ah yes, and just one other point, tell me of any fault in her that you are aware of, please,' he concluded.

'That's no problem. I know most but not all. As to faults, I will have to think that one out as, off the cuff, I cannot imagine any!' answered Angus wondering still the purpose of the questions. So he gave as many names and addresses as he could recall and after another drink offered him, he left to make his journey home.

233

'Mr Meredith, thank you for seeing me. May I sit down, thank you again,' opened Gerry Peck, as he was ushered into Mr Meredith's office.

'I see your name is Peck and you are a journalist. What would I be wanting with a journalist and enquiry agent?' questioned Mr Meredith.

'I have been asked to make up a profile on one of your employees. I must first add that I am not at liberty to indicate by whom I have been instructed. I would be pleased if you could give me as much as you can on Miss Anne Hopkins?' he asked as he looked across at his contact.

Mr Meredith was astonished to hear the request. What presumption this young man had to ask about *his* Anne. He could ask him to leave and tell him nought or answer him. In the first case, he would possibly jump to wrong conclusions, but in the second, he could hear the question.

'It is rather astounding to get such an enquiry my young man. What on earth is it for?' he questioned.

'Sir, as I have already said, I am not at liberty to divulge the name of my client, but I hope you will give me some information for which I will be grateful, and truthfully, I too do not know the reason for the enquiry,' he answered with a feeling that here he may not be too successful.

'What exactly would you wish to know?' he asked as he stared at his visitor over the top of his glasses.

'Can you tell me about her workability, her social life and anything else that you may know of her, please?' came back the reply.

'On the work front, I can say that she is perhaps best described as a jewel among jewels. On the social front, she is extremely pleasant and polite. I have had her as my guest at an hotel for dinner and her manner is impeccable. Is that what you wish to know?' asked Mr Meredith still looking at him over the top of his glasses.

'Thank you, sir. That is useful information. How is she, however, on the sexual front, sir?' came the next question.

Even though Mr Peck's face retained its composure, Mr Meredith's face tinged slightly red and flustered a bit before he could reply.

'Indeed Mr Peck, you are going a bit too far in your quest. But nevertheless, I can add that as far as I am aware, Miss Hopkins is probably still a virgin. Does that answer your question?' perjured Mr Meredith still a bit hot under the collar from the unexpected question.

'Mr Meredith, please do not be offended by my questions. But I must ask you. Have you ever indulged in sex with her?' he asked still wearing a straight face.

'Well I never!' expostulated Mr Meredith suffused still more in the face, which his visitor presumed to be because it offended his standard. 'When you are a boss, you will learn never to make a mess on your own doorstep. As I have said, she has been my guest for dinner and have only reached the stage of courtesy of a handshake. No, not even a kiss has passed between us even though we have known her here for a considerable time. Does that answer all your investigations to your satisfaction, Mr Peck?'

'Thank you very much, sir. It seems that I will have to build a pedestal for her. She appears to be a paragon of all the best virtues. Lucky guy that will get her, eh sir? But permit me to ask one final question. You have extolled her integrity and virtues, now tell me of her faults, please?'

'Faults, faults,' echoed Mr Meredith as he rose from his seat with a great show of umbrage. 'If a great sense of loyalty is a fault, that is it! Now I must ask you to go, as I have work to do. I hope you are satisfied with the information so far,' he added with a glint of temper.

'Miss Fawley, may I come in. I have asked Mr Meredith if I may speak to you on a private manner. Here is my card.'

Felicity took the card proffered and looked at it. It spelt out that he was a Mr Gerry Peck and a Journalist/Enquiry Agent.

'That's right. Mr Meredith did call me to say that you would be dropping off here to ask me some questions. What would you be wanting me for, Mr Peck?'

'Thank you Miss Fawley. Let me preface my remarks and tell you that I am commissioned to make an enquiry about one of your colleagues. I am not at liberty to indicate whom it is for. But as your senior Mr Meredith obliged me with a very nice report and answered all my questions, I hope you will be equally candid. I am seeking as much information as you care to give me on Miss Anne Hopkins.

Will you answer a few simple questions please?' he asked as he looked at her and appreciated a very smart and attractive young lady.

'It is not our custom to disclose such information unless we know the reason. However, please ask your question. But I think before you do, could you let me know what Mr Meredith told you?' she asked.

'Exactly as I have said, I cannot divulge my client, and for the same reason, I cannot divulge what has been imparted to me. All the information I glean is confidential and only for the eyes and ears of my client. What I should like to know is about this young lady's workability and as much as you can tell me of her social life. I hope you can give me some guide on those easy points?' he asked as his eyes dwelled on her.

'Well, on those points, I will not be giving away any secrets. On the work front, if we had a few more like her in the firm, we could reduce the number of staff drastically. She is both competent and reliable. She is a super master of her job. Everywhere she is posted to has asked for her again. In almost every post she has been offered a job to remain at a highly inflated rate, but she has loyalty to her credit and refuses every offer made. Does that answer you or is there anything else that you wish to know?' answered Felicity, who felt that she was the right person to answer such an enquiry and boost Anne as she deserved.

'Thanks, that is what I wish to know. Now can you also give me an equal appraisal of her social and sexual life?' he asked without any embarrassment.

'Now that is asking a bit too much! But I will tell you just the same as there is nothing to hide as far as I know. On the social front, she is a very jolly person. She gives the impression of being a bit stern, but that is only a first impact, a natural veneer. Once you get to know her, you warm to her straightaway. On the question of sex, you are asking the wrong person. I am not a man to whom you should direct your question. But hearsay, if that can be trusted, indicates that she is a no-nonsense woman and does not sleep around as appears to be common today,' glibly replied Felicity.

'Thanks again. You have been most helpful. But on the question that you are not a man, that I can see for myself,' he said with a chuckle. 'It is not unknown that a woman can have a liaison with another woman, too. Has she to your knowledge, Miss Fawley?' he asked as he continued to stare at her.

'If you are suggesting that I have such a liaison with a member of the staff, you are insulting and had better leave!' she lied as she stood up somewhat heatedly, as she stared back at the offender.

Mr Gerry Peck also stood up and apologised for her misconstruing his question. 'Please forgive me, Miss Fawley. With a man, you can ask directly if there has been any sex between the parties. But with a woman, that question is always in the third person. Never direct to the person in front of you. I hope you understand now?' he begged, realising that he had ruffled her the wrong way and that he would not get any more information from her – that is, if he needed any more.

'Then let me, please, ask one final question,' and without awaiting for her reply, added, 'You have indicated a very fine person. But nature always leaves a spot out for fault somewhere along the line. What are her faults, Miss Fawley?'

'That my man is easier asked than answered. The only fault that occurs to mind is that she is a workaholic. Now I must ask you to leave, if you would not mind. I am on leave for a few days and do not really wish to be disturbed. Thank you for calling.' He thanked her again and took his leave.

Mr Peck returned home that evening with his mind full of the latest information about his quest on Miss Anne Hopkins. From his point of view it made dull reading. Only nice things had been said and not a bit of scandal anywhere on the scene. Was it worth seeing anyone else in the search for something against her. He still had a few more names and addresses to check out. 'Perhaps one more, so let's see which is the nearest and will try to see them on the morrow. Ah, there's that fellow Jack Courtney. Perhaps I will try to see him.'

'Mr Courtney, so nice of you to accept my request to chat with me. As I explained on the 'phone, I am making enquiries about a young lady and would be pleased if you would answer a few questions. Can I suggest that we pop into a local café for a coffee, that would make it more compatible and comfortable at the same time.

Shall we?' Gerry Peck proposed to Jack to lead to the local café. That they did and entered, ordering the coffees as they passed the counter.

'I'll come straight to the point, Jack – you do not mind me calling you Jack, I hope,' he began.

'It makes it less formal, Gerry,' replied Jack in a pleasant frame of mind as he accepted the coffee paid for by his new companion.

'The point is that I am making an enquiry about a friend of yours, a Miss Anne Hopkins.' And before he could utter another word, Jack raised his voice in temper and said, 'The hell you are! All I will tell you that we have known each other for a long time and as far as I am concerned she is as straight as a die. You get no hanky-panky with her, but you can still have a good time as she is so jolly. Thanks for the coffee, that's all I can tell you about Anne. But you can tell me who the devil wants to know?' Jack remonstrated in a most indignant tone.

'Thanks Jack, you have answered all I wanted to know. As I told you on the 'phone, I am not at liberty to disclose who is paying me to check her out. Actually, I would like to meet her myself. Everyone I have spoken too has given me glowing reports of her. Can she really be living in this generation. I have never met such a presumed virtuous person. It will be a novelty for me. But thanks again, Jack. Just one final point, if you please. You have indicated her good points, but what of her bad points – everyone has them, so what are hers?' he asked as he peered at Jack with his eyes wide open and wondered if at last he might hear of at least one poor item against this creature who appeared so blameless.

'Do you ever give up?' asked Jack with a show of mollified wrath. 'The only fault Anne has, is her generosity of spirit. It is so infectious. Is that what you wish to know, Gerry?' returned Jack still in mind of resentment.

'Thanks, Jack. You have given me all the confirmation I need, so thanks again. Perhaps we will meet again, eh Jack?' he added as he stood up to leave.

Anne was asked on the telephone to call in and see Norman that evening. She excused herself as she indicated that she was dining with Sir John. She promised that she would first thing in the morning prior to going to Sir John's establishment, look in to see him.

As soon as she hung up on the call from her boss, Norman, she was told that another call was awaiting her attention. She gave the OK for the call to be put through and heard Felicity asking how she was. Anne replied that she was well and indicated that she could not spend too much time on the 'phone, and would Felicity please tell her what she wanted quickly.

'Both myself and Norman have had an enquiry agent asking questions about you. He would not indicate who his client is. As far as we are concerned, we have blown your trumpet as loud as we can, but have you any idea who can be behind this enquiry, Anne dear?' posed Felicity into the mouthpiece of the telephone.

'I'll be jiggered! No, I do not know who is behind all these questions. I have had a call from Norman but could not speak and promised to call in tomorrow. I presume he is going to tell me the same. Thanks, Licy, I must hang up now, but will pop in as soon as I can, you can be sure, so cheerio, my love.' And as she concluded, she hung up and leaned back and looked up to the ceiling and wondered who was asking questions.

'Now why should anyone want to know anything about me,' mused Anne as she remained rooted in her stare into the plaster of the ceiling. 'When one is married one gets an enquiry agent seeking information that leads to a divorce. But I am not married, so what is all this in aid of? Then I have no lost relatives that may be searching for me to tell me that I have inherited a fortune. I have not filed any forms of late that may be the cause of an enquiry. I know what I will do. I will ask Sir John tonight during dinner. He may be able to give me a clue.' So she cogitated until interrupted by a further call.

'Yes, Sir John. Anne here. Was there something you wanted?'

'Just to clarify our arrangements for tonight. Shall I pick you up or what?' asked Sir John.

'I'd rather make my own way to the theatre if you do not mind, and then we can go together to the Ritz. But you can give me a lift on the homeward trip. I will meet you in the foyer, at about seven tonight. Will that be OK John?' she posed.

'Very well, Anne. I will be happy to see you there. I look forward to that.' And with that he hung up.

'A Mr Peck on the telephone to speak to you, Sir John. Shall I put him through or shall I ask him to call again, sir?' asked the telephonist.

'Err . . ., I think I will speak with him, thank you.'

'Sir John here. What have you to tell me Gerry?'

'I have interviewed a number of people about that enquiry I am conducting for you. So far, I have not come up with one measly little blemish! I do not think that even Nelson's column pedestal would be big enough to hold the subject of my enquiry. I can give you a written report in a couple of days unless you would wish me to keep searching for faults. What do you wish me to do, sir?' asked Mr Peck.

'Just let me have a full report with the exact comments, so that I may draw my own conclusions. What you have told me appears to be as I expected, so take no more action until I have digested your narrative. I will get in touch with you after that. So thanks again.' And as he concluded, he hung up and leaned back with a broad smirk of satisfaction on his clean-shaven face.

Chapter 19

Anne returned home that mild evening to shower and dress for the meeting with Sir John Cuthbertson at the Palace Theatre. Her mother gave her a black coffee, which she drank whilst awaiting the head of water to reach the temperature she desired. She showered leisurely and luxuriated in the fountain of hot water. She eventually turned off the jet and left the shower cubicle and donned a bathrobe. When she was satisfied that she was dry enough, she let the robe fall from her shoulders and stood there in front of the cheval mirror reflecting herself in full length *in puris naturalibus*.

Without a smile on her face, she posed in front of the mirror that imaged her body to her. She swung round on her toe sideways as she raised one of her neat and developing tight breasts and stood momentarily studying the reflection she saw portrayed in the glass. She moved her head one way, then she moved it in the opposite direction. The while she did so, she still cupped her breast in her hand. She then gyrated into other poses, still with a stern look upon her face. Although the mirror showed that her scrutiny did not change, she appeared to be appeased with the physique she saw and then made a rueful smug face.

Anne realised that she had spent too long in her musing, so now she hurriedly dressed and did her make-up in record quick time. She called down to her mother to call a taxi for her as she was almost ready and did not wish to be late. Her mother did as she was requested and a taxi came to the door just as Anne descended the stairs to make her exit for the theatre.

Just as the local clock sounded the hour, Anne entered the portals of the theatre and saw Sir John Cuthbertson standing nonchalantly against the wall facing the entrance. They spotted each other almost immediately. He came towards her and greeted her affably, to which she responded in like manner. Anne noted that he was in a well-pressed dress suit and looked the part of a gentleman. It pleased her greatly.

'You look very attractive tonight,' said Sir John as they closed up and he espied that she indeed did look very glamorous in her beautiful ball gown over which she had draped a three-quarter length light cashmere coat.

'Does that mean that at other times I do not meet your acclaim, but I think you look very smart too sir,' she grimaced in mock humour.

'Far be it that you read me that way, Anne. You have always appeared smart and attractive to me, but tonight you are exceptionally so. Now we have just under a half-hour before curtain up. Would you care for a preliminary sherry, my dear?' asked Sir John as he kept his gaze on his companion.

'Just one,' answered Anne with one finger pointed upwards as an indication that she meant just one only.

'Very well then. Let us see if we can squeeze through the crowd to the bar,' he replied as he took her arm and led her towards the direction where it appeared most of the assemblage was moving towards and thronging around.

It was not possible to find a seat in the overcrowded bar, but they managed to get themselves wedged into a corner that gave them the partial privacy that pleased them. They conversed of the evening just prior when they met at the Eastbury Hotel in company with her two friends. When they tired of that topic, he gave her a glossary of the actors and actress that were appearing that evening. So the conversation continued until the bell summoned them to their seats.

Without doubt, both enjoyed the show. They were ushered to a loggia seat for two and he deliberately sat as close to Anne as he could. The moment the lights were dimmed, he took her hand into his and held it almost the whole evening during the show. She felt very contented and happy in that position and could have stayed on for ever. But the show came to an inevitable end and they left to walk to the car park for the short ride to the Ritz for late dinner.

The moment they arrived, they were welcomed by the *maître de hôtel* who called Sir John by his name. They were shown to a table set in the opposite corner to the orchestra. This gave them pleasure, as they could then converse without having to raise their voices above the din of the band. The opening subject was what to choose from the extensive menu, then what to drink with it. They made their individual choices and whilst they awaited the service, they discussed the play. With little time lapse, the dinner began to be presented to them in reasonable succession of plates.

The dinner over, they both reclined in their comfortable seats and, whilst Sir John puffed at his cigar, Anne took greater stock of her surroundings. It delighted her with what she witnessed and voiced her opinion to her companion. He was pleased to have her approval, not that anything could have been achieved if it were the other way round.

Anne decided that now they had reached the coffee stage, it would be appropriate that she raised the point of the enquiry that involved her. Without preliminary she began, 'John, let me thank you again for this wonderful evening you have given me. But I ask for your indulgence for a moment as I have a problem that you may be able to assist me with.'

'Why Anne, whatever is it?' he asked her looking into her face and observing her serious expression. He continued, 'Of course I will help you any way that I can. Now what is bothering you, my dear?' said Sir John as he removed his cigar and again looked at Anne with an intent stare.

'It is not really a problem. I should have phrased it saying a puzzle rather. I had a call from my boss Mr Meredith and following that, a call from his secretary, my senior. They informed me that both of them had been subjected to an enquiry concerning me. Now why should anybody want to know anything about me. Mark you, I am not disturbed as I have nothing to hide, but all the same I find it mystifying nevertheless. Can you give me a clue about that, John?' appealed Anne as she raised her head to face and watch for any reaction from him.

'Well, let me see,' answered Sir John as he flicked his ash off his cigar into the silver ash tray at the side of him. He then took another heavy puff and blew out the smoke towards the encrusted ceiling, then gazing into her face answered, 'There can be a number of reasons for that but I cannot reconcile any to you or, at least, I cannot see that they would fit in. Enquiry agents are involved in divorce, but you are not married. Or are you secretly and no one knows?' he posed in a humorous vein. Not expecting or getting an answer, he continued, 'Then they are involved in checking apparent wealth for the grant of a loan and I do not think you come into that category either. Then if you broke a speed record, you would be newsworthy and you would have enquiries too. Then if you angled for a high security post, you may get an enquiry, and that does not fit you either. Quite frankly, I must confess that I am equally puzzled. But what else did your firm tell you? Any other clues, then we may be able to analyse them?'

'Then let me dispel any element of doubt. I am not secretly or otherwise married. That answers that point. I only had the message on the 'phone but will be seeing my boss first thing in the morning before I call at your office. Perhaps I will learn a bit more then and I will tell you.'

'Sorry Anne, my dear, that I cannot be of help in this instance, but do let me know if you glean any other clue, then will put my thinking cap on again for you,' added Sir John with a mock perplexed look on his face.

'Then let us say no more about it then and let us wend our way homewards. It is getting rather late and we both have work to do on the morrow,' she added as she rose from her seat.

Sir John came round her side of the table and pulled her chair away for her to rise more easily; then taking her by the elbow walked towards the foyer.

The drive back to her home was uneventful, except that he insisted that she placed her hand on his knee as he drove the car quietly along to her home. She found it rather a stretch to reach his knee in the Rolls and said so, but did her best to comply.

On reaching her house, he switched off the engine and leaned over towards her inviting her to his embrace. Anne accepted his overture and moved towards him and entered his enfolded arms. She readily accepted the kisses and reciprocated.

After a few moments of passionate kissing, he moved his hand downwards towards her knee. She became aware that he was attempting to raise her long dress above her knee by taking in handfuls of the fabric until it was all above her knee. He then surreptitiously let his hand travel up her knee to the top of her legs. All the while Anne made no move to discourage him. But the moment she felt that his hand was upon her panties and his fingers moving under them, she slapped his hand heavily and moved back out of his reach.

'John please, do not spoil a wonderful evening and stop this immediately,' she demanded in an urgent and irritating tone.

'But my dear, I am not going to seduce you, so why the excitement?' he responded with a look of hurt surprise.

'I do not care what you intended. You are not going to touch me there. So the question of seduction does not apply and never will. So if you have no objections, I will leave you here and pop in home,' she retorted with a slightly angry tone that he discerned.

He realised that he had taken too much advantage particularly after the information of the enquiry. But it did prove the point in the intelligence that she was not a free and easy girl but a respectable one that did not permit interference.

'My apologies, Anne. Please forgive me! I know I should not have been so bold, so will you please forgive me?' he pleaded as he looked into her face and saw that her colour was still heightened.

'I am not accustomed to being mauled about for one thing, and for another I do not like it. I hope to retain my privacy for one man yet to be found. I will forgive you if you promise to behave as a gentleman should!' she countered still with a stern look upon her face.

'I repeat my apology, Anne dear. I promise you will never have reason to be upset with me again. So can we kiss and make up?' he acknowledged as he again held out his arms to receive her.

'Well,' she mumbled in a long drawn way. 'But please remember, there will be no second time!' and with that she returned to his embrace that pleased both and gave them the return of a happy countenance.

'Hullo Norm, can I come in?' asked Anne as she pushed open Mr Meredith's door. She did not await the answer but proceeded to the chair in front of his desk and sat down.

'Anne, you have forgotten something,' answered Mr Meredith as he looked over his glasses at her seated in front of him, with a broad grin.

'Sorry Norm, you are right. I am forgetful this morning,' she replied and rose from her seat, pranced behind the desk, bent over his upturned face and gave him a good morning welcome kiss.

'Now that we are back as we should be, please buzz for some coffee like a good boy!' she suggested with a wimpish smile on her face.

He did as she bid and whilst awaiting its arrival made conversation on inconsequential topics.

'Now that I have had a sip, tell me what all this is about Norm – about this enquiry?' she asked as she replaced the cup down on the mat on the desk.

'Well, I had this chap along and he would not say what the information was for or for whom. He wanted to know what sort of worker you were. Of course I told him, the best. Actually, I said that you were the "jewel among jewels",' he chuckled as he repeated the phrase.

Anne's face lit up on hearing this extolment and replied, 'Oh surely not, Norm. You did not say that, now did you? What else did he want to know and why did he want to know that?' she added.

'Yes, I did tell him that and will repeat it to anyone else that asks,' he beamed at her. 'He also wanted to know if we have had an affair together and I blew my top at him for suggesting such a thing. Of course you know that we never have, now have we?' replied Norman in a scintillating glitter that was infectious.

'Thank you, Norm. Of course we do not know anything about such things! What cheek to ask or suggest it. Thanks again for your wisdom in your reply,' returned Anne now very much pleased with the outcome of the enquiry.

'Another coffee, my dear?' he asked as he held up the coffee pot. She accepted a refill and as he resumed his seat he said with a devilish twinkle in his eye, 'And to prove that such a thing could not happen between us, when do we have a night out together, my dear?'

'I have been thinking about that,' she replied with a look of devilment in her eye. She continued, 'I think we may have to wait until I take possession of the flat. You had better be concerned about

246

Licy first, then we will get together, you can be sure,' she rejoined with a look of love in her posture which he observed and felt happy about.

'Yes, I suppose you are right as usual. Do you think that Licy will be back at work soon or will this morning sickness last much longer, my dear?' asked Norman as he feasted his eyes upon her.

'I am going in to see her tonight – that's if you are not dated up with her. I will check out what's what and give you a call tomorrow morning. Will that be OK, Norm?' she asked, still with her face turned up towards him to his delight and pleasure.

'That will be fine with me. Now come and kiss me and then you can go off to that ogre John. By the way, are you getting on all right with him?' he enquired.

Anne replied that all was well between her and Sir John and told him that they had been out together last evening. She did not mention his attempt to touch her though. She then rose and walked round to Norman's side of the desk, and again he turned his face upwards to receive her kiss. And as she bent to kiss him, he moved his hand up her skirt and over her panties and fondled her. Anne ignored the action, but for his delight, she lingered over the kiss so as to allow him a longer caress.

'Please come on in, Anne. Why did you not use your own key, my love?' asked Felicity as she opened the door to Anne's knock.

Anne first embraced her friend and then closing the door behind her, entered the flat and sat down.

'I have seen Norm this morning and he told me about that enquiry chap. Perhaps you will tell me your story to see if I can get a clue out of all this?' she asked as she looked at her friend for a reply, but failing to respond to the question raised about using her key. She did, however, observe that Felicity was fully dressed and appeared pleasant and jovial.

'Well, he started off asking about your work. I told him that with a few more like you we could dispense with some surplus staff. Then I blew my top when he suggested – no, that's not quite how he put it – I really don't know how to put it either, but he wanted to know if we are a pair of lesbians. He apologised when I shouted at him and told him to get out. The damn cheek of the man, don't you think, my love?' she said as she now had the mirthful urge to burst out in laughter at the way she huffed him. Instead of replying to the tirade, Anne got up and moved round the table to Licy and pulled her up and threw her arms around her. They both went into an embrace that continued for many minutes, during which time they allowed their hands to roam over each other to the sexual delight of both.

'Now Licy, you had better get back to work tomorrow and the moment your menstruation begins, let me know. OK my love?' ordered Anne as she smiled at her lover.

'You're the boss, Anne,' was all the reply she made.

It was a fresh, cool Saturday morning that Anne went to the flat by taxi to collect Felicity. She asked the driver to wait whilst she ascended the lift to collect her friend. Felicity was ready with but her topcoat to put on. They descended and together they entered the waiting taxi. Anne gave the instructions to the driver to take them to the registry office.

On the steps of the registry, Norman was stamping his feet more in apprehension than to dispel the dampness of the morning atmosphere. He hastened down the few steps the moment he saw his bride with Anne arriving. Licy acknowledged his desire to press kisses upon her, but asked him just to allow her but a peck so as not to disturb her carefully applied make-up. He then thanked Anne for escorting her, and all together they mounted the steps and then entered the portals of the registry. In the hall, there were a few friends, clients and a couple of staff of the firm. Among the clients were Sir John Cuthbertson and Mr Charles Harrington. Both recognised the bride Felicity but they knew Anne the better, and after making their greetings to the betrothed pair, and giving them their blessing, they joined Anne.

With but ten minutes, the assembly was called into the registrar's room for the ceremony. Everything went as planned without any hitch and in the same length of time they were pronounced husband and wife. Together, they all left the marriage room and returned to the entrance hall. Anne announced that there were three taxis outside to take them all to Norman's home, now the home of Mr and Mrs Norman Meredith.

After a short drive, they entered the carriageway of the house. Anne asked everyone to proceed and enter the abode as the door was opened by the maid. Anne settled the charges with the taxi-drivers, then followed the remaining guests into the house, too.

It was the first time Anne had been to her boss's house. She had but a glimpse of the exterior as she arrived, but she was taken aback at its apparent splendour and opulence as she traversed the tiled porch and entered the hall. Although it was still before noon, all the lights, both inside and outside, were ablaze, which gave sparkle to the beautiful surroundings, which helped to diminish the outside atmosphere. Although the hall was squarish with doors leading off on all flanks, the upper gallery that went around the walls was circular and access was gained by a central stairway in the entrance hall. As she stood staring and marvelling, a set of doors were flung open which gave access to a very large room. With the doors held back, it enlarged the hall to extra dimension. This enabled all present to move around without having to jostle. Apart from the three taxi loads of friends, there were also many others that constantly kept arriving, so within half an hour of her arrival, the house appeared to be quite full.

A buffet lunch had been prepared and was available to all guests. The maid that appeared at the entrance was assisted by another and more elderly person. Anne gleaned that the person was the regular house-keeper. Before Anne had time to consume her plateful of goodies, she was called upon to make the traditional toast to the bride. Anne rose to the occasion and without preparation, delivered a very nice speech with a few jokes interspersed, to the acclamation of the assembly. Mr Harrington was called to make the toast to the groom, which he executed with equal aplomb. After that episode, Licy was able to ask Anne if she wished to look over the house. Anne proposed to defer that pleasure until all the guests had gone. Licy concurred with that view.

The last guest did not leave until near four. Anne suggested that Norman sit down with his brandy and cigar, whilst she with Licy take a stroll around the house. Norman gave the OK, but hoped that they would not desert him for too long. Amid some mirth, the two mounted the stairs to begin their tour of the upper floor. If Anne was surprised at the entry into the house of its sumptuousness, she was overwhelmed at the sheer luxuriance of the sleeping quarters.

At the first door they entered, Licy announced that it was the main suite which she and Norman would henceforth occupy. Anne stared with open mouth, and for a few seconds could not utter a word. When she had recovered her faculties, she declared that the bedroom was beyond description.

'Thanks to you, Anne, who has made it possible,' quoted Licy as she came forward to place a kiss on Anne's cheek.

Anne did not answer but stood momentarily looking first this way then the other, taking in the beauty of the room.

'This is just the bedroom. Now if you open that door that appears to be part of the wardrobing, it will lead you into the dressing-room, then the bathroom,' added Licy as she pointed towards one of the doors and, as she approached it, flung it open to show that indeed it was not part of the wardrobe but the entry into another area that held additional wardrobing, plus dressing-table. Beyond was a further door, partly ajar which Licy opened to its fullest extent, and as she did so, she pulled the switch cord for the interior lights to make the marble-tiled bathroom come alive.

'Licy, you have struck gold here. I wish you every happiness in your new home. And please make Norm happy as he deserves it, too!' quipped Anne as she viewed the suite.

'My dear Anne, I can promise you I will do everything in my power to please Norm. I know that without you, my dream would never have materialised. I hope that you do not come between us, Anne dear?' asked Licy in a pleading voice.

'Licy, if I ever hear you ask or say that again, I will be very cross with you. It shows an element of doubt in our friendship which I do not like. I know you would do anything for me, as I would for you. So be happy and I will for your sake be happy too!' answered Anne in a somewhat sterner tone than she wanted to.

'Oh Anne, please forgive me. Of course I trust you implicitly. But everything is so new to me that it makes me doubt even myself. Please say that you forgive me my foolishness?' begged Licy as she looked appealingly towards Anne.

'Say no more, but let us see the rest of the rooms please?' replied Anne.

Felicity then showed her the various bedrooms and bathrooms and indicated the guest suite that Licy hoped Anne would occupy whenever she felt like it.

'When Norm is away, then I will come and keep you company,' responded Anne to the invitation.

Altogether, the two spent something like more than half an hour touring and commenting on the upper floor before they descended to the ground floor to return to Norman. He looked up on their approach, and commented that he was of the opinion that they had got lost, but was pleased to see them again. He asked them to join him for a drink, which both accepted.

'Well, Anne, how do you like my home? It was my house, but now it will be my home?' questioned Norman as he smiled across to Anne.

'Norm, it must have felt like a mausoleum on your own but now with Licy at your side, it will be truly a home worth coming home to. I wish both of you every good fortune and happiness.' And as she finished, she went over to him and bent forward and kissed him on the lips.

'When will you be moving into Licy's flat, Anne?' asked Norman with a broad smile of satisfaction on his face, after that exercise of care and friendship.

'I have not yet made up my mind. Probably be a few weeks yet, I think. I will want to redecorate first after introducing my parents to it. I have not told them, so feel the best way would be to take them there as a surprise to announce the object. What do you think, Norm?' asked Anne with an interrogative eye.

Norman replied that he was of the opinion her idea of introducing the flat to her mother was fine, and Licy concurred.

'So glad you like my idea. Now I must get home, you two! You do not want me around on your wedding night, now do you!' questioned Anne with a look of serious amusement.

Anne reached her home rather later than anticipated. She found the house all quiet and knew all were abed. She entered as quietly as he could so as not to disturb the sleepers and went directly to her room. With a quick rinse she jumped into bed to get warm, as she felt the cold air of the night. She mused over the events of the past few days, being still too lively to succumb to sleep. It then occurred to her that

251

she had not given a second thought to the comment Sir John had made to her a few days ago of 'something else in mind.' It could not have been the theatre and the following dinner and it did not allude to her work. So what could he have meant by that remark? 'He made the illusion before we went in company of Angus and Joan to the Eastbury Hotel and before we had a meal together. Could he know more about that enquiry than he is letting on to? He appeared to be sincere when we discussed the enquiry agent. No, I cannot think what he meant by that mention.'

Her mind then switched to Licy and the plan for her taking over the flat. She had better tell her parents soon, as it would not look good if she delayed much longer. Perhaps she would get some paper patterns and of curtain material too, and have them at the flat so that her mother could assist her in making a choice. She did not think that any of the furniture needed replacing or discarding, so on that point, all was well. But she would mention the flat on the morrow without fail.

'Licy, yes Licy. So far she has acted very well and she has married the boss as planned. I hope she can act the last episode equally well,' thought Anne as she lay pondering. 'Fortunately, they have deferred the honeymoon holiday until later, otherwise it would be a show-down between them. And obviously, Norman would blame her more than Licy. Well, we will know within the next week or so.'

'Hullo, Joan. Anne will not be long as she is upstairs getting changed. But why not go up. I am sure she will not mind,' said Mrs Hopkins at the threshold of the house as she opened the door to Joan.

'Thanks, perhaps I will go up,' responded Joan as she entered the hallway and proceeded to mount the stairs to Anne's room.

'Come in,' shouted Anne when she heard a knock on her door.

'Only me,' answered Joan as she entered the room and witnessed Anne still in her underclothes, but her outfit laid out over the bed neatly.

'Why, hullo. It's nice to see you. Anything special though?' questioned Anne as she continued to dress.

'Angus was a bit apprehensive of calling himself to tell you a story, so he asked me to call instead. He has had an enquiry agent chatting him up and asking all about you. He does not know what it is all about, but thinks that you should know. Did you know anything about this enquiry, Anne?' asked her friend as she sat down on the corner of the bed.

Anne could not reply just at that moment as she was struggling to get a garment over her head. But as soon as her head emerged from the neckline, she replied, 'I've already had some other people telling me about an enquiry, but I have not discovered the reason or who initiated this investigation. Think it would be better if Angus told me himself, as I may wish to question him and feel sure that you may not be able to answer them all. Thanks for calling to tell me though. It was nice of you. If you are going round to his house, perhaps you will not mind if I tag along too, eh?' asked Anne.

Both Joan and Anne called on Angus together. After the usual salutations, Anne asked if she could have a chat about the enquiry privately. Joan indicated that she had no objection when Angus put the question to her. Anne then followed Angus into the next room where they both seated themselves.

Angus gave a resumé of the agent's questions and his answers. When Angus mentioned that he also asked if they had indulged in any sexual matters, Anne's face tinged.

'How did you answer that, Angus?' questioned Anne looking slightly perturbed.

'Why, that was easy to answer. I told him the truth as you know it, Anne, that we have not gone beyond the kissing stage despite my attempts to improve the action. That was correct was it not, Anne?' he asked as he peered at her with a twinkle in his eye.

Instead of answering him, Anne leaned over towards him and kissed him on the mouth and said, 'Of course, Angus.'

That night, as she lay in her bed, Anne began to cogitate on the problem of these enquiries. So far they had all given her a clean bill of behaviour, despite what actually happened between them. She decided that on the morrow, time permitting, she would make a round of calls to check if any other of her friends had also had questions to answer about her.

'Hullo Jack, Anne here. Hope you do not mind my calling you, but have been making a round of calls, and you are the last on my list.'

'Why Anne, how nice to hear from you! I am glad however that you phoned, as I have some news for you. I had a chap asking me questions about you. Is that what you wanted to know, Anne?' he asked.

'Yes, that's it. What did he want to know and how did you answer?'

'The only relevant question was concerning your sexual habits! I told him there was nothing doing or words to that effect. He seemed put out as it appeared that everyone told him the same and reckoned you are a Miss Perfect! But what is it all about, Anne; have you found out?' questioned Jack in solicitude and sympathy.

'I have not yet discovered who instigated this enquiry, but you have confirmed that one has taken place alright. And thanks for your reference. I will do the same for you one day, eh Jack!' answered Anne as she felt relieved by the apparent support given her by her friends.

Anne listed all those that told her they had been interrogated. Then she listed all the ones she had called that knew nothing about the enquiry. She studied the list and could not ascertain a clue out of it. For the present, she decided to forget the subject until she could collect more material about the affair.

Felicity had returned to work, but at the request of Norman, she left a little earlier. It was so that she could supervise the eating and menu arrangement at home. She had begun to discuss the menu with the housekeeper before she left for work and checked again on her return. Then she would go upstairs to her bedroom to have a quick shower before changing for dinner. She had never had to change before, but Norman insisted upon this ritual. So this evening she showered and donned a bathrobe and sat at the dressing-table to make up.

'Hullo darling, all's well I hope?' asked Norman as he entered the dressing-room where Felicity was still sitting in front of the mirrored table. As he bent forward to kiss his bride, he observed that her bathrobe was held very loosely around her and that she showed cleavage. As he kissed her he put his hand down her bare breasts and took one in his cupped hand and gently squeezed it. He felt an erection coming on, so he pulled her up and as she rose, he threw the robe off her shoulders.

'Do you want me, my love?' asked Felicity understanding that she had excited him.

'Oh yes darling. I need you very much!' he replied in eagerness as he followed her back to the bedroom.

Felicity was about to throw back the bed cover and enter beneath the blanket, when her husband spoke.

'Now darling, just lean over the bed. That's right, put your elbows on the bed and then just push your back out, and it will be just fine, my love,' he responded as he approached her incumbent body. He had already dropped his trousers and removed his underpants and stood with his thing fully extended in front of him. He approached her and placed it in position from behind her, and pressed forward as she pushed backwards towards him. It was her first encounter in this fashion and she screamed as it entered her as it felt twice the normal size. Nevertheless, as much as it hurt, she kept time with his motion. He had his hands cupped around her two breasts and each time he pressed forward, he pulled them towards himself. This created the pain she felt as it entered to the hilt. He repeated this action in frequent quick succession and each time she gave a high pitched moan of pain coupled with delight. As she reached her climax she screamed louder still, calling on him to give her more and more. Then he realised that in this way he had given her greater satisfaction than ever before. He asked her when he should let himself go and finish. She pleaded with him to hold on still more even though it hurt her terribly until eventually she begged him to satisfy himself.

Even then, she craved him to remain within her until she felt her orgasm returning again. She raised her voice in a high pitch and asked him to once again repeat the exercise and motion as before. This return of Felicity in her demand for more renewed his appetite too, and he found that he had an extraordinary erection develop, that compelled him to repeat the motion as demanded. He even began to wonder at his own ability to do this twice in very quick succession! But nature provided the impetus that gave him both the strength and ability to recapture the urge to give his wife the satisfaction she sought and at the same time to give himself more-than-expected gratification.

It was about two weeks after the wedding of Felicity and Norman that Anne called at the office for a chat. She had been waiting for Licy to tell her when her periods had begun. It was she felt, well over a month, and that she should by now be with it? She opened the door to Licy's room and put her head round the door and asked if she could disturb her for a few minutes.

'Of course you can. Come on in, Anne?' answered Licy as she looked up with a broad smile of contentment on her face.

'It was only to ask that you have not yet mentioned that you have your menstrual periods, that's all,' asked Anne as she sat down.

'Oh dear, I have forgotten all about that. It is well overdue now! He ho! Surely not!' she mirthed with a grin across her face.

'What do you mean, Licy. Is it really overdue or what?' demanded Anne with a look of puzzlement.

Before Licy replied, she took out of her desk drawer her private engagement book and thumbed the pages.

'It was due three or four days ago. The recent excitement may have caused it to defer. Give it another day or two before we get agitated,' countered Licy as she held her head back and started to wonder herself.

'OK then, I will leave you to tell me as soon as you can, otherwise there is sure to be an inquest,' answered Anne as she rose to leave the room.

Chapter 20

'This is your room, sir,' said the luggage porter as he handed the room key to Angus on his arrival in the Clinton Hotel in New York.

'Thank you, but can you offer me some information. Where exactly are we in the city and where can I get a meal at this time of day?' questioned Angus from the porter after he had handed him a tip.

'If you look outa the winder, you c'n see Penn Station on the corner o'Eighth that can get you up State very quickly. To the left o' the station is an exc'llent restaurant The Bake Oven, or you may eat in the station buffet unless you wisha to stay in the hotel and eat here. You can eat in the restaurant downstairs or call room service on the 'phone. You have your own carffee machine in the room and any thing else you wanna, just ring room service, sir.' replied the porter.

'Thank you very much. I feel a bit lagged after the scramble at the dockside. I think I'll make my self a coffee and hit the hay, but thanks again.'

'You'r welcome, sir.' responded the porter and left the room.

So without further thought about food, Angus unpacked his clothes and hung them up in the wall inset robe. He then made himself a pot of coffee. Whilst sipping the hot coffee, he undressed preparatory to taking an inviting shower. After the ablution, he flopped into bed and was asleep before his head touched the pillow.

Angus was awaken by a loud knocking on his room door. As he had failed to draw the window drapes the night before, there was

257

sufficient light in the room to enable him to read the time on his watch. It told him it was almost seven o'clock New York time. He called out to the knocker to hold on, he was coming. Somewhat dishevelled and still drowsy, he donned his dressing gown and opened the door. He was confronted by a young man about his own age, pleasantly attired and wearing a broad grin.

'Angus Finch, I believe, eh?' asked the caller.

'Yes, and who are you so early in the morning?' asked Angus.

'I'm Ira Mellows and have come to join you for breakfast then take you to work. At least I have been asked to collect you, the breakfast bit is my idea! But you look as if you have not been to bed. Never mind, a good hot shower will liven you up! So off you go and I'll loll around for ten minutes whilst you get ready', and as he spoke, he entered the room and closed the door behind him.

'Nice to know you Ira,' said Angus as he put out his hand for an acknowledgement shake. 'Forgive me, but I feel that I had just put my head down when you came a'knocking. I'll skip the shower, as I had one on getting here last night. So sit around whilst I wash and shave', and as he spoke, he took off his gown and left his early morning visitor, and entered the bathroom.

Within a quarter of an hour, Angus had washed, shaved and dressed. He asked Ira to lead the way to a good breakfast bar, which he indicated that he would. They descended in the elevator and left the hotel and crossed the road to the very restaurant referred to him last night by the porter.

As they entered the restaurant, the waft of newly baked bread invaded his nostrils. Ira observed the reaction and said, 'This place is famous for its variety of breads, and as you can see, it is hard to find a seat even though it is early in the morning. Just take a pack here – its a napkin wrapped around a knife, fork and spoon, then come to the shelves and help yourself. If you wanna something cooked, just go over there to that high counter', as he pointed to where a few customers stood.

'Thanks Ira, I will try their eggs on toast this morning,' he replied and turning towards the high counter indicated, whereon one of the attendant women behind asked him what he would like.

'Eggs on toast, please,' asked Angus.

'How d'ya wanna d'eggs – sunny side up?' queried the coloured counter hand without looking up.

Angus not knowing what he would get, but nevertheless gambled on the result and answered in the affirmative. He was told to take a seat and it would be brought over to him when ready. He looked around and found his colleague already seated, munching some cornflakes. He moved over and sat opposite him.

'Your eggs n'toast, sir. D'ya wanna a carfee now?' asked the same counter hand.

'Thanks, that looks good. Yes, I would like a coffee now if you please,' replied Angus.

'You only pay for one cup of coffee, but you may have as many as you care to drink. How's the food – to your liking, I hope, Angus?' asked Ira helpfully.

'Well, I do like a second cup and that should be enough for me. But have you had enough yourself?' queried Angus looking at his companion's plate.

'Oh, don't worry about me. But tell me, how was your journey over?'

'Well, I was seen off by my girlfriend and we left on time. I'm happy to say it was an uneventful passage and I hope it will be on my way back home too,' detailed Angus whilst chewing his toast. 'But tell me, what time are we expected in the office in the mornings?' he added.

'Normal time eight o'clock. What time do you begin your day at home?'

'Eight o'clock! that's a bit early. We commence at nine and finish around five in the afternoon,' sponsored Angus.

'Its the same, except we start at eight and finish at four. That gives us time to get home, eat and change, then get out on the town for fun. Have you any acquaintances here, for if not, you can join me for the evening, Angus,' replied Ira in a very friendly manner.

'That would indeed be nice, as I am a complete stranger here,' answered Angus with a broadening smile.

'I do not think you will be a stranger for long here. Look to your half right; you are being ogled by a beaut. Just give her a nod to come over and she'll be here, I guess,' said Ira with a mirthful expression.

Angus in as innocent manner as possible, turned himself as suggested and witnessed the 'beaut' referred to.

'Gee, that's quick. I did not expect a dame to be waiting on me here. As I've told you, I have a girlfriend back home to whom I'm engaged, so had better not play around. What you say, Ira?'

'Well, I would not say 'No' to her, so please yourself.'

'I think I'll not look over in that direction again. I do not feel that I should make dates so soon here. Would rather accept your kind invitation for this evening.'

By this time, both had completed their repast, and Ira rose followed by Angus as they both left the eating house. Ira led the way to work on foot, as it was but a block or so away.

Josefina Lozano's mother was born in Spain, and at the age of some twenty-two, realised she was pregnant. Within a couple of days of telling her boyfriend Ramon, he vanished. It did not take her long to find that he had been shipped to America to relatives. By devious means, she obtained his exact location. Ramon was but a week in Portchester, upstate New York, when Josefina knocked on his door, much to his surprise and anguish.

After a preliminary bout of accusations, she was invited to meet his uncle and aunt. Mr and Mrs Garcia were both past middle age, but welcomed Josefina, and in a way reprimanded their nephew for his attitude towards his once-betrothed. Many hours passed before a solution was reached as to the baby to be born, that Ramon did not deny he was the father.

As Ramon had come to America to avoid the consequences of his action in fatherhood, it was now agreed that he return home to Spain and that Josefina could come and stay with his relatives. As the Garcias were childless, they agreed to look after the child in its infancy, so as to give Josefina the opportunity to obtain a job of work. Mr Garcia, an employee for the Department of Immigration & Naturalisation, then advised Josefina what she would have to do, if she proposed to remain in America, which she did to avoid the embarrassment of having to return as an unwed mother.

Josefina followed the instructions given her and in due time her baby, a girl, was born. She was duly registered as an American citizen and given her mother's name. After the initial period, the baby was cared for by the elders whom Josefina called 'Tia' and 'Tio' the Spanish for Aunt and Uncle. Josefina, the mother, began to find the ties of looking after her own infant too much and irksome for her. This became apparent to the elders, who thereupon proposed that she return home to Spain and leave the infant behind.

After a lot of soul-searching and first agreeing then countermanding her own proposal, she was eventually encouraged to return home. So in the end she did, and apart from one visit when little Josefina was about ten years of age, mother and daughter had never met again.

Little Josefina had been encouraged to call the elders her parents, which she found compatible. They in turn lavished parental care and affection upon their adopted daughter, and saw her through high school until she reached the twelfth grade at the age of eighteen, when she left to commence a career as a stenographer.

At this point in time, Josefina was twenty years of age and had already tasted the fruits of love. Although she was by no means promiscuous, she liked to change her boyfriends rather sooner than later. As soon as she espied someone that she liked the look of, she made a beeline for them and at the same time dismissed her latest beau. So it was that she saw with refreshing delight a handsome young man in the restaurant. She was disregarded by the male she espied to acquaint, as he did not even look towards her. At least he turned round, but she was sure he could not have seen her. Her determination was such that she knew that she would hound the restaurant a few days until she struck up a friendship with him.

On the second morning, Angus satisfied he did not need an escort. He arose from his slumbers and left his hotel room to meander out and venture to the same restaurant that he had entered but yesterday. This time he studied the menu more leisurely, then ordered. Getting his order, he took the tray and looked around for possibly an empty seat. As he surveyed the tables, he heard someone call out, '*Hi*'. He turned to look in that direction knowing full well that as a stranger, it could not be for him. At as few tables away from where he stood, an attractive young lady raised her hand and beckoned him.

'You calling me?' questioned Angus in a surprised tone. Could that be the 'beaut' that was here yesterday morning, wondered Angus.

'Come and sit here,' was her only reply, except that she again gestured with a beautifully shaped hand the invitation.

'Thank you very much miss,' replied Angus as he reddened in the face, as he took the seat alongside this beauty. 'Very nice of you to offer me a seat especially to a stranger.'

'We are not strangers, we have already spoken – haven't we?' she chirped with a broad smile on her happy countenance.

'Thank you very much again then. I'm Angus, and this is my second day in America, so I am a bit lost. But you are not new here nor lost, so what is your name?'

'You can call me José. No, I'm no stranger as I was born in upstate New York. But what brings you here, may one ask, as you are obviously English?' posed José.

'I'm on a course with the American section of our firm. I reckon to be here at least a few months, or possibly it may be longer, then to return to London again. It is very nice to be greeted so early in my stay and I appreciate it very much. Thank you for making my day so bright!' Angus added as he looked more into his new found friend than his meal.

'Well, as a good American, I will show you round the town. Where are you staying and will pick you up tonight – that's if you would like to join me?'

'Nothing would delight me more. I'm at the Clinton opposite. I hope to get back about half four to five. Would that be OK with you?'

'I'll call for you at six-thirty which will give us both time to prepare. But what is your room number Angus?'

'Room 520, but I'll be downstairs waiting for you.'

'OK then, until tonight. I must fly now, otherwise I'll be late for work,' said José as she rose from her seat and accepted his hand in a friendly shake, then turned and left.

For all intents and purposes, Angus was liked by his American colleagues. They found him very amenable and charming. He appeared to be an extremely happy employee, although it was but his second day at work, his cheerful attitude appeared to be reciprocated all round. It was a while before he realised, that the constant requests to repeat everything that he said, was because they found his British brogue fascinating. He found it somewhat difficult to avoid the offers of escorting him that night.

'Bet you had your breakfast same place as yesterday,' probed Ira when he among the many other offers to take Angus under their wing that night.

'Yes, but why? It's the only place I know and as you rightly said yourself, it has good food there, so why should I look elsewhere, when I am only here for a short while?' Angus threw back.

'I guessed that you returned there. You met up with that dame that was trying to attract your attention yesterday. Is that right, Angus?' asserted Ira with a smirkish grin on his face.

'It so happens that again you are right. Yes, I am meeting José tonight. She is calling for me and that's why I've had to refuse offers. Hope I have not done the wrong thing though!' challenged Angus with a slight worried frown showing.

'Well, do not allow her to monopolise you the whole time you are here. Allow an odd day or so for man to man entertainment. But be ready for the works with her! Have you brought any preventatives with you, for if you have not, you can get them in the staff toilet,' offered Ira with a grin that seemed to get bigger and bigger.

'What do you mean – on the first date you expect me to get the "works"?' blushed Angus.

'Nothing wrong in that. So take one with you, then you can be prepared if needed, that's all,' Ira threw back in an off-handed couldn't-care-less attitude.

Angus visited the gentlemen's room a couple of times before he found that he was the only occupant. He then plucked up sufficient courage to insert a dime into the slot-machine, and so found himself with a sealed envelope of small size bearing the legend 'Use once only, handle with care'. Angus secreted his purchase that made him engender a slight guilty feeling, though he could not see why.

The early evening was still light and also very bright. Just a few clouds hovered the grey-blue sky. But the noise he found somewhat very heavy, as it throbbed and pulsated with the screeching brakes and hooter sounds. He approved of the behaviour of the pedestrians that awaited patiently at the kerbside until the traffic lights turned to

263

their favour – then *en bloc* they all flocked across the road. Angus was able to negotiate the solid mass of people and vehicles in about twenty leisurely minutes walk from his place of work to his hotel. He enjoyed the newness and novelty of his exhilarating yet carefree walk through the crowds. He wondered how anyone could hear let alone understand each other, as the minions walked along in the terrific hubbub that made New York what it was. Angus walked with a happy smile, enjoying the unfamiliarity that was present.

'Now what shall I do,' thought Angus as he entered the room. 'Ah, I'll get myself a coffee then have a nice hot shower and will be ready well before six-thirty.' So he switched on the coffee pot then turned to divest himself of his jacket and tie, which he hung in its proper place. He then extracted the suit he proposed to wear for the evening. But before he was able to get the suit out of the hanging closet, the coffee pot had boiled. He thereupon returned to attend to his refreshing hot coffee, and pouring out a cupful, he left it awhile to cool whilst he returned to retrieve the suit. Having laid it out neatly across the back of the settee, he began to undress preparatory to taking his shower.

Having laid out all his apparel in readiness and having enjoyed the coffee, he was now humming to himself in the shower, as he heard a clock strike the hour of five. There is no hurry, thought Angus as he soaped himself for the second time. Lashings of lovely hot soft water and plenty of time to enjoy it, were a bonus he had not anticipated. So ten minutes later he was still wallowing in the shower when he heard a knocking on his door. He ignored it, presuming that whoever it was, had made a mistake and would soon realise it and go away. The knocking however, instead of fading out, became louder and louder and more persistent. Angus was now somewhat very ruffled and a trifle annoyed. He turned off the shower and quickly stepped out of the cubicle, wrapping himself in the heavy towel supplied around his midriff.

'All right, all right, just hold on, I'm coming if you will wait!' shouted Angus in a gruff and annoyed voice as he traversed the carpeted floor of the room towards the offending door. He withdrew the security latch and held the door open but a fraction so as to see who the hell was making that racket and disturbing his leisure and

264

shower. His face changed immediately. His head flung back and with a gapping mouth, espied standing outside his room door, with a broad happy grin on her face, no other than José.

José did not stand upon ceremony, but pushed the door wide enough for her to make an entrance, then closing the door behind her, replaced the security latch.

'You did say six-thirty, now didn't you?' stuttered Angus as he looked at her with pleasure, anticipation and heightening colour, when he was able to close his mouth and regain his equilibrium.

'Sure did, but guessed it might be nice to surprise you a bit early. See you have not wiped yourself and you had better, otherwise you will catch your death of a cold. No, no, don't you do that. I will, as I am good at wiping, so let's be having the towel!' proclaimed José as she ripped and pulled the towel off his midriff, as his face now shone in a heightened strong red hue. He endeavoured to avoid his embarrassment by holding on to the towel, but too late. So there he stood without a stitch on!

'Now turn your back to me and will soon get you dry,' suggested José, and like a lamb to the slaughter he turned round. She rubbed his neck vigorously and he realised that he was become sexually excited, but in the circumstances could do nothing about it just at that precise moment in time. She then asked him to turn to face her, but he felt reluctant to do so.

'No bother,' she said, as she moved around him and now stood facing him.

'Now that is what I call a real man down there!' she quipped as she gave him a very quick wipe across his chest, then stood back to view him to advantage.

'Please, let me have the towel so that I can finish then get dressed,' pleaded Angus reddening still more, if that was possible?

'That's what you think. It is just as quick for me to undress as for you to dress!' replied José as she made a quick grab at him for a split second, then began to disrobe, much to Angus' consternation.

In less time than he imagined possible, she had removed all her clothing and stood as he did with none on at all!

'Well, we are now both the same. How do you like it Angus?' she asked, knowing full well what he would reply.

265

Angus was by now over-excited and wondered if he could contain himself long enough to enjoy this sudden gift bestowed upon him so unexpectedly. Still somewhat abashed, and still red in the face, he put bravado to the test and pulled her to himself, and she responded by placing her two arms around his neck.

So they stood for an indefinite period kissing each other on the lips and neck. As they stood there, she wiggled and he squirmed, until they became locked together. As soon as they reached that proximity, she manoeuvred him gently backwards until they reached the bed, at which point, she, rather than him, pushed, so they both fell together on top of the bed.

'I've a French letter, José; shall I get it out and put it on?' speculated Angus.

'You dare do that. Just let me have you as you are now and do not worry,' she replied still gripping him tightly.

'Then you have got me as I cannot hold on any longer – sorry, but I've got to come, and I did hope to last it out a bit more to please you, but you have taken me by surprise,' flushed Angus, delighted, yet not delighted as having to finish so soon such a pleasure.

'Told you not to worry, Angus my boy. When we get back tonight, you will be able to last out longer, now that you have had your initial shot-off, and that will be something now, won't it Angus?' she replied in raptures of anticipation.

Angus could not reply at that moment as he was in a state of over-excitement as he clung on to José as if life depended on it. In turn, José took full advantage of the situation by drawing him yet closer, if that were possible, as she wove her legs around him so that they remained locked together, whether he desired it or not. By his ecstasy and reaction, he began to call out in a loud tone for her to hold him tighter. Thus they remained for that interminable time that cannot be countered nor measured, until eventually they broke apart, as if by unstated mutual consent.

After they both regained their calmness and composure, José dismounted from the bed. With an exclamation, she pulled Angus off too and drew him towards the shower. Angus was so overwhelmed by what had happened to him, that he just followed in a semi-dazed manner as she pulled him towards, and then pushed him into, the

266

shower cubicle. As he entered, she followed suit and turned on the hot water.

'Now isn't it nice to have a shower together, Angus my boy?'

Angus could not reply as promptly as he should, as he still felt the ardour around him of still being in close proximity of that lovely creature José, who was now rubbing him down, he felt tongue-tied.

'It's lovely,' was all he could mutter in reply when his faculties returned to him. He continued, 'Please, please, don't keep washing me there, as it is getting big again and it will get sore!'

'That's all right, my boy. If you won't to get it big and get it off, that's OK with me, but it's time you give me a rub down – and up!' José answered with a giggle, as she continued her frenzied attack where he did not want her to, but he enjoyed the episode nevertheless.

'Hullo Angus, you look nice and rosy this morning. Been shaving close or is it from the night before?' smirked Ira, as Angus entered the offices the following morning.

'Must be the cold wind making my face red I suppose,' answered Angus in a slightly tempered tone.

'And how did you make out last night? Was she worth while? Let's be hearing about your adventures?' asked Ira as he took his seat opposite Angus and continued to look at him to his discomfiture.

'Well, what do you want to know? I had a nice time and was shown around this lovely city – is that what you want to know?' responded Angus as his mind raced over the exploits of the previous night. How could he tell Ira that he had such a liberty even on his first night. In truth, even after a number of nights out, he had never yet been able to seduce a partner, and here on a first date and without a fight or struggle, it was *that* easy. It was virtually put in his proverbial lap. No, that's not quite the right expression, but then it must be No! he could not tell either.

'Come now Angus, you know what we want to know, so don't be so coy. Did you have her or did you?' questioned Ira with a face that said, 'I know you had it so own up'.

'I think you had better join us for breakfast tomorrow morning, then you can ask her yourself. I'm not backward in coming forward, but we behaved ourselves, apart from a kiss and cuddle!' lied Angus in a bravado and cavalier manner.

'And we suppose you have dated for tonight again. Are you going to act the English gentleman then old buddy?' sniggered Ira as he began to turn over papers on his desk.

'Sorry to disappoint you Ira, but I can only act English for whatever that implies. And if you would like to join us tonight, you are welcome,' replied Angus, getting somewhat frazzled by the inquisition.

'Thanks for the invitation, but decline. Some of the other lads here, wish me to invite you to a party tomorrow night. Can I tell them that you will be coming, but suggest that you say 'yes' for yourself alone. Don't get me wrong, you can ask José when you see her, but for now just answer for yourself.'

'I'll say "yes" for the moment as we had better get on with our work, as I see we are being watched,' finalised Angus, as he began to shuffle papers on his desk in a semblance of order.

Chapter 21

'Good morning, I'm Mrs Meredith and have an appointment to see the gynaecologist.'

'Ah yes, do take a seat. Mr Brown will not keep you long,' responded the young efficient-looking receptionist.

Felicity was now three weeks overdue and had made an arrangement to see the gynaecologist to confirm her suspicion that she was indeed pregnant. She could not believe that she was although she had all the apparent symptoms. She knew that Norman had long indicated that he could not make her conceive presuming to be infertile, and yet he accepted that the impossible had happened when he was falsely told that she was pregnant. As a result, he married her! Now it seemed that she was indeed pregnant and Norman was the father, as she had not been near another man. She surmised that it must have been that evening when she tempted him and he entered her from behind. She remembered that occasion more than any other, as she thrilled over it and asked for it again that way at every opportunity. From Norman's point of view, he was delighted to give it to her, as undeniably it thrilled and excited him, too.

Felicity saw the gynaecologist who confirmed the possibility that she could be pregnant. She was to visit him again in a very short while to reconfirm.

'Licy, what is the matter with you? You look as if you have overdone your rouge this morning, or is something bothering you, my dear? Whilst I am here, is it not time we announced to Norm that you have aborted!' asked Anne after she had entered Licy's office the morning after the consultation with the gynaecologist and obstetrician.

'If my face is red, it is because I have an important announcement to make and do not know how to start,' blurted out Felicity in deference to Anne's question.

'Then let me ask you Licy, when, if not now, shall we mention your abortion? You could get up right now and complain of severe tummy pains, and I would insist that you get home immediately. That would be the best clue to the problem. But say, why are you looking at me like that Licy; what is the matter?'

'Oh Anne, Anne! I went to see a doctor yesterday and he confirmed that I was indeed pregnant and wants to see me again in two weeks time to confirm firmly. That is why my face is so red. So I will have to cover for about four weeks overdue. What shall we do Anne; you are the brains here, so what shall I do?' pleaded Licy as her face reddened still more as she looked across the desk to Anne.

'*What!*' exclaimed Anne in a higher pitch than was her normal, 'are you telling me that you really are pregnant after all our deception and scheming?'

'I do not know if I should laugh or cry Anne,' came the response from Licy. She looked across to Anne whose face showed utter amazement. 'Now you know all, what next?' added Licy.

'Well, I'll be jiggered. To think that we engineered a betrothal when nature could have done the job for us in truth. But do not be alarmed about the overtime; it would make it I suppose about ten months then, would it Licy?' questioned Anne. Then she continued, 'Then you must recall that you remained at home after the wedding as you were supposed to be feeling a bit unwell. You were afraid to mention to anyone, not even me, as you thought it would upset Norm, that whilst at home you aborted. Now, happily, you can again announce the happy event will after all take place a wee bit later than originally planned. You tell Norm right now, and then officially tell me. That would please him to think that you put him before me!'

'Anne, you are a genius. As soon as you go, I'll buzz him and see if he is free and announce it,' replied Licy now looking not just red in the face, but shining with radiance that had to be seen to be believed.

'Norm, Licy here. I know it is unusual, but could you pop in here instead of me coming into your office, please?'

'Why, of course, my dear. You sound ominous, so hope nothing is wrong. Is there my dear?' queried Norman.

'Yes and no, but in the finale, all's well. So will you please pop in?'

'OK, expect me in about ten minutes,' responded Norman, then hung up.

In less than the forecast ten minutes, Norman was moving along the short corridor towards Felicity's room wondering what could be the cause for this new approach.

'Well now, what's in the wind that you ask me to look in to see you?' asked Norman as he entered Licy's room and took a chair in front of her desk.

'I hope you will not be cross with me, but have to tell you that when I was at home some weeks ago, I aborted, but feared to tell you, as you may think I tricked you into marrying me. Yesterday, I visited a Doctor Brown of Harley Street, an obstetrician who has confirmed that I am indeed pregnant and he asked that I call to see him again shortly to establish precisely the fact. Now before you ask, let me explain. Yes, I did abort, but you know the way we now enjoy sex. That has cured your infertility. Isn't it marvellous, Norm?' said Felicity with a bewitching smile to beguile her husband.

Mr Meredith looked at his bride for a long moment and could not bring himself to utter the words that ran in his mind. 'Was she pregnant in the first place? Would it not have been wise to have asked her to get that fact checked before he rushed into matrimony? Now she says that she is indeed pregnant. I do not think it can be mine after all! Yet she has not had any opportunity to indulge with anyone else.'

'Does Anne know what you are telling me, Licy?' was all he could say.

'Actually, no. I thought you should be the first to hear and learn of the pending birth. I hope you are not cross or anything like that with me, my love?' said Licy with a look of subdued smiles beaming across her face towards him. She could not quite fathom his look. Was it a look of doubt or was it a look of puzzlement. Whichever it was, it was up to her to endear him to her, otherwise she would have to

271

plead her cause to Anne for her assistance. She did so wish to win this round on her own.

'I'll say the same as you – actually, no. I am pleased to learn that you consulted me first, but your news, to say the least, is a bit staggering. Yes, I am delighted that we are to have a child, and the delay will look better, as it will now be well over the nine months after the wedding. But you have now raised the old question of fertility? Perhaps you will permit me to attend the appointment with your doctor?'

'Why of course you can come with me,' responded Licy with a smile that should have conquered him, and added, 'I am delighted that you concern yourself. That is very proper and I appreciate it my love.'

'Then you will let me know as soon as you get the appointment fixed. Now if you will excuse me, I must get back.' And as he concluded, he rose from his seat and was about to depart when she called him back.

'Darling, have you not forgotten something?' she said looking askant towards him with her head slightly on one side.

'Sorry, my love,' came the answer, as Norman returned to her side of the desk and bent forward and kissed her lightly on the cheek. 'In future my dear, I think we had better keep the door open whenever we meet and behave in an employer/employee manner,' he retorted brusquely as he made a second attempt to leave her office.

Mr Meredith walked straight out of the room without turning round to see the reaction on Licy's face. He was very disturbed by the news. He was contented before he accepted that he married a pregnant woman, but now to be told that she had an abortion and was again pregnant, seemed to him a bit more than a puzzle. There was no question that not only was he in love with his wife, but he also admired her as a fine woman in many respects. But the news was shattering to say the least. Now he questioned the advisability of going with her to see the obstetrician. What was the point? Perhaps he could arrange a private chat with him before he saw Licy.

Then should he confide in Anne as had become the pattern of late? Then was Anne exerting too much influence on him? What was the alternative? He wanted Anne for his own ends and she was very useful commercially too. To keep confiding in her also held Anne to him, and that would assist his plan with her. He would check to see where she was at that moment in time.

As Norman left her office, Licy mused as to the revelation she expounded to her husband. She felt that she did not put her case over sufficiently well, as he appeared to leave her in a quandry. He now proposed to accompany her to see the doctor. Where had she gone wrong? Should she have had Anne to break the news first after all? She had better find out where Anne was and get her to smooth over the ruffled feathers of her husband for her. Although she felt she owed a lot to Anne and also was in love with her as far as a woman can profess love for another woman, she did so desire to work this one out on her own. She did, however, feel that things had gone awry between her and Norman. He had never spoken to her so sharply as he did when leaving her room, not even before he wed her.

'Braddely here, sir; can I be of help to you, sir?' he responded into the telephone on getting a call from his boss, Mr Meredith.

'I want to speak to Anne. Could you please transfer me to her Brad?'

'Sorry sir, but she is out and has not yet returned. She did say when I spoke with her last that she expected to be finished by this evening, sir.'

'All right then, just ask her to pop in to see me when she calls.'

'Brad, Miss Fawley here. Let me speak with Miss Hopkins please.'

'Sorry Miss, but she is still out. Have just had a call from Mr Meredith asking for her, too. Hope there is no trouble?'

'No, that's all right Brad. Just let her know that I asked to see her; that's all and thanks again.'

'That's unusual Ian. Both of them asking for Anne! She must have done something wrong this time, I bet! I kind of like her but at the same time would like to see her taken down a peg or two. How do you feel about her, Ian?!'

'Well, Brad, as far as I am concerned, Anne has made it clear that she is not interested in me, and although I still would like to go out with her, I do not think it is in me to see her hurt. But you amaze me! Because she has shown merit, you feel usurped or something. I respect her ability and go along with her and feel you would be wise to also. I bet she can answer your exam questions off pat, too, if you approached her. So you just pass on the message and forget it.'

'Perhaps you are right, Ian. But to think that she had jumped over us both in seniority. Have you noticed that she simply marches into the boss's office as if she owns it! She is taking on too much in my opinion and is due for a mighty big fall; mark my words, Ian!'

'Don't kid yourself, Brad. She knows where she is going and she will get there with or without us. The difference between us is that I like her, so have watched her and have seen her brilliance. I only wish that she would be interested in me. Nothing would please me more, I can tell you. So be prudent Brad, and play your cards right way; otherwise you will be the loser. As we are all three of us due for the finals at the same time, we should get together rather than follow your stand and separate.'

'I'll say again, perhaps you are right Ian, but I still cannot alter my feelings against her. She is not like any other girl that is friendly towards her workmates. She huffed me from the very beginning and have not got over that. Then when we go out on assignments, the air she portrays as if she is the boss herself, is a bit more than I can tolerate.'

'Well, if you want to be antagonistic, that is your privilege Brad, but I still think that you are wrong. Let's say no more for the moment,' replied Ian as he turned from his colleague and proceeded with his labours.

'Thanks, Mum; it was very nice and enjoyable,' said Anne as she pushed her plate an inch further forward onto the table, after finishing her evening meal in company with her parents.

'It was a new recipe I tried and am glad you approve, Anne dear,' replied her mother as she looked across towards her daughter with a happy smile on her face. 'Does your father also approve of my new recipe?' added Mrs Hopkins as she now looked across towards her husband.

'I think it was very nice too, Mary. In fact a second helping would go down extra well if there is any left, my dear?' replied Mr Hopkins.

'Sorry, but there is no more, but am delighted that you both enjoyed my culinary prowess. Would you please, Anne, help me clear the table?' she added as again she looked across the table towards her daughter.

'Why of course I will Mother, but first I would like to ask you both if you would come with me on Saturday morning to see my new flat. I have taken over Felicity's place and think you should visit it with me, as I propose to get it redecorated and would like your opinion,' Anne ventured as she glanced towards her parents on the other side of the table.

'What do you mean you have taken over a flat? Does that mean you will be leaving us here, your home, to live alone or with whom?' asked her father in a quiet, subdued, yet stern manner. Her mother meanwhile just sat and looked at her husband to fathom the point raised with their daughter.

'I shall be on my own exactly as Felicity was. As you know, she recently married, so I have the option of the flat and I feel I would be foolish to let slip a good deal. I will still let Mother have her monthly allowance as before, as I will be due for a raise very soon, so can meet that contingency easily. Now will you both come with me to look it over on Saturday morning?' pleaded Anne as she continued apprehensively.

Neither of her parents replied but stared at her until her father said, 'I think it would be foolish to leave your comfortable home for a doubtful pleasure of living on your own. To cook and clean for yourself and come home to an empty flat is to me not luxury but idiocy, so I would suggest that you just forget it, my dear.'

Anne thought quickly that she would have to overcome her father's objection to keep the prevailing smoothness between them.

'Dad, I'm nearly twenty-one and am considered by my firm to be an adult and responsible, so why you should raise these objections, I cannot see. In any case, surely it is for me to find out if living alone will prove to be compatible. If not, I will ask to come back. I hope you will not refuse me if such should be the case, so please do come and see before you raise any more objections. Will you please, on Saturday?'

'Well, John, perhaps we should go and see what Anne has got to show us and then we can discuss it there if needs be. Shall we?' As she ceased speaking, she continued facing her husband until he voiced his reply that he would, but that should not be taken that he felt it was a correct move.

Although it was but four o'clock, and by the time she would reach the office, it would be almost home time, Anne decided nevertheless, to return there instead of going directly home. Then the atmosphere at home was not as it should be since she requested her folks to visit with her to see her proposed new home. So she made her way back to the office, where she arrived to be welcomed by Braddely.

'Got some messages for you,' he announced in an untoward manner.

Anne walked over to his desk and stood waiting whilst he rummaged to unearth two scraps of message-pad paper. He handed them over to Anne without a word.

Anne accepted them and noted they were from her boss and Felicity.

'Which came first, Brad?' asked Anne as she still stood at his desk.

'Mr Meredith buzzed through, then a couple of minutes later, Felicity did,' replied Brad in a terse, could-not-care tone.

'Thanks for the notes,' she replied as she left the office to pop into her boss's room.

Anne traversed the short corridor to her boss's room and without the courtesy knock, opened the door and noted that he was alone. She entered and closed the door being her, as he gawked at her with a full flush smile. As had become their custom, she walked behind the desk and bent her head to kiss him on the cheek. He too had developed the custom of rubbing his hand up and down her leg, a custom that she ignored for compatibility. Anne then moved away and asked him what he wanted her for.

'Its a quarter to five so did not expect you back, but it is appreciated that you made it. Now please sit down Anne, my dear. I wish to have a grave discussion with you. Ah – now you are seated, tell me, did you know that Licy aborted then became pregnant again?' He asked with his eye fixed on her every movement.

'Norm, is it fair that you discuss this with me, as you should really be talking to Licy. I did know that she aborted and was afraid to tell

276

you. I had been pushing her to tell you, but she feared you would be upset and think that she wheedled you into marriage. It is, though, news to me to learn that she is pregnant again; so what is it then?' asked Anne as she pondered what had happened between husband and wife that she was now questioned. It seemed apparent that things had not gone too smoothly for Licy.

'You have become our referee! I do not know how that happened but it is so. This is the first time she has consulted me before informing you. I am flattered. But please, for the sake of my sanity, tell me the truth. Was she pregnant and can she become pregnant now, as you know I am of the opinion that I am infertile.'

He looked across towards her with a stern but not unkind face awaiting her answer. She looked back at him and tried to probe his mind to ascertain what he knew and what he did not know.

'I think you yourself told me you were infertile, so that you could indulge without preventatives. But from what I understand, even if you are infertile, that does not mean that you do not produce the eggs that fertilise the womb. What it means is that you do not produce sufficient. Of course you should check this up with your own doctor. In your case, it is feasible that due to excess of zeal and over-excitement, you did on an occasion produce more fertilising eggs than usual and perhaps you also indulged twice in succession and that caused the pregnancy. Surely you are not suggesting that Licy tricked you or that she has been unfaithful, surely not!' she emphasised still looking at him as he portrayed a shocked manner at the very thought of being tricked and cheated.

Norman half closed his eyes as he attempted to fathom Anne's mind and ideas. Could it have been the new approach he has had with Licy that makes her scream with delight! Licy has suggested that it was this new way, too. He stared at her without blinking until she asked for his reply.

'Anne, I do not know what to think or believe. But it appears that despite my conviction that I would remain childless, Licy is for the second time carrying my child! Should I ask for a blood test, because I still cannot believe it is true!'

'What you mean, Norm, is that you do not believe Licy, and that is nasty even by your own standards. If that was me, and you suggested a blood test, I would say 'yes' but think very little of your faith in me. Has she had time to play around with anyone else – you know that cannot be – her time is as on the clock accounted for to the minute. So where are your suspicions? What I'll do is have a chat with her, but be warned Norman, if you want to lose the second, then carry on with your present attitude – that will assuredly encourage an abortion again!'

She faced him and showed far from a pleasant manner. She appeared to get heated and showed that too.

'Anne, my dear, you know I trust you both, but this is a shock to me and I am not thinking straight. But I take your point – if I antagonise her, it may cause her to lose it again. I did not do anything to cause her to lose the first, so what?'

'My tip to you for what it is worth, is that you be extra kind to her and solicitous. She loves you and you know it. The margin between love and hate is so infinitesimal that it is impossible to define, so do not take chances. Act and mean it, that you love her and emphasise it as much as you can. You should wrap her in cotton wool, because in your case you have probably only given her very few eggs or genes, and that can abort easily! She should not be at work but stay in bed twenty-three hours a day for safety, at least until she is about six months. So go to it Norm for your own sake!'

They sat staring at each other, both awaiting the other to speak first, each weighing up what had been said and what had been unsaid.

Norman spoke first, 'Anne, again I must agree with you. Why is it that you always appear to be right? I sometimes wish it was you that I married. But we will be having our private arrangements just the same, won't we, Anne dear?'

Anne's face spread into a broad grin at his suggestion of a liaison with him. She recalled her promise to that effect which, to date, was limited to the kiss they exchanged on greeting and his probing hand. She felt pleased with the outcome of their conversation, as at least it gave him to feel that Licy was honest and could be trusted and needed cuddling, not condemning.

'Norm, you know you can count on me day or night. I have never let you down in private or in business, now have I? We will get together as promised, but please do not sour our relationship by your attitude towards Licy. She deserves the best you can give her. I will give her anything that I can, and both of you know it, so be nice to her and I will be nice to you! That is our deal, eh Norm?'

'Anne, come and kiss me, then go and see her. I will wait until you are through, then take her home. How would that be, my dear?'

Without replying, Anne arose from her seat with a look of great satisfaction shining on her face and walked around to his side of the desk. As she approached, he stood up and took her into his arms in a strong embrace and kissed her harshly, to which she reciprocated. As he held her tightly, he rubbed himself against her, until she felt his manhood become rigid. Anne moved back out of his grasp and as she stepped back she grabbed him and said, 'Sorry to get you heated up ol' boy, but save it for Licy, and for me later on, eh!'

'Gee, you are twisting me again. See what you do to me? But I will not forget your words. I will give it to you that you will never forget and neither will I, so off you go before I make a fool of myself!'

As she left the office, he began to dwell on his prospects with her in the very near future. If only she would take it from him as Licy was now doing and twice in succession too. 'I wonder,' thought Norman, 'was that "twice" the possible cause for Licy's condition?'

'Hi, Licy, how are you?' called Anne as she entered Felicity's room and walked across the floor in a joyous manner to take her seat alongside her desk.

Felicity looked up at her friend with a solemn face that spoke a lot of her anguish she felt and which Anne recognised.

'Anne, I'm glad you made it tonight. I feared that you would be going straight home tonight, and I did so wish to speak with you. But first, have you seen Norm since you got in?' questioned Felicity as she gazed at her friend in earnestness.

'I have just come from his office and he is waiting for me to have a chat with you before he comes to take you home. Now do not look like that at me. All is well! He will be taking you home and requesting that you stay abed for a while. I have suggested twenty-three hours a day for at least the next six months or at least until your pregnancy is sufficiently advanced and strong enough not to abort. And you had better do that, and if needs be, get the gynaecologist to visit you, then it would appear natural for Norm to be at home when he does visit.'

'But does he believe me, that I am for the second time expecting; that's what I would like to know Anne?' questioned her friend as she gazed appealingly at her.

'Licy, everything is fine. I am satisfied that he accepts the fact. I explained the reason why it happened, so do not worry; you are in the clear.'

'Gee Anne, I do not know how to thank you enough. It does not matter what the wicket is like, you always manage to clear the pitch for us! But how can I lie in bed all day – it would bore me to tears. So put your thinking cap on for that section and tell me what to do?'

'Licy, you are being a trifle absurd. You have a telephone at your bedside, so you can carry on your work to a limited extent. Then you can read and I hope you learned to knit in your youth, as you could start that for the nipper now. Then you will have the housekeeper to see to, so you would not, or should not, be bored. And I suspect Norman will leave later in the morning and get home earlier in the evenings. Then I will be popping in too, so your day will soon disappear. So be sensible my girl; you told me that he was infertile and you are now pregnant; so be wise and hold on to it for love's sake – you may not get a second – or should I say, a third chance!'

Felicity stood up wearing a broad smile of satisfaction on her face and walked around to the front of the desk, and as she approached, Anne arose from her seat and faced her. Unashamedly, Felicity pulled her friend towards herself into a strong embrace, and rained kisses on her in appreciation for her assistance in the present problem. After but a fleeting few seconds, they broke apart, when Anne suggested that Licy reseat herself, while she would let Norman know that she was free to be escorted home.

Felicity danced back to her seat and with a happy laugh in her voice, commended Anne for her astuteness and asked her to proceed as suggested.

Chapter 22

It promised to be a glorious summer to come by the token of the present fine few days. The sun shone through Mr Meredith's office window, as he summoned both Ian and Braddely with Anne to his room. He requested them to be seated around his desk and opened with –

'Now you all know that tomorrow and for the day after are momentous days for you all. You all sit your finals and I wish you all good luck and success. I feel confident that you will give me a hat trick by the three of you passing the first time. Do you feel as confident as I do?'

Both the lads looked towards Anne and gestured for her to speak first, giving privilege to females first. Anne took the bait and responded.

'Well, sir, you can be sure that we will all endeavour to pass for our own sake and we also hope that in doing so, it earns us the respect that we so far have enjoyed in this firm. I am sure that my two colleagues feel the same; is that right boys?' asked Anne raising her eyes to them.

'Speaking for myself and am sure for Brad too, we endorse Anne's remarks and thank you sir for your good wishes. We all hope to succeed.'

After a few more pleasantries, the three dispersed back to their desks. None of them felt very much like working with the examination pending. So they spent the next short period of time in idle gossip, until as if by mutual consent, yet unspoken, they bowed their heads and got on with their labours.

'Ah, you must be Doctor Brown,' posed Mr. Meredith as he answered the door of his own house, to receive a well-dressed gentleman that stood on the threshold with a Gladstone-type case in his grip.

'Yes, that's right. I have come to see Mrs Meredith and presume you must be her husband,' replied the doctor as he stepped across into the hallway.

'She is upstairs awaiting you, so please do follow me,' replied Norman nodding in acknowledgement to the question, as he led the way across the hallway to climb the one flight of stairs, then advanced to his bedroom. Flinging open the door, he invited the doctor to enter. As the doctor cleared the entrance to the bedroom, Mr Meredith followed him into the room, closing the door after him.

The doctor observed a very pleasant and extremely well-furnished room and reclining on a comfy bed, sat Felicity to whom he addressed himself.

'Ah, good morning, Mrs Meredith. Glad to see you looking so well. I hope therefore all will be well with you.' Then espying her husband also in the room, enquired if he wished to remain during the examination.

'Well, if you have no objections, it would save a lot of time and questions after, to repeat all the instructions and advice given my wife if I remained, don't you think Doctor Brown?' responded Mr Meredith who wished to be present yet not too keen, as he was apprehensive, yet could not define why.

'In that case, by all means, but please do not interrupt me in my examination. It will be my duty thereafter to explain to both my diagnosis and proposed treatment, if any,' indicated the doctor as he divested himself of his jacket and donned a white coat, that he extracted from his case. Then, by instinct, entered the bathroom to rinse his hands.

Some twenty minutes later, the doctor announced that he had finished his examination and was satisfied that his patient was pregnant. He reckoned that she was about two months advanced. He endorsed the suggestion that she should remain abed at least to the sixth month. He also recommended that a midwife be engaged now, and she would attend to all the needs until his attention was called for. The doctor was thanked for his services and escorted out.

'That means you are due about December, my dear?' reckoned Norman to his wife.

'Yes, that's right. Are you now satisfied, my love, when we indicated that the impossible, as you thought, has happened. It must be due to the new way we make love now and twice in succession too!' chortled Felicity emphasising the question of his presumed infertility.

'Cannot argue my love and am very happy at the prospects.'

Anne questioned herself and instead of getting a taxi, proposed that her parents join her on the journey to her new flat on a bus. Very little was uttered during the excursion and Anne suspected that she was going to have a fight against strong opposition, more from her father than her mother! Her father looked sour throughout the tour of inspection and then voiced his opinion that the flat might appear all right on the surface, but it was lonely there. Anne responded to the augment that she was really surrounded by a lot of people in the adjoining apartments. Anne tried her best to use her gilded tongue to convince him. After a lot of toing and froing, a provisional understanding was reached, whereby Anne should stay at the flat after the redecoration for a while, then reconsider. From Anne's point of view, she was happy to have attained that understanding.

Angus took stock of his attitude and realised that to entertain José each and every night would disenhance him at his office, so he agreed with Ira to join in with the staff and accept their offer of entertainment. As he now began to get almost daily letters from back home, both from his parents and Joan, he realised that he would have to lie in his replies if he just remained with José, but if he went out with the boys, he could tell the truth omitting mention of José.

All the letters that Angus received spoke of the prospects of peace but with an element of doubt. This made him wonder at his own disposition. What would he have to do should war between Britain and the German dictator be for real? Would he have to return home as he thought he would have to! He had already been asked if he would like to remain indefinitely, which would given him freedom from the war effort back home.

The news and press here in the United States all gave the strong indication that Britain was alone and should not anticipate help from them! This said to Angus that his country would then need every man, and he felt that he would have to return to do his best for the war effort, should that day dawn. He, as well as thousands of others, sincerely hoped that that day would not come about.

Angus began to settle down at his work and was admired for his enterprise. He was well-thought-of. He enjoyed the fun generated by his colleagues, knowing that José would be happy to meet up with him for the two allotted nights that he nominated, and she did concur with him. He was happy in the knowledge that she at least was co-operative, that he could settle back to his work with his mind free from frustration that he always suffered back home, from getting so near yet never achieving his objective and goal. If the world could stop still, he was happy to stay as he was!

Yet Angus did have thoughts of Joan. Her letters to him were clear that she missed him and constantly begged to learn in his 'next letter' how much longer he expected to stay away from her? As always, he was indecisive. He wondered at himself if he would have been keener to get back home if Joan had been more co-operative with him as José was? Perhaps he pondered this absence was a test of his love for her. His current attitude of not hurrying to get back, did that mean that he did not love her as much as he thought he did! He did so wish he could master his own destiny and come to a concrete decision.

Angus knew that if he returned home soon, he would miss José very much. So did he love her too? That troubled him! He endeavoured to analyse his true feelings and considered that his attraction to José was more physical than ethereal, but he would miss that interlude very much. Then perhaps, if he found another partner for those engaging episodes, he would not then be so beholden to José? Yes, that appeared to be a solution, surmised Angus. So he would seek out another female for special attention, and then he could re-arrange his timetable again. Would he have to shorten his time with his colleagues or forsake José for those two nights or ask her to consent to just one night alone with him? He somehow knew she would reject and refuse, as she would suspect the reason. 'Oh dear, life is not so simple and "Love's Like That"' bemused Angus.

284

On the advice of her boss, Anne requested the help in redecorating her flat from a client of the firm. With a modest amount of reluctance, Anne approached Mr Seymour, famed for his inspiring designs, and asked if he could give her a few tips on her quest. As Anne was known to him by attendance for accountancy work, he offered his assistance without hesitation. He met her at the flat, and after making copious notes, promised to let her have some suggestions within a few days.

True to his promise, three days later, he called Anne to visit his studio and to look over the proposals. With great excitement, Anne found time to rush over to view that which Mr Seymour had sketched out for her.

Anne's visit proved well worthwhile. She was not only shown a scaled plan, but also swatches of the suggested wall paper proposed for her to consider. The plan also showed her the re-arranged setting of the existing furniture. It gave Anne inspiration to view the proposals, and with little comment agreed for him to proceed with the work as planned. A schedule of time was then agreed as to how long the work would take, and the costing also agreed to. Anne was assured that the work would be completed before the end of April, so the planned party for the May Day celebrations coupled with the house warming gathering could coincide.

Sir John Cuthbertson had met up with Anne now a number of times, and had become quite popular with her. She still, however, looked upon him as a client and latterly as a friend. Never for one moment had she looked upon him as a lover, suitor or anything else! As originally she had huffed him in his attempt to be brazen with her, he had behaved since, as a true English gentleman. Though they might have kisses somewhat passionately, that was as far as any scene went. This was not to say that from his standpoint, he would have refused to make advances to Anne, had he the confidence that she would not spurn him. He regarded her with too much sincerity to risk losing her by making untoward advances upon her. He feared her reaction again, which might cause her to turn away from him. This he could not countenance. So he exercised great caution despite his feelings and growing desires.

From Anne's point of feeling, she would have relished a little more adventure, but having once made her stand, maybe as a prude, she felt it inappropriate to change her tactics. She really enjoyed the entertainment afforded by Sir John, and somehow felt that it was his desire to behave correctly. She did not think it could be her initial attack upon him, on his first sexual attempt upon her, that restrained him. She therefore, viewed his detachment to be of his own inclination, whilst he in turn, presumed that it was her attitude of refraining from those entanglements, so left it as it was! He also had in mind very forcefully, those comments presented to him by that private agent.

On this occasion they both sat opposite each other in a restaurant enjoying a meal after a theatre show. As had become their habit, after a show, they both went into realms of assessing the merits or otherwise of the artists and the play as a whole. This evening, he had determined to broach the subject that had been on his mind ever since he first laid eyes upon her.

'Every occasion we meet, you always evince your satisfaction as you apparently enjoy being with me, I hope that you really do enjoy my company as well as the entertainment seen, my dear Anne?' entreated Sir John as he peered across the table into her eyes and wished the table was not between them.

'Why of course, John. To attend these shows or munching a meal in a restaurant without you sitting near me, would not be so nice or pleasant! It is the company to me that I value more than the entertainment that goes with it. But surely you suspected that John, otherwise you would not have invited me so often, now would you?' reiterated Anne gazing at him with a beautiful bewitching glint in her eye that made it hard for him to control his emotions.

'My darling Anne, you delight me more and more each time we meet, so I think it time I spelt out what I wished to say since we first met. In fact, I'm sure you may remember the vague proposal I made to you in the presence of your boss, now do you, my dear?' queried Sir John as he continuously peered into her eyes as if mesmerised to one stance.

'Please John, we have met so often that I cannot remember everything that you may have said just like that. So please do not make a mystery of whatever you wish to say. I promise I will not bite you,

286

how about that, eh?' quipped Anne with a smirkish smile on her face that said a lot yet admitted nothing.

'I repeat, my darling, it may have been, not very romantic the first time I broached the subject, and this too may not be considered the ideal place either. I must, however, ask you just the same. Would you be my wife? I know this is not perhaps the best or proper place to propose, but there it is, I have, so what does my dear Anne say? I hope it is the "Yes" that I crave?'

Anne's glint of devilment vanished and in its place a look of amazement spread across her face. For all the affection she held for Sir John, she had never dreamed that she meant so much to him. Then her affection suddenly developed on hearing the enunciation, so she felt love. Now could she be in love with him or was it because he entertained her so royally. 'What was love anyway? Was it proximity with another to mutual desire or was it habit of frequent meetings. Then frequent meetings may lead to boredom, as one gets acquainted with the routine that develops. Now we have met numerous occasions and have not reached the stage of boredom! Was that a clue that it would never reach me? Should I consider if I love him, or that I could love him yet? Well,' she mused, 'even if I am doubtful as to whether I am in love – for that feeling is so hard to define – can I live with him for the rest of my days in, shall I say, contentment? Is Love Like That?'

'Anne, my cherrie, I have proposed to you her in this restaurant of all places, and all you do is stare into me with a glazed look. What are you looking for in my face? I love you and have done so from the first time I saw you, so I repeat, will you marry me?'

'John, I do not know how to respond. I love being with you, but did not for one moment anticipate or suspect that you had those intentions towards me. After all, I am from a different station in life than you, so for that reason I did not consider ourselves more than agreeable friends. To propose to me here is a bit of a shock to say the least . . .'

'Anne darling, forgive me interrupting you, but I do not care about stations or all that. I love you and wish to wed you, so please say yes and make us both happy,' interjected Sir John as he still stared into her face endeavouring to analyse her innermost thoughts. He stretched out his hand towards her across the table and took her hand into his and held it whilst awaiting her reply.

'I remember now your first suggestion when I was in your office with Norman. I took that as a leg-pull and forgot it soon after. But are you serious now or are you still playing silly buggers. If you are, I do not relish it for one moment, John!' responded Anne still with a look of amazement.

'Anne, would it please you if I went down on my knees here in a public restaurant – will if that will satisfy you as to my seriousness. I repeat for the umpteenth time, will you marry me, Anne dear?' he declared, still with his eyes looking appealingly into her and still holding her hand.

'John dear, you have staggered me, hence my hesitation in replying to your unexpected proposal. I am very attracted to you, so presume that is the same as being in love or is it? You had better tell me. If you are asking to marry me soon, I must decline. I must await the results of my exams, for if I have flipped, I intend to resit and cannot do that married, now can I? Then I have my new flat being decorated. What am I to do with that? This all too sudden, and I think I must ask for time to think it out carefully!' returned Anne with a puzzled frown on her brow.

'My dear Anne, all I ask is that you say 'yes' now and details can be sorted out afterwards. To be engaged should not prevent you having to resit, but then I feel that this would not be necessary in your case. As to your flat, how would it be to combine the celebration of the flat with the announcement of our engagement there?' added Sir John now with a more happy feeling, having heard her comments which he understood but did not consider a problem.

'If I said "yes" now, and then after a night's reflection, I changed my mind, would that be nice of me? Hope you do not mind if I think aloud John, as you have jumped me unexpectedly,' posed Anne still puzzled as to know the best way to resolve this question to the advantage of both. 'But then why am I hesitating? He had made me a very valid suggestion that we can make it a double celebration at my flat, so that takes care of that. Then he is not proposing marriage right away as he does not press the point. So why am I shilly-shallying – look at the advantage to me – I would be considered a fool to throw

288

away such a chance and in any case, I do like him a lot, so say "yes" and be happy.'

'John dear, thank you for your patience with me. I have tried to look into my own mind and have come to the conclusion that my attachment to you is more than just friendship, but is the first blossom of love, so John dear, I will happily marry you and hope that you will continue to be patient with me!' answered Anne now with a radiant blush on her cheeks, that made her look, if that were possible, still more beautiful.

'Darling, you have made me very happy and I promise you I will make you equally happy, too!' he answered, as he raised his hand to beckon the waiter to order some champagne.

The news of the betrothal of Anne and Sir John Cuthbertson spread rapidly and astonished many, but not Felicity nor her husband Norman Meredith. Although they knew of its probability, they still did not really think it would be realised. Yet both had that happy feeling for her, however, for its accomplishment, having known of its portend a long while ago. From Felicity's point of view, she was extra happy, as she now felt that any possibility of a liaison between Anne and her husband Norman would now be nonexistent. She could not imagine that shrewd Anne would spoil her opportunity by an intrigue. Then her mind raced ahead, would it affect her own attachment with her? She could see no reason why it should. After all, both of them would now be ladies of leisure so could meet up for a quiet tête-á-tête. Anne would have the reasonable excuse of visiting her to see both her and the infant too. So opportunity was there.

And Norman smiled to himself with the thought that she had made a promise to him. She always kept her promises in the past, so saw no reason for her not doing so in the future. If he had an affair with her once, she would then continue, again and again. Obviously, she would not need the flat, so it would revert back to him! He would propose to meet her there as a love-nest between them both. That gave him happy thoughts that made him feel erogenous.

'What's making you smile like a Cheshire cat, Norm?' asked Felicity as she witnessed his face beaming after discussing that piece of good news, or maybe wishful thinking?

'I do not know why, but the thought of our Anne getting away with it has got me sexy, so what shall I do, my love?' Norman replied.

'Norm, my love, you had better jump into bed with me quickly, as soon, at least in a few months time, you will be starved of my love, so take advantage whilst the going is good, so come on in,' Felicity urged, as she turned back the blanket and moved to make room for her husband to get alongside her and . . .

Everyone now hoped that war would not come, but preparations had to be made in case it did happen. Everybody had to register for a ration book should that eventuality be necessary. Instructions were blared out for the benefit of the public as a whole. Instructions about food, instructions about blackout, instructions about petrol, instructions about rationing! Every day more instructions and all hoped and hoped despite the wild preparations that the day would not dawn to bring war again to the country.

Life carried on superficially as if nothing untoward was disturbing the public's equilibrium. Beneath the surface, however, all were alarmed at the vile prospects that would develop turmoil where peace now reigned.

Most will still remember the Prime Minister Mr Neville Chamberlain returning from a meeting in Germany with the Führer Hitler, waving a sheaf of papers saying, 'Peace in our time'. This now seemed very distant and far away. Yet the preparations that were made appeared only half-hearted, as without conformity to anything concrete. So life continued under a cloud of apprehension!

So summer and autumn were well over and the winter had set in, when Felicity gave birth to a bonny baby girl. And the child was born but a month after war was eventually declared.

The birth of a daughter to Felicity and Norman gave both of them great joy and happiness, only marred by the recent declaration of war. After a lot of wrangling, they decided that they would name their child after the Mother and Godparent, Anne. So the child was named Felicity Anne, with the injunction of the proud mother, that the name was not to be corrupted by shortening.

The joy was not dimmed by the greatly increased war effort. From Felicity's judgement, she was secure in her housekeeper as being well over the age of being likely to be called for National Service. So she was in her maid, who though not passé, as in the age bracket, that led Felicity to feel secure in her household's continuation.

Norman however, found that he lost a small number of his staff. This imposed a greater workload on those remaining, which included Anne. With so many men being called to the Colours, additional work and clients came to the firm for help. At Anne's suggestion, he called a meeting of all staff and proposed that they all from then on, should work an extra hour per day to keep the workload in proportion. This was agreed as were the compensatory pay for the extra hours worked. It was at that period that our three entrants for examination had had the results of their efforts. Happily, both Ian and Anne passed, but with sadness Braddely failed and was asked to resit.

'Sorry you made a muck of it, Brad,' said Ian to his colleague after the results had been announced.

'Really thought I did it OK. Wouldn't have minded if she also flipped it, but me and not her makes me mad. Perhaps should have done as you said and been sensible, as you did and work together with her. Don't like to ask her now,' winced poor Brad.

'If you believe in the adage, *Once a fool always a fool*, then keep to yourself and don't ask. For crying out loud fellow, what has it achieved you by your antangonism against her? She is a cracking girl and feel sorry for you being so dumb and blind not to realise that she is going to pass us both by, and to be on her side will be to my eventual advantage. Remember Brad, that if she does marry that Cutherbertson guy, she will become a titled girl, too, and that will lead to somewhere, I bet!' resounded Ian to his crestfallen partner.

'Perhaps you are right, Ian. I'd feel a fool now to approach her after I refused her help. Would you be a pal and sound her out for me?' begged Brad in a self-pitying voice.

'Sure I'll ask her, but in the meantime there is one saving grace for you. I will get called up, but you can get a deferment until you have resat. And I am not to keen to get called up until I have had at least a year postgrad experience,' Ian responded.

'Thanks pal, I'll owe you one,' replied Brad as they resumed their work in hand.

Angus had enjoyed the pleasure of work and play in New York almost a year now. He had presumed that he would have been sent back home after no more than three months, but his progress was so appreciated, that he was requested to remain a further indefinite period. Now that the war appeared too imminent, the Company President had contacted his English counterpart and suggested that he retain Angus for the duration of hostilities – if the war did erupt.

From Angus' disposition, this proposal helped him to come to terms with his indecision. He did wish to return home to his commitment with his betrothed Joan, yet desired to remain in New York to continue the pace of enjoyment he encountered. The frequent mail he received from Joan, indicated that she was becoming suspicious and doubted his explanation of living a loveless life! She demanded in a way that he return home very soon, otherwise she would have to consider their engagement off. After scribbling a number of letters and then throwing them away, he eventually wrote and agreed that under the prevailing circumstances, that it might be as well that they called off the engagement, with the hope that he would yet return to her. Joan accepted this rejection very badly and determined to overcome her pangs of both anger and frustration by not responding to his final letter.

Not having a reply to his last letter, Angus again wrote to Joan. Failing again to get any response, he wrote for the first time to Anne. He did get a reply from her that did not please him, as he was duly reprimanded and admonished by Anne for his *laissez-faire* attitude. Anne presumed, that knowing him, he had already made other attachments that prompted his sang-froid disposition. He was also told to refrain from any further correspondence as it would be ignored! For the next few days, Angus's behaviour showed his troubled mind, but in the end, he reconciled himself to remaining in America. Other than José, he found girls easier to get along with, as having a different philosophy to those back home. This was not to say that he succeeded with them as he did with José but he enjoyed their company more than his female friends from England. His patriotism also diminished as he Americanised himself.

When the question arose as to why he did not return to fight for his country, Angus glibly indicated that he wished to remain in the USA, and hoped after the statutory period to apply for citizenship. He found that this manifestation removed the growing stigma of being a coward.

The war had been devastating many areas now for about two years. Joan had completed her course and was successful in obtaining her degree in Science. She was directed to apply to the Ministry of Employment to do war work! Having met a number of girls that she knew at college that were on war work, she became unhappy. She mentioned this fact to Anne with whom she still retained firm friendship. Anne proposed that she would obtain for Joan a post in the war effort with a firm that she was acquainted with that she would possibly enjoy and appreciate.

'Hullo Charles, Anne here. How are you?'

'Fine, fine, and how are you? Well, I hope, but what can I do for you, my dear?' answered Charles Harrington.

'Two things. First I have you down for a visit within the next couple of weeks, and the second, I wish you to consider a friend who seeks a job.'

'Oh, that's nice to know that we will be seeing each other again. It's been a long time since we have met. And who is this friend, Anne?' requested Mr Harrington.

'Charles, I only saw you less than a week ago, so be a little more patient. Now, I would like you to consider a very great friend of mine, a Miss Joan Marchant who has just completed her B.Sc., and is to be directed to war work! I feel that you may appreciate a girl of that calibre rather than see her wasting her brain on some humdrum, mundane job, don't you think Charles?' advised Anne.

'Gee, she sounds just like the person I am looking for,' came his enthusiastic reply. So after a few more banters, provisional terms were agreed and Anne was requested to entreat Joan to report for duty Monday next without the formality of an interview.

'Miss Joan Marchant, sir. I have been told to report to you sir.'

293

Thus Joan entered and was ushered in to her new boss, whom she recognised from the description Anne had given her. Despite the fact she was informed that he was a hard man and somewhat diffident and perhaps a bit autocratic, she found him stern, but pleasant. He stared at her for a full minute before he spoke to her. He first requested that she be seated and than ran over the information that Anne had imparted to him about her. She concurred with the facts and had little to add and found none to amend. She also indicated that the terms proposed to her were acceptable. Mr Harrington then told Joan that he would like her to work in the technical and research department. He then called through the intercom for a person named Tom.

'You called for me, sir?' said a tall thin man that looked into the room from the doorway.

'Yes, Tom. I would like you to take Miss Marchant with you. She is your new assistant. Let me know how she progresses by the end of the week, will you Tom!' instructed Mr Harrington, still in the same tone of sternness.

'Thank you, sir,' he replied, then looking towards Joan, he just beckoned her with his index finger, and just said the word 'come' implying that she should follow him.

Joan arose from her seat and with a 'thank you, sir' she turned and followed Tom out of the office along the corridor and down a flight of stairs to a very large and light studio-type of room or office. Along the longest wall it had the most natural daylight, a bench type of fixture was apparent. On this work bench, as it appeared to be, a number of scientific instruments were rooted. Within the room were a threesome of staff working away. Tom first took her through to a small office adjoining the general area and asked Joan to be seated. He then asked her and obtained all the information that was already known to Mr Harrington. Then Tom indicated that he was to be referred to as Mr Thomas, and then with her, walked out to the main area to introduce her to the three operatives she observed when entering.

'Joan, this is Harry Firkin, my assistant with whom you are to work. This is Vanessa or Nessy as we call her, and him over there in the corner is Bill Boldinger. Now you know everyone, I will leave you to Harry to show you what to do.' And as he finished speaking, he turned towards his room again and retreated therein.

Chapter 23

All will remember that September 1939 was not many days old when war was declared. Every one then knew that we were in earnest and that any half-hearted effort must now be made with full vigour. Great effort was being made to evacuate many of the population away from the considered vulnerable areas. Railway stations would become crowded with flocks of children carrying their meagre possessions, plus over their shoulders, hung the cardboard box containing the issued gas mask. By now, Ian had asked Anne if she would help Brad with some coaching, to which she responded that she would. At infrequent intervals, he stayed behind after hours to accept the assistance and tuition she afforded him. He found that her theory and exposition elucidated many problems that he had a mental blockage on. During these short periods with her, he found that his former antagonistic attitude diminished, so much so, that he found himself falling in love with her much to his own perturbation.

Each and every evening he stayed behind with her, he found it extremely difficult to control his feelings. He craved to take her in his arms, but knew that would spell disaster. He could not understand his own feelings and became erratic and unsettled in his work. Anne quietly observed his attitude and suspected his mental turmoil. Prudently, she spoke to Norman about this and suggested to him that he should be granted extra day release time for him to study in a different environment. In the interest of Brad, Norman agreed and requested Anne let him know, so that he could organise his schedule.

'Brad, the boss suggested that you extend your half-day release to perhaps two or three sessions. Would you please contact your Head at college and have a word with him and arrange accordingly?' proposed Anne at the next evening that they stayed behind.

'We are short-staffed, so how come the boss suggested that Anne?' posed Brad as he looked up into her face solemnly.

'That's an order Brad, so no need to discuss it but get on with it tomorrow morning!' instructed Anne without any rancour.

'Does that mean that you will not be helping me any more, Anne?' pleaded Brad as he looked at her with drooling lips and wishful thoughts running through his mind.

'As you must appreciate, Brad, I too have a heavy workload. But you can count on me to assist you when you need my help. So don't look so downcast,' she appeased, hoping he would feel that it was the boss that directed the extra tuition and not her.

'Hullo Joan, don't see much of you these days. So how are you? You got the job at Harrington's?' questioned Anne in a confirmatory way, as she met up with Joan over a coffee one evening prior to them going their respective ways home.

'I'm fine Anne, but thought that you may like to know that I have that post in the factory to work on research and development that you referred me to.'

'That's good news. How do you get on with the boss, though?'

'Well, I only saw him that once at the initial interview and haven't seen him since to talk to, but see him around at times. Found him quite mellow actually and not as you hinted as a bit tough. The others at the plant are inclined to agree with you on that point.'

'Glad to learn that he has mellowed down as he was very awkward the first time I met him and, as I understand, that was his normal manner too. I'll be seeing you there then in a couple of days time, as I am due to visit them. Will look in to see you then.'

'That will be nice if permitted,' Joan questioned, with a glance of awe at her friend.

'Hullo Tracey, thought I'd ring you to tell you that I've got my call-up papers. So can we meet tonight to talk it over, eh?' asked Andrew with as calm a voice as he could muster.

'Oh dear. I knew you would get them sooner or later but had hoped against hope, that it would be later. Then shall we meet as usual, the same place and time tonight, Andy dear?' came her immediate reply from her troubled mind.

'OK then, the same time and place. So long till then, darling,' replied Andrew and then hung up.

By gradual established custom, Andrew met Tracey as she left her office that evening and took her to a nearby restaurant for a meal and chat over the news imparted her. By mutual agreement they deferred discussion of the major topic until they reached the coffee stage. At that point, she asked what he had in mind for the future between them. He rejoined that he felt it might be better if they wed before he reported for duty. Tracey was thrilled at the prospects, but felt a little squeamish. Nevertheless, they discussed the plan, and after much debating, agreed to fix a date as soon as it could be arranged. He promised to see his vicar to have the banns called, and then try to get an extra week or so deferment for the wedding. They finished their coffees, and departed the restaurant.

It was then that Andrew discovered that he was not the only applicant for having banns read, as the call-up had accelerated the demand. However, he managed to get the date asked for and also a note from his vicar to be presented to the recruiting officer for a week or so's deferment. This he applied for the very next morning and received a very sympathetic response.

In the interim, Tracey found herself with the customary duties of preparing for the happy day. She found an obliging printer for the invitation cards and dispatched them after booking the church hall for the reception. The parents of both sides not having met each other then made arrangements for so doing. The young couple had already met their prospective in-laws. It was agreed between the betrothed, that they would reside at his flat, and that she should continue to occupy it whilst he was absent. She could then periodically return to her former home, should she feel lonely at any time.

By the time Joan had been at Blackstones Engineering Works a month, she had attended the wedding of her friend, Tracey, with her beau, Andrew. Due to prevailing conditions, it was not the patriotic thing to have a big function, so after the Church ceremony, they had a modest reception in the church hall. Again, Anne was called upon to make the speech to the bridal couple. Now with more experience, she again excelled to the mutual acclaim of the bridal pair. Andrew was given a matter of three days deferment of the original call-up date after the wedding for a honeymoon. Andrew then attended for drafting to the Royal Air Force.

Now as Mrs Tracey Gilmour, she continued her post knowing that, before long, she too would be called for interview with the theme to be drafted to a more needed occupation. She had already discussed this prospect with her husband, and they had come to the conclusion, that as he was in the Air Force, that she too would join up in that branch of the Service, if called up. In the meantime, she continued her hitherto post.

But Joan's month saw her beginning to get happily involved in her new task. At first she found herself lost and not understanding the projects that were being performed at her place of work. But gradually and by the kind disposition of her new colleagues, she gradually became absorbed. The atmosphere that prevailed there was very intense, but not dolorous. She was not confined to that area alone, but was encouraged to meet up with the general workers in the staff canteen during meal times. Here, she found the noise somewhat heavy but not oppressive, not even the background music. She enjoyed the banter that emanated from the friendly atmosphere among the workers and it was not very long before all knew that she was a new employee and worked in the lab.

The majority of staff were men, as the work was of a manual nature, but with the advent of war, women had been drafted into the workplace to take over the function of the men called up to the Services. At this point in time, there were more men than women, even though with each man that left, he was replaced with a female. Joan found them all very sociable and a happy bunch of mortals, and enjoyed her mealtime breaks among them. In true democratic manner, each employee sat at whichever table happened to be available without differentiation. Thus she was not surprised to be greeted outside the factory by workers, even if she was perhaps vague as to who they were exactly.

'Ullo Joan, would y' like comp'ny or y'r way 'ome t'night'?' asked an employee of the works that Joan recognised but could not recall his name. She looked at him before replying, and observed that he was a man of some thirty years of age with thinning hair that blew in the breeze, with an old suit of clothes that appeared had not been cleaned since its long-ago purchase. It was apparent that he had recently scrubbed his face, as it shone like that of a new-born babe.

'That's nice of you but see no point in taking you out of your way, though,' she replied wondering if she should accept his offer.

'Well, I know y' drek'shn y' take an' vats me way 'ome too. An' if y' like t' stop fer a drink first, vats OK wiv me too Joan,' he added, as he gazed at her staring at him.

'But you have the advantage of me. I know you from having seen you, but I do not know your name even or where you live!' Joan responded wondering if she should or not accept his company.

'I'm Jimmy, an' I see y' git on t' same bus vat I do, so y' mus' live in v' same drek'shn too. So what y' say, shall we go' t'gever?' he answered looking at her as she stood there in a neat two-piece costume that emphasised her trim figure, that contrasted against his scrawniest.

'Jimmy who?' was all she could think of replying.

'Sorry, should 'ave said Jimmy Seaton. I werk in v' foundry section, an' 'ave bin 'ere a long time an' can reckon will still be 'ere f'r a long time t' come!' he ventured as he smiled at her whilst she still wore a vague expression on her face that showed.

'How do you know that you will be here and not called up though? You seem sure of yourself?' questioned Joan now looking at him wondering how he could say such a thing.

'I 'ave bin rejected by v' Board for Nash'nl Service as I 'ave a club-foot. Av'nt y' noticed?' he expounded in a nonchalant manner.

'No, I have not observed your infirmity. How do you come by that, or may one not ask?' she questioned now looking at him in a different way.

'Born wiv it but am not really 'andicapped as can still do a damn good day's work, but am 'pparently not fir fer mil'try service, so will stay at Blackstones. So now, c'n I see y' 'ome Joan?' again asked Jimmy in a quiet voice.

Joan looked again at him and could not quite resolve her own mind. She still thought of Angus and tried to contrast them, but could not. Then she unkindly thought that she was not keen to be out walking with a cripple. And his diction left a lot to be desired, too. But his broad smile was so captivating that she replied in a subdued voice, 'Well Jimmy, why not.' And as she spoke, she turned and commenced walking towards the bus-stop.

'Good,' was all he said as he walked alongside her.

Joan did not observe any apparent difference in his walk as she expected to with a club-foot. He just seemed to have a slight wobble from side to side that was not too obvious. This pleased her as she still felt she did not relish being with a cripple, as she referred to him in her mind.

'Do y' wish t' go straight 'ome or would y' like t' stop fer a drink first, Joan?' posed Jimmy as he continued alongside her.

'If it's a pub, the answer is no, but if its a cuppa, then yes please,' she replied as she turned half towards him as they continued walking.

'Vats fine. Take 'v next left an' a little way down is a nice café,' suggested Jimmy in a very happy frame of mind, now that he had this bright young girl from a senior department with him.

So they walked in silence for a matter of minutes until they reached the proposed café. They entered the half-empty place and took a seat. He questioned Joan if she would like anything more than a cup of tea. She declined, so he arose from his seat and approached the counter and ordered, then returned to his seat. In the short distance of perhaps six paces, Joan watched Jimmy traverse to the counter and noted that he slightly rocked as his feet apparently had different pressures or dispositions. Perhaps if she had not known of his disability, she may not have noticed his walk. His return to the table was the same, as was his broad smile.

'Be 'long in a mo,' said Jimmy as he took his seat facing Joan. He continued, 'An' 'ow d' y' like workin' at Blackstones?'

'Well, in the short while I have been there, I have found enjoyment both in the work and friendliness. Can say that I am very happy in my job. But tell me about yourself Jimmy?' she asked as she looked up towards him.

At that moment, the proprietor placed two cups of tea on the table in front of them, then withdrew.

'Not much t' tell. I've bin at Blackstones all me workin' life. I've bin put t' diff'rent departm'ts so I can claim vat can work anywhere in v' fac'try. I also enjoy me work, an' 'av 'ad a good deal o' v'riety, as I've said an' feel vat I am be'n schooled fer promotion vat way. When I first came vere, I was subjected to a lot o' catcalls an' laughter because o' me deficiencies, but soon showed 'em fools vat I was as good as vey were an' vat put a stop t' vat. Now I'm treated as one should be,' confided Jimmy without any rancour.

Joan soon found his diction somewhat jarring, but otherwise found him quite polite and attentive. She did at times find it difficult to understand him. How could she raise the question without causing embarrassment to both of them? But she took the opportunity when he asked her if she would care to join him at the weekend. She indicated as gently as she could, that she found his vocabulary beyond her comprehension and did not feel that she would care to sit and listen to that for an extended period of time. He sat looking in her direction with his mouth agape for a few seconds before he replied that he was not aware that he had been clipping his words. He indicated that when he first came to work at Blackstones, his diction was very good, but it drifted into the vernacular of the other members of staff with whom he worked. He promised to endeavour to improve his speech and renewed his request to Joan about the coming weekend.

'I was intending to go dancing this weekend, Jimmy,' Joan replied, wondering if that would get her out of the awkward situation.

Jimmy drew his breath in an apparent effort to get his words correct. He exhaled then said, 'That's OK with me, as I like dancing too, so can I pick you up on Saturday night, Joan.'

Joan was now in confusion. She now felt the embarrassed one, having broached the subject of his speech and getting his responses in an effortless reply without his having dropped an 'H'. Then also he had a club-foot – could he dance with that disability. She would rather not accept the invitation but his smile and general demeanour counterbalanced that notion. Her hesitation became apparent to him, so he added, 'I can dance despite my foot, and you will find that I can hold my own on the floor, so shall we meet? Just say whether you would prefer me to pick you up at your home or meet at the dance hall?' he added still looking into her face with an intenseness that made her avert her own eyes.

'Oh dear', thought Joan. 'He is persistent. Am sorry now that I accepted the cuppa with him. He now says that he can dance with his gammy leg and also wishes to call for me. Can I be rude and hurtful and get up and say, "Sorry old boy, but would rather not be seen with you," then walk out on my own and not look round at him!'

'I can see that you are finding it difficult to say yes to me because of my foot, and also I suppose because I am somewhat untidy. Please be assured that I *do* dress up when going out, and feel sure that my pronunciation now meets with your approval. Then may I propose, that we meet at the dance, if you tell me which one you will be going to?' and he still kept his eyes glued to her but in a subdued way, so as not to offend her. And again, Joan found it difficult to come to a decision. She thought it may be compromising to have him call for her, as apart from her parents, most of the neighbours were aware that she was engaged to Angus.

'Well, I'm still awaiting your reply, Joan. Shall I meet you there? Just tell me which hall you patronise and will be there, too,' he added still with his eyes affixed on her.

'It would be rather embarrassing for you to call on me, Jimmy, as I'm engaged. But if you happen to be at the Palais, you will find me there with a crowd of friends.' And as she concluded her comments, she rose from the table as a clear indication that she had no more to add to the subject. Jimmy understood the inference of her getting up from the table and realised that it would not serve his purpose any more to press his point any further. He arose too, then walking past the shop counter leaving some coins thereon, followed Joan out.

'Then I'll look out for you Saturday night,' said Jimmy as he tagged on to Joan as she continued to walk to the bus-stop.

Joan alighted from the bus and walked the short distance to her home. Her mind was in a turmoil over the last hour's adventure with Jimmy. She was inclined to regret that she accepted his offer of a cup of tea and being escorted onto the bus jointly. She pondered her wisdom, yet could see no alternative in having accepted, other than being crass rude, which she could not countenance. Then a solution

302

must be reached as she had, wisely or otherwise, agreed to meet him at the Palais on the coming Saturday night. Of course, she could deprive herself of the entertainment and not appear at the dance. That action she knew would indicate to Jimmy that she desired to spurn him. However true that may be, she could not tolerate such gross action. But then to attend, and take her usual place among her regular friends, she would naturally be obligated to introduce him to the assembly at the table. Then he might not attend himself, she mused. Somehow she was confident that he would be at the dance and she could see no choice for herself but to accept the irrevocable and hope that he did appear better dressed than hitherto! Turning the question over in her mind did not produce any other solution, so with prudence, she accepted the inevitable.

Despite her indecision of mind over the prospective meeting with Jimmy that evening, Joan did not have a disturbing night's sleep as she imagined she would. General family matters, and the usual Saturday morning shopping, took those thoughts away from her, at least for the time being. By evening, her mind and inclination was of cool-headedness with imperturbable indifference as to the consequences of meeting up again with Jimmy. She viewed the situation as she re-called his change in diction on her criticism. She herself would not have realised that he had a gammy foot, so she presumed that her companions sitting at the table would not notice this defect either. She began to grow in calmness that he would arrive nicely attired, and maybe, maybe even be a credit to herself for the evening's entertainment, looking forward to seeing how a university graduate could mix her metaphors with an otherwise uneducated man!

That Saturday night at the Palais de Dance the crowd was less than usual. The war had reduced the dance-goers, but it did indirectly create a more pleasant space to exercise the art of dancing. Now among the throng was the inevitable uniform present. The wearers of the uniform all appeared to be jollier – if that were possible – than the others at the dance that evening. When Joan arrived, she only found Tracey on her own at the table. She was but seated a few minutes, when Wynne and Richard arrived. Joan knew that Anne would not be coming that evening, having already spoken to her earlier that day. So that made three ladies to the one man, Richard. So perhaps with Jimmy's arrival, it might reduce the odds. No sooner had she reached that conclusion that Jimmy, the man in her questioning mind appeared in front of her. All he said as he came to the table was, 'Hullo Joan!'

Joan looked up towards the voice and saw Jimmy standing in front of her at the other side of the table. Much to her surprise and pleasure, he was indeed neatly attired in a well-tailored suit of pinstriped grey with a well-laundered shirt and a neat tie and matching handkerchief protruding from the top pocket of his jacket.

'Why, hullo Jimmy,' responded Joan, and as she spoke she looked around to her companions, and noted with satisfaction that they peered at Jimmy with an appearance of delight and wonder as to who he was.

'May I join you, Joan?' was all he replied.

'Why, of course, Jimmy, and now let me introduce you to my friends. This is Mrs Tracey Gilmour and next to her is Richard Crosby and his friend Wynne Roxbee.' And as she announced each one, Jimmy extended his arm to reach the individual and shake them by the hand. 'And this is Jimmy Seaton who works with me for the same company,' she added.

'Happy to meet you all. Now can I buy you all a first round of drinks?' he asked whilst still standing alongside Joan, who responded for the rest, by indicating that they invariably leave refreshments until the interval. With that explanation, Jimmy sat down alongside Joan and engaged her in local conversation. Then as the music restarted, he asked Joan if she would care to dance with him, and as he spoke he stood up.

Joan again had her mind racing with the premonition of disaster, but saw no alternative but to arise and take the floor and hope for the best. So without much enthusiasm, she rose from her chair and moved the few paces to the edge of the dance floor, at which point he placed one hand feather-light on her shoulder, and the other, still more lightly, behind her waist and led her out onto the floor to dance. With his very first step, he was inadvertently jostled, which caused him to tread slightly on her foot.

'Oh heck!' Joan exclaimed wondering if this was to be the evening's adventure?

But Jimmy with a somewhat reddened face ignored the comment and with a brief exclamation in a very low tone of the word 'sorry', he led her forward, and much to her amazement, she realised that she was dancing with one who knew how to dance!

'Everything OK, Joan?' questioned Jimmy, after traversing the floor a couple of times to the correct tempo to the music.

'Why yes, Jimmy, of course everything's OK,' replied Joan not knowing now how to respond and realising that what he had indicated was in fact true – he could dance, and well too! She also noted that his otherwise 'wobble' as she cared to refer to it, seemed to be lost in the general motion and swing of dancing. Now her new appraisal was confirmed at the conclusion of the dance when together they made their way back to the table to join the friends. Joan flopped down alongside Tracey, who leaned over and whispered in her ear, 'You've got a good dancer there Joan. Where did you find him?'

Joan immediately realised that her perturbations were unfounded, and that he had won the day, for which her innermost self gave a contented expression of happiness. Her facial mien changed imperceptibly to a cheerful flush of delight. All her misgivings of the past days and hours had diminished to now happy things. But she was soon awakened from her reverie, when Tracey asked her if she would object if she could ask Jimmy to give her a dance, too. She then realised that Jimmy's infirmity obviously was not apparent. This added to her delight and instead of responding direct, she turned towards Jimmy and proposed if he would care to invite Tracey for a dance. Jimmy replied in a very cavalier manner that it would be his pleasure, and so saying, rose from the table to escort Tracey onto the dance floor.

So the evening passed pleasantly for all of them. Even Tracey, that was otherwise unescorted, enjoyed an occasional dance with Jimmy. He also took pleasure for a couple of dances, partnering Wynne, too. So it seemed that the evening departed much too quickly.

Wynne left the hall escorted by Richard. That left Jimmy with both Tracey and Joan. As both of them took a different bus route, although they did not live far apart, Jimmy volunteered to see Tracey first onto her bus, then he proposed to escort Joan to her home. This was agreed even though they had let the bus pass that would have suited Joan.

'Would you like to stop for a snack first before going home?' asked Jimmy soon after they entered the bus.

'Thanks, Jimmy, but it would make it too late. Perhaps next time, eh!' responded Joan peering at him now with a more settled expression on her face. In fact, she could be said to be wearing an expression of great happiness as of having lost something of little value and having in its place found a greater prize.

'Shan't press that but will hope that next time you will join me for a snack. And I hope you enjoyed yourself tonight, Joan. As far as I am concerned, I did, and thank you for that!' added Jimmy who had by then proffered and paid the fares for both of them on the bus.

'Thanks, Jimmy. Perhaps next we meet up, you can take me for a meal.'

'Well, what about tomorrow then? What do you say to a film tomorrow evening. Can call for you if you wish?' volunteered Jimmy, eyeing Joan in an askant way and hoping that her otherwise doubtfulness had now dissipated sufficiently for her to accept his proposal.

Joan hesitated for a moment to assemble her thoughts in a proper order. She now realised that Jimmy was a very pleasant fellow and that his otherwise infirmity was of little consequence, as it was not even observed by her friends that evening. She had in her own mind already forsaken Angus as a lost cause, so why not accept this offered treat!

'Thanks, Jimmy. Call for me around seven tomorrow night. Would that be OK with you?' questioned Joan, who now considered she could see no legitimate reason why she should hide any more, as if her engagement with Angus was still valid!

So the night ended for both of them as he left her at the doorstep, with the promise to meet again on the morrow.

But Joan lay awake that night, going over her adventures with Jimmy. First his apparent coarseness, then his change in manner and speech on her mode of correction. Then his discernible mastership on the dance floor coupled with his magnanimity with Tracey. And surprise of surprise, he did not even venture to kiss her the anticipated good-night kiss! Was he really a gentleman that she had not recognised! Perhaps she would accept his invite and see where it led. But how would her parents react to him if they became aware of his questionable leg! Perhaps she would not make mention of it and see if they observed it. After all, her friends at the dance did not mention it as apparently they did not notice, so why have any trepidations? Her pondering went no further, as sleep conquered her as it invariably does to all.

Chapter 24

T he war had run its course over two drastic and cruel years. The country as a whole has suffered greviously, both in loss of life and vast tracts of buildings, both commercial and residential, have been bombed. The Americans are helping financially but have not come to the physical aid of the United Kingdom. During these two eventful years, Angus has remained in New York now for more than two years. In that time he has developed a strong American accent, but it was neither a true reflection of any State or creed. It was presumed by a stranger that he was an American, but the listener could not be sure from which State. Angus became aware of this attribute and that helped his conscience in remaining where he was. In the period of his sojourn, he had not returned home even once, although he had had that opportunity given him. By now, only his parents communicated with him, as all his otherwise friends had lost touch with him. This did not disturb him as he began to feel American and had decided to remain, as he enjoyed what the country had to offer in return for what he gave!

José had long ago forsaken Angus after a year or so of tumultuous bliss. This he shrugged off as of small moment, as other ladies of easy virtue appeared on the scene for him! He found love life so much more fun here than back home. Not only did this give him his physical satisfaction, but indirectly he found that his daily tasks became an enjoyment to him. As a consequence, he was looked upon as a brilliant and eager member of staff. So much so, that had it not been for the war that now raged, his Company President had indicated that he would like to have a few more English staff. But under the prevailing conditions, that was not possible!

In Angus' reconciliation to remain rooted where he was, did not give him periodical moments of anguish of his old country in its trials? He somehow managed to divorce his mind entirely from everything English! He rarely thought of Joan to whom he had once, not so long ago, become engaged to. If he did, he merely shrugged his shoulders and forgot the point in thought, just like that? In fact he thought more of Anne than of Joan. He still hankered after her, yet he could not eliminate her from his mind. The fact that she was engaged to Sir John Cuthbertson a long time ago had not reached his ears until recently. This newsflash renewed his thought of her much to his anguish and regret that he had not persevered still harder for her. He still craved for her! When he was appraised of the news, he let it be known among his colleagues that she was once his escort. This he presumed enhanced his masculinity among them!

Despite Angus' attitude to England in its hour of need, others around him had visited the British Embassy to join the Forces. At the same time, a larger intake of recruits to the American Forces became apparent, possibly by fear of a spillover in the war. This tempted Angus as with the other members of the firm, as together they elected to join the American Navy. This action assured Angus that he would be accorded citizenship early, which delighted him no end. The fact that he had to forego so many weekends to training did not deter him from his otherwise pursuits.

Joan had been keeping company with Jimmy Seaton now for a couple of months and had already introduced him to her parents. She made no reference to his disability, yet her parents did not observe it! This reconciled her to ignore the fact, as apparently it was not so pronounced to be discerned. She still attended dances with him and began to enjoy the pleasure they brought her. Her friends also seemingly approved of him by requesting to dance with him, if they happened to be short of partners that evening. During this period, Joan was commended for her work in the laboratory and became quite popular with the other members of the lab team.

About the same time, Jimmy was called to the Head of Works and promoted to Charge-hand of the Foundry. This pleased Joan, too, as it now allowed that he had an office to himself, where he was able to hang his outdoor garments and change to overalls to work in, and for home going, change back, so that he appeared now quite reasonable when they were in company together. In deference to Joan, he retained his grammatical speech without slipping into the vernacular. And, as he was now a senior at the works, he brooked no criticism. The liaison between Jimmy and Joan became known throughout the firm.

From Jimmy's reflection, he had a great passion for Joan, and as a result, a great respect for her. Thus he made no physical approaches to her beyond the greeting, and later the parting, kiss! He had been told by her that she had broken off her engagement with Angus, as he had failed to return as expected. During the early times together, she constantly mentioned Angus, but happily, she now rarely referred to him. He also perceived that when they met, she had a spontaneous smile spread on her lips in greeting him and came forward to meet him enthusiastically. This pleased him greatly, so much so that he was now pondering if he should propose to her. He considered it might be proper if he deferred yet a while longer, perhaps after they had been together for at least three or more months.

Tracey found her loneliness of being separated from her husband Andrew, even after less than a couple of months too much to bear, so she wrote to him that she was joining up and hopefully they might be able to meet up. She attended the recruiting officer by appointment for her medical. It was then that she discovered that she was pregnant and thus not acceptable for the Forces. This gave her mixed feelings. On the one hand, she was delighted that she bore Andrew's child, but on the other hand she dreaded to raise a child during the years of war. She dwelt a long time if an abortion was appropriate or not. She discussed this with her parents who suggested that it might be prudent to defer raising children during wartime, but in correspondence with Andrew, he raised many objections and insisted that she carry to term. So she progressively became morose and miserable, despite the efforts of her friends and companions. She still attended the Saturday night dances and still accepted an invite to an odd party here and there, but this only formed an interim relief.

Despite her otherwise sophisticated attitude to life, she found all and sundry monotonous. She missed Andrew very much and particularly the complete and forceful lovemaking to which she grew to look forward to with more than a modicum of relish and anticipation, so much so, that she found it hard to go through the day without that pleasure. She discovered a temporary cure when awakening one morning, she found her fingers within her. This gave her some relief!

When she did attend the Saturday night dance, she appeared to lose herself in a new atmosphere that was foreign to her before. Whereas she was known to be a little snooty, she now seemed to throw strictures to the wind and seemed to play fast and loose. This was a disguised temperamental attitude that she endeavoured to raise, in her effort to throw the scent of her anguish aside. It did create a gathering of lads around her seat, as they now found her full of fun and so unlike her old self. Initially, she refused an escort homewards, but now knowing that she was frustrated from joining the Forces, and being pregnant too, she threw discretion to the wind and accepted offers.

Our friend Jack Courtney, who was Anne's escort until he learned that she was to marry Sir John, was among the most ardent admirers of Tracey. He became her favourite too. It was not considered odd that they should be found together, as they had known each other over a long period of time, and Jack was also acquainted with Andrew too. For the first and second time he escorted her home to Andrew's flat, which was now her home, she accepted his token good-night kiss, and so parted. But the third time he accompanied her back there, she felt so depressed at the thought of entering a lonely place all by herself, that she threw discretion to the wind, and invited Jack in for the proverbial coffee. She mixed the coffees with a shot of rum, which was possibly the cause of her romantic attitude. As they sat together, she asked Jack to place his arm around her shoulder.

Jack was in a quandary. Was her disposition borne from frustration or from some other uninhibiting reason? He felt only a little qualm of attempting to make love to a friend's wife. He knew that she was in the early stages of pregnancy and that encouraged him. He was cognisant that she did not need to take any precautions under those

311

circumstances. But he also knew that he had better make up his mind very quickly, as these moods pass as quick as a puff of wind. So taking the axiomatic view of the situation, he turned towards her and took her glass out of her hand and placed it on the side-table alongside him. Then turning back towards Tracey he placed his arm around her shoulders and gently turned her to face himself, and as they faced each other, he moved to place his lips on hers, to which she responded in a manner of relief and happiness. Within a matter of a few seconds, he had his hand at her belt around her skirt which somehow he managed to undo. Having achieved that, he drew back momentarily and asked her divest herself of its encumbrance, which she did without uttering a word. As soon as she did that, her hand began to feel under him until she found the buttons to his trousers and endeavoured to undo them. She found that task not too easy, so she whispered into Jack's ear to take them off.

'Tracey, darling, shall we go into the bedroom and strip?' said Jack realising that her sexual temperature had risen to an all-time high?

'You won't tell on me, Jack, now will you?'

'We know each other too well and in any case, it is safe as you are pregnant, so cannot get pregnant again, so let's go!' he added, as he led her willingly to the bedroom and drew the curtains. Then with the inner door open, which gave them just enough light without switching any on, they disrobed each other to mutual satisfaction.

'You have a beautiful body, Tracey, and it doesn't show yet that you are pregnant,' said Jack as he allowed his hand all over her much to her pleasure and gratification.

'Please, Jack, I want it, so leave the admiring to later,' was all she said as she moved towards the bed and pulled back the bedspread to reveal the blanket which she threw open. She then mounted the bed herself and then held her hands out to Jack. Without answering her, he too moved to her realising that by the time he got to the bed with her, it may be too late, his erection and heat was so great. Jack said to himself, 'Control yourself, and then both of us will have fun!'

Tracey held the blanket up so that Jack could slip under it, at which point Tracey dropped her arm and placed it around Jack, snuggling up to him very passionately and manoeuvring herself so that he could get it into her. As soon as he achieved that posture, she let out a scream of delight and crushed his ribs in her pleasure. But he had consummated too soon, as he could not hold back any longer and this upset her, as she was craving for more and more. He promised to repeat the exercise if she would bide with him for a few minutes, during which time she could play with him. She insisted that he play with her, as she was in dire need at the moment, so he sat up in the bed as she lay there, and manipulated his hand all over her to her jubilaton and bliss, until he thought that he could re-erect his phallus once again to her thrill. This he did, but she would not permit him to move away, even after he had spent himself for the second time. So he remained within her until sleep captured them both.

It was about six o'clock in the morning that he awoke and found that he was still in bed with Tracey beside him. His sitting up to switch on the bedside light, awakened her. She opened her eyes wide and looked in surprise to find the situation she was in!

'Oh my God, Jack – you're still here! We must have both fallen asleep. What are you going to do, Jacko?' she asked looking at him as she pulled the blanket up towards herself to cover her young breasts that shone out like twin pinnacles.

'Tracey, my dear, what *we* are going to do, is do it again, so that you do not feel frustrated again until we date up. No need to let anyone know, and we could meet discreetly, eh my dear?' he said in response as he took her hand and opened it so that the blanket dropped away from her, exposing her once again.

'Do you think we should, Jack? I'm afraid now!' she murmured.

'Now why should you be afraid now of all things. What can go wrong if we are sensible and mind our own business, eh, my lovely lover?' answered Jack in full earnestness.

'What happens if Andrew finds out. He will kill me, I'm sure!'

'And why should anyone find out unless you tell them – which you should not, even in the strictest confidence, even to your best friend. So say no more and let's make love!' he speculated as he slipped down between the sheets and moved to lie over her, as she again placed her arms around him and drew him in.

They lay side by side panting, after thrilling each other to mutual satisfaction. Their reverie came to an end as they heard the local church clock striking the hour of seven. Almost simultaneously they arose, and arm in arm in a frolicking mood, they both resorted to the bathroom where their fun and games did not abate. After a quick wanton gambol, they both emerged to dress and eat a modest breakfast, then make their respective ways to work, after agreeing a further meeting in a couple of days time.

Richard was in the age bracket for call-up and attended for his medical examination. He discovered that he had a slight cataract on one eye and a parental history of epilepsy. He was downgraded, and declared unfit for military duties. He must perforce accept a change in occupation to a military establishment in a clerical capacity. He now finds much to his pleasure and surprise, that he will be in receipt of a higher pay packet than as an insurance salesman! When Wynne is given the information, she asks if his reticence to marry her is now any longer valid? After an hour of debate, they agree to wed with the proviso that only a few intimate friends be invited, as for one reason, he did not wish to expend too much cash, and on the second consideration, it may be considered unpatriotic to hold a flash party during wartime.

When Tracey learns of the pending wedding, she immediately proposes to Wynne that she should use her flat for the party, and she and Richard could stay on for a few days there, too, in lieu of a costly honeymoon. Tracey indicated that she would return to her parental home for the while.

It did not take much discussion between Wynne and Richard to agree to the proposed plan. Within some six weeks they celebrated the occasion and utilised the flat as arranged. The bridal couple then resorted to the bed they once used before to make love, but incompletely. Richard reminded Wynne of that occasion. She admitted to remembering the time and said that now they were married, Richard had a free hand in his demands – nothing would be refused him.

'Darling,' responded Richard in a flush of joy of what was to come, 'let us mutually agree, that what is mine is yours, too, and what is yours is mine. In that way we should have no reason ever to argue. What do you say, my love?'

'Does that mean that if I am not in the mood for you know what, that you can demand it and I must consent?'

'It will be a two-way street, so cannot see why you or I should refuse to please the other. After all, the object is to give what the other wants and accept it, and not what either wants without regard to the other – hope that's clear, darling,' echoed Richard.

'Does that mean that if you ask me to put that thing in my mouth, I must agree then?' queried Wynne looking askant at her husband of a few hours.

'Darling, it is as I've said, a two-way street. Whatever you ask of me I must give you, or at least try to. And the same goes for you – if I ask you to do what you have just mentioned, I can see no reason why you should refuse me. But please do not let us forget the clock, as we waste valuable lovemaking time. So you now help me undress,' he replied, as he put his hand forward to reach her blouse to undo it, and then remove it, then follow that by disrobing her completely until they both looked at each other for the first time without any clothes upon them.

They stood both of them with their eyes wide open staring at each other in complete astonishment and love. Wynne was the first to move, as she stepped forward and threw her arms around him. He responded by moving her backwards until they reached the bed, then he gently laid her down upon it and followed her. Without any resistance, she succumbed to his physical pressure and demand to mutual fulfilment.

How many times Wynne reached an orgasm was not counted, but it can be said that it was a number of times! Richard for his part, held back as long as he could, but after his first ejaculation, remained within her until his ardour reached its peak once again to their requited joy and bliss.

'Tracey, I've an idea,' so said Jack to her at Wynne and Richard's wedding reception at her flat.

'Hope its a good one,' replied Tracey that she was hoping that he could come up with an idea where they would meet clandestinely, as they found it was not easy to enter and leave her flat without being observed by the other residents.

'On the last day of Wynne and Richard staying here, we could join them for a last welcome drink, and then stay behind. I could then

315

leave early or if not, then late at night so as to avoid the obvious; what you say, my love?' asked Jack as he looked upon his bedmate with growing desire that never seemed to slacken off.

'Only if you agree to me stopping at your place tonight, as I must have you!' whispered Tracey looking at him with overflowing passion and desire.

'That's agreed then. You will let them know whilst I am talking to them, then you can invite me up at the same time in front of them. That will make it look natural, eh?'

Chapter 25

Sir John Cuthbertson had been pressing Anne now for some two years to name the day for them to wed. Her repeated reply to his quest was, that had it not been for the war, they would have been married a long while ago. But under the prevailing circumstances, she did not feel it prudent, as she feared more than anything else was to be a war widow. Sir John kept repeating that he had a reserved occupation, so could if he chose to remain, as it was up to him to volunteer or otherwise. This argument still did not convince Anne.

'Look at the bombing that has occurred around us. Up to now we have been lucky not to have been hit. How can we guarantee that we do not get it in the end, eh?'

'I'll buy you a gypsy's crystal ball, and then you can look into it and see the future, my dear,' retorted Sir John more in jest than otherwise.

'No, I for one do not wish to know what the future holds for us. As far as we should be concerned, is to pray that we live to see this futile war over and we all get back to peace. Then we can plan assuredly and can anticipate the future. But I will promise you, if the war is not over by this time next year, we will wed. Hope that will give you some peace of mind, John.'

'It's now near the end of '41 and that means the end of '42. You are asking me a lot. Surely you can be more accommodating and suggest an earlier date, my love?' returned Sir John more in hope than expectancy, having learned that Anne had a very strong will, that even he so far had not been able to prevail upon.

'John dear, you know nothing would please me more than to say "yes" to you, but you do understand the awkward circumstances we live in today, so please be patient with me a little longer!'

'What could change your mind to propose an earlier date, my love?' he pleaded.

'Really cannot forecast the future so as to answer that question, but if, for example, the news indicated that we stood a better chance of success than it seems at the moment, then I may be tempted.'

'Then we will all have to work harder in the war effort to make that wish come true,' threw Sir John, showing a happy countenance but underneath, somewhat disgruntled at having to wait. He was no less in love with Anne than before, but this prevarication was trying him sorely. He still recalled the huff and admonition he received from Anne when he raised her ball gown, in his venture to make love with her. He has kept his promise of refraining to approach her in a sexual manner since, but he was frustrated almost beyond control. He feared he would lose her if he gave her an ultimatum that she should marry him earlier than she suggested. So he writhed in agony of thwarted discontentment bordering on vexation.

Sir John continued, 'My dear, you do realise that you are putting me under a great strain and am not sure that I can hold out that length of time you are now proposing. In all earnestness, I must plead with you to consider an earlier betrothal for the sake of my sanity. You know, Anne, that I love you to distraction, and my body is crying out for you, so please, be a bit kinder to me.' Sir John concluded his prayer-like speech, retaining his eye upon her in a sorrowful stare that spoke for him.

'How do you suppose I feel my dear, also awaiting that moment of bliss when we mate together! Do you think that only men think of these things? Women are human too, and also have feelings for the unattainable. But I promise you, I will give it more serious thought tonight before I fall off to sleep – that's if the sirens do not disturb me.'

Norman was by now showing his displeasure of Anne, who continued to fox him. Each and every time he proposed a meeting with her, she managed to concoct an excuse or reason as a magician fetching a rabbit out of the hat. He was nonplussed each time, as it appeared the reason was immovable! But he was determined that time was running out for her to keep her avowed promise to him. He left a message for her to look into his office on her return from an assignment.

'You want to see me, Norm?' asked Anne after she had entered his room and in the customary manner, kissed him.

'Anne, my dear. You will be coming with me tonight and no arguments, please. Either at the Eastbury or the flat. Where would you like to go?' he demanded as he glared at her; but not unkindly, as he stretched out his hand to take hers into his.

Anne realised that she had played him along now for some many months and appreciated that he must be mad at her. She had hoped that now he was married to Felicity, he might have lost his appetite and ardour for her. But it appeared as not! At this precise moment she too felt that it was time for her to have a bit of fun. She, too, was getting frustrated, so why not!

'OK then, Norm. Give me five minutes and pick me up as you reach the High Road. Will await you at the corner, and then you can drive me home to the flat. Don't keep me waiting long, now Norm, as it looks like it's going to rain!' teased Anne, and as for once she failed to give him his courtesy kiss, but left the office and dashed out to be at the tryst before he reached her with the car.

Within half an hour they had reached her flat. During the drive, Anne suggested to Norman, that he should tell the truth as to where he had been and not hide the fact that he had not given her a lift to her flat in view of the rain. She was confident that Felicity would not see anything wrong in being offered a ride home in the rain. Norman complimented Anne on her strategy in that regard.

Although her folks had expected that she would feel very lonely at her new abode, and return soon after she took up occupation, she relished her new home and made known that she was staying there. The new decor that she commissioned and Norman paid for, was truely very attractive and that gave her more incentive to live there. And this was not the first time Norman had visited her for purposes other than business.

'I'll make a quick sandwich and a cuppa first, Norm, then I'm ready. OK with you Norm?'

'It would be nice if you kept to tradition, my dear. I am supposed to be the boss at the office, and you are supposed to be the boss here. But it always works out that you are the boss in all places! I'm not grumbling but thought I'd mention it. So let's have the sandwich, my love.' And as he concluded his inference, he took off his jacket and loosened his shoelaces.

Whilst she prepared the snack, she enquired if he was getting his sexual appetite satisfied at home?

'Is it fair to discuss that with you, my love?'

'See no reason why not. Is there anything I do not already know – I doubt it. For example, I know that you achieved the miracle of baby's birth by giving it to Licy twice, but not the usual way. So presume you still practise it that way, do you Norm?' she quizzed viewing him at his discomfiture at her revelation.

'That is how I would like to give it to you, my love – so shall we tonight, eh?' perked Norman more in expectancy than otherwise.

'Norm, if we got as far as we have before, will that make you happy, because if you press for further, I will say a big NO to you right at the beginning before we strip! So what will it be?' challenged Anne with a deal of humour in her inflexions.

'Then shall I tell you what we can do and still be within your strictures. If you pose as Licy does, I will put it under you, but not in you. How would that be, eh my cherrie?' chortled Norman again more in expectancy.

'Norm, you will have what I offer you or go without – now do we agree? As to letting you try a back scuttle with your do dah that close, I would be mad to let you try it – it would slip in as sure as eggs are eggs. So, shall we strip, or do you want to go home?' asked Anne chuckling and knowing full well that he would not refuse and accept any offering she would make.

By the time Norman could reply, he was more than half undressed and needed but a couple of seconds before he stood in his birthday suit!

'Oh come on then, and give me all you have to give, as I am very much in need of you, my dear!' he added as he approached her and began to remove one garment after another from off her without any remonstrance. And before many seconds had passed, they both stood

320

with their two hands on each others shoulders, viewing the other to mutual delight.

Norman could not help himself, but his erection was that great, that he did not have to move forward before it touched Anne. She retreated a pace backward and with a giggle in her inflexion, grabbed at his arm and led him to the bed. Together they mounted the bed after removing the spread. As they lay down, she grabbed at his extended rod with one hand, and with the other she placed under his shoulder. Simultaneously, he closed up to her as near as he could without infringing her instruction, and moved his hand and fingers beneath her. As soon as she felt his fingers within her, she squirmed and wiggled towards him until they left no space between them. Heavy motion by either hand was now very much restricted.

'Now you stay where you are and that way it will last longer for both of us,' proposed Anne who was getting very excited and had already lost count of time, then added, 'but tell me what to do when you are ready to explode, Norm, as I haven't a catcher at hand!'

'Then it will have to go over us both as we are, my sweet!' replied Norman, with a titter in his throat as he thought of that happening, and wondered how Anne would react.

'Roll over towards the edge of the bed, Norm, and you will get a face towel out of the bedside cabinet,' ordered Anne, as she prepared and lightened herself for the roll-over, which would entail his weight on top of her momentarily.

But as he rolled over from the position of both of them being on their sides, to him now being on top of her, he hesitated and remained there. For a few seconds he thought that she was lost in sexual haze and did not appreciate that he now could exercise his desire to a greater extent as he lay over her. But his pleasure was short-lived, as she let out a yell of temper that he had better continue to roll over, otherwise she would get away from him. He responded even before she had completed her sentence of illumination, such was his fear of her leaving him, not just in bed but in other ways too!

'Really, sorry, my sweet; got carried away and you must realise that now, don't you!' he put forward as his excuse in his humblest manner possible.

'Guess it is a bit provoking as we are Norm, so say no more and let's enjoy ourselves, eh?' Anne answered, now in a good even temper and realising that perhaps she was a bit hasty to yell at him. So they rolled over once more so that he was able to reach and pull out the drawer of the cabinet and extract a small cloth, and not too soon, as he called out to her that he could not hold back any longer.

Altogether they remained on the bed for perhaps over a half-hour, giving each other the pleasure and satisfaction each sought within the limits set by Anne. As far as Norman was concerned, it was all too quick when Anne proposed that it was time they issued off the bed and resorted to the bathroom. He was enjoying the pleasure even after they had both spent themselves, but he knew that he must not antagonise her, so he acknowledged accordingly.

Subsequently, they both returned to the lounge after helping each other cleanse themselves in the nether regions in the bathroom, to added mutual delight in their sexual frolicking.

'It was topping, Anne my sweet, but tell me, how far have you progressed with John?'

'Really, Norm, you must not ask such questions. It is not fair, but I will tell you all the same. About the second or third time he gave me a lift home, he tried to put his hand up my skirt, whilst in his Rolls. I pushed him away and told him in no uncertain terms that he must never do that again, for if he endeavoured to behave like that, I would refuse to go out with him. Since then, he has truly behaved as a gentleman, and apart from a greeting and parting kiss, he has not made a pass at me since. Do you think I'm hard on him, having in mind what we do, Norm?'

'Anne, my sweet, you are exercising prudence and I commend and compliment you. He is like all of us – we have a real and great regard for you, and you know it. We all love you too! But we had you on our field and gave you your first feed off our pasture and you are wise to remain in that field and keep enjoying the fruits of that meadow, for if you let John into that field, it may be open to question from him that others have also been in the field with you for a nibble. But I cannot understand that you have managed to keep him in check – how do you do it my love?'

'That's easy, Norm. Apart from any regard I have for you, I also owe you a lot, and am not unmindful of the bounty that I have enjoyed through you. So what we do is my way of saying "Thank you, Norm". And you remember, I told you that we should get together, even if you married Licy, and we have. Our secret remains our secret!' sermonised Anne as she moved closer to him on the settee, and placed her arm around his neck and drew him down and kissed him full and passionately.

'But he stayed behind here when you had your engagement party. Did anything happen then? How will you respond my sweet, when you do eventually marry John?' queried Norman in a cool tone.

'Norm, we have managed so far and can see no reason that we should forego our fun. After all, you are married and we still enjoy each other's company, so why should we change if I marry John. Of course, we will still have to exercise great caution, as an exposure would ruin both of us without any shadow of doubt, don't you think so? And John has stayed behind here, on more than one occasion and nothing has happened; not like us, eh Norm!' provoked Anne as she looked at him for an answer.

'Tell me, my sweet, if John gets you pregnant as I am sure he will sooner or later, would you do it properly with me then, or still only give me half a loaf, eh?'

'Norm, you ask too many questions of the future. But once I get preg' from John, we can throw caution to the wind and go the whole hog! That would be real fun, eh Norm?' Anne responded with a beautiful grin across her face and a twinkle in her eye as if to say, 'I can't wait.'

'My sweet, then get married tomorrow, as I cannot wait much longer to give you all I've got!' he replied in earnestness blooming in his flushed face.

'Norm, do you know that I look forward to having you, but the only worry I have is that it is so big and will kill me, I'm sure!' countered Anne.

'Let's get to that stage then we can argue, eh my sweet?' proposed Norman.

'And how is my Anne this evening?' asked Sir John Cuthbertson, as his greeting on meeting up with her for an evening out.

'Oh fine, fine John, and how have you been the last few days since I've seen you?'

'Then we are both well and that's good,' was the response from Sir John, as he led her to the table set for them in the restaurant.

'Are you finding the pressure of business getting heavier daily as I do, John? If this war goes on much longer I will have no energy left in me. We have lost another chap yesterday and the load has to be spread around. Now it's my job to get everyone to agree to accept part of the load – and believe me, John, that's no easy task – they all plead they are at full stretch and I know they are, but must still insist that they accept the extra!' bemoaned Anne as she picked up the menu and noted that many items that she otherwise enjoyed were now no longer available.

'Anne, my dear, I too find it hard to get our work out with more or less a skeleton staff to what we should employ. You are lucky if you have only lost one fellow; we have lost in the last week about six men and have only replaced three, and women at that. It makes it very hard going, but the worst loss we have sustained is the Works Manager – how can I replace him with a woman?' opined Sir John in as placid tone as possible.

'Do you know, that I hear that your friend and one of my clients has also lost his Works Manager. Old Charlie Harrington has lost his! Now you know him, so can I propose that you suggest to him that he considers Jimmy, you know, the fellow that's a'courting my friend Joan. Then if that comes off, we could also name the day – what you say, John?'

'Actually, you are thinking along the lines that I have. He has been schooled in all departments, so I understand, and is a fairly good disciplinarian and is well-liked,' raised Sir John in reply to her proposition.

'You could become a fairy godfather if you did, as Joan would marry him on his promotion as I feel sure. So give it some extra consideration, John.'

'In deference to you I have given it all the consideration needed, and will call Charlie tomorrow and suggest it to him. That should make a few people happy, I'm sure, eh my dear?' Then he added, 'But what about us two getting wed? Can I suggest that if they fix a date, then we should too; what you say my love to that? You match your proposal for your friend and we marry too!' chortled Sir John more in hope than ever before.

'John, my dear, I've been fighting you to put if off for too long, and I feel that I cannot wait any longer. To the outside world, I should not contemplate matrimony during wartime, but we are mere humans and our needs must be pacified too, so I will agree with you John. And to please you my love, regardless of the outcome of Joan and Jimmy, we will fix a date just the same next week. Happy now, John?' Anne beamed at him with a most captivating smile upon her face that radiated love.

'Whoa, whoopee!'

'John, John, not so loud, you've got every one in here ogling us now. You are making me feel embarrassed and red in the face – am I red, John?'

'To me you are as lovely as ever and more so now if that's possible. Never expected this turn of events. I'm thrilled and cannot wait to get young Jimmy appointed and hear the news that he has also popped the question. Whoa, that's wonderful my love!' bubbled Sir John in ecstatic delight.

'John dear, can I confide a secret with you – you will not get cross with me now will you?' asked Anne as she looked down at the table in front of her instead of facing him.

'How can I get cross with you after getting you to agree to fix a date with me?' Sir John replied as he looked into her face, or what he could see of it being turned downwards, wondering what the confession would be?

'I do not know how to say it, so please look away,' she asked, and in compliance, he half turned his face away from her and indicated that he had done so.

'John dear, I am getting frustrated and cannot hold out much longer and need you badly. Do you understand me, John?' whispered Anne in a very low tone and inwardly she felt like an executioner telling the victim that he is her first!

'Why Anne, my love, I too am getting frustrated by this long wait that you have imposed upon me, but have gladly accepted that tribulation for my love of you. So I'm not surprised that you feel the

325

same, which is human after all. But that means that the date will have to be sooner than later, won't it?' added Sir John in delight to learn that she craved his body as he craved hers!

'So that's agreed then, eh John?' finalised Anne.

Tracey had met up again with Jack at her flat that evening. It had become a regular feature between them. At times, she resorted to his flat and at weekends, they went off together as husband and wife to various hotels. It seemed that both, not only enjoyed the illicit love, but became enthralled with each other.

They did not answer the telephone if it rang – and that was not too often. This was so that any caller should presume that she was out. On this particular evening, just as they had reached their climax, perhaps for the first or even second time, they were disturbed by a loud knocking upon the door. This was unusual, as visitors could not enter the lift without the hall porter's permission. Both looked at one another in dismay.

'Hell! who could that be. Shall we open it or what?' queried Jack very alarmed.

'Can't be Andrew as he has his own key, unless he has lost it! And if it is him, we would be in dead trouble! Do you think we can ignore it?

'Buzz down to the porter and ask him who let him in?' suggested Jack still somewhat alarmed.

Tracey concurred the suggestion by lifting the handset and pressing the appropriate button and so connected with the porter.

'Mrs Gilmour here. Did you let some one up to my flat? He's knocking the door down. Who is it please?' questioned Tracey.

'Sorry, Mrs Gilmour, but had to let him in as it was the telegram boy and thought it might be important,' was his explanation.

'Oh, thanks,' was all Tracey could respond as she replaced the receiver.

In the meanwhile Jack had attired himself so as to be presentable, and understanding the drift of the conversation, motioned to Tracey to get into the bathroom with her clothes and he would answer the door.

'Yes, what is it?' questioned Jack as he opened the door to a diminutive telegram boy.

326

'Telegram for Mrs Gilmour,' was his only reply.

'OK, then let's have it, and thanks sonny; here's a tip,' said Jack as he took the telegram from the boy and handed him a coin in exchange, then closed the door on him.

'You can come out, Tracey. I've got the tele. Here it is. Hope it's good news whatever it is,' Jack said in apprehension, knowing that at this period in time and history, telegrams only spelt one thing – someone had died on active service!

Tracey took the proffered enclosure, and for a few seconds just held it and looked at it in trepidation without any motion, until he suggested that she open it. With quivering fingers she ripped the envelope of the missive and extracted the contents, then opened the folded sheet it contained. She looked at the printed words of the message, and Jack saw her face turn blanched white as she collapsed in a heap on the floor.

'Oh my God!' cried Jack in nervousness. He immediately bent down and placing his hand under her armpits drew her up and laid her on the still-warm bed, then rushed into the kitchen for a glass of water. By the time he returned with the glass in his hand, she had rallied and was half sitting up on her elbow.

'Here, drink this. It may help you to compose yourself,' commiserated Jack, now more concerned about her than the telegram.

Tracey took but a sip, then placing the almost full glass down on the side-table, opened her crunched hand and held it out to Jack to take the offending telegram.

Jack took in the contents of the message in a flash and almost swooned himself. He sat alongside Tracey on the bed and said in a subdued voice, 'Oh dear me! That's terrible! What now?' was all he could say in compassion.

'And me six months pregnant, and no husband. *Failed to return from a mission and presumed dead.* That's fine; what of me?' poor Tracey blurted with eyes swimming in tears.

All Jack could do, was to turn towards her and place his arm around her, and take her into a passionate cuddle which gave her but momentary satisfaction.

'Jack, what am I to do?' pleaded Tracey in a muffled voice and still very tearful and yet still reclining in Jack's embrace.

'Tracey, it is not what YOU will do, but what WE will do. Tomorrow morning, you will go with me to the War Office and get to the bottom of this message. It does not categorically say that Andrew is dead but "presumed dead". That may mean he is a prisoner. What we will do if he is without a shadow of doubt dead, is that we will marry quickly, so the nipper will have a father and a name. I presume you would marry me, Tracey?'

Without answering him, she rallied her strength and flung her arms around him and in almost unaudible whisper, said the proverbial 'yes' in his ear.

The storm had lifted somewhat from Tracey; even though the cloud still hung in their midst, she felt a feeling of freedom in herself. Her conscience of having an illicit love affair with Jack over the past few months now dissipated in a flash as of no concern. But she felt an inner satisfaction despite the reasoning behind her mood.

Chapter 26

December in America as far as Angus was concerned, had many recollections and similarities of what it was like back home in England. The major difference to Angus was that here it was at 'peace', whereas back home they were bearing the brunt of a vicious war. Life was the same every day – fun, coupled with work, which made good companions, one bolstering the other in harmony. Time inexorably moved on and the first weeks then months to a stay of a couple of years, vanished to become but as memory. When Angus awoke the morning of the eighth of December and switched on his bedside radio as he moved towards the bathroom, he paused on hearing the newsflash. He turned and went back to his radio and raised the volume a trifle so as not to miss the relayed message. The announcer kept repeating something about Pearl Harbour, wherever that was?

'By jiminy,' expostulated Angus when he got the drift of the announcement. 'The Japs have overrun Pearl Harbour and declared war on the United States of America after this action!' He could hear but not understand the extra loud hubbub that was growing immeasurably outside his room. He dressed as quickly as he could and made his way to his office. But it took him longer than usual, as the streets had developed an unusual heavy crowd and on everyone's lips were the words 'Pearl Harbour'. He knew that if war had been declared, he would be called up to join the American Navy.

He eventually reached his office and found that nobody was physically at work! All were debating the current crisis. From the work output that day it was poor indeed. And when he reached his home that evening, not surprisingly, except for the promptness, he found a directive to report within three days to his naval base for enlistment.

Three days later, on the eleventh of December, he was on his way to the naval base when he was again stunned by the latest news. America had now declared war on both Germany and Italy, too. So after all, he could be drawn into battle, a little later but still in it!

Angus was assigned to extensive naval training at the base for a period of time before being accredited to a boat as a Naval Lieutenant. Initially, he was aboard transport carriers taking military equipment to the Allies. Eventually, he was assigned to the S.S. *Conway*, a very large vessel that had the capacity of carrying over one and a half thousand passengers or troops. All the voyages were now on convoy duty, helping cargo vessels to reach the shores where directed, to assist the allied war effort.

He had been in the Navy now about a year, when he was commissioned to convoy a number of vessels towards the United Kingdom for his last port of call, Gibraltar. When he had traversed about half the distance, his ship was instructed by the British Admiralty to proceed independently.

'Joan darling, I've got some grand news for you,' so began Jimmy as he met up with Joan that evening, as had become their custom. He peered into her face with glee roaming around his countenance like a child that had been given a favourite toy.

'Well then, spill it out and don't keep me in suspense!' threw back Joan, wondering what news he had that made him look like that.

'You remember I told you that I was being schooled for promotion? Well, I'm the new Works Manager as from tomorrow!' he preened at her and awaited her acclamation.

'Gee, that's fine. Must I call you "sir" when we meet in the works, though?' asked Joan in a harmonious way.

'No my sweet, but I want to call you Mrs Seaton. What you say to that my love?'

Joan looked at him for a full minute digesting the import he had just said before the intent fully sank in!

'Are you proposing to me, Jimmy?' was all she could think of saying just then in reply to his statement.

'Yes my love. Will you marry me and be Mrs Seaton. Just say "yes" then we can go out and celebrate. So let's be hearing you!'

Instead of replying, she flung her arms around his neck and shouted in a loud voice that she would happily accept him. With that agreement reached, they took themselves off to the nearest restaurant to enjoy a celebratory meal. It was not long before the news of the betrothal reached all ears, including Anne, who passed on the information to Sir John.

Sir John Cuthbertson on hearing the news of the espousal of the new Works Manager, partly through his instigation, having been prompted by Anne, with his friend Harrington, then again formerly proposed to Anne. As she had already promised she would consent to wed Sir John, it just remained therefore to fix the date. They mutually agreed to name a day in December so that they may be able to have an elongated Christmas vacation as a honeymoon.

Anne retailed the information to her superior, Norman, at the first opportunity. His immediate reaction was that they meet that night at her flat, to which she consented. On arrival there, she indicated to him that she engineered the betrothal of Jimmy to her friend Joan by recommending him for promotion via Sir John.

'You know, Anne, you astound me. There does not appear to be the slightest vestige of cussedness in you. You even go out of your way to help another, true, your friend. But to "engineer" your Sir John to speak for you to Harrington, takes some beating! And I bet the lucky couple haven't a clue you had a hand in the affair; am I right my dear?' questioned Norman.

'They don't know, and I for one do not think it proper that I should tell them. It may take the sails out of his promotion if he thought it was gained by favouritism! Am I right there, Norman?' posed Anne as she peered at him for his acquiescence.

'Yes I think you are right. And I think you are right to fix your own date, too, for marrying your John. Suppose you will be away with him over the Christmas then, eh? But no more of that; let's make love my dear!' answered Norman as he took her hand and led her to the bedroom.

It was now a couple of weeks since Jack had committed himself to marrying Tracey. During that period he did not have a moment of peace. He was now having doubts as to his own sanity for jumping in with that proposal. What had possessed him to do that! Yes, he did like her but was it love, if there was such a thing? Perhaps it was love of sex and not love of herself – could that be the reason for his over prompt reaction? Somehow he wished he had not been so bold and quelled her insatiability of despair on learning the unfortunate news of Andrew's demise.

But he had committed himself and now wished he had not. How could he confront her with the retraction of his affirmation? And not for one moment did Tracey suspect that he was now dithering. They did go to the War Office on the morrow and that took many hours of being shuffled from one department to another before they located the right individual. It did not take that person very long to check and declare that Andrew regrettably was dead! Tracey was torn between anguish at the loss of a husband and elation of the prospects of remarrying right away to Jack. Whatever he said, she accepted as being in her interest and never for one moment did it dawn upon her that Jack's proposal was a rash one made in a moment of overwhelming pressure of seeing her in such a miserable state. He now regretted his spontaneous outburst.

On the day following after going to the War Department, they planned to meet. He dreaded to tell her himself, so connived to get a message to her that he could not see her for a couple of days and that he would be in touch with her as soon as possible. For the first few days she did not think anything was amiss, but after four days and not hearing from him, she became apprehensive but not too anxious, as to her future status was concerned. Tracey determined to call upon Jack at his home. Up until now, she had never been there nor invited. This did not alarm her, as she accepted things as they were. She checked for his address in the A to Z and found the right bus to get her there. The helpful conductress told her where to get off. She found the house in the main road, but a few doors from the very bus-

332

stop she had alighted at. Apprehension now entered her thought of knocking upon the door to face whoever it was that responded and explain herself! She observed that all the houses appeared to be the same – a whole row of identical small terrace houses with hardly any depth of front garden that she considered essential to any abode. After a moment's hesitation, she approached the correct door and knocked thereon.

'Yes, can I help you?' was the response uttered by a reasonably dressed middle-aged woman who answered her knock.

'I'm looking for Jack Courtney and I believe he lives here?' was her reply.

'Jack is not at home at the moment. I'm his mother; can I be of any help to you?'

Tracey held her hand out to greet the woman in as friendly a way as possible. After all, she was to be her future mother-in-law.

'I'm Tracey and feel sure that Jack has mentioned me to you, and am glad to meet you Mrs Courtney,' Tracey said as she gripped Mrs Courtney's hand and gave it a shake of greeting and acknowledgement.

'I'm very sorry but he has never mentioned you to me. Should he have done so you think?' responded Jack's mother looking at a pregnant but very pleasant attractive girl, and wondered if her son was the responsible party for her condition.

'I am surprised that he has not, seeing that he proposed to me and I have agreed to marry him! But when will he be home then?' replied Tracey now beginning to feel a trifle uncomfortable.

Mrs Courtney was for a moment speechless. She could not understand what was going on. Could she very well ask this perfect stranger, that had suddenly appeared at her door, if her son was responsible for her obvious condition. They both looked at each other and both at a loss how to continue the conversation. At last Mrs Courtney spoke.

'To say you surprise me is an understatement. But I feel that you should come in and sit down. Then we can wait until Jack gets home. Then we will learn what there is to learn! So please, do come in and sit down! In your unmistakable condition you should not be standing when you could just as well be sitting.' And as she concluded, she

333

held open the door wider to admit Tracey into her house. She was led into a modest small lounge and asked to sit down on a comfortable but old armchair, which she did.

'Tell me, what did you say your name was?' asked Mrs Courtney as she sat down facing Tracey.

'My full name is Tracey Gilmour. Jack proposed to me a few days ago as we have known each other for quite a long time. I am really surprised that he hadn't mentioned that to his mother though!' replied Tracey now feeling very uncomfortable and uneasy.

'Then tell me if you would, and I hope you do not think me impertinent to ask, was he responsible for your apparent condition then?' ventured Jack's mother who was more than a trifle rattled to have this exposure of her absent son.

'Oh no, no! Perhaps I should have introduced myself more correctly. I am Mrs Gilmour and my husband has been killed whilst in the Forces as Jack knows. He was with me when the telegram came to let me know,' stated Tracey, now beginning to feel shivers in her whole body as she spoke.

'Ah, that sounds like Jack coming in!' said Mrs Courtney, as she rose from her seat to go to the door to call Jack in, if it was indeed him just entering the house.

Tracey sat awaiting the entry of Jack in great trepidation. She felt far from comfortable, thought she could not think why she should be so. After all, he did make a promise to marry her, so why should she be nervous. She heard Mrs Courtney speaking with Jack in the small entrance lobby. She could not hear what was said, but presumed that she was relating what had been said between them. She did, however, hear both of them raising their voices, yet she still could not distinguish the comments between them.

Chapter 27

J oan and Jimmy had fixed the date for their wedding for the
nineteenth of December. This pleased her as well as it did Anne,
for she was to wed Sir John on the very next day. It was not
possible to arrange the two weddings simultaneously. Thus, they both
could attend each other's big day before going off for their respective
honeymoons. And it was on the day before Joan's wedding that she
had a visit from Mrs Finch, Angus's mother.

Joan had met Mrs Finch on a number of occasions when she was
courted by Angus, so they knew each other fairly intimately. This
was, however, the first time his mother had called on her. Joan
discerned that she had a drawn look upon her face as if she carried a
heavy burden. She was sorry to see her like that, as she really liked his
mother, even if Angus did not play fair with her!

'Why, Mrs Finch, how nice to see you! Do come on in. I say you
do look a bit pale; are you unwell or something?' was Joan's compassionate greeting, as she opened the door to the unexpected caller.

'Thank you, Joan, for inviting me in. I have some very sad news to
tell you. I know that you are getting married tomorrow, but feel just
the same that you are entitled to the news. Angus is dead! His ship has
been lost at sea with all hands on board. Apparently, the ship has been
lost without trace, so it is presumed that it has been sunk!' blurted out
the distraught woman who could not contain herself any longer and
burst into a flood of tears.

Joan put her arm around her to give her some comfort and said in a
soft voice, 'I am indeed very, very sorry to learn this. May he have

335

everlasting peace wherever he may be now!' she said with a full heart, but feeling now herself getting facially pale, too.

'Joan my dear, I did so look forward to you being my daughter-in-law and regret now that he went to America to all our hurt. And you are now marrying someone else. I do hope that you have a good life, and that you do not think too badly or unkindly of our dear departed Angus — although I know that he did not treat you fairly. You have my blessing for you future and please, do keep in touch, as I should like to see you from time to time. It will remind me of my son. Now can I hope for that, my dear Joan?' sobbed Mrs Finch, still enfolded in Joan's arms.

'You have my promise. And if you would like, may I call you mother, please come to my wedding tomorrow,' declared Joan in a strong feeling of condolence and sympathy.

'Thank you, my dear daughter. I will endeavour to hide my misery and bask in your sunshine tomorrow,' responded Angus's mother with a trifle more happiness in her demeanour than hitherto.

'Why Wynne, this is an unexpected pleasure. But do come in!' said Anne as she opened the door to her friend's knock. Wynne followed Anne into the front parlour and plopped down on an armchair and went into a sob that shook her violently.

'Oh dear, something the matter and you have come to tell me and it is not good news?' asserted Anne with a look of discomfort at her friend's distraught manner, as she herself took the chair opposite. Anne just sat and looked at her colleague without saying a word, wondering what it was all about, but kept her counsel until Wynne had recovered sufficiently to speak.

'Would you please come with me to the hospital in Frien Barnet to see Tracey. She was taken in yesterday and her mother, who was very hysterical and agitated, called me and when she spoke, told me that she had had an accident,' blurted Wynne amidst tears.

'But that hospital is not a maternity hospital. If I'm not mistaken it is a mental hospital, so why is she there?' questioned Anne, as she contemplated her friend strangely.

'Tracey's mother phoned me and in a somewhat vague and rambling way, I pieced the story together. It appears that she has been keeping company with our mutual friend Jack Courtney. He was with her at her flat when they got the damn news that Andrew was killed in action. He, it seems, committed himself to marrying her, even though she was about six months pregnant. Now it seems poor Tracey called on Jack and that his mother knew nothing about it, but they sat together until he came in. Then there was a frightful row and she got so worked up, that she ran from the house straight into the road and got herself knocked down. She was taken by ambulance to the General Hospital where she lost her baby, but was transferred to Frien Barnet as she is raving and uncontrollable now!'

'Oh dear, poor girl!' sympathised Anne, who for once was lost for words just then, so remained silent for a moment to reflect. 'Do you know if Jack is aware of what you have told me?'

'The accident happened right outside his house, so he must know. But I cannot say if he is aware that she has gone nutty and has been transferred elsewhere, though,' was the reply that Anne heard uttered.

'Then in that case, we will forget Jack for a moment, but will not put him out of our minds. Let us go right now to the hospital and see poor Tracey. If she's there, she must be in an awful state and she will need her friends around her to help her rally back to normal. So let's go, and you can fill me in on the way if you know of anything else.'

Norman had a very long discussion with his wife, Felicity, prior to attending the wedding of Anne to Sir John Cuthbertson. Due to the war effort, Anne had indicated that she intended to continue with her work in consideration of the shortage of staff and in anticipation of promotion. To this, Sir John, her future husband, acquiesced. From Felicity's point of view, she too would do anything for her Anne, but she still harboured a secret dread of Anne's attachment to her husband Norman. This was despite the assurance from both her husband and Anne, that nothing was happening between them since their marriage – but she still could not put it out of her mind that may be, may be, she did have a secret liaison with her husband. After all, she reflected, was it not Anne that engineered them together with her scheming! And Anne was always the instigator and innovator if anything had to be worked out. She was accepted as the 'brain' between them, so could she not also be pretending to be innocent whilst still having fun with her husband. Yet, surreptitiously check as she did, she always failed to get even the slightest hint or any proof. So why was she so obsessed. She could not answer but nevertheless, she was.

And Norman was keen to retain Anne on the staff, as not only was she an asset in both work output, but also as a fine example to the few other staff that were still with the firm. But overall, he still had his secret tryst with her to apparent mutual satisfaction! He was still infatuated with her on more than the sexual level, and still craved to be with her even though he had never reached his goal with her. He thrilled to be cosseted by her and accepted any injunction, so long as he could be close to her. Then he admired her commercially for her quick wit when it came to a problem – she was always ready with a solution however difficult, or seemingly so, the dilemma.

'Well, I suppose Love's Like That where Anne's concerned,' ventured Norman then added, 'And it would look good to have her as a junior partner with her name on the letter heads as "Lady Anne Cuthbertson, F.C.A.", would it not my love?.'

'Yes, I agree with your Norman.'

Acknowledgements are due to the US Navy Department in Washington DC, and to *Troopships of World War II* by Roland W. Charles, in particular for the information of ship movements during the War, except that I substituted the true name of the ship to S.S. *Conway*. The information, however, of its loss without trace is regrettably true.